TAKE ONE YOUNG MAN

Vivien Kelly was born in York in 1973. She read Modern Languages at Magdalen College, Oxford and then moved to London after she graduated in 1995. *Take One Young Man* is her first novel. She works in advertising and is currently writing her second novel, which will also be published by Arrow.

Praise for *Take One Young Man*

'Lively and sharp ... a well–observed picture of contemporary life' *The Times*

'Clever, witty and well written' *Express*

'Brilliant ... moving and hilariously funny' *Woman's Own*

'The advertising world should tremble at the sharp wit behind this work' *The Times*

'An exceptional first novel which mixes fluent storytelling, thoughtful insight, sensitive observation, seriousness and humour, all in perfect proportion' *The Richmond Review*

D1135666

October 2004

Joanie & Scott——

Enjoy it all

with love & luck

Robyn
xxx

TAKE ONE
YOUNG MAN

Vivien Kelly

ARROW

Published by Arrow Books in 2000

5 7 9 10 8 6

First published in the United Kingdom in 2000 by Arrow

Arrow Books Limited
20 Vauxhall Bridge Road, London, SW1V 2SA

Random House Australia (Pty) Limited
20 Alfred Street, Milsons Point, Sydney,
New South Wales 2061, Australia

Random House New Zealand Limited
18 Poland Road, Glenfield
Auckland 10, New Zealand

Random House South Africa (Pty) Limited
Endulini, 5a Jubilee Road, Parktown 2193, South Africa

Random House UK Limited Reg. No. 954009

A CIP catalogue record for this book
is available from the British Library

Papers used by Random House UK Limited
are natural, recyclable products made from wood grown in
sustainable forests The manufacturing processes conform to
the environmental regulations of the country of origin

ISBN 0 09 940983 6

Typeset by SX Composing DTP, Rayleigh, Essex
Printed and bound in Great Britain by
Bookmarque Ltd, Croydon, Surrey

For Terence Kelly and for Leokadia Syga

With love and thanks to:

colleagues who became friends, Harley, Janet & Zoë, Julia
& Jon, my mother, my father, Kate, Patrick and Barney.

ONE

Sam Glass lived in London, but he didn't like the noise. He was aware of a hum, a background rumble that continued through the night, not only the pounding of the city's heart, but the rumbling of its stomach, the creaking of its joints, the straining of its intestines. The noise made Sam anxious. It made his own heart beat alongside, faster and louder. It made his head race and his ears buzz. Sometimes, when a plane passed overhead or a motorbike zoomed by, Sam would freeze, suddenly paralysed by the din. When he lay in bed at night he listened hard to the London night noises, trying to find a silence somewhere among them.

Sam used to spend a lot of time alone, either on the flat roof outside his bedroom window or just at his desk, looking at maps. He looked at any maps, tracing the edges of continents with the chewed nail of his index finger, and folding his bottom lip in half with the fingers of his other hand. He would sit and stare at the expanses of light blue that made up the sea, imagining how the pieces of land on either side once fitted together. Sometimes he took off his glasses and cleaned them on his shirt. When he sat on the flat roof outside his window he stared at the sky, watching the stars and occasionally the moon. Sometimes, when he was on the roof, he would talk to himself, quietly, under his breath, chewing his nails, polishing his glasses. Sam Glass was looking for something. Sam Glass was twenty-five years old.

'Full stop apply periods contract minimum and rental line full stop close bracket VAT ex open bracket ninety nine pound sign costs package start–up ISDN CC's to connection colon example full stop 03 full stop 12 full stop 31 by installed lines on 02 full stop 11 full stop 31 ends offer.' Sam finished and looked at Chloe. Chloe wanted to be a costume designer. Instead she worked in advertising. 'Are they okay?' Sam asked.

'Yeah, fine,' she said, flicking her eyes along the tiny words. She turned over the press advertisement and signed it on the back so that it could be supplied to the papers. 'Thanks, Sam.'

'No trouble,' he replied.

Sam sat down at his desk and pulled his chair underneath, so that he could rest his feet on the bin on the other side. He had noticed, in recent months, that he could no longer pull his chair as far under as he used to because the edge of the desk constricted his gently expanding stomach. His phone rang.

'Sam speaking.' He picked up a pen with his left hand.

'Sam, it's Clive.'

'Clive, how *are* you?' Sam asked, speaking like a game show host.

'Sam, where is my ad?'

'Right. I know I said it would be with you today but we had a bit of a hitch. I rang Carol this morning to explain. Did she tell you?'

'She's at lunch.'

'Okay. As I told her, the account team weren't happy with the concept, so the creatives are doing some more work on it.' Sam started to draw circles on a post-it note. He had worked with Clive Reason, the UK brand manager for Shadows, for nearly two years.

'You told me it would be here today.'

2

'Well, I probably said that subject to internal approvals it would be with you today. Carol seemed to think that it wouldn't be too much of a problem for us to get the revised work to you next week.'

'I'm not Carol.'

'Right.'

'You'll be hearing about this, Sam.'

The phone went dead. Sam shut his eyes.

He started to sift through the pieces of paper on his desk. Angela approached. She was tall and thin, with long dark hair and a pale face. She looked like a Modigliani, but slightly more distorted. Her natural expression was one of anxiety: a furrowed brow and down-turned lips. Even when she was relaxed she appeared anxious. Angela was Sam's boss.

'Have you been to see the boys yet about their work?'

'No, I've been –'

'Why not?' She was pulling bits of fluff off the bottom of her jacket with scrawny but well looked-after fingers.

'I've been doing other things. I had a meeting. I'm sorry.'

'But you *know* that it's really urgent.' She raised her voice. 'Why aren't you up there now?' The office noise dropped as people started to listen in.

'I'm just about to go. I was looking for the brief.' Sam took his time with each word. His mobile phone rang. He reached for it. Angela glowered at him. 'Sam speaking . . . Beth, can I call you back? . . . No, I will. I promise, as soon as I can. Bye.'

'Why haven't you done it?' Her voice had become a mixture of a screech and a whine. 'I don't think you understand how important this is. Why are you so – ?' She looked as if she wanted a fight and her eyes glistened.

'I think we should have this conversation in private,' Sam ventured, phrasing it as a question. His heart was pounding.

3

'I'll decide whether our conversations are in private or not.' She glared back at him. 'You have to go and see the boys. Now.'

'I'm going,' said Sam. His phone rang. Without looking at Angela he picked it up. 'Sam speaking . . . hi . . . yeah, okay. What time are they coming? . . . Okay, so he wants a bacon sandwich, and the other two want croissants . . . herbal tea, okay . . . What about Jay? . . . Okay, I'll give him a ring and see what he wants . . . Fine. Yes, I'll make sure it's there by half past eight. Okay, bye.'

By the time he hung up Angela had walked off to pick a fight elsewhere. Sam's head was spinning. He had a list of things to do that was longer than the day ahead. He looked at the circles on the post-it and imagined himself stuck, circling, day after day after day. All the jobs were urgent, it was just a question of what was more urgent than urgent. At the moment the most pressing job was to talk to the creative team on his main account: Shadows, the market leader in sanitary towels.

Sam worked at McLeod Seagal Gale, or McLeod Seagal as it was known for short. McLeod Seagal was the ninth largest advertising agency in Britain. It was located in Soho: a tall, white, glassy building with a wide lobby where two lissom girls sparkled during the day and a security guard recited the Koran through the small hours. It had 254 employees, 239 of whom were under thirty-five. The remaining fifteen were all male. It had a staff turnover of twenty per cent: about sixteen per cent left and four per cent were fired. Last year about sixty million pounds had been through its books, about twelve million of it profit. It was responsible for some of the most technologically advanced ads on TV. Lines such as *Blitz those Bitz with Glitz* (Glitz washing-up liquid), *When*

4

the Seed Arises (Titan condoms) and *Wherever You Go, There You Are* (Hitsui mobile phones) were thought up on the fourth floor of its sexy building, sold to the client by Sam's department and dropped into the bottom right-hand corners of press ads by the studio in the basement. Between its walls meetings were held to find more effective ways of selling sweets to adults, cigarettes to kids, cars to mothers and vitamins to businessmen. For most of the day and most of the night it throbbed with life. There was rarely a time when the building was completely calm. When Christmas came it threw lavish parties where there was much snorting of powder and sucking of flesh, and occasionally a streak of flaming vomit. In the summer it threw another party where there was much snorting of powder and sucking of flesh, but fewer clothes. McLeod Seagal was founded by three men – Oliver Seagal, a board account director, who had gone off to run a vineyard in LA; Robert Gale, an art director, who now lived near St Tropez, and Robert McLeod, a copywriter, who currently occupied the best office in the building and paid himself approximately seven hundred and fifty thousand pounds a year – almost more than the salaries of the entire agency put together. And about fifty times as much as Sam earned. Every day at McLeod Seagal was chaos and crisis. The agency lurched like a ship in a storm, from one side to the other, always threatening to capsize and sink, as Sam and his workmates ran from port to starboard, trying to counterbalance the tipping of the waves.

Sam had worked on Shadows (*Have You Ever Felt Your Shadow?*) since he joined McLeod Seagal as a graduate trainee. He also worked on Reynolds, the automobile exhaust manufacturers (*Exhaustingly Low Prices*) – but it was a small account, and their advertising amounted to a bank of a few press ads. Sam had asked to move accounts. He did not enjoy working on sanitary towels, nor did exhausts particularly interest him, but his request was seen as peculiar: Shadows was one of the agency's biggest accounts, the clients liked him a lot and after two years of working with them he was familiar with their business. And so his request was ignored, and Sam continued to plough through research documents about 'stay-dry top weaves' and the benefits of 'wings'. He picked up office-speak quite quickly, but it still baffled him. He could not understand why, as a student, he could just *tell* people things, but now he had to *brief* them. He used to be able to *show* things to people, but now everything had to be *presented*. And he didn't have *chats* any more, he didn't just swing round on his chair and have a natter. Suddenly two people together was a *meeting*, as though some strange curfew laws had been introduced, and Sam, without really realising it, had become an *Account Executive*.

When he was still a trainee, one rainy day in November last year, he had had to go out and actually buy sanitary towels. One packet might have been okay, but he had to assess all of Shadows' competitors, and as he approached the supermarket he felt his heart in his throat. He lingered in aisles, staring at washing powders and tins of beans as other shoppers came and went. He was waiting for the aisle to clear, but just as the last person found what they were looking for, another would round the corner and stroll past the piles of goods, their blinking slowed and their decision-making faculties dulled. Eventually he reached the queue at the till, cheeks stinging and with a basket positively bulging with soft plastic pastel packets. His mind was racing with sentences to present to the cashier: 'it's my job' (simple enough, and true too, but what kind of job would she think he had? Sanitary towel tester? Was he the guy in the white coat who poured the blue liquid from the test tube on to the towels, and then dabbed it with a tissue?); 'my girlfriend – she's going on holiday'; 'my sisters – they're housebound'. He was so worked-up by the time the packets began to be swiped through that he could no longer think, and, as soon as the cashier glanced at him from under her groomed eyebrows, he blurted out, before he could stop himself: 'they're not for me'. She did not reply, but carried on swiping the packets through the till. All the remaining blood in Sam's body rushed to his face, which did not return to normal until he got out into the open air.

Sam was on his mobile when he spotted the script he was looking for under a folder of competitive advertising. He pulled it out and tried to concentrate as he read it:

Product: Shadows
Production budget: £400k
Team: Kid/Dan

This commercial will be shot in the style of a II world war news real. All black and white and grainy. The music will be the 'Damn busters'.

A young boy, is walking in the countryside.

Somewhere else a damn is starting to heave at the seems. Straining with the weight of water behind it. With a pop a small bit breaks away and water starts trickling threw. We see images of tidal waves and hurricanes go through the boy's head.

The boy approaches the damn. He sees water leeking out. He puts his thumb in the hole and the leek stops. He stands there; the camera pans along his shadow, and a female voice reads:

'Shadows. When things need to be kept in.'

Sam sighed. Lauren, with whom he shared a desk, was having a heated conversation on the phone. Michael, who sat behind him, was having a tense meeting with two Germans at his desk ('I don't know what it is, I can't quite put my foot in it . . .'). Gina, who sat in front of him, was listening to a CD of technological soundtracks. Sam could not concentrate. He reread the script. The account team had decided not to present it to the client, and it was Sam's job to explain to them why this was the case. What could he say? Because it was shit? The client was looking for something new and radical in the field of sanpro advertising. Their last campaign had been shots of shapely bottoms clad in white with a strident soundtrack and some wolf-whistling men. This time they wanted something new and improved.

His pager buzzed: *Pls call Clive URGENT.*

'You're going to have to wait, Clive,' he said and picked up the Shadows script and went upstairs. He could feel Angela's eyes on him as he left the floor.

Kid and Dan were both in their office. Kid had his feet on the desk and was watching cricket on the TV. He was in his late thirties, tall and quiet. Dan was a different kettle of fish. A kettle of particularly rotten fish, with blue hair. Younger, more conventionally attractive, he always had the most up-to-date trainers. At the moment they were Donna Karan. He was looking at the pictures in *Loaded*, or rather he was hoping that somebody was looking at *him*, looking at the pictures in *Loaded*.

'Hi, Dan and Kid. Do you think I could talk to you about your Shadows script, please?'

'Come back in half an hour,' said Dan, his Somerset lilt ringing through the office. Regional accents helped on this floor. They meant that you were better at thinking up good ads.

'I can't really. I've a meeting. I'm sorry. Would it be possible to do it now?'

Dan scratched the back of his head and sighed. He shut the magazine. 'What is it?' he said with a sneer.

'Your script. We need to do a bit more work on it before we can present it.'

'You mean I need to do a bit more work on it. Well, I'm not going to. It's a top script. If you don't think you can sell it that's your problem. I'm not having some arse client telling me there's something wrong with it.'

Sam sighed gently and bit his tongue.

'What is it?' Kid looked away from the cricket for a moment.

'It's a number of things. We can't have . . . well, put it this way: we feel that a boy sticking his finger in a dam is not an appropriate simile for how Shadows work. Then there's the tonal values – the music, the fact that it's in black and white – they say completely the wrong things about the brand. And the new endline –'

'It's a damn good idea, if you ask me,' replied Dan, running his hands through his hair. 'Damn good – geddit?' he chuckled and nodded at Kid. Sam felt his pager buzz: *Call Clive. VERY URGENT.* He clipped it back on to his belt.

'Well, it's just that the idea of a dam with all that water behind it, women don't like to think about menstruation like that.'

'So how do women like to think about it then?' Dan asked. Kid sniggered. Sam's mobile rang. He pressed the *busy* button. Dan raised his voice, so that the rest of the department, through the thin plywood walls, could hear: '*Quiet*, Kid. Sam's going to tell us how women think about periods.' He laughed. Sam's pager went again: *Where are you? Angela.*

'Look. Perhaps I'll get Angela to come and talk to you about this. I think that might be more productive. The only thing is that it is really urgent, so we need to turn something around fast. Thanks anyway, guys.'

Sam went back to his desk. Now he had to face Angela and tell her that he had failed. Lauren was on the phone. Björk was blaring out of a stereo. All around him phones were ringing. He looked at his new e-mail messages: five, two from Budget Control, one from Beth in the TV department, one from his secretary, Gail, and one from a friend. One day soon Sam hoped to add the prefix 'girl' to that description. He and Gilly had been flirting over e-mail for a good few months, and Sam was slowly trying to muster the courage to ask her out.

dear sam, hi! how are you? can you help me out? my sister wants to get a job in advertising – do you think you could have a chat with her? maybe we could all go out one evening . . .
   let me know
Gxxx

PS. I met a friend of yours the other day – Henry? Maybe you could bring him along too?

Sam shook his head. His phone rang. 'Sam speaking . . . Oh, hi Mum. How are you?' He breathed out with relief as he realised it wasn't a client.

'Fine. How about you?' She sounded a long way away.

Gail put a note on his desk: *Dean wants to see you asap.*

'Errr . . . yeah. I'm all right.' He mouthed 'thanks' at Gail. She really wanted to be a physiotherapist, but for the time being she worked in advertising.

'Isn't it wonderful news about Mark?'

'Yes, it's great, Mum. Just great.' Sam's brother had recently announced his engagement.

'I really think she's perfect for him, don't you?'

Sam looked up from his desk. His heart sank. Angela was approaching, weaving her way around the marshes of desk lamps, computer terminals and cables that made up their floor of the agency. She came to rest opposite him.

'I've got to go. I'm sorry, I'll call you back as soon as I can. Speak to you soon.' He hung up. His phone rang again. Since he needed Angela to be in a good mood he let it ring. She would be pleased that she was more important than taking his calls.

'Why didn't you return my page?'

'Oh, sorry. I was about to come and see you.'

'Clive rang me. About getting the script over to him this morning. He was not happy.'

'I explained it all to Carol this morning. Clive was in a meeting.'

'When *you* fuck up *I* get it in the neck. So don't do it, okay? What happened upstairs?' she asked, fiddling with her jacket buttons, her mouth corners twitching.

'Not very successful. Do you think you might be able to go and talk to them?'

'Why?' she said, her voice raised, wiry and whining.

'Well, they weren't very co-operative. I think it might be more effective if you were to talk them through our issues with the work.'

'Of course they weren't very co-operative. It's your job to *make* them do it. I don't think you quite understand how this works. The more times we go and see them, the more our position is undermined. You've got no idea, have you? You've completely blown it for me now. For how long do I have to pick up the pieces after you?' Her face had become completely red.

Sam didn't know what to say. He was beyond words. Angela looked like a cornered animal, dark eyes flashing, top lip curled.

'The thing is Sam, you don't seem to get it. You completely miss the point. The point of your role in all this is to make things happen. That *is* your point. And if you can't do that then there's no point you being here.' She turned and fled, slamming the door to the stairs behind her.

Sam let her words wash over him as he imagined the idea of 'points'. What did she mean? He saw a sharpened pencil in his mind, its lead razor-sharp and long like a spire. He saw a ballet dancer up on her pointe shoes, strangely named when one saw them and realised that they had squared-off ends. He saw points of a compass and points on a graph, tiny black one-dimensional things. He heard his mother telling him that it was rude to point. Was he missing the point? Well, points were small, so they were easy to miss. He didn't know what to say. 'Sorry,' he mumbled, to nobody in particular.

Sam looked at his diary and saw that he had half an hour free before his next meeting. He looked at his 'To do' list and saw that he wouldn't have any spare time between now and the end of the week. He decided to rewrite his list in order of what was most urgent, knowing that by the time he got to the end of it he wouldn't actually have time to do anything. List rewriting, however, was an important part of his job. His phone rang.

'Sam speaking?'

'Sam, Henry's in reception.'

'Henry who?'

'He said you'd know who he was.'

'Oh, okay, thanks – I'll come down.'

Sam got up from his desk with a frown and went downstairs.

'What are you doing here?' Sam asked with a half grin.

'Hi Sammy, how's it going? Got time for a coffee?'

Sam shook his head and sat down beside him on the metallic bench.

'I've a meeting in ten minutes. What's going on?'

'Well, the thing is, I'm supposed to be catching a flight to Paris in an hour and I left my passport at home. So I thought, maybe I could borrow yours?'

'What?'

'I thought you kept it in the top drawer of your desk?'

'Yeah, but Henry, it's *my* passport. What are you going to do with it?'

'Well, they never really look at the picture, do they? All they do is glance at the cover. The thing is I have to get this flight, and I haven't got time to go home.' He tapped his watch. 'Will you get it?'

'Okay, but it's not going to work. They check it against your tickets too,' Sam said as he stood up and headed for the door to the stairs.

'Mmm, I know,' Henry nodded. 'I've just had my secretary change the name of the passenger.'

Sam was back down in a flash, clutching the small red book and skidding to a halt on the marble floor.

'By the way,' he said as he handed it over. 'You met a girl I know.'

'I've met a lot of girls you know.'

'Gilly. She's got long brown hair, and a nose-stud.'

'Is she pretty?'

'*I* think so.'

'Oh yeah? Is she in the running to relieve your singledom?'

'Perhaps.'

'Well, I can't remember her.'

'She remembers you. She wants to meet you again, but I've told her you're on holiday.'

'Hello? I'm here. If she wants to see me again, I think you should help her. She'll thank you for it one day.'

Sam laughed. 'I wouldn't be so sure.'

'Don't be cruel, Sam. You shouldn't deprive women of me. I'm their accessible, flexible friend. Speaking of which, I'm meeting up with Sara at eight and a friend of hers. We're going to the cinema – I've got tickets for some new film called *A Baby Ate My Dingo*.'

'Aren't you going to be in Paris?'

'I should be back by then. I'll give you a call. Cheers,' he yelled and swung through the doors into the street.

Sam and Henry had been friends since college. They had first met in the library where Sam had been reading for an essay on return immigration one evening in the first term. A fair-haired boy stomped up the stairs and began to pile books on the desk next to his. The boy strode around the library with such purpose, and plucked books from the shelves with such conviction, that Sam assumed he was a second year, bored and unimpressed with the new batch of freshers, keenly scribbling into the evening. The boy placed a pencil on the desk, sat down next to Sam, produced a pencil sharpener from his pocket and began to sharpen the pencil. He examined the point carefully under his desk light and then glanced sideways at Sam, so that Sam, slightly embarrassed, looked back down at his textbook. The boy shuffled in his chair and opened a book, pressing the pages open in the middle and smoothing them to the sides with his palms. Then he shuffled once again, cleared his throat and stretched out his legs. The desk lights went out. The blond boy muttered something, looked under the desk and realised that he had kicked the plug from the socket. He tutted and got down on his knees to put it back in. He got up and went back to his book. Sam realised that although he had turned the page, he could remember nothing of what he had read, and so he flicked back and started again, urging himself to concentrate. The blond boy shuffled in his chair and the lights went out again. And Sam thought: 'does not learn from his mistakes – not very bright'.

'Oh, really,' said the boy and bent down again, wiggling the plug until the lights flickered back on. He sat up again and returned to his book, clearing his throat again and pushing back his hair. Sam read a sentence for the third time, but still failed to understand it. He listened to the noises of the town around him: to the distant rumble of buses going over the bridge, to the occasional squeals of eighteen-year-olds fresh from boarding school and having fun in the streets, to the rattle of the few pipes that circled the library, attempting to keep it warm. Then the blond boy looked around at the shelves of books, shook his head, blew out through his lips, letting them vibrate against each other like the sound of a car engine, and said into the silence: 'I can't be doing with this. Let's go to the bar.' Sam looked at him, and found that the boy was looking directly back. Sam shrugged and smiled. 'All right then,' he said, and they left their unread books, spines intact and pages untouched, in a pile on the table.

As it turned out, their rooms were almost opposite each other's and whenever Sam went in and out of his room in the first few weeks there was a group of girls hanging around in the corridor, chatting, smoking and trying to look cool, waiting for Henry. Sam didn't understand why Henry didn't invite them in and have them sprawl all over his room, examining and admiring his possessions. One night, when all had been quiet for a while, Sam knocked on

Henry's door to see if he wanted to come and eat with him. He heard a shout and he went in. His attention was immediately caught by a black suit hanging against Henry's wardrobe, along with a white shirt and a black tie. A funeral outfit. Henry saw him looking at it.

'My grandmother. She's going to go any day, and I thought I should be ready. I might need to leave in a rush, to get there just before she goes.'

Sam asked. 'Is she old?'

'Seventy-seven, but she lived with us when I was growing up, so I'm used to having her around.'

'My grandad used to live with us too,' Sam replied. He paused and tried not to look around the room. 'Have you time to eat?'

Henry nodded and picked up his wallet from a spartan desk.

'Have you done any work then?' Sam asked. The desk looked like nobody ever sat there. Henry shook his head.

'I can't concentrate. I'm just waiting for the phone call.'

'You can borrow my essays if you want,' Sam said.

Henry looked at him for a second. 'Thanks,' he said.

As it happened Sam did not see Henry that evening. He had to work until half past eleven. Angela had come to see him towards the end of the day and informed him that she needed a presentation typing up by the following morning. He had explained that he had plans, but Angela had answered as she always answered in those situations: 'that's the challenge of the job', and she went and put her coat on.

As Sam sat there in the increasingly calm and silent office through the hours of the evening, typing away, he felt that the only thing that was being challenged was his patience. He was tired and dehydrated and fed up. He could not be bothered to have anything to eat. He could not type properly, and so the job took over twice as long as it should. At least it was quiet, although the air-conditioning hummed in the background.

Once he had finished he had to copy and distribute the presentation, and just as the photocopier was spitting out the last pages it stopped and beeped. He looked at the red light on the display, calmly flashing at him. His eyes were stinging and his head throbbing. His throat felt sore. He wanted to give up. He wanted to go home and never, ever return to this office. He sighed. Then he swore. All the rude words he had ever heard came flying out of his mouth, quiet but fast. He removed his glasses and polished the lenses on the bottom of his shirt. Then he went over to the windows and stared up at the March sky.

As he walked up the hallway of his flat he heard muffled giggling coming from around the illuminated edges of his flatmate's door. Gray had been single for a good few months, so he had been ruthlessly pursuing all the single (and some of the attached) girls that he knew. Sam kicked his shoes off, went into the kitchen and had a bowl of Frosties followed by some toast and Marmite. Then he felt bad, so he opened the fridge and took out a carrot. As he did, he heard his mother in his head: 'make sure you eat at least one vegetable a day.' That was fine but, working his hours, it was more difficult than it sounded. Where was he going to find a vegetable in an advertising agency? Vegetables were not cool, nor were they often advertised. The closest he could come would be a *brand onion* – used by the planning department to impress clients, with its banal assertion that brands, like most other things, could be seen as made up of layers.

Just as he was halfway through his second carrot, his tie undone and crumbs and Marmite strings around his mouth, a girl appeared in the doorway.

'Hi,' she said, serious and grown-up. She had long blondish hair, a few strands of which were repelling each other as they danced about her shoulders.

'Er . . . mmm . . . hi,' he managed, nodding and swallowing as fast as he could.

'I just thought I'd make some tea.'

'Sure.' He moved out of the way. 'Go ahead.' He didn't really know what else to say. He leant against the counter and she turned the tap on and picked up the kettle. As he watched her he realised that her movements were unsteady, and she had trouble removing the lid of the kettle.

'There you are!' Gray appeared in the doorway. 'Why don't you come back?' He pushed himself up against her back, pressing her into the sink. Sam sighed. It was time for him to leave the room.

'Hiya, Sam. How's thicks?' Gray slurred at him.

'Yeah. Fine.'

'Oh right. This is Aphrodite. Aphrodi . . . this is Sam.'

'Hi' he smiled at her back. She was miles away, trying to plug the lead into the back of the kettle. She was wearing a T-shirt, and, it appeared, no pants. Her skin looked smooth and her flesh firm. Sam felt sick with jealousy. Once she had managed to connect the right parts of the kettle she wandered off in the direction of the bedroom.

'Who's that?' Sam hissed. Gray grinned.

'She's dancer,' he said through his smile. 'We are currently dancing to the music of lurve in my bed.'

Sam didn't really want to ask. He knew that asking would just make it worse, but he could not help himself. 'Really?'

'Her bum is amazing. Just . . . ' he shrugged his shoulders and held his hands up as though they were cradling it there and then '. . . just really . . . edible.' Gray kissed his fingers and let them fall through the air. He laughed too much and scratched his bollocks through his dressing gown. Then he went back to his room.

Sam heard the door shut, words being exchanged and more giggling. He was toying with the idea of washing his plate up when he heard a yelp – a high-pitched yelp that echoed through his head – and in his mind's eye he saw the laughing girl being flipped on to her tummy by an excited Gray, ready to interfere with her amazing piece of anatomy. Sam went to his own room, at the other end of the flat, and shut the door.

He took off his clothes. He turned off his mobile phone. He brushed his teeth. He turned out the lights and pressed his forehead against the coldness of the window pane, staring out into the darkness. He tried to think back to that morning, but it seemed like such a long time ago. He realised that he was frowning and that his mind was replaying everything that had happened in the office that day. He looked for the moon but it was hidden by clouds. He looked into the sky instead, into the milky billows of cloud, sitting up there, doing nothing. He climbed into bed and fell asleep with images of Aphrodite in his mind.

TWO

Kasia Mentrak walked quickly up to the house and let herself in. It was a large Victorian house in north London which had been badly renovated and was constantly needing repairs which meant that workmen were frequently clomping up and down the scrappily carpeted stairs. She headed for the door leading to the ground floor flat, her key already poised to slot into the lock. Once she had pushed the door wide enough for her to squeeze through (it caught on the carpet) she called out: 'Mr Glass. It's Kasia. Good morning.' Her voice was a little boisterous and harsh: her Polish accent flattened some vowels and spiked consonants. She stood in the hallway as she removed her orange coat and dropped her plastic bag on the floor. Then she walked through to the front room, the largest in the flat, with a bay window that overlooked a street in which nothing much happened. The room had dark red wallpaper with stains and worn patches. There was a large pair of faded purple curtains hanging, like dog ears, on either side of the bay windows. She stood directly in front of Mr Glass, who was sitting in an armchair. His head was tilted backwards against the antimacassar on the chair. His mouth was open. He did not stir.

'Mr Glass. Hello, it's Kasia,' she said, in a quiet voice. He still did not move. 'Hello Mr Glass,' she repeated, a little more loudly, prodding his shoulder as though she was scared of catching something from him. Then she remembered her training and she picked up his wrist, which felt cold and hung limp in her hands. Her heart thumped.

'Kasia!' he cried all of a sudden, making her drop the wrist and start backwards. He started to laugh and waved his hands in the air to show that he was well and truly alive.

'That's not funny,' she said, shaking her head, her heart still pounding, 'not funny at all.'

'Brightens up the day,' he said, shuffling in his seat and rearranging the blanket on his legs.

'Some of us have a job to do, Mr Glass.'

'I know, I'm sorry, Kasia,' he replied, still smiling at her. She shook her head and looked sullen. 'I know, I know. You're right, of course.'

She picked up a cup from the floor and a bowl and spoon from the table to his right. She took them through to the kitchen at the back of the flat and began to put on a pair of washing-up gloves.

'How are you?' Mr Glass asked from the front room, his shout barely louder than a strained whisper. She came and stood in the doorway, folding up one of her sleeves. She looked fed-up.

'I'm fine, Mr Glass. How are you?' she said, letting the words form slowly and then drop on to the floor, with the weight they bore from being over-pronounced. She talked to him as though he was not very bright, his brain dulled by the years of sitting by himself.

'I'm old. And I'm older today than I was yesterday.'

'Umm. But you can be other things too.' She started to pull the gloves on, right hand first.

'Very good point. Let's see. I'm old and . . . decrepit? Manky? Grumpy? Overweight? Insensitive?'

Kasia shook her head, stretching out her left hand as it found its way into the glove, and walked back through to the kitchen.

For someone who had travelled so much Mr Glass, who now spent his days sitting in an armchair, had a peculiar fear. He was not afraid of the dark, he was not afraid of spiders and he was not afraid of being afraid. Most remarkably of all, and this is true, he was not afraid of death. That is to say, he did not *want* to die, but at the same time he was not afraid of it: he had no fear of pain, or of his life ending or of never living, ever again. The thought of not being around did not make him shudder – he had not been around before, when he was far away, travelling in another hemisphere, and he knew that the world would continue without him. He did not believe in Heaven, or ghosts, or any kind of afterlife. 'We don't have a *before*life, do we? We just spring from our mothers with no warning of what is to come. There is no decompression chamber. Why then is there any reason to think there is an afterlife?' he used to say, gently and with a shrug of his shoulders, if ever the subject was raised.

No, what scared Mr Glass was not *being* dead; what scared Mr Glass was being *mistaken* for dead. He was terrified that one day, while he was sleeping deeply (which he had a tendency to do – once, on a boat in a storm just off the southernmost tip of Argentina, he slept for fourteen hours as the boat crashed round the rugged coast of Cape Horn), somebody would think that he was dead. He knew already that, on occasion, people had thought him dead. How many chances did he have? Sooner or later, somebody, would, for whatever reason, think that he had died. Even in this day and age, mistakes were made and factors over-looked. And where easier to make a mistake but with the 'corpse' of an eighty-six-year-old?

He knew that when his grandsons or his daughter-in-law or his home-help saw him sleeping, the first thing that went through their minds (and who could blame them?) was that he might be dead. Popped his clogs? Kicked the bucket?

Thrown in the towel? The thought that one of these people could pronounce him dead made him quake, for were that to happen he knew he would not wake up until the coldness and dampness got into his bones, and he would open his eyes to a darkness till then unimaginable, an odd, damp smell, and the cramping confines of a wooden box. Or he would wake when he began to sweat, dreaming he was in the forests of Brazil again, until the heat made him uncomfortable and he could no longer sleep. Then, when he woke, it would surely be too late. The flames would have started work on the box, on the wood, and he would be powerless to stop them consuming his suit and then his flesh. He could yell, but no one would hear above the music. Would anyone in the congregation, were they to lift their nose to the wind, be able to tell that they had cremated a body whose heart was still beating?

'Just make sure,' he used to say to his family. 'Just make sure that you're sure. Sure as the floor.' But he knew in the end that it would not be up to them. They would call a doctor who would look him over and then utter the irrevocable words: 'he's dead'. Well, the good doctor probably wouldn't say that. He would use an idiom or a gentle phrase to keep it all nice and distant. 'He's no longer with us', 'he's passed away' or the delightfully ambiguous 'he's gone', which always left the relatives hoping for more: 'to the loo'; 'insane'; 'and won a million pounds on the lottery'. Mr Glass lived in fear of this good doctor's announcement, and his family's acceptance of it.

When he reached the age of eighty and realised that he might pop the bucket or kick his clogs any day he wrote out a long list of things that he wanted his family to check on the announcement of his departure. Once he had composed his list he folded it up and slipped it into a clear plastic bag. He put this in his pocket, and at night it was propped against his bedside light. Now and again he tested his family to make sure ('sure as the floor') that they knew where it was. It reassured him to be able to ask them and get the right answer. There were a number of things that Mr Glass, in his copperplate handwriting, requested of whoever the unfortunate witness should happen to be:

Instructions to be followed in the case of Leonard Glass's suspected death:

1. Place a piece of paper to my lips and leave it there for a good few minutes. Observe it carefully (your eyes should ache *because you stare at it so fiercely). If it moves at all (even if you think that it might have been a breeze), then there is some doubt as to my physical state.*

2. Cross my right leg over my left at the knee. Take a thin hardback book (I recommend Configurations of the Southern Hemisphere *by P. H. Hamilton) and tap the spine against my right leg, at a point just under the kneecap. Tap at least ten times, varying the point of contact each time. Watch my right foot closely for any movement or twitching.*

3. There is a torch on the left-hand side of my bed, on the floor. Take it and lift each eyelid in turn, shining the torch beam into each eye. Watch carefully for any contraction / dilation of the pupil.

4. Pick up my right arm. Support the arm at the elbow with your left hand. Place the first two fingers of your right hand over the artery just beneath the palm of my right hand. Do not apply pressure. Leave them there for at least one minute, standing absolutely still so that any pulse (however weak) will be felt.

5. Turn on my gramophone. This may be a little complicated, because the television may need to be unplugged and the gramophone plugged in before it will work. I have found that the best position for doing this is to stand as close to the wall as possible, and slide your arm down the back of the piano until you reach the socket, keeping your arm straight and pressing your left cheek against the wall.

Once the gramophone is on, select Encores by David Oistrakh, side 1, band 2. The piece of music is called Jota, and is number 4 of Falla's 7 Canciones Populares Españolas. Make sure the settings are at 33 and 12". Set the volume knob on 7, and let the recording play to the end. Watch me! If there is any sign of movement, then there is some doubt! Remember – a negative result means nothing!

6. Open all the bay windows. Each has a catch halfway up that demands to be unscrewed. Open all four of them as wide as they will go (regardless of the time of day or the weather outside) and make sure the door of the room is open too. Leave them open for fifteen minutes. Watch my body for signs of chill.

7. Tear a sheet of newspaper off the pile on top of the piano. Fold the sheet diagonally in sections an inch wide, so that you are left with a long flat stick. Set fire to one end with a match. Bring this burning end to my face and hold it against the end of my nose. Watch carefully to see if the skin reacts. Any sign of redness or blistering means that I am still of this earth, and do not yet require interment.

8. If all of the above proves fruitless do not give up! Positive results show that I am alive, but negative results do not necessarily mean that I am dead. Fetch a doctor, and then another one.

9. When you are sure, I am sure.

Mr Glass had told Kasia about this list on her first day with him. He had explained where he kept it and, to a certain extent, why. He ran through it with her and she became convinced that she was looking after a crazy one.

The thing that confused her most was instruction number nine: 'When you're sure, I'm sure.'

'That's clearly not true,' she said. 'Why do you write that there, as though suddenly you trust this person, when you have made them do all these ridiculous things, as though they are a complete imbecile.'

Mr Glass shrugged. 'By then, once they have done all those things and the doctors say I'm dead, it's all settled. All I mean is, if you're convinced then I'm happy.'

But Kasia wasn't so sure. It seemed to her that he had written it to make the reader doubt themselves. And so oblige them to double-double-check, and check once again, because most people find being sure hard.

'I'm going to start on lunch in a minute. There's lamb and broccoli and carrots. Is that okay?' She hovered in the doorway, thinking that it was too bad if it wasn't because she hadn't got time to sort anything else out.

'If I've told you once I've told you a million times. I want beef. In a last glorious gesture I want to save the British public from slowly killing themselves, by eating all the beef in the country, so that there's none left for them to buy. I'll die before I start to shake and fall over, so I feel that it is my duty to eat it all up. Beef for breakfast, beef for lunch, beef with cream and jam for afternoon tea, beef for supper. Beef sandwiches, beef salad, beef hot dogs, beef biscuits, even beef pancakes!'

Kasia shook her head and let the corners of her mouth relax into what was not quite a smile. More a kind of gentle mouth-stretch. She walked into the kitchen where she began to wash up, a frown slowly forming on her brow as her mind wandered.

Back in the living room Mr Glass was still talking.

'There's a beef mountain in Europe, you know. I don't know where. Maybe in the Pyrenees, towering above all those craggy granite monsters. Or perhaps in the Alps, covered with pine trees. The bottom layer is sausages and steaks, well done, so they're easy to walk on. Then come the ribs and things get slightly trickier. Once you get towards the top it becomes T-bone steaks and things get damn near impossible. You're a hero if you climb Beef Mountain. In fact, it's actually a beef volcano, and every few hundred years it spurts boiling hot gravy over the locals. And Yorkshire puddings are shot into the air and settle on rooftops, fields and gardens. Of course, they're not called Yorkshire puddings over there. Even then, with all those trimmings, the locals can't eat it all.'

Mr Glass cleared his throat and, staring straight ahead of him, at the dark red wallpaper, inclined his head. He could just hear Kasia washing up in the kitchen. He lowered his voice 'You see, that is what I don't understand. Why is it a *beef* mountain? Why is it not a *cow* mountain? If we've too much beef, why doesn't somebody just say: right, stop killing the cows and let them run around for a few more years until we've eaten the mountain. A surplus of cows wouldn't be so bad, would it? I'd have one in my garden, if they asked me. Wouldn't mind a bit of bovine company. You can use a cow for all sorts of things,' and he laughed. A whispery laugh that shook his shoulders and would have made Kasia think of a cartoon character, had she heard it.

Leo Glass was eighty-six. He was slightly overweight and wheezed like a bicycle pump. He had a gentle voice that sounded almost like a whisper, and when he spoke his eyebrows raised themselves involuntarily. He gave the impression of a slightly shambolic polar bear with white bushy hair and large hands. He wore fine corduroy shirts in either blue or green that had no collars and buttons too fiddly for his old fingers. He often used to put a button through the hole either above or below the one that it was supposed to be in, so that his shirts hung over his stomach like wallpaper falling off a wall. He had a thick pair of glasses which he wore when he tried to read, but if he were honest with himself he would have to admit that even with his half-inch thick lenses he could not really make out the text in the books.

He still picked up books every day. Most days he would wander over to the bookshelves and choose a book, sometimes spending a good hour trying to decide which to read. He would reach out and run his fine fingers up and down the spines, feeling the dry dustiness of the paper. And he needed to pull the books out, one by one, so that he could read the titles. But once he had selected one he could not stop himself from looking at the others, from continuing along the shelf, and then along the next. And he would pick out book after book, whispering to himself the whole while. Then, when he finally had five or six books in his hands he would look them over, and pick the one with the best cover. And when he had finally chosen one, he would return to his seat, and sit with it between his hands, as though the information that it contained could be transmitted just by holding it. And that would be it.

This morning Mr Glass had selected *Birds and Flowers of Our Country Lanes* by B. E. Holmes. It was a thin hardback book which was now placed on the stool to the left of his chair. He had sat with it for a good ten minutes, trying to remember the last time he read it (by which he meant really read it, actually opened it and read it) and came to the conclusion that it was probably when he still lived with his grandchildren. When he lived with his grandchildren he used to read all his books a lot. He used to take one through to their room at night and open it, and begin to tell them about European shrubs or wildlife in Scotland.

'Boring!' they would scream, and quickly hide under the covers, giggling and thrilled by their own audacity. 'Boring, boring, boring,' they would chant sometimes, one always deserting the other on the third refrain, so that one of them was left, usually the younger one, guiltily looking keener to condemn his grandfather than the other.

'Tell us about the moss,' they would cry, 'yeah, the moss!' as they wriggled in their beds and made farting and burping noises, giggling all the while. And so he would tell them the moss story, for what seemed like the millionth time in his life.

The last time he had read *Birds and Flowers of our Country Lanes* must have been when he was living with them. Were somebody to open the book and read it to him he would realise that he still knew much of the detail in the book. But he didn't know that he still knew it and the book lay unopened on his table. Instead he waved his fingers in the air like a magician, a gesture which looked silly – but was actually an expression of frustration.

Kasia came through with a cup of tea. She handed it to him silently and he put it down straightaway because the mug was too hot.

'I've left my shirts in a pile in the bathroom. If you could bring them back on Wednesday I'd be very grateful. I've only got one more clean one.'

Kasia nodded and tightened her lips. She could not understand what it was about old people that made them always do things in the same way. Would the world stop if he didn't have a corduroy shirt to wear on Wednesday? Were there not more important things to think about?

She began to tidy up the front room, conscious that she

needed to be gone in an hour. She could feel Mr Glass watching her as she tidied, and she moved nervously, trying to dust and shuffle and rearrange as quickly as she could but at the same time trying not to break anything. Compared to some of the old people she visisted, Mr Glass had a lot of junk. She had never seen so much stuff in her life. He had millions of books for a start, all gathering dust and housing mites. Then he had loads of pictures on the walls – prints of plants and flowers, carefully dissected and labelled, and now fading from being left in the London sun for too long. There were some prints that didn't even make it on to the wall, stacked in the corner. Against one wall was a piano, with two standard lamps either side. Along the other wall was a sofa, pink and dusty like the rest of the room. And then, as a final touch, there were plants everywhere. On almost every available surface (and the floor too) stood a tub of some description, filled with bits of green, and, very occasionally, a flower. Some grew up and others tumbled down. Some had thin spiky leaves that rose into the air like huge blades of grass, and others large shiny expanses of green that clustered towards the window. When she first saw this room she refused to tidy it at all.

'Missed a bit!' he said.

She looked over her shoulder.

'Where?'

'There.'

'Here?'

'No, there. Down a bit, left a bit, nearly, left a bit more, now right, up a bit.'

She turned to look at him once again.

'Where?' she said, despairingly. There was a rawness to her face – a vulnerability. She looked as if she was going to cry.

He paused. 'I'm joking,' he said at last, clearly

uncomfortable. 'I'm sorry.' She left the front room and sought peace in the kitchen.

Kasia lived by herself in a small council flat. She had been in London for a few months and was trying to settle: she was searching for a routine, for familiarity, for habit. She worked three evenings a week in a newsagents, behind the till and stacking the shelves. The stock that needed to be replaced most frequently was the beer, closely followed by cigarettes, milk, chocolate and biscuits. She was never left in the shop by herself – the man she worked for did not trust her and he was right not to: if she had the chance she would empty the till and disappear. At least, that was what Kasia thought she would do.

She felt her life was split into three parts. The first section was the daytime, when she visited Mr Glass and other old people, chatting about the weather and their lives. That part of her life was civilised and good: she was looking after others, caring for society's has-beens. The evenings were brutal. The shop smelt of bad milk and smoke. The customers were rude and lewd and drunk or drugged. For this part of her life she narrowed her eyes and hardened her mouth and got on with her job. The nights and weekends she spent alone, sitting quietly in her flat, reluctant to make any noise that would disturb the silence. Or maybe reluctant to make a noise so that she didn't miss anything. The sound of someone coming to get her, for example.

On Saturday nights she would take a bath – as a treat, and as something to do. She would take something to read with her, perhaps a magazine that she had borrowed from behind the till at the shop, and she would lie there, listening to the whooshing of the water tank filling up once again, and underneath that the sounds of the street below – squeals of young people, the heavy footsteps of old. It was then that Kasia would allow herself to admit that it was hard. All the time she felt the hardness of being here, of being alone, of being. Her isolation grated on her every day, like an ill-fitting shoe, rubbing a blister over and over again, refusing to let it heal. The odd thing was that, although she was almost used to it, it didn't seem to get any easier. When she sat by herself in the bath on Saturday nights, not having uttered a single word all day, she felt the terrible oppression of being alone. Of having to distract her mind at every turn, just in case it might accidentally admit its loneliness, and she would have to spend the rest of the night huddled in tears on her bed. It boiled down to this: a person who lives alone feels everything more keenly than those who live together. Solitary people are necessarily more sensitive. And Kasia's sensitivity had become almost raw.

Sometimes, when she sat by herself she had long periods of despair. Despair that she had no one to talk with. Despair that she had no one to go out with. She sat by herself and suddenly everything in her flat looked strange and unfamiliar, as though she was sitting in the flat next door by mistake. Mr Glass referred to her as a 'young thing' and imagined her staying up all night and lying in the sun with her friends. But she did none of these 'young thing' things. And she knew it.

She was supposed to be rebuilding her life, but she did not know what to rebuild it with. She clung as tightly as she could to her jobs, to her flat, to her patience. But she worried that she might, at any moment, become the way she used to be. She lived in fear that she would return to that life, that the impulse to live her old existence was stronger than the urge to live a normal life like most other people.

The thing was, she did not know how she had come to that in the first place, and that was why she cowered in her flat at the weekend, terrified that at any minute she would abandon everything and undo all her hard work.

Kasia was stressed. She was going to be late for work at the shop and her boss, a young man called Ian, would shout at her, exactly as he had done on the one other occasion that she was late. As soon as he saw her come in the door he began to shout and swear at her, in front of customers and colleagues alike. She had not understood a lot of the words that he used but she knew they were unpleasant. What disturbed her more was the fact that none of the customers had paid any particular attention to the barrage of obscenities that he had spat at her.

Kasia brought Mr Glass's dinner through and left it on the table next to his chair. She went back to the kitchen to get on with clearing up, anxious to be gone as quickly as she could. There was a crash from the front room. She dropped a cup into the soapy water of the sink and went through. Mr Glass was still sitting in his chair (when was he not sitting in his chair? she thought). The blanket covering his legs had pieces of lamb and beige sauce on it. The broccoli and carrots had made it to the end of the slalom and were scattered on the carpet. Joining them, at his feet, was the plate, upturned and surrounded by bits of food. It looked like he had been sick, or like a toddler had refused to eat its food and flung it, in a fit of tears, on the floor.

'I'm terribly sorry, Kasia,' Mr Glass said, a grave tone in his voice. And his jaw continued to move after he had stopped speaking, as though he was speaking in a foreign language, and had been badly dubbed into English.

'*Damn*,' Kasia sighed heavily. 'I'm late already.'

She went back to the kitchen and left Mr Glass sitting there, the sauce slowly seeping through the prickly wool of the blanket. And Mr Glass? Mr Glass looked out of the window, desperately remembering a time when his hands didn't let him down.

She came back through, this time wearing her orange coat and carrying a bucket, and she started to clear up the plate and the food. She handed him a clean blanket and wiped the food off the carpet with a cloth that she kept washing out in the bucket. She packed her cleaning tools away again, and then left the flat, shouting a loud 'bye' from the hallway.

Mr Glass had been about to call her, when he heard her voice, shrill and jagged, come through the hallway and into his room. He sat there for a while, looking out of the window, muttering to himself and stroking his sideburn with his left hand. As he got up and shambled towards the kitchen, he noticed that his corduroy shirts were still in the bathroom, in a pile and ready for the launderette. He served himself some more lunch and returned to the front room to eat it. Once he had swallowed the last mouthful he put the plate on the table and sat for a long while looking out of the window.

Eventually he got up and went to the kitchen, where he took a large blue book from the counter. He opened it and looked for the letter 'G', stopping the page with his thumb when he found it. He picked up the phone and dialled. A moment later he began to speak: 'Hello, Mark, it's me. I was just wondering whether you could do me a favour. The current girl I've got from Clarks, I don't want to make a complaint about her, but I was wondering whether it might be possible to get her changed. I don't think we're compatible, and it's my fault as much as hers. Could you find out whether they've still got Inge? Anyway, let me know how you get on, and please don't say anything bad about the current one. Thanks then. Goodbye,' and he replaced the receiver.

THREE

Seven o'clock in the morning and it was still dark outside. Sam looked at his reflection in the office window. It was nice that his desk was next to a window. But not so good that the window was next to a brick wall. Not that it mattered when it was dark. He could see himself reflected in the shroud of light from his desk lamp. He studied his reflection and, although he was not near enough to the window to pick out individual wrinkles, he got the impression from his face that he was getting old. At twenty-five he was not in the least bit old, but he still felt that he was ageing quickly. Every morning as he left his flat in the dark he felt as though another wrinkle had formed on his forehead. Every night, as he emerged from his office into the darkness of the street he felt his heart shudder, as though the stress of the day had shortened its lifespan.

He looked around him at the whiteness of the office. The walls were white, the ceiling was white, the piles of paper everywhere were white, and things that weren't white were a light grey – a dirty snow grey, slush grey. Sam squinted and tried to pretend that, instead of sitting in the office, he was out in a snowy landscape. He could just about do it. He could just about imagine that the wall in front of him was a mountain rising out of nowhere, that the computer terminals were hillocks, that the pieces of paper sprawled on the floor were patches of ice. He peered into this landscape for a while, turning his head slightly so that he could look at things from different angles, transforming the objects in his imagination. The snow-scene transfixed him. The prospect of all that white paralysed him with its beauty, its power, its wholeness. And that was only how it looked. What would the scene be like with the right sounds? With a brutal wind, with cracking ice and crunching snow? What would it be like with a coldness in his nostrils, a blueness around his lips? What would it be like with a huge blue sky overhead?

'Sam? Earth to Sam?'

'Oh morning, Lauren. How are you?'

'Have you been here all night?'

'No. Feels like it though. Out at eleven, in at seven.'

'Got time for a coffee?'

'Sure.' Sam walked to the lift with Lauren. He liked sitting with her because not only was she nice, but she was also pretty. Hers was a good face to see first thing in the morning. She had gingery blonde bobbed hair which ended just where her lips began. She had resisted dyeing it any blonder, though most of the other girls in the department had peroxide-enhanced hair. Her eyes were green, but unusually dark and she had great breasts. They were a perfect size, though Sam did not know what size that was. The fact that there were two components involved in breast sizing completely threw him. If it were just 34, 36, 38 and so on, then he might have been able to manage it. But the letter thing was just too complicated. So Lauren's breasts were just perfect: large enough to be womanly, but small enough to be pert. And sometimes she didn't wear a bra. When she took her coat off in the morning and Sam saw the shadow of her nipples against her shirt he knew that he was in for a good day. Lauren really wanted to make documentaries. The first one was going to be about the mice that live on the train tracks of the London Underground (*Town Mice* was its title) but no one had wanted to commission it.

They went to the wine bar in the basement to smoke and to have coffee. It was a quarter past eight, and there were a few people sitting around, trying to orientate themselves.

'How are you this morning?' Sam asked.

'Mmm. Could be better. I went out with Richard last night and –'

'*You did not.*'

'*Un*intentionally,' she said, as though he ought to have known. 'We *happened* to end up in the same bar. You know I told you I was meeting a friend at 101?'

Sam nodded. Richard had started at McLeod Seagal at the same time as Sam. He was tall and blond, with a long fringe and a loud voice. Sam knew that as long as Richard continued to talk loudly he would be successful.

'And?'

'Well, we were both quite drunk, and we had a long chat. Did you know he used to go to ballet lessons?'

'No,' said Sam, full of disbelief, half of his face smiling.

'Yep. His mother sent him from an early age. Apparently he got too muscular and had to give it up.'

'Too muscular? For a ballet dancer? I think not.'

'Yeah, I know. But can you imagine: Richard in tights?'

Sam smiled. 'Are you sure he was telling the truth?'

'Well, why would he lie?'

'To impress you?'

She shook her head and furrowed her brow. Her hair bobbed around her ears. She was wearing a light blue jumper. He looked at her breasts, gently rounded in the fluffy wool.

'Sam, are you mad? If he was trying to impress me he wouldn't have told me that he went to *ballet classes.*'

'Maybe he thought you would see it as all sensitive and nineties?'

'Anyway, I was with a bloke already. He'd have to be a

fool to try and pull a girl who was with a guy.'

'And he's not?' Sam said, eyebrows raised.

'Yeah, but not that much of one.' Sam sighed. Richard walked past their table, his shoes clipping on the lino, a cappuccino in one hand and a paper bag of croissants in the other.

'Morning, Sam. Lauren,' he boomed. 'How are you feeling this glorious Tuesday morning? The worse for wear?' Sam looked at him, saw him decked out in his tights and tunic, and smiled.

'Oh, I'm okay. Or I will be once I've had my coffee,' Lauren replied with a gentle smile. She was very good at insincerity. Sometimes it made Sam feel a bit insecure.

'After you left last night, my friend and I went on to Chez Emile's where we did shots till three this morning. Then I chucked all over my shoes.' He laughed. 'Yeah, I felt like fucking *shit* when I woke up this morning. It was then that I started to regret not having taken you up on your offer. At least I wouldn't have woken up with my clothes on.' Richard laughed again from his belly, and raised his eyebrows at Lauren from under his fringe. He balanced his croissants on top of his coffee cup and massaged her shoulder with his right hand. Then he walked off.

Lauren looked pale.

'Now I see why you were so adamant that he wasn't trying to pull you. Because *you* were trying to pull *him*.' Sam smiled at her.

'Yeah, right. About as likely as me trying to pull you.' She tapped the ash off her cigarette.

'Gee, thanks.' Sam pulled his pager off his belt: *phone Janine ASAP*. He replaced it. 'So who were you with last night?' Lauren looked at him and laughed. She had a nice laugh.

'Since when did you care?' She got up and pushed her

chair underneath the table. They retraced their steps to the lift.

'Since when were you so secretive? Was it anybody I know?' His mobile phone rang. 'Sam speaking. Hi, Janine. No, sorry, I was just about to ring you, I got your page . . . Yes . . . yes, I know. Right . . . Yup, two o'clock is fine . . . Okay . . . Bye then.'

They got into the lift. 'So how many times do I have to ask you who you were with?'

Lauren unclipped her pager and looked at a message. She raised her eyes to the ceiling. 'I was with my brother,' she said, shaking her head at him.

As Sam came round the corner he saw that Angela was standing by his desk, rummaging through his papers. She looked especially fragile this morning in a tight white top stretched across her bony shoulders. His throat felt dry.

'Hi,' he said as he approached. 'What are you after?'

'Those notes you did last night.'

'I put a copy on your desk.'

'Yeah – I just want to check it against the originals.' She looked up from his desk and fixed her birdy eyes on him, holding the original set of notes in her left hand, fingers twitching. She looked cross. But she usually looked cross.

'Is there something wrong with it?' he asked gently.

'It makes no sense,' she said, loud and clear. 'Did you not realise? There are notes on *both* sides of these pieces of paper. You've only typed up half of them.'

Sam took the sheets from her. He flicked one over. And then back. He took another. Notes on both sides again. She was right. He had only done half of what he needed to. Fuck.

'We need the whole thing for the meeting at eleven. I'd make a start now, if I were you,' she said, a little glint in her eye. 'What's the matter with you? Can't you do anything right?' As he looked at her, Sam couldn't help thinking of the evil stepmother in Snow White. He waited for her to walk off, then straightened the notes and left them on his desk. He took the lift down to the ground floor and walked straight out of the door.

Sam strode down the street in no particular direction, shoulders hunched over, looking down at his feet. He felt better being outside. There was something about being in an office day after day that threw Sam off balance – he became twitchy and impatient, fidgeting in his chair or tapping his foot. Walking along in grey, brutal weather, there was something about Sam that made him appear tough, almost brittle, but Sam was not really tough. He was generally mild-mannered, and would be described by most of his colleagues as quiet ('it's always the quiet ones' would be heard many times round the office in years to come). He was tall and well-built, and had once played a lot of sport, but in the past year had been too busy, and this, combined with drinking with clients, had softened his stomach. Sam spoke slowly, taking his time over each syllable. He had a funny little habit of staring off into the distance mid-sentence, as though thinking of something far away, or groping for a fugitive word. He had short thick dark hair and a nose that he had got from his grandfather – largish and bent. His eyes were blue: a cold blue, cyan blue, ice blue. And he had an odd look in them. A look that had always been in Sam's eyes, and that had inspired his father to call him *Crazy Horse*. 'Hello there, Crazy Horse,' he would say as he sat down at the dinner table in the kitchen and flicked his fork over by bouncing his finger on the tines.

'Darling,' his mother would say, looking disapprovingly at him as she placed straw mats on the checked tablecloth.

She thought that Crazy Horse was not a suitable nickname for a child.

'But look at him,' his dad would cry, 'look at those eyes. They're all your fault, Dad,' and he would turn to Sam's grandad who had by now appeared in the room, book in hand, spectacles hanging around his neck on a string, white hair slicked back.

'What, me?' Leo would protest. 'I don't know what you mean,' and he would shake his head as he began to help his daughter-in-law with pots and plates and bits of cutlery.

'Sam's got your crazy eyes, that's what I mean. And one day he's bound to do something as hare-brained as the stuff you did. And that's why, although we all call him Sam,' and at this point he lowered his voice to almost a whisper, 'his real name in this world is *Crazy Horse*. Isn't that right . . . Crazy Horse?' Sam's dad would wink and look over at Sam who, all eyes on his dad, would nod and, for special effect, emit a loud, whinnying neigh, rolling his eyes and flaring his nostrils while his father's laugh filled the whole kitchen.

'Oh darling,' his mother would start, but with a smile in her voice, 'don't encourage him,' and she would remove her oven gloves and sit down at the table with them. 'It's just like Mark and the roof. You're not fit to be a father, you really aren't.' And then she would turn to Sam and say, 'Sam, you're *not* crazy. And there's nothing odd about your eyes,' but even as she said it she would wonder whether her husband was right, and whether Sam would do something crazy one day.

The argument over the roof had been an argument that Sam's parents had had for as long as they had been together. His mother did not feel that she should stop her husband going up there, even though the neighbours often commented on his peculiar behaviour, but she felt she had to draw the line at their children. Sam's dad of course agreed that it was dangerous and irresponsible. He put his arms around her and blew on the end of her nose and tried to explain that although she was right, she could not understand how much fun it was up there, up above Cheltenham, above the buildings, with only the sky far away.

'The thing is,' he said, 'they'll see me going up anyway, so they're going to want to come up at some stage. I think it's better to let them see what it is like and then they'll get bored and start to go out with girls instead. If we stop them now, it'll always hold a fascination for them, you see?'

And in a way both Sam's mother and his father were right. By the time the boys were adults, Mark would never go up on a roof again. But Crazy Horse, whom their mother had always been the keenest to protect because he was the youngest, Crazy Horse would spend a large part of his adult life negotiating drainpipes and broken tiles, just to get up to where his dad had once been.

Sam's nickname worried not only his mother but also, from time to time, Leo, his grandfather. As he watched his youngest grandson tear around the back garden, a large pair of white pants tied to a walking stick trailing behind him, he knew that Sam's father was right. Occasionally, when Mark pushed Sam over and tickled and wrestled with him, Leo would see Sam suddenly start upwards, looking around him as though he had just heard something odd, ears pricked and eyes darting everywhere. Or when Sam was chasing Mark, he would suddenly spurt ahead, seeming to have a burst of strength and energy out of nowhere, and easily overtake his elder brother. And Leo knew that this was what Robert meant when he called his son Crazy Horse, and he also knew that he was probably partly responsible for this behaviour because, although it was a long time ago, he could remember doing the same things himself. He could remember the feel of that crazed look in his own eyes. He could remember how it felt to have that little buzz just behind your pupils, that shortness of breath, that conviction that the world was set to end at any minute.

And so Leo worried that the name might make Sam anxious, that it might, in some way, concern him that his entire family called him crazy. Because it wasn't really crazy. It wasn't institution crazy. It wasn't straitjacket crazy. Leo knew the feeling, and he wanted Sam to know that it was, all in all, an okay feeling, an okay crazy, a crazy that could be joked about. And that was why, one day, when Sam's dad and Mark were sitting on the roof and Patty was in the kitchen, Leo came into the front room to see Sam.

'Hi there, Sammy.' Leo came over and sat down in his chair. Then he got up again and took one of his maps of the world from the bookcase, spreading it over the coffee table and fetching a box of pins from the top of the TV. He looked over at Sam who stopped what he was doing and came to sit near by. Leo and Sam played this game at least once a week.

'Sam, what's that doing there?' Sam had a paperback stuffed into the top of his trousers, pressing into his tummy.

'I was reading it and I kept losing it,' he said as he looked up at his grandad, only becoming aware that his behaviour might seem curious once he had uttered his explanation. Leo nodded and took the top off the box of pins, holding it out to Sam to select one.

'Where's your dad?'

'Up on the roof. With Mark.'

'They're a pair those two, aren't they? If you could have seen your dad when he was a boy, you wouldn't believe how like Mark he was.'

'But he doesn't look anything like Mark,' Sam objected, scrunching his eyes shut and reaching out his hand, ready to find a home for his pin in the map.

'Not now, no. But as a boy he looked just the same.'

'Was he as awful as Mark is?' Sam asked, jealous of his brother's resemblance to his father and opening his eyes to find that he had to travel to Sweden. Sweden. How boring.

'Do you mean was he as awful *nice* as Mark is?' said Leo with a smile and a shake of the head. 'Yes, they're quite similar in behaviour too, really,' and he stretched out, eyes shut, and stuck his pin in the southern coast of Portugal.

Sam looked at the map and wondered where he should go. It appeared, to him, that he wasn't really a part of this family. Mark fitted into the snug embrace of genetics, his mum and dad were two halves of a whole, and Leo was, well, Leo was a founding member. But where did Sam come into it?

'You know who you're like, Crazy Horse?' asked Leo, seeming, as he often did, to be able to read Sam's thoughts. Sam shook his head and took another pin. He pressed the sharp end into the soft part of his finger to see how much pain he could stand. He held his breath as his grandad stared off out of the window. 'You're like me,' Leo said, 'just like me', and tilted his head to one side, scratching his cheek.

Sam looked at his grandfather. He certainly didn't look anything like him. Sam was seven. Leo was sixty-eight. Sam had thick dark hair, bright blue eyes and a small child's nose. Leo had thick white hair which stuck up off his head, bright blue eyes and a largish bent nose.

'And that's why I wanted to say,' Leo continued, aware that he had finally come to his point, 'that when they call you crazy, they don't mean a bad crazy. Your dad says you get it from me, because he thinks I'm crazy too, but I'm not. You know, it's just something that happens every now and then, I just get stuck on things. You'll probably do so too, but don't let it worry you.'

Sam nodded at his grandad. He didn't really know what he was talking about. All he had taken in was that it wasn't bad crazy. So Sam wasn't going to be bad. He felt relieved.

'And it has its good parts,' Leo continued, staring down at the map, letting his eyes wander over vast continents, over mountains and seas, and smoothing his hands over it, as though brushing away crumbs. 'I'm glad I did the things that some people consider crazy. I couldn't really help myself at the time, but now I'm glad I did them. They don't make me better than anyone else, but they were important to me. They really were. It means that when, on this planet, the last animal takes its last breath, at least I was slightly crazy. At least I let myself be slightly crazy.'

Sam leant over the map and stuck his pin into the bottom of it. Then he climbed on to his grandfather's knee and waited for the story to begin.

These were the thoughts going round his head as Sam walked along the streets of Soho, waiting until he felt calmer, waiting for his crazy look to subside. And as he walked he dropped his shoulders and held his head high in the cold air, enjoying the biting wind blowing round his neck and ears.

He walked on, past closed restaurants, sleeping strip bars and barely open offices. He couldn't help thinking that Soho in the morning seemed like a performer in her dressing room, her make-up half-finished, her costume half-on, her expression businesslike. Soho was not a morning place, and as she struggled to life Sam noticed that almost everyone was carrying a polystyrene cup. He looked at the pavement beneath his feet, stained with streaks of darkness and littered with prostitute cards, burger wrappers and cigarette butts.

He turned the corner back into the street where his office was, took a deep breath and walked back into reception.

His phone rang. 'Sam speaking.'

'Sammy. How are you? How late was it?'

Sam had just dropped a copy of the presentation on to Angela's desk.

'Hi, Henry. About midnight.'

'Oh well. You didn't miss much. Sara's friend went home early and then we had a row. Anyway, I'm off to New York for a few days so I won't see you.'

'Not on my passport, I hope.'

'Nah, don't worry, I've got a temporary one. I'm going to interview a *very* sexy human rights campaigner.'

'Henry, you cannot make a move on a human rights campaigner.'

'Why not? She'd be the last one to deny my right to try, wouldn't she?'

'So how's Sara?'

'Not so good. Well, she's fine, but I'm just not that keen any more. You know when you get that feeling that they're more into you than you are into them?'

'I don't think I've ever experienced that. I think I've always been on the keener side.'

'No, you know what I mean, Sammy. She sends me cards and things. I think it has to end. I don't think she understands me at all. And I find talking to her about stuff kind of difficult. Actually that's a complete lie. What I mean is that she thinks I flirt with other girls too much. And she's bought this pair of white dungarees which she insists on wearing all the time, despite the fact that they make her look like she's pregnant, which really worries me.'

'Why? Is she?'

'She says she's not. But, good God, can you imagine? Having to have babies with her? That's what made me realise that it wasn't going well.'

'So are you going to chuck her?'

'Dunno. Thought I might go for the constructive dismissal option instead.'

'Which is?'

'Oh, you know. Making myself suitably annoying until she chucks me. It shouldn't take that long – about three weeks of leaving my pants on her floor, putting empty cereal boxes back in her cupboard, begging for blow-jobs, not to mention getting completely rat-arsed at the weekend. That should do it. I'll tell you something else though. Late at night, lying in bed, I say "What's your favourite sexual position?", guess what she says?'

'Goal attack?'

'Military. The military position,' and Henry went silent at the other end.

Later that day, Sam was in a cab back to the agency. He had been to a Reynolds shoot in Essex, where he had had to check the model of the exhaust, the angle of photography and the positions of the shiny tube. He was dazed and tired, staring out at the rows and rows of suburban houses, wondering who was in them and what they were doing.

Then suddenly they were in a street Sam recognised, but for a split second he didn't know why. He sat up and instinctively looked to the left, waiting for the house he knew, for the familiar bay window to flick by. He wondered whether he might even be able to catch a glimpse of Leo, sitting in his armchair by the window, looking out, and Sam felt a wave of guilt knowing that he didn't have time to stop, that he was needed back at work. Just as the house was approaching Sam saw a young girl in an orange coat walking along on the same side of the street. As the car sped past her Sam turned his head and tried to see her face, but he caught only a sliver of her profile. What, he thought, is a young woman like that doing in a street like this in the middle of the day? What was someone like her doing in these dreary streets where nothing ever happens and everything looks the same, day after day? Yet her presence there seemed to change those streets, it seemed to block the road and fill the front yards, towering high into the sky and saying loudly, confidently to Sam: these streets aren't so sad after all. And he waved at Leo's window, which reflected the street and the sky and didn't let Sam see through to his grandfather inside.

Back in the agency he started on the pile of Reynolds press ads that had appeared on his desk. When he had just started on the account he had run a batch of ads with the wrong phone number on them, and an unsuspecting household in Kent had a barrage of calls from people wanting to know more about the free-Reynolds-exhaust-with-every-tyre-refit-at-selected-garages-offer. Jeff had gone mad, and the agency had to pay for the ads and the space in the papers. Ever since then Sam had been extra careful with these ads. He started to read the small print backwards.

'Is this your idea of a joke?' He knew, without looking up, the expression on Angela's face. He looked up. Red cheeks and neck. Eyes with a clear sheen. Curled lip. Keep calm, Sam told himself. She might be right, she might have a point. She must have a reason for being so worked up.

'What do you mean?'

'This,' she said, thrusting a sheet of shaking paper in front of him. He looked at it. It was one of the charts he had typed up that morning. One of the charts she was now presenting to the client downstairs in the boardroom. He read it through. He still couldn't see what she meant.

'I'm sorry, Angela, I –'

'How could you? Are you intent on embarrassing me and making me look foolish?'

'I don't know what you mean,' he said slowly.

'Read out the headline.'

Sam did his best to read from the piece of paper that was now positively jumping around in front of his eyes.

' "What are we doing for Shadows?" '

'Yeah right. Read it again. Jesus, you're *so* slow.'

Sam looked at it again. He saw that he had read it wrongly the first time.

' "What are we doing Shadows for?" '

He had to stop himself smiling. He bit his cheeks.

'I'm really sorry. I –'

'How many times have I told you: check and check again. Have you any idea how this looked when I presented it downstairs? I know you're trying to catch me out, Sam. I know that you're doing this on purpose, but it's not a very good idea to try and take on your boss. Especially when your boss is me.' She stormed off, knocking the wires out of the back of somebody's computer as she went.

Sam didn't have to stop himself smiling. It wasn't funny any more.

FOUR

The first thing Sam saw as he entered Le Matelot was his brother, leaning against the bar, his mobile phone in one hand and a crisp tenner in the other. Sam made his way over and raised his eyebrows at him as Mark shouted into his phone, 'I'm in Le Matelot.'

Sam smiled. 'You don't say,' he murmured and mouthed 'lager' at him a couple of times until he'd got the message. He looked around and spotted Mark's fiancée at the other side of the bar. The fiancée was blonde and petite, and she spoke with a lisp. She had the misfortune to be christened Clarissa and she chose to live in Sloane Square, and so basic conversation (what's your name? where do you live?) was rendered embarrassing and difficult. Henry called her the Square Sloane from Sloane Square, and he was not far off.

'Hello, Clarissa. How are you?' He kissed her. She smelt of something floral.

'Jutht wonderful,' she smiled. 'How about you? Tham, this is Janie. Janie, thith ith Tham.' Clarissa was indicating him with an open hand, as Janie came back from the loo and sat down opposite him. 'Janie workth in PR, tho you two will have thomething to talk about.'

Sam looked at Janie and smiled. She had even features and long brown hair, tied up with black ribbon. She was wearing a beige cashmere sweater and a thin gold necklace. Sam's spirits sank.

Sam frequently asked himself how Mark had ended up being friends with girls like these, and he always came up with the same answer: his job. Mark worked as a fund manager for a large Japanese bank in the City. He worked like a lunatic, but he was paid by a lunatic too, so he came off all right in the end. He used money as a buffer, as something that would protect him, as best it could, from things that he didn't expect. Sam had no idea what it would be like to earn so much but he had watched Mark gain a certain confidence, a certain laid-backness, as his payslips rolled in and his credit cards went from blue to gold. Sam knew that money made things easier, that it dispersed anxiety as warm water dissolved sugar.

'How you doing?' Mark brought the drinks over.

'Thanks. Yeah, I'm fine. How about you?' Sam yelled to make himself heard above the noise of the music.

'Mmmmmnnn.' Mark gave a small nod. 'Yeah. Though I can't stay out late tonight – Andrea's not very well.'

'Oh really?'

'Mmmmmnn. Vet says it's flu.'

Andrea was a pure-bred Pyrenean Mountain Dog that, as a small bundle of fluff, had set Mark back about six hundred pounds. She was insured – against injury and death but not disgrace or acts of God. She was walked twice a day by a professional dog-walker who lived round the corner. She had a lovely large beanbag bed made for her out of thick wool, her own fridge and her own neatly packaged food from an up-market grocer's on Notting Hill Gate. Mark had actually bought a book of names before he decided what to call her (he objected to 'silly gaga names' because he thought of dogs as people, complete with a dark and destructive side). Sam suspected that he had tired of it rather quickly and never got past the A section.

Mark was actually quite a funny person to have a dog. He liked drawers shut, cupboard doors closed, surfaces clean and empty and everything packed away. When he opened his jars of instant coffee he pierced the gold paper and then carefully peeled it all off, so that no trace remained. His leather brogues, placed side by side under the table in his hallway, were always supported with wooden trees when they were not on his feet. They were polished once a week, and the laces replaced once a year. He was wedded to order, symmetry, proportion and, most of all, peace. The kind of peace that came from everything being in its proper place. He kept his tea towels — washed, ironed, folded and then rolled up — in a special drawer in the kitchen. There were three states of tea-towelness in Mark's flat. In the drawer, in use or in the wash. These were finite states, and there was no in-between. A tea towel could not be kind of in use but kind of in the wash. Neither could one that had been in use be returned to the drawer without first going through the wash. In his last year at university when he was looking for a job Sam used to come to London for interviews and stay in Mark's flat. They once spent a whole evening sitting in silence in front of the TV because Mark had come into the kitchen to find Sam taking a tray of pizza out of the oven with one of his regulation white tea towels, encrusted with molten cheese and singed by the heat.

Right now Mark was piling up his change on the pine table, grouping the coins and then stacking them, and then arranging the piles into something symmetrical. Sam glanced along the bar, hoping that Henry would soon appear to give him someone to talk to. He was supposed to be coming along with some other friends from college, Jack, a policeman and Clare, a newly qualified solicitor.

As Sam looked around the bar he couldn't help wondering what all these people were doing here. Sam was here because, well, because everyone else was. That's not a very good reason, he thought to himself, as his gaze homed in on the female faces at the bar.

'Sam? . . . Sam?' He turned to see Janie looking at him.

'Oh, sorry. I was miles away,' he smiled.

'You weren't. You were right here, I promise you,' she giggled. He nodded. 'What accounts do you work on?'

He drew breath. 'Shadows.'

She coloured a little. 'That's great. What a great brand to work on. I mean, that's a huge brand. A huge brand. A really meaningful brand.'

'Yeah, it's okay. What about you?'

'Groughtons.'

Sam nodded again. Who? he thought.

'They make toiletries and cosmetics. It's great. I love it. They don't have any money for advertising so they care a lot about their PR. We do all sorts of things. Last week we all dressed up as the herbs and plants they use in their products and stood in Covent Garden to draw attention to the fact that all their products have natural ingredients. I was witch hazel,' she giggled again, fiddling with her necklace. 'I dressed up as a witch. Witch Hazel, you see?'

Sam smiled.

'So, did you never think about working in PR?' she said.

'No,' Sam shook his head. His eyes scanned the table to see who else was there.

'Oh right. Of course, Daddy says that PR's all common sense, but then he would. But my brother's the company accountant for Groughtons, so he'll be able to back me up when sales shoot up after our herb day. It only cost the company five thousand pounds' worth of money.' She smiled.

Sam smiled back and looked over at Claritha for help. She was playing with Mark, leaning forward on her stool and pinching his cheeks and stroking his hair. They looked like a pair of puppies, fascinated by their own reflections. Sam knew that Mark had not always been faithful to

Claritha and wondered now that they were engaged, whether all that had stopped, or whether Mark was just more discreet about it.

Henry, Jack and Clare arrived and joined the table. Clare looked pale and stressed.

'Working you hard?' Sam asked, knowing the answer to the question before he asked it.

'It's not that,' she said. 'Something really weird just happened.'

'What?' Jack said, rolling a cigarette and raising his eyebrows.

'Well,' she paused and looked off for a second, 'for the past few weeks someone's been sending me my own underwear in the post. And then today –'

'Hang on. Someone's been doing what?' Henry interrupted.

'Sending me my own underwear,' Clare said, and raised her eyes to the ceiling. 'I know it's odd, but I'm kind of used to it by now.'

'But how do they get it?' Sam asked.

'I don't know. Or I didn't know until –'

'Was it clean?'

'Oh Jack. Yes, it was clean. And it wasn't particularly racy either. And the envelopes were typed and posted from WC1,' she paused and flicked her eyes from one face to the next, 'and then today my boss came into my office and told me that . . . it was him,' she said, anxiety draining into her face.

'Bingo,' said Henry.

'You're kidding,' said Jack.

She shook her head. 'Straight up.'

'His is, I'm sure.'

'Henry, that's not funny,' she replied. 'It's really freaked me out.'

'I'm not surprised,' added Sam, 'he's clearly a lunatic. So how *does* he get it?'

'I don't even want to think about that part. He said that he had a *method*.'

'You should tell the police,' Henry suggested.

'That's exactly what I am doing,' she replied, looking at Jack.

'Mark, what shall I do?' It was an idle question. The kind of question they used to ask each other when they were young, sitting in their bedroom when it was raining outside.

'What do you mean?' Mark was scanning the wine list. 'They haven't got that Sauvignon on their list any more.'

'I want to give up my job.'

'Really? Mmmmmmn. I thought you loved it. Dunno.' Sam looked around as more and more young people in suits came in off the fashionable Soho streets to be in the fashionable bar.

'Sometimes I think I just don't want to work at all. Well, not doing a normal job, anyway.'

Mark laughed. 'Yeah and? Most people, given the choice, imagine that they don't want to work either.'

'But what's the point of it all? Is there any other point apart from having a nice life for the three seconds that you're not in the office?' Sam looked off into the distance.

'Well, now you're getting all philosophical on me. I don't know. Who knows? All I'd say is that I used to feel like you too. Don't worry about it, it passes. As you get older you accept it more. You're twenty-five. I'm twenty-eight. As the years pass you become less poetic.'

'Tham, there you are! What are you two nattering about? Janie ith all alone, and I thought I charged you with keeping her entertained. Get her a drink and be charming!'

Sam did as he was told and bought drinks for Janie for the

rest of the evening. In fact, he bought more drink for himself than for her, because he couldn't face her without it. She talked about her daddy, her old banger of a car, her career and her Tiffany necklace. As the evening wore on and Sam became more weary Janie started to grow on him. He had drunk enough to think intimate conversation with her was a good idea, and they talked meaningful rubbish, shouting at each other, their mouths touching each other's ears in an effort to be heard above the music, as the bar slowly emptied. They moaned about London, about work, about being old before your time. Janie invited Sam to come and live with her in the countryside.

'No, go on,' Janie shouted. 'I think we should go. Exit the rat race. Become country bunnies.'

'Yeah, well, I'm fed up with London, that's for sure. It's taking years off my life living here,' he yelled at her.

'Well, come on then. Daddy has a house in Norfolk which, if I ask nicely, he'll let me live in. We have to be totally self-sufficient, that's all. Well, apart from the dishwasher maybe. But we have to grow our own food, and mine our own electricity. I'll leave you to do that bit,' she giggled.

'You know what really gets me down?' Sam began, tilting his head on one side.

She took a sip of her wine and shook her head. 'No. What?'

'This,' said Sam, and he began to dig around in the inside pocket of his jacket. He found what he was looking for, pulled it out and put it on the table in front of Janie.

'Your tube ticket?' She looked confused.

'But what *kind* of ticket is it?' He leant closer to her ear. She smelt of something. Something nice.

'It's a travelcard. So you can go on the buses and the tubes and the trains and everything.' She still looked confused.

'Yes, but how long is it valid?'

'Oh,' she said, picking it up so that she could read the date. 'It's an annual one. Valid for a whole year.'

'Exactly. My point entirely.' Sam said, satisfied, in a drunken way, that his point had been made.

'So what?'

He looked at her again. He went back to the beginning: 'This depresses me,' he began, pointing at the card in the plastic wallet, 'because it is valid for a whole year. That means that I am supposed to be in London for the next year of my life. It means I am supposed to be here, travelling to work every day, for another year. Another whole year on the underground. I *know* what I will be doing for the next year, and I don't like it. I don't like what I do, and I am sentenced to another whole year of it. *That's* why it depresses me.'

'Oh, I see,' she said, and fiddled some more with her necklace. 'Maybe you should get a car?'

When Sam finally staggered up his stairs and into the hallway it was two thirty, and he was drunk. Gray wasn't in and Sam lurched through to his room to play the game he always played when he was drunk and melancholy. He sat on his bed and removed his shoes. He took off his jacket and his trousers and then his tie. He left them in a pile on his chair. Then he picked up a clear box with pins in it. He took a pin out, concentrating so that he did not drop it, and walked carefully over to one of his maps, shutting his eyes for the last few steps and stretching out his arm.

The pin struck home in the sea just off China. In the East China Sea, south-east of Shanghai. He looked at the place names dotted on the land near by: Hangzhou, Nanjing, Fuzhou. *Hang-zhou, Nan-jing, Fu-zhou* – he mouthed them in his best Chinese accent, bowing his head at the start of each word. He looked at the colours on the map, at the green delta where the place names gathered and at the yellow mountains. Those were real places, he thought. All those little words and symbols and lines and colours – they indicated life. They meant flesh and blood. They meant breath and hair and ligaments. And shit and piss and semen. They meant that there were things there, that there were people there, that right now, as he sat there, there was somebody like him sitting in Fu-zhou, staring at the same moon as him.

He looked at the map. He looked at it some more. And then he thought that maybe a map was actually the prettiest picture in the world. Maybe this functional thing, this sheet of information, this lovingly detailed and crafted diagram was also the nicest thing he could look at. Forget Matisse, Rembrandt and Hockney. Maps should be hanging in galleries, maps should be auctioned for millions of pounds. Look at the use of colour! Look at how gently the gradations slide down the mountains, and how cleverly all the lines fit so snugly together and yet do not cross each other! And what would happen if the place names were removed from the map? Sam looked at the map in front of him and tried to see it without any words on it. Then it really would be art, wouldn't it? A still life, perhaps?

Sam looked at his pin. Should he go to China? Tea, communism, Mao and pandas. Something Mark had said kept coming back into his head, like a cat that has been fed once, and keeps returning just in case there's more: you become less poetic, you become less poetic. *You become less poetic. Less* poetic? Sam didn't think he was that poetic now. If he was only going to get less, what would he be when he was thirty? The most trivial philistine on the planet.

He took the rest of his clothes off and got into bed. He

lay and stared at the diagonal line of light that lay across his ceiling, formed by the orange of the street lamp falling through the gap between the curtains, his head full of thoughts of the Great Wall.

Eventually he slept, waking at half past three, anxious that he had forgotten something for the Shadows meeting he had in the morning. He put on his dressing gown and went out on to the roof. As he sat there he thought about the scene with Angela from the day before, and what he could have said to help the situation. As he replayed the conversation in his head, Sam thought that he should leave. The only trouble was that the logical path he saw after giving up his job went from unemployment to eviction to alcoholism to friendlessness to heroin to impotence to insanity to death. And Sam Glass did not want to die.

He counted as many stars as he could see, having to start again about seven times over because he kept forgetting whether he had counted particular ones or not. Then he counted the number of roofs he could see. Then he counted chimney pots. And then tree tops. Next he moved on to the hairs on his big toe.

Sam shivered. He was cold, sitting out there just in his dressing gown. But Sam quite liked being cold. There was something about it – a kind of simplicity and alertness – that attracted him. He did not feel hungry when he was cold, and his thinking was at its best when his skin rose in goose-pimples. Of all weather types snow was his favourite. Grimy pavements and tacky shops could slowly transform into a scene from a postcard. He liked the way it fell too, in no hurry to be anywhere in particular. Ice-crystals, sitting together in intricate formations, falling when the mood took them. Water, Sam knew, had more solid forms than any other known substance. But only one of those forms was silent when it fell. It was possible to go to bed one night, sleep soundly and wake to a white world in the morning. And when it was on the ground it silenced other things too: it absorbed footsteps and car noises and pram rattles and bicycle judders. It absorbed everything into a world of quiet whiteness.

Sam couldn't help feeling, after he had left university, that his life had somehow stopped. That everything had been put on hold for a few years. In fact, when he thought about it, he wasn't even sure that his life had ever begun. School and university were all preparation, they were all part of the process of getting ready, of building up knowledge and ways of thinking and skills that would be used later on. But used later on doing what? Sam couldn't help thinking, 'is this it?' Over and over he refused to believe that it was. But when he asked himself what *it* was, he had no answer. And so he felt that he was waiting. Treading water. Fire-fighting. Taking two steps forward and two back. Twenty-five and waiting for a different life. Waiting for the real thing. Waiting to become somebody. When he chewed his fingers that was what he was thinking. When he stared at the sky those were the thoughts that went through his mind. And it always started with the same question: Is this it?

He got up and went back into his room, where he shut the window and gazed for a moment at his maps, remembering the game he had played when he got in last night and looking at where the pin had struck home. Climbing into bed he thought that the answer must lie on one of those maps. There must be some place where things would make sense, where he would do the right thing, where he would stare at the sky to admire its beauty and not to look for an answer.

For the second time that night he fell asleep, and slept, twitching, with more of his duvet off the bed than on. A few hours later, just before dawn, the pin fell out of the sea on the wall and landed, with a tinkle, on the floor.

FIVE

Robert Glass was sitting in his chair. He had a tray on his lap, and on the tray was a plate with beans on toast on it. He was watching tennis on television. The room in which he was sitting was long and thin. There were a lot of plants in it – a spider plant on top of the TV, a begonia on the table, a yucca on the mantelpiece and a large aspidistra by the bay window. His wife was upstairs doing the hoovering, a walkman straddling her head. As she pushed the hoover under the edges of their bed, she was listening to a song she used to sing as a teenager.

Downstairs Robert was watching Björn Borg playing at Wimbledon.

'Superb,' he said, nodding his head. 'Bloody superb.' He glanced up and looked out of the window at a ginger cat jumping into their garden. He stared for a second. Then he picked up his knife and fork and began to cut his beans on toast. As he lifted his left arm he felt something squeeze his chest. He breathed in, and the squeezing increased. He gasped for breath, but the tightness held on, and he felt pressure building in his head. He had never felt this way before. He was confused, and he panicked.

'Pat,' he called out. 'Patty,' he called again, louder this time, but also with more of a rasp. And he thought: she will not be able to hear me. What with the TV, the hoover and the walkman. He didn't know what to do. His children appeared in his mind. He tried to get up, but the pain in his chest was so great that he stumbled, his knees giving way, and fell on to the carpet by the armchair. The tray and the plate fell through the air, landing face-down just in front of him. He could no longer hear the TV, but he could see the sports commentator smiling out of the screen. He was trying to cough – there was something in his throat – but he could not breathe. He could no longer feel his arms or legs, and he did not know that he was grasping with his hands, reaching out into nothing. The only thing he could feel was the bursting in his chest and the stasis in his lungs. Breath would move neither in nor out. He felt as though his face was being pressed against a plastic bag. He could not understand what was happening. He defecated in his underpants. He was looking at the paisley pattern on the carpet. At the way the big paisleys were filled with smaller paisleys, something that he had never noticed before. He stopped being able to see the paisley as his body became deprived of oxygen. His arms gradually fell to the carpet. His heart, the root and cause of all this, stopped. It had a final large muscle spasm, and then lay still. His breathing stopped. He thought of his wife upstairs, of the mess he had made and asked himself how she would clear it up.

The boys knew there was something wrong when they saw their neighbour at the school gates. She had no kids, so she was not here to pick up anyone but them. 'Bad news', she said, as they got into her car.

'What?' asked Mark.

'Wait till you get home.'

They travelled in silence. It was a filthy car. Dirty on the outside from dust and mud and strewn with tissues, empty mugs and boxes of Tampax on the inside. The boys were normal children: boisterous, lively and curious. They would not usually let themselves be fobbed off with 'wait till you get home' as an answer. But this was different. They thought that their neighbour was weird. They thought she was a lesbian (or a 'lesley bean', as Sam thought they were called). To them, as twelve- and fifteen-year-old boys in a small Gloucestershire town, lesley beans were really weird.

They twitched and fidgeted in her car, desperate to get out just in case she started doing whatever it was that lesley beans did to them. The expression on her face told them not to ask questions. So they sat in silence and panicked quietly. Sam's heart pounded and he nearly wet himself with worry. Most likely, he thought, something was wrong with his grandad. He was old. And old people die. He thought about that expression: *something wrong with*. Well, if he was dead then there would be nothing wrong with him. There's nothing wrong with being dead, is there? And once you're dead, you can't have anything wrong with you, can you? So let's just hope there's something wrong with him, he thought.

Their house looked normal. Their mother and grand-father were in the kitchen. Their grandfather was sitting at the table, holding a salt cellar tight in his right hand. Their mother came to them when she saw them and embraced them both. She had a walkman around her neck that dug into their cheeks. She was shaking and crying, as silently as she could. She held them so tight that they thought they would choke. Neither of the boys had ever seen their mother cry. They were shocked. She was crying just like they used to – her mouth down-turned, her brow furrowed, tears streaming from her eyes. They both realised that it must be something really serious. They wanted her to stop and be how she usually was, but they knew that they could not stop her. They couldn't do a thing.

Their grandad told them to sit down. Their mother held their hands and tried to talk, but she just sobbed, her eyes swimming, her chin wobbling, her mouth making unintelligible sounds in front of them, choking sounds and snorts and shudders as she tried to breathe in. Sam wet himself. He sat there horrified as everyone heard the urine drip on to the kitchen floor. He saw a blackness. An end to what he had known. Their grandad said something, and Lesley Bean came into the kitchen and helped their mother out of the room. She shut the door behind them and they could hear the stairs creak and the sobs grow louder.

And so their grandfather told them: their father — his son — had died. At first they didn't understand. They sat there in silence for about an hour as their grandad tried to talk. Then all of a sudden Sam cried. He could not help himself. Just like his mother he sobbed and sobbed, his sleeves gradually becoming as wet as his underpants. He felt like a young child again, like a toddler, and he was ashamed. Mark tried his best. As he sat there tears ran down his cheeks and noises came from his throat, but he was no longer a child. Their grandfather did his best too. His eyes shone, his fist clenched the metallic salt cellar, and his jaw tightened, but he did not shed a tear in front of them. If he had sobbed there would have been no hope.

Sam excused himself and went to the loo. He removed his trousers and his Aston Villa pants, put them in a plastic bag and took them through to his bedroom, where he hid them underneath his bed. He did not want to bother his mother with them. And he was embarrassed. His thighs were red and stinging from the urine and he wiped them down with a flannel. His parents' bedroom door was shut (it was rarely shut) and all was now quiet. He had a terrible image of his neighbour kissing his mother, trying to comfort her in her grief. He saw his mother's face with swollen eyes and a pink nose being pressed against the lips of his horrifying, predatory neighbour, a tall wiry woman with grey short hair and unforgiving eyes.

He stood outside his mother's door for a few minutes,

listening as hard as he could. He wiped his nose on his sleeve and looked at the snail track that it left on his green woollen cuff. He got another plastic bag from downstairs and went back to the bathroom. He had to help his mother. In the bathroom he opened the cupboard and began to put all his father's things into the carrier bag. There were canisters of shaving foam, bottles of Old Spice, his old, blue razor, his plastic comb, his tablets in brown bottles, the labels worn with corners curling. From the sink he took his toothbrush and his mouthwash. He worked quickly and in a frenzy, scared that his mother's door would open any minute, and she would come out and sob again. He didn't want to see her crying face. He filled the bag and put it in his wardrobe. Then he went back and started on the dirty laundry, removing everything that was his father's and that had his peculiar smell of musk, mints and age.

They heard snippets of whispered conversations about them, about what would happen to them, about how they would turn out. They caught the eye of other mothers or fathers who lived in their street, and saw their expressions clearly. And when they saw those expressions they realised that there was nothing that could be done to change their situation. Their father would never come back.

When Sam looked back on it, a few months after the event, all he could think about was how it was like sucking a boiled sweet and accidentally swallowing it too soon. Having his father around was like having the sweet in his mouth. And then it was gone. And he coughed a little, startled and shocked, thinking he might cough it back up. He could feel it stuck in his throat, and eventually it went down. When he swallowed that sweet too soon it was the last thing he expected to happen, and he had not realised how good it tasted before he accidentally swallowed it. It was only then, when it was gone for good, that he tasted its traces in his mouth and remembered how sweet it had been.

One day after school, a few weeks after his son's death, Leo sat Sam down at the kitchen table. He served him soup with toast. Mark had stayed at school for cricket practice. Sam could taste that his grandad had mixed chilli sauce into the soup.

'Hello, Sam,' he said gently.

Sam nodded, his mouth chewing slowly, cutlery chinking against the plates. Whereas once he used to race with Mark to see who could finish first and then bolt upstairs to start playing, he now ate slowly, chewing every mouthful properly. When he had finished eating he helped his grandfather clear up the plates.

'Don't worry about your mother,' Leo began, 'she'll get better. She'll be how she once was.'

Sam sat down again and looked at the tablecloth. It was plastic, small green and white squares, all crammed together. He didn't want to look at his grandad. They sat for a while, listening to the pipes under the stairs wheeze and bubble.

'And don't worry about yourself either, Sam.'

Sam looked up, confused by his words.

'You probably don't know this but I've seen it: you have a star that watches over you, looking out for you. Whatever you do, she'll always be there. So when you next look into the sky, remember that one of those stars is looking back, directly at you. She's a star sent by your dad. And she'll make sure you're all right.' His grandad shrugged at Sam and nodded, and the two sat there, unaware of the symmetry of their profiles.

They became a very quiet household. Sam's mother no longer listened to her walkman. Mark began to watch the

TV with the volume off. Sam let his tape collection gather dust. Their mother preferred to sweep the carpets rather than hoover them. She no longer listened to the radio. Only Leo still made some noise. He sang loudly in the bathroom ('It's a long way to Tipperary, it's a long way, to go . . .'). He clattered around in the kitchen and he danced in the living room, knocking things over and falling against the door. The rest of them tiptoed around the place, scared that they might miss something.

Sam had a lot to thank his grandfather for. Not just the singing and the dancing. Not just the cooking and the cleaning. Not just for becoming the cement, the centre, the sanity of their family. What he had to thank him for most were his stories. When Sam's dad was still alive his grandad told them all stories. They were the best stories Sam had ever heard, better than any of the stories his friends knew, better than any of the stories he had read. Stories of the secret lives of trees, that dance around at night and freeze as soon as dawn breaks. Stories of magical flowers that shimmer gold in the moonlight and grant wishes when you inhale their smell. Sam's grandad had been a botanist and had travelled the world searching for unusual specimens. He had been around most of Europe. He had been to China. He had been to South America. But best of all Sam's grandad had been somewhere so amazing that Sam had to run and touch him every time Sam remembered it. He had to go and feel this man – his hands, his face – and ask him questions over and over to check that it really was true. Sam's grandad had been to Antarctica. Sam grew up in a house where somebody had been to (actually set foot in!) the South Pole. *The South Pole!* And Sam and Mark had more questions about it than could ever be answered.

They had both grown up hearing about 'the sleeping princess'. 'You can fall in love with her, but whatever you do, don't try to kiss her,' he used to say, 'she'll freeze your mouth before you even finish thinking about it', and he would laugh to himself. 'Come here, Sam. Mark, Mark, come here,' and the two of them would stop whatever they were doing and go and sit with him, frequently on him, or at least on the arms of the chair in which he was sitting. 'I'm going to tell you about her,' he would begin, stroking Mark's head or placing his hand on Sam's shoulder. 'What is the driest continent on earth?' he would ask, looking off into the distance. 'The desert,' Sam would yell, closely followed by Mark's superior answer, 'The Sahara.' Leo would shake his head. 'What is the highest continent on earth?' he would try. Sam would run off to get his dad, 'Wait a minute. Don't say anything more before I'm back', dragging his father into the front room, demanding that he whisper the answers into his ear. Mark would take a guess: 'Scotland?' Leo would shake his head again, turning the corners of his mouth down and scratching his sideburn. 'Now where, on this earth, is the windiest continent?' This would make them both pause for a second. Mark would try 'the Grand Canyon?' with a little shrug. Sam would furrow his brow and then, excited by a flash of inspiration, blurt out 'Holland?' Leo would smile and shake his head again. 'You'll get it this time,' he would say. 'What is the coldest continent on earth?'

'Antarctica!' they would both yell, pleased to be able to answer something at last.

And then Leo would begin in earnest: 'Antarctica is the driest, the highest, the windiest and the coldest continent on earth. She has a mountain range as high as the Appalachians underneath her polar plateau. She makes up one tenth of the earth's land surface. She is one and a half times as big as the United States. *One and a half times as big as the United States.* She is at the very bottom of the earth, underneath everything. For most of the time, she is forgotten. And that is how she likes to be, for she is a bashful creature, who at best will only ever whisper to you when you are looking away, and she closes her eyes when you turn back to look at her.' Their grandfather would wave his fingers about in the air as though performing a magic trick, and look off into the distance. 'She is blue and white. Sometimes the blue is almost see-through, and sometimes it is the brightest blue you have ever seen. The white is bright too, brighter than you ever imagined white could be – as bright as red almost, or as orange. The white makes you shield your eyes. And this white is empty. It stretches as far as you can see and further still, for miles and miles and miles, all empty and all white. There are few things that can live here, but one of them is the hero of our story', and his fingers twitched again and he cleared his throat.

'Well, when I got to this white wonderland I was, at first, completely focused on my job. I talked only of my job, I dreamt of my job, I almost ate my job. I saw my work in my mind at every moment. But you know, after a while, you get used to it and you start to look at, and think about, other things and it was then that I made friends with Mr and Mrs Snowball – *those were their real names,*' he would whisper, in a theatrical aside. 'They lived on a ship in the Antarctic Peninsula which had a wonderful drawing room and spare cabins for visitors passing through. Mr Snowball was a marine biologist investigating miniscule life in the huge lakes that were trapped under the ice. He spent his time working mainly with bacteria. Now Mrs Snowball was also a very interesting lady,' at this point Sam and Mark used to giggle, 'she was interesting because she was one of the first women to come to Antarctica. Moreover she came as a wife, and not as a scientist or a researcher. She came to accompany her husband, and her arrival caused a bit of a stir on our base. There were a number of people, well a number of men, who thought that Antarctica was no place for women and that their presence would be an unwelcome distraction, a frivolity, a chastising presence. There were others who simply believed that only people who actually had something to contribute should be allowed to witness this fantastic landscape. And they refused to acknowledge that Mrs Snowball contributed anything worthwhile, despite the fact that she sang beautifully in concerts once a week and looked after a lot of the men.

'Anyway, I struck up a friendship with both Mr and Mrs Snowball, and I used to spend long evenings describing, particularly to Mrs Snowball, my work with moss. One day Mr Snowball noticed something peculiar. His wife had gradually been becoming more and more distant, and there were a few odd things happening around the ship. He had noticed some strange marks on the parquet floor in the drawing room, and when he got home at night his dressing gown was never where he left it in the morning. Then one night Mrs Snowball whispered all sorts of things in her sleep about "a dear fellow" and "such a sweetie". Well, Mr Snowball was a kind man, but not a very trusting one. And Mrs Snowball was a very attractive woman who was popular with a number of the men on the base. Indeed my weakness for her had already been commented on. Over the next week or so Mr Snowball watched his wife very carefully and, from her faraway stares and the excitement she showed each morning, he came to the conclusion that Mrs Snowball was having a man around to entertain her.' Leo spoke each of these words carefully, with raised eyebrows and a stern expression. He adjusted his glasses and scratched the side of his head.

'Now, Mr Snowball had a fairly good idea about who was entertaining his wife. There was a young man who had recently arrived from Argentina looking, he claimed, for a specific type of moss. He had spent a lot of time with Mrs Snowball and his face took on a certain expression when she stood by the piano and sang. Mr Snowball was so sure that it was me who was making love to his wife that he started to spread rumours around the base and soon none of the men would talk to me.' He shuffled in his chair.

'Suddenly I found myself a guilty man. I was ignored when I came to dinner, and my trips out of the base, crucial for my work, became difficult. There was nothing for me to do but try and clear my name so I decided to take a week off from my research and find out who the real Casanova was. I got up early on the Monday morning and set up camp on the side of a glacier by their ship. I watched Mr Snowball leave for work, head down and muttering to himself, at eight-thirty. I sat there for the whole morning and only the base cook came and went. And then, just after lunch, when you might have expected her to be napping, Mrs Snowball came out on deck. Well, whoever she was expecting clearly did not care for appearances. She was wearing a thick pair of canvas trousers with wellington boots, a tatty fisherman's jumper, a woollen scarf and a cloth cap. But she was definitely expecting somebody. She walked along the rail on the deck, looking over the edge and all around. She was calling something too, but I couldn't hear what it was she said. And then I held my breath.

'Along the side of the ice, where the ship was anchored, he came waddling along, dressed, would you believe, in a tuxedo. He crossed the drawbridge and she came to meet him, bending down, her hand outstretched and I saw her touch him. Right in front of me I saw her stroke his face and neck. She was smiling and cooing gently. But it wasn't just any old face that this guy had and it wasn't just any old neck. When she stretched out her arm to touch him, this is what she must have felt,' and at this point their grandfather would root around under his chair and tell Mark and Sam to shut their eyes and hold out their hands. The boys would do as asked, with only a little peeking, and their grandfather would find what he was looking for and hold it against the outstretched palms of the boys. 'Stroke that,' he would say, holding a worn black velvet cushion out for them to touch.

'But that doesn't feel like a person,' one of them would say, as he ran his fingers across the soft pile, 'that doesn't feel like you or Dad. It doesn't feel like a man.'

'That's because Mrs Snowball wasn't stroking a man,' their grandfather would chuckle. 'Mrs Snowball's visitor,' he would whisper, 'was a penguin. A penguin with feathers like velvet. A slightly oily velvet, but velvet all the same. Can you believe it? I laughed when I saw it. I sat on the side of that glacier and laughed. He followed her on to the ship and I went after them, fascinated to see where they were going. Watching them enter, I walked round the ship until I came to a porthole through which I could see the large drawing room. Looking through the window I saw the penguin standing, as good as gold, by the piano and Mrs Snowball seated at it playing Bach. I thought I was dreaming. I just stood there dumbfounded and stared.

'Of course, after a little while Mrs Snowball saw me and invited me in. "Come and meet Magnus," she said and took me inside. As I got closer Magnus just stared at me from the corner of his eye and I felt that I was intruding. He was taller than I thought he would be and sleeker than you could imagine. He looked like he had been sucked smooth by a toddler. I could see now that he was wearing a pair of woollen booties – "to protect the parquet", Mrs Snowball told me, "his claws are quite sharp, especially when he dances". He was, it transpired, a musical penguin, who enjoyed nothing more than to spend the afternoon listening

(or dancing) to Bach and being fed sardines by Mrs
Snowball. She was experimenting with him in the most
gentle way possible. She tried out different composers on
him and watched his reaction. He liked Bach, couldn't bear
Wagner and was currently under observation for
Szymanowski. And Mrs Snowball enjoyed his company. He
filled her otherwise empty and long afternoons. "And I like
the fact that he doesn't say much," she told me with a shy
grin.'

'But did he sing?' Sam would suddenly ask, clearly
perturbed by the thought of a singing penguin.

'No, he didn't sing. He just listened. And now and again
he waddled around the room, twitching his wings. The
three of us sat together for the rest of the afternoon and
waited for Mr Snowball to return, taking it in turns to play
the piano and watch Magnus. Mrs Snowball, of course, had
had no idea of her husband's suspicions, and was horrified
to hear of my treatment. And, when Mr Snowball came
back and she explained everything to him, he too was
horrified and begged my forgiveness. And they decided
then and there to throw a dinner party to mark the
occasion, so we all went to get changed except, of course,
for Magnus, who was already ready.'

Leo told this story on the evening of Robert's funeral. The
boys did not yell and shout. Nor did they even attempt to
answer the questions. And when their grandad asked about
the highest place on earth, Sam did not go off and get his
father, who was currently, in Sam's opinion, in the coldest
place on earth. Sam and Mark did not enter into their
grandfather's story the way they used to. They did not
imagine themselves battling through ice and blizzards with
a team of huskies and a sledge. They did not imagine
anything very much. They just sat and listened to the story,

grateful that their grandfather was telling it, grateful that, although their lives had undergone so much turmoil, at least one part of it had not changed.

From then on they still enjoyed listening to their grandfather's stories, but they listened to them as most adults would. With a kind of politeness, a kind of mature observation. They listened with their heads, and not with their hearts. From the day their father died they did nothing with their hearts.

When Sam asks Mark now about what he remembers of that time after their father's death he always has the same reply: *that* doctor. *That* doctor was thin and wiry and tall. It wouldn't have surprised Sam if he was the tallest person in Gloucester at the time. He had a large forehead too, the kind of forehead that befits a doctor, the kind of forehead that Mark and Sam called a 'Tefal' forehead because of an ad that was running on TV at the time. Once all these elements were added together, his appearance, it has to be said, was like something from *Close Encounters of the Third Kind*. His head, swelling at the top, was too big for his body, making him look as if he might topple over at any minute. His wiry limbs flailed about as though they were too long for him to control, and might, at any minute and completely of their own accord, lash out and catch you round the ear or on the nose, or worse still, sweep your legs from under you in a particularly powerful spasm.

That doctor was called Dr Hatte, and their grandfather took them to see him about nine months after their father had died, to be checked, as soon as possible, for potential heart problems or tendencies. Their father's post mortem came, as Sam had expected, through the post. It confirmed what their mother had already been told: that their father died of a *myocardial infarction*. So their grandfather let them take the day off school and explained where they were going to the boys' mother, although she just looked at him blankly.

'And this is my youngest grandson, Sam. Sam, this is Dr Hatte.'

'Hello, Sam,' chimed the wiry doctor, a lopsided smile on his face. He looked as though he should have been dribbling too, to complete the alien effect. Sam's heart lurched and he didn't know what to do, but Dr Hatte told him to take a seat, so he did. He measured Sam and weighed him and took his blood pressure. Then he took a blood sample. He shone a torch in his eyes and ears, and then he looked in his mouth. Then he asked him questions about his diet, about his 'bathroom habits' as the doctor called them.

Sam was embarrassed, and a sickness rose in his throat as he thought the doctor was going to ask him about wanking. Not in front of my grandfather, please, he thought. Please God, don't let him ask me whether I wank while my grandad's in the room. When Sam realised that he had changed the subject he was still shaking with anxiety.

'Sam, tell me, do you play sport?'

'Yes,' he replied. His grandfather looked at him. Eyebrows raised, he was asking Sam to behave himself.

'What sports do you play?'

'Football and rugby.'

'Do you like it?'

Sam had liked football with his father. He still liked football with his father, but his father wasn't here to play it with him any more. He didn't know what to say.

'No,' he said.

Dr Hatte got up from his seat. He really was tall. Sam was scared again, and he wondered what he might do. He could just fall on them both, on Sam and his grandfather, and they would need to go to hospital because of their injuries. He came round to the other side of the desk and squatted next to Sam. Tall when he squatted too. Sam looked at his triangular face, at the huge dome of wrinkles right in front of him and at the little eyes darting around beneath it. He could smell him, a kind of musty, fruity smell, and he could feel his breath on his cheek.

'Sam,' the doctor said, almost whispering, 'you need to run.'

Sam's heart was pounding. Run. What did he mean, run? Run now, away from him? Was he going to inject him with the alien substance, so that he too would become long and stringy with a swollen head? Was the alien inside him about to burst out of his face, tearing through that wrinkly dome and lunging towards him?

Sam looked at his eyes again, hoping that would give him a clue. He was scared. He wanted him to go away. The doctor got up and went back to his side of the desk where he began to speak with Leo. Sam sat there, his heart pounding and his mind racing, until he felt his grandfather's familiar hand on his shoulder, and he got up to leave.

Dr Hatte had told Sam to run. And after that visit Sam did start to run. He used to run when he got in from school at night. Sometimes, in the summer, he would run in the mornings, before he went to school. How Dr Hatte had known, Sam could not say, but running suited him. First, he had a runner's physique. He was lean and athletic. Secondly, he had a runner's mentality. He liked to be by himself, inside his own head for long stretches of time – the isolation of it never bothered him. And it relaxed him. Since his father's death Sam had become tense and anxious. School made him nervous. The other kids worried him. And the prospect of exams made him want to spend the rest of his life under the covers of his bed. One of the few things that could get him up was the idea of a run, of starting something that he knew he could finish.

Sam wanted to become strong too. He wanted to become an adult as quickly as he could, so that he could pick up the pieces left by his father's death. He wanted to have a job, to earn a wage, to buy food, to change light bulbs, to clean the car that never went anywhere, to get a lot of post. He wanted not to cry any more. He wished that he did not need the star that looked out for him in the sky. He wanted to stop being a kid. He wanted to grow up.

Aged two months Sam was a rather fat baby. Aged one he had learnt to crawl. Aged two he wanted to be a fireman. Aged three he wanted to be in the circus. Aged four he wanted to be a motorbike man. Aged five his grandad told him the story of the sleeping princess ('The *other* sleeping princess' he would say to his friends at school, when they thought he was talking about *Sleeping Beauty*). Aged six he wanted to go to the South Pole. Aged seven he wanted to go to the South Pole. Aged eight he wanted to go to the South Pole. His mother told him that he would never really be able to go. Not really, but pretending didn't hurt. And so he spent a lot of time pretending. When Sam was twelve his dad died. Sam forgot his dreams and grew up.

SIX

Zach was swanning around the floor, waiting to be wooed. As soon as he came through the door heads turned and false smiles replaced genuine frowns. People approached him from all directions, desperate to share jokes, talk about new ads, or just smile and giggle and ask him for an opinion on something topical which they could then memorise for conversations with clients and friends.

Sam looked at his screen, suddenly fascinated by the fax he was sending to Clive about the air date of the TV campaign. He could hear Zach making his way over to his side of the building: 'How do you make your girlfriend cry when you're having sex?' He paused for effect. 'Phone her up and tell her.' A peal of girly laughter followed. 'So, it's Thursday, where are we going for lunch? What about Giorgio's? Or The Circle? Emily, we have to talk about that new work for Hitsui. Do you think the client will buy it? Yeah, yeah, good. I love it, you know. I fucking love it, and if they don't buy it they need their fucking heads sorting out.'

Sam glanced over. Zach certainly needed his head sorting out, if it wasn't too late already. He had had his mucous membranes rebuilt on many occasions, but there was nothing that could be done for his mind. Too much white powder in the grey matter and paranoia sets in, along with a multitude of other minor personality defects. There were four girls on his heels as he strode through the desks, and they had to move quickly because Zach had just had his first snort of the day and he was hyperactive.

He approached their desk. Lauren too was glued to her screen. He passed her end of the desk, and stopped to look down at her. 'Nice tits,' he said. Lauren raised an eyebrow. Sam couldn't help himself: he shook his head gently.

'Thanks,' Lauren replied. 'My girlfriend likes them.' Zach snorted, and laughed. 'Maybe her and me should form an appreciation society. We could have viewings and tastings and stuff like that.' He guffawed, impressed by his own wit, and walked on by, eventually reaching the end of the row of desks where he began to practise his golf swing.

'Why aren't blondes allowed to have a lunch break?' He looked up at his entourage. Chloe and Annabel were still hot on his heels, like seagulls after a trawler. They shook their heads and shrugged. 'Because it takes too long to retrain them afterwards.' Chloe and Annabel did their best to laugh, suddenly conscious of their artificially enhanced hair.

Zach looked pleased with himself for the second time that morning. He swung through and watched his imaginary ball arch through the air, oblivious to the Soho bricks.

Zach was one of the two creative directors of McLeod Seagal Gale. He had a royal blue Porsche, a penthouse flat in Pimlico, a continuous supply of cocaine, a two hundred and fifty thousand pound salary and a white rabbit called Franny in a cage in his office. He claimed that she helped the creative juices start to flow, and if anything was wrong with Franny – if she was off her food, or generally apathetic – then no ads could be written and Sam and his department would have to think up excuses to tell their clients. Zach had recently ordered two garden sheds to be erected outside on the balcony of the creative floor, for 'his boys' to go and sit in when they needed to create. Zach had shagged at least half of the attractive women in the building, and over half of the unattractive ones. When he wasn't shagging, snorting or communing with Franny he was playing golf on what were called *Management Awaydays.*

Sebastian called Sam over.

'Sam, come and have a chat in my office. Have you got five minutes?' (He was head of the department. It was not a real question.)

'Yeah, of course.'

'How's it going, Sam?' He had a smile from an ad for teeth-whitener.

'Well,' he nodded. 'You know that I'd like to move accounts, so the sooner I could do that the better, but apart from that, well.'

'Good, glad to hear it. Yeah, we will be moving you, but it's a question of waiting for the right opportunity to come along. You know, I think you've got really specific, rare skills, and I want to give you the opportunity of developing them fully. Now, there are a couple of things I'd like to talk to you about. Completely confidential, of course, but I know I can trust you.' He flashed Sam his smile once again. If Sebastian hadn't been a man, he could have won Miss World. Hands down.

'Okay.' Sam looked around the office. There was a tastefully framed poster on one wall, one of the agency's finest ads. A large macho stereo stood in one corner next to a large TV and video. The phone had been ringing ever since they sat down. As each new call came through Sebastian leant over to see the number of the caller displayed on the body of the phone. Now and again he picked up.

'Right, well, first of all I've some great news for you. We had a discussion at last week's board meeting and we came to the decision that we'd like to promote you. I'm going to make you and Richard account managers as of next

Monday. Congratulations, Sam. You deserve it.' Sam was a bit taken aback.

'Thanks,' he said.

'You're pleased?' Sebastian looked at him as if he had just healed Sam's sick mother or told him that he had won the lottery. He clearly expected a show of gratitude.

'Yes.' Sam nodded. He felt stubborn. That was as good as it was going to get.

'Now, the only thing is that, as I'm sure you're aware, business is a little unstable at the moment. We've resigned Havelot which is worth about six million and things are shaky with Euroair who, as you know, is one of our biggest clients. Now there are a number of sacrifices that we all have to make because of this. The board will go without their profit-related pay for the first half of this year. And that's a major thing for most of them. So, the sacrifice I'm asking you to make, temporarily of course, is to go without a payrise for a few months. We'll sort you out as soon as we can. I'm sorry to ask you to do this, but we all think you're doing a great job, and that needs to be recognised. All I ask is that you're sensitive to the agency's financial affairs. And I know that you are mature and far-sighted enough to be able to do that.'

Sam nodded and made noises of agreement. He was not surprised by what Sebastian was telling him. He would have more responsibility, probably work even longer hours, but he would earn the same.

'Now, we're going to have to shed some people because of reduced profits, so there may be a gap sooner or later for you to fill. I think Chloe will go first and then Phil, but I'm not quite sure when. The other piece of good news is that I'd like you to work on a pitch. We're pitching for Thermlex, and I think you'd be perfect for it. It's a small pitch, last year they spent about three million on advertising but it's really exciting because they want to relaunch their brand, and it would be amazing if we won the business. It's a creative pitch, and we've got two weeks, so it's fairly intensive. Angela's working on it too, and I know that you two work well together.'

Sam nodded again. After his first year of asking for a better desk (when he first arrived he had sat, like a bell boy, at a temporary desk next to the lifts), for a different account, for a pay-rise, he now realised that these were all things that he could have no control over. He did not have a choice, although management would pretend that he did, to make him feel better.

'Well, thank you, Sam. Thanks for all your hard work, and for being so understanding about the current situation. We knew that we could rely on you. And in this job, that'll take you far.'

Sebastian slapped him on the shoulder and Sam thanked him and left. Sam went back to his desk and began to sort stuff out for the pitch. He thought about what Sebastian had said about Chloe and Phil, and wondered whether it would happen, or whether it had actually been a veiled threat.

Sam went through to his bedroom and changed his clothes. Then he went to lie on the living room floor. Gray was sitting on the sofa smoking dope. He was wearing some of his best gear: snowboarding shoes, dark jeans with huge turn-ups, a three-colour fleece. He was waiting until it was late enough to go out.

'I am fucked,' Sam announced.

'Oh yeah?'

'Mmmmm. I don't suppose Mark has rung, has he?'

'Uh-uh.' Gray shook his head and held out the spliff. 'Want some?'

'No.' Sam rolled on to his front and lay examining the pile of the carpet. It was funny how it was actually made up of lots of different coloured threads, but it always looked brown and nothing else. Like light, he thought. Full of all those different bright colours, but white in the end.

'Gray. I – fuck, I forgot: *who* is Aphrodite?'

'Just a girl.' Gray held the spliff between his lips as he began to relace his shoes.

'Oh, don't act cool with me. Who is she?'

'Okay okay. She's a ballerina. Well, she dances for some company. Met her at a theatre during the interval. She is extremely fit, and er, accommodating. And her real name is Lucy.'

'So what is she then? A one-nighter? Or shall I clear some space in the bathroom?'

Gray finished with his shoes and stood up.

'Right. I'm off. Don't wait up, Sammy-boy. Oh, listen, are you around at the weekend? I spoke to Henry. Thought we could have dinner here tomorrow. I'll bring her along then, so you can meet her properly.'

'That'd be good. Have a good one.'

Sam slithered across the floor until he could reach the remote control. He flicked on the TV and dialled the number of the local Indian restaurant from memory. The voice on the other end of the line laughed when, after requesting home-delivery, Sam gave his address. The take-away was four doors down.

The take-away arrived and he ate it in the kitchen, out of the silver tubs that it came in. There was an ad for the local dry cleaners on the lids of the tubs, as though they knew you were going to spill it down your clothes. When he had finished he threw everything away and took the rubbish downstairs. Then he went back to his room, and looked at his maps. There was a large one of Australia which could keep him occupied for hours. He would stare at the contours, the colours, the marks and symbols and wonder what the place would really look like when the two-dimensional turned into the three-dimensional.

One of the nicest things about maps, he decided, was that there were never any people on them. It was possible to flick from London to Athens to Bombay to Mexico City and not see a soul, but knowing all the while that each of these cities was densely populated – huge sprawls of pulsing bodies, crammed together on top of each other. They always looked so empty and clean and, of course, this was part of their great deception. Sam sometimes thought that maps should come with a health warning because they made even the most inhospitable terrain look accessible and friendly. It was possible to see everything on a map: hills and mountains no longer blocked views, distance disappeared, scaled down into manageable, comprehensible gaps, so that far things became close and craggy gulfs and icy lakes became symbols, pretty pictures that made one want to go there, the sheer size and overwhelmingness of the place forgotten.

It was Friday. Regardless of how busy Sam was things had to slow down. He was always slightly less tense on Fridays, though it didn't stop him from chewing his fingers and staring off into space, wondering. His phone rang.

'Sam speaking?'

'Sam, it's Clive. Sam, the brief was late.'

'Hello, Clive. I did send it at quarter to nine this morning.'

'And I had told you I needed it by nine.'

'Yes.'

'You know that my secretary checks the fax machine at half-hourly intervals, so in order for me to get something by nine, it needs to have been faxed by eight-thirty. Is that clear?'

Sam nodded into his phone. 'Yes, Clive.'

'Now, as it happens I'm not in the office, so could you refax it to me at home?'

'Yes, Clive.' Sam hung up. 'There is nothing more I would love to do in the whole wide world,' he said, and then picked up his phone again, listening for the reassuring dialling tone that meant the line was no longer connected.

Sam's pager buzzed: *Are you still on for tonight? Call me, you fat puck. H.* Henry still found it amusing that the pager women would not let you use swearwords in your messages. In fact, they censored *damn* and *blast* too, which only served to further aggravate the sender of the angry message, usually leading to an even longer stream of expletives, this time directed at the women themselves. So Henry always sent messages with the sibling of an expletive in them. And in fairness, they did make Sam smile.

As he sat making his phone calls Angela approached. Sam bristled. He looked up at her and noticed that she had been crying – her eyelashes were slightly wet and she had two shiny triangles of pink skin underneath her eyes.

'So Sebastian spoke to you about Project Warm?'

'Err . . . yeah.' Sam presumed this was the name given to the Thermlex pitch.

'Right. I want all the information from here circulated by lunchtime. Then I want a vox pop done this afternoon. I've written out the questions upstairs, they're on my desk. And I hope you haven't got any plans for tonight.'

His heart sank. He couldn't work tonight. It would be physically impossible. He would collapse, he was sure of it. His hair was falling out, he was so tired. He had not eaten anything today, and he had dark patches around his eyes. He needed some time to himself.

'I have, actually. It's Friday night.'

'Cancel them now. We've only got two weeks.'

'I'd rather come in at the weekend than work tonight.'

'It's not an either or situation. It's both. You're working tonight.'

'I'm not – I'm sorry,' Sam replied. 'I'll get everything done today, but I'd rather not stay tonight.' Chloe was eavesdropping in the background. A fight would make her day.

'Jesus Christ, don't you care about this? Can't you take responsibility for once in your life?' She was shaking, her face contorted into a poisonous expression. She was going to cry, Sam could tell. He couldn't deal with this. He ought to stand his ground, he knew, but he really didn't want to get into an argument. He didn't have the energy.

'Fine, I'll work tonight.'

She walked off, pleased that she had won. Sam's Friday was ruined. And he probably wouldn't have much of a weekend either. And it wasn't really necessary. Head down, nose to the grindstone, he worked solidly for the rest of the day, answering phones, returning pages, highlighting and copying reports and every now and again running a hand through his thick hair to see if any more strands had come loose.

There was a sentence that had been cropping up in Sam's head recently and it appeared there now, as he sat in the Library department making phone calls with one hand and flicking through Outdoor Clothing 1997 reports with another. It was a tie-breaker sentence, the sort of sentence that would appear on the back of a cereal packet, as the clincher for the moulded plastic cocker spaniel with moving tail. It read: *If I hadn't left advertising when I was twenty-five, I*

would never have . . . Please complete in no more than ten words.
Sam did not particularly want the spaniel, but he would not win it anyway. For although he knew, without a shadow of a doubt, that something went in that blank space, he had no idea what it was.

By the time Sam's day was nearing its end Gray had cooked dinner for Lucy, Henry and Sara. Well, Gray didn't really cook. Instead he assembled food and warmed bits of it up. Sometimes he warmed up the packaging too, but after a few drinks you didn't really notice. And he was good at assembling food. He bought a lot of it and mixed cuisines with abandon. By the time Sam got there the plates and dishes were empty, and the bin was bulging with plastic cocoons of spring rolls, garlic bread and chicken legs. Sam cut some bread and cheese and went to join the others in the living room.

'Sammy! Glad you could make it!' Sara squealed out of the fug of smoke and alcohol vapour, and came over to embrace him. The downstairs neighbour banged on the ceiling. Sam quite liked Sara, but he knew she wouldn't last long. Henry had a three-word response to almost everything Sam said to him: 'Is she pretty?' Sometimes he would shorten it to 'ISP?', if the girl in question happened to be within earshot and he couldn't quite get a good look himself. Sam remembered a time when he had taken Henry to task about all his girls. They had been sitting up late, as was frequently the case during their time at university, in Sam's room drinking whisky and playing snap. The curtains were open to reveal the night sky, Henry was lying on his stomach so that he could peek at his cards before he put them down, and Sam was sitting, cross-legged, leaning against his bed.

'But doesn't it bother you, that sometimes . . . I mean, you know, you can't fancy all of them, can you?' Sam said, as he flicked a card into the arena between them.

'All of whom?' Henry asked, tilting the top card up so that he could see what it was and then placing it carefully on top of Sam's.

'All the girls you get off with. I mean, have you actually been attracted to *everyone* you've snogged since the first term?'

'Ah,' said Henry, nodding slowly. 'Why shouldn't I have been?'

'Because you just seem to go for anybody. I mean, it's not like you hold a flame for one particular girl and pursue her. You know, you don't seem to *discriminate.*'

'I am,' Henry cleared his throat 'an equal opportunities employer. I do not deny anyone access. I have a diploma to prove it.'

Sam dropped another card gently into the centre and poured some more whisky. His eyes were feeling heavy and his body relaxed but it was only two in the morning. He looked up at the maps that were pinned over his walls.

'I'm not like that, anyway,' Henry suddenly said, pushing up off the floor and sitting cross-legged opposite Sam, balancing his glass of whisky on one knee. 'I just like girls, you know.'

'You don't say.'

'No, but what I mean is that I like *being* with them. I like them for company. I just like being around them. And the easiest way of getting them to be around me is to snog them. I don't know where it came from,' he said, brushing his cards, one by one, face down over the carpet, 'but I'm just no good with boys. You know, I never really had any male friends. I never had a best mate. My friends were always girls. I mean, you're probably . . . you're probably . . .'

'Right,' said Sam and drained his glass. Henry stared at the carpet for a while and then picked one of his cards and threw it on the pile. Sam did the same, and as he reached for his cards he felt vaguely honoured that Henry was his friend.

'Snap!' yelled Henry, before his card had even reached the pile in the middle. It was the queen of hearts, shyly smiling at them both in duplicate under Henry's palm.

'Henry, you are a fucking cheat,' Sam said, pronouncing each word carefully.

'Better than a cheating fuck,' he replied, still straightening all his cards. '*And* I get all the girls,' he continued, pointing at the the two queens with a grin.

'Hi, Sam.'

He turned. Janie. He looked again. It *was* her. The last time he saw her flashed through his head. He looked to Henry and then to Gray for an explanation. Gray was lying on the sofa, Lucy playing with his bare feet. He winked at Sam and giggled. He was drunk. Or stoned. Probably both. He must have spoken to Mark. Sam turned back.

'Hi. Nice to see you,' he bleated. She leant to kiss him and he made sure that she got his cheek. He sat down and began to eat his sandwich. She sat down next to him and watched him closely. This was the last thing he needed, after a tough week. The only thing he could recall about the evening he spent with Janie was being very drunk and spending a lot of time looking at her small ear. He might have kissed her, or he might not have. He just couldn't remember, and he was sure that she, on the other hand, would have remembered every detail.

He looked again at Gray, draped over the sofa. He would kill him. He had half a mind to expose Gray's most painful secret here and now. Gray had been at university with Sam and Henry, and Sam and Gray became friends in the first week. Gray was the coolest bloke in the year. He had the hippest gear, went to unheard-of clubs and got crazy women. At university he had had a long relationship with a sociology tutor called Henrietta, but it ended messily and he had never been the same since. It was during the first week that, one night late in Gray's room, Sam happened to catch sight of a postcard, written in old-fashioned fountain-pen handwriting, *Hope you're settling in. We're very proud of you. With love from mum and dad.* Something caught his eye when he looked at it. As his eyes flicked over it for a second time, more slowly than the first, he realised what it was: the card was addressed to *Gary*. For a second Sam thought it belonged to somebody else, but then the penny dropped.

'So where did you get the name Gray?'

'My parents. They were hippies in the seventies, you know how it is. Dope, caftans, auras, unusual names.'

'Is that why they call you Gary then?'

Gray looked at him, aghast. He did not know Sam very well, and he didn't know what to do. He was terrified that his secret would be out and his reputation ruined. He asked Sam not to tell a soul. He pleaded, begged, threatened. Had he known Sam better he would have realised that he didn't need to. A simple request would have sufficed. And Sam hadn't told a soul. But sometimes he was sorely tempted.

Janie patted his shoulder.

'Sam. Do you think we could have a chat somewhere?' she smiled.

'Sure. Let me just finish this,' he indicated his sandwich. There was half left. He would have to drag it out. What did she want to talk to him about? His mind was racing. He was still in work mode, and Janie's presence made him tense. He considered his options. Take her to bed and shag her (but he didn't fancy her and he really didn't want to shag her. It would be a bad thing. Did it matter?). Take her to bed and fall asleep (but then there was always the morning to get through). Take her to the kitchen and set her straight (I only snogged you – did I? – because I couldn't think of anything to say to you. Because I was drunk, and I thought you were too. It was a one night thing).

Sam sat and listened to his friends arguing about whether feet were sexy or not. He took off his shoes and his tie. Eventually Sara, fed up with hearing Henry go on about a pair of feet he had once encountered, announced that she was tired and wanted to go home. Henry wanted to stay. He wanted to make a night of it.

'You look terrible, Sam,' Sara said as she kissed him goodbye. 'You need to get some sleep. Take care of yourself. And look,' she said, touching the hair just above his left ear, 'here's your first grey hair.'

'Pull it out, will you?'

She laughed. 'No, I think it makes you look quite distinguished.'

'I don't want to look distinguished. I'm twenty-five.'

Gray and Lucy went off to bed and Sam, Henry and Janie were left in the front room. It was two in the morning. Despite having to work the next day Sam was determined that this was going to be a Friday night like any other. He had given up on what to say to Janie. She had kept up her requests to talk to him throughout the evening, and he had kept up with the pretence that he kept forgetting. She was sitting opposite him now, smoking with her right hand and playing with a cork with her left.

'We were talking about dogs earlier,' Henry said. 'Janie's got a beagle. I almost told her about the time you saved Mark's Pyrenean Mountain Dog, but I thought I should let you tell her yourself.'

'Really?' Janie turned to Sam, face alight.

Sam looked over at Henry. What was it with his friends?

It seemed that they were all determined to give him a hard time tonight.

'Well, it was a completely natural reaction. I was walking it in Kensington Gardens. It was just a puppy and it's a mountain dog, you know. Not very good with water.'

Janie nodded, sympathetically. Henry went out of the room because he wanted to laugh. He and Sam played this game every now and then when they were bored. One would cue up an unlikely story that the other had to finish. They took it in turns and you were never allowed to back out of a story. Sam finished his fiction as best he could. Janie made appropriately impressed noises. Then she noticed that Henry had left the room. Sam shut his eyes. Here was her opportunity.

'I like your friends, Sam.'

'Really? So do I.'

He twitched his feet and reached his hand to his face, feeling the rumble of stubble under the skin on his chin. He stroked his sideburn.

'Janie. Look. The other night –'

'Yeah?' she giggled.

'Well, I was drunk. Well, *you* were drunk too. You know. I think we should forget about it.'

'Forget about what?'

Shit, thought Sam. Shit shit shit.

'Err. You know. Whatever happened.'

'I gave you my number. You seem to have forgotten about that anyway.'

'No. I've just been rather hectic, that's all. I've still got your number.' Had he? He couldn't remember where he had put it, if he had. He had a vague recollection of throwing it in the bin.

'Well, will you ring me then? At some point. I'm going away this week to Daddy's house in Norfolk. But perhaps the week after? I should go now, I'm riding tomorrow. Got to get up at the crack of dawn.' She stood up, gathering her things from around the room: camel coat, Mulberry bag. Sam followed her to the door. He kissed her cheek, grateful that whatever had happened had obviously been forgotten and also slightly offended: half of his mind had imagined a girl dumbstruck with love and passion after one meaningless snog.

Sam wandered back into the front room to find Henry peering between his toes.

'She's gone.'

'Take her outside for a goodbye snog?'

Sam shook his head. 'How the fuck did she come to be here, anyway?'

'You'll have to ask Gray,' said Henry, as he flicked on the TV. 'Anyway, she's not that bad. I quite liked her myself. She's got a nice voice. And a kind of inner something, an inner –'

'Tube?'

Henry shook his head again. 'Besides, there'll be all sorts of perks going out with a rich girl.'

'How do you know she's rich? She's posh, that's all,' said Sam as he lay on the floor, arms spreadeagled. He undid his shirt. There were penguins on the TV, running along a large patch of snow.

'Nah. She's a millionaire. Her dad's the Chief Exec of Barclays Bank.'

'Yeah, right. And I'm a flying penguin.'

'He is. She is Janie Brookes-Smith. Her dad is Guy Brookes-Smith, Chief Exec of Barclays Bank.' Henry had a habit of making things up, especially when it was dark. It was part of being a journalist, Sam thought. It annoyed him. He wished he could do it too. He looked at the penguins on the TV again.

'And, as we stalk through the undergrowth, we catch a rare glimpse of the common bullshitter, or *bullshittius communis*. Their natural habitat is, of course, the public house, but here we see one at rest in the home of a friend.'

'It's true,' Henry protested. 'Honestly, have a look at their annual reports tomorrow.'

'The sad fact about *that*, Henry, is that I could actually check that tomorrow. We're pitching for thermal underwear. I'm in the office all weekend.'

'Jesus shit, Sammy. Give it up. The pay is shit. The hours a nightmare. Why are you still doing it? You'd get more working in McDonald's. Children weaving carpets in Africa work fewer hours than you do.'

'Yeah yeah,' said Sam. He looked at the TV. The penguins had gone, but in their place was a huge bluey-white glacier, with tiny people on it, recognisable only because of their brightly coloured snow-gear.'

'Whack the volume on, will you?'

Henry passed Sam the remote control and poured them both some more wine. Sam let the wine seep through his body. He relaxed. Friday night. Janie had left. His brow became smooth, he stopped squinting, and he loosened his shoulders. Half-past two in the morning and the street outside was silent. Apart from the noise of the TV, everything was quiet. Everyone was sleeping.

Sam breathed deeply and watched the images on the screen. He saw empty landscapes and vast white areas of nothingness: 'in winter the temperature can drop as low as −70°C as wind speeds reach 120mph. The Weddell Seal is the only mammal that can winter in the Antarctic with its . . .' He muted the TV and just watched the images. He did not need to hear the narrator: he knew most of that stuff already. His body seemed to relax limb by limb, gradually going limp. His breathing slowed, his heart-rate calmed.

Yet he did not feel tired. He felt detached and separate. Almost light. A kind of white lightness. A spacious lightness. An airy lightness. He could see himself, slouched against the sofa, watching television in his front room. More penguins (Emperor penguins, Sam knew) came along and laid eggs, rolling them on to their large feet as soon as they were laid, so that they did not spend too long on the ice.

In this rare state of absolute calm something stirred within Sam. Like a bulb deep under the frozen winter soil that starts to sprout, somewhere inside Sam, in the ashes and destruction that had been left by his dad's death, something came back to life.

SEVEN

It was actually April who brought about a reconciliation between Mr Glass and Kasia. Not that they had actually had a fight – they did not know each other well enough to fight – but from the very first instance neither of them liked the other. Kasia thought Mr Glass lazy and irritating; Mr Glass found Kasia lacking in humour and grace, which was why he wanted Inge back. Inge, however, had moved on to other things and so it was with a sinking heart that Mr Glass awaited Kasia the following week.

April was called April for a reason. She was called April because, like the month with its sunshine-filled promises of spring that make you leave the house in a summer jacket only to be chilled to the bone minutes later when it begins to hail, April could not make up her mind. She had never been able to make up her mind. And so it was that when the call of 'Hello, Mr Glass. It's Kasia' rang through the flat, April was hovering in the kitchen, unable to decide whether to go out or not. She was standing there looking unsure when Kasia rounded the corner and came in.

They looked at each other in silence, their eyes meeting for a second or more and then Kasia spoke: 'Hello,' she said, extending her hand and squatting as she did so. April wasn't sure. She sniffed, lifting her nose in the direction of the outstretched hand, but before she could make up her mind Kasia had scooped her up into the air, and rested her against her shoulder, so that she could see right over it, and view the flat from a totally new perspective. Leo had never done this. And as April thought: 'do I like it?', Kasia said '*Kiciús*,' and stroked her under the chin.

Now it must be said that April was a striking creature. She had come through friends as a kitten, and while her father had been a roving moggy, her mother had been a Maine Coon. A Maine Coon is a remarkable cat. It looks like a mountain leopard that has been through a carwash – all long, fluffy fur but with primitive, Tarzan markings. April had mostly taken on the colour of her father, but with bits here and there from her mother too, and the end result was tortoiseshell. She had also kept her mother's long hair, and had dramatic, tusk-like wisps and thickly furred ears. These features were not brushed as often as they might be. She was, all in all, quite a sight.

And so on that day, in the second week of her visits, when Kasia went through to see Mr Glass (who had decided that pretending to be dead would not have been sensible under the current circumstances) the first thing she said was the rather formal 'you have a very nice cat'.

'You like her?'

Kasia nodded. 'She's lovely.'

'She's called April.'

'April,' Kasia replied, as though he had just given her directions and she was confirming them. 'I will call her *Prima Aprilis.*'

Mr Glass raised his eyebrows and explained how she had got her name, how his youngest grandson had bought her for him and how she came to look so odd. He told Kasia everything about her, and Kasia stood there, weight on one hip, and listened. He only omitted one piece of information, and he did so on purpose.

April could do a trick. Mr Glass had taught her to do it when she was a kitten, much to Mark's surprise ('you can't teach cats anything. It's a good job they have holes in their fur where their eyes are, otherwise they'd never learn to see'). But Mr Glass had taught April a trick, and the trick was this: whenever he had a visitor or guest arriving he would leave the front room, pull the door to, leaving a gap of about six inches and slide April up through it, until she was standing on the top of the door. Then he would show his guest in, letting them lead the way, shouting directions from behind. As they pushed the front room door, April would leap on to their shoulders, claws extended for good purchase. It would be understating the case to say that this trick of Leo's, in each and every case, terrified his visitors. And of course that was what Leo loved about it. He loved the unexpectedness, the anticipation, the sheer shock of the leap. The look on the visitor's face made Leo's eyes light up, and he would laugh as April jumped down to the floor and ran off to find something else to amuse her.

So Kasia stroked April, unaware of her unusual gift and Mr Glass talked about her. And they looked at each other properly: Kasia let her frown dissolve, and Mr Glass took off his reading glasses. The afternoon passed as Kasia did what she was paid to do. She made fish and leek pie for lunch, she cleaned up the kitchen and the bathroom and this time she remembered to put the pile of corduroy shirts into a carrier bag to take away and launder.

The rest of their conversation that day was straightforward and almost meaningless. It revolved around practical questions and concerns, around what to eat, what to clean, when to come again. But it did not matter because their friendship had found a foothold. They were living in different worlds but they had stumbled upon a point of overlap. And that was all they needed.

'Mr Glass, what's a gerund?'
   'A gerund?'

She nodded her head and stood in the doorway, arms folded, leaning against the doorframe. She had learnt, over the past couple of weeks, that Mr Glass knew a lot. It was as simple as that. He was one of those people who knew a lot.

'Where did you hear that used?'

'I was listening to a programme on the radio.'

Mr Glass stroked his sideburn. 'A gerund is a small mammal. Larger than a gerbil but smaller than a rabbit. It has pointed ears and a long tail, and it lives in forests.'

'Oh,' said Kasia.

'Its young are called gerundives.'

Kasia frowned 'On the programme they talked about how young people don't use gerunds as they should, about how schools don't educate them properly.'

'That's right,' Leo continued. 'Gerunds used to be used by farmers to control insect populations, but now they're increasingly popular as a household pet.'

Kasia unfolded her arms. 'So how come I've never seen one?'

'They only live in Britain. Never introduced to the Continent,' he said. There was a silence.

'Could you show me a picture?' she asked, eyebrows raised, her face like a child's.

'Yes, yes of course,' he said, a little smile appearing on his lips. He picked up a pen and notepad from his stool and began to draw on the paper. Kasia came towards him and perched on the edge of a blue armchair, tilting her head so that she could follow the lines he was creating.

'There,' he said, and held out the notebook for her appreciation, his mouth corners twitching. She looked at what he had drawn for a little while, and then she looked up at him. Her brow was furrowed. Then it released.

'You . . .' she was shaking her head, 'you,' she put her hands on her hips, '. . . that's not fair,' she said, her face breaking into a smile. She took a cushion from behind her and threw it at his head. It missed and landed on the floor on the far side of his chair. 'Taking advantage of a foreigner, just because my English is not that good. That's terrible,' she said, pretending to be cross. She stood up and headed for the door. 'For that you are going to get slugs for dinner. Slugs and worms, and perhaps some birds' legs. You are a liar, Mr Glass, and you should feel ashamed of yourself,' but as she looked over her shoulder at him, she could not help smiling.

The following week Mr Glass judged the time right for April to do her stuff. He briefed her thoroughly on the Wednesday morning before Kasia was due to arrive. April wasn't sure whether it was a good idea or not. She liked Kasia because of the way she picked her up and lay her over her shoulder like a baby. On the other hand, April couldn't deny that she shared Mr Glass's love of practical jokes, and it seemed like a very long time since she had participated in one. She liked the leap. She liked the challenge of hitting a moving target, and, at the same time, not inflicting too much damage.

Mr Glass loitered at the window for most of the morning. Staring at the sky, predicting the weather to himself, identifying clouds, looking at his watch. At one point he went over to the living-room door and spent a little while positioning it – so that it was an inch off being shut. April hung around the front room, chasing after nothing-theres. When Mr Glass saw Kasia coming down the street he scooped April up and held her against the door until she climbed on to its thin top. Then he jigged over to his chair, waved his fingers in the air, sat down, arranged the blanket over his legs and placed a book spreadeagled on his lap, as though he'd been sitting like that all morning.

'Mr Glass, good morning.' Her call came echoing down the hallway.

'Good morning,' he called back, sure that, with his weak voice, she wouldn't be able to hear him. He heard her go into the kitchen and then walk up the hall. It has to be said that Mr Glass did not know Kasia very well when he decided to play his best joke on her. He did not, for example, know how old she was. He did not know where she had grown up, where she had lived, what she wanted to do. He had no idea how she had looked as a little girl. He had never heard her sing. He had never heard her scream.

As he heard her footsteps get closer his stomach tingled with excitement. He wanted to wave his fingers around, but he stopped himself, mindful of the fact that he had to look as if he'd been having a quiet morning. The door started to move. Kasia started to walk over the threshold and suddenly, seemingly out of nowhere, April leapt, legs stretched, on to Kasia's shoulder. And as soon as Kasia felt something foreign brush the back of her neck she opened her mouth.

By the time she felt the weight of the thing that had attacked her she was screaming. And what a scream. Mouth wide open, teeth bared, back of throat clearly visible, it was the scream of a horse. It was a scream that was shocking in itself and it echoed through the flat and around the building. It was a scream that terrified Mr Glass. It quickened his pulse and shook his hands, and made him assume that something had gone wrong. It was a scream that disposed of April before Kasia had even reached the top note. She became a streak in the otherwise static picture of which Mr Glass was a part. He sat there, mouth open, heart pounding, hands shaking, trying to work out what was going on.

Kasia's scream stopped as suddenly as it started. There was

a silence. Kasia looked at Mr Glass and he looked at Kasia. He was pale.

'Are you all right?' he whispered.

She looked at him.

'It was a joke . . . I just – a joke,' he said. Please smile, he thought. It's important to have a sense of humour.

She walked across the room and sat down in the chair next to him. She pulled her legs up and hugged them, laying the side of her face on her knees. She didn't say anything.

'What's the matter?' Mr Glass asked. He was imagining all sorts of terrible things. Perhaps she had once been attacked by somebody leaping on her? Perhaps her parents had been killed by a falling piece of masonry? Perhaps her first childhood cat had leapt to its death, mistaking the laundry that was billowing in the wind off the balcony for a row of cushions?

Still she said nothing, staring blankly at the wall behind his head. Mr Glass was experienced enough to recognise the symptoms of shock, and he knew how a person in shock should be treated. He got up and shook the blanket off his legs. He placed it around Kasia's shoulders, noticing that she was trembling. As he went around to the other side of the chair to make sure she was tucked in he saw the corner of her mouth move. It was a small movement – just a little twitch – but it made him stop. Then it moved again.

She could control herself no longer: she gasped for breath and let forth a torrent of laughter. Mr Glass shook his head slowly, a look of admiration on his face. He had met his match.

The phone started to ring.

'Shall I get it?' Kasia asked, half getting up from her chair.

Mr Glass shook his head. 'No,' he said, 'it's good for me

to get up,' and she watched him rise slowly from his chair, and find his balance.

'Hello?' Mr Glass said.

'Oh,' Sam paused. And then, 'Grandad . . .?'

'Hello, Sam.' His grandad's voice softened.

'Oh, I didn't . . .' Sam had meant to phone Henry. He thought better of saying anything. 'How are you, Grandad?'

'I'm old, Sam. What about you?'

'I'm fine, thank you.'

'Listen,' he said, and he lowered his voice so he really was whispering, 'I've got a visitor at the moment, Sam.'

'Oh, right,' Sam said with a frown. 'Shall I call you later?'

'Yes, do that. Thank you. Bye now.'

'Bye.'

'Kasia, have I ever told you the moss story?' She shook her head and sat down in the dusty blue chair, slipping off her shoes and curling her legs underneath her. She had just cleaned the bathroom and had brought his tablets through for him to take.

'There was once a young man called Leo Glass who learnt all about plants and flowers at university.' Mr Glass paused for the interruption ('that's you, isn't it, Grandad?' 'Of course it's him, stupid'), and then he remembered that he was not telling the story to his grandchildren. He cleared his throat. 'One day, he decided to look for some moss. Now, this wasn't any old moss. Leo had travelled to South America and learnt all about moss from El Professero del Mosso at the University of São Paulo' ('but what was he really called?' 'Lorenzo Lopez,' Leo would reply. 'Lorenzo Lopez, Lorenzo Lopez,' they would chant, making it all one word so it sounded like 'laurensolopez'). 'He had learnt about small moss, moss that is so tiny that it grows only on the grains of sand in an egg-timer far away in a forgotten hut on the beach of a lonely island. He learnt about large moss, about moss that is so big that the smallest of its specimens covers a whole mountain in the Himalayas. About moss that can grow on the cliffs of Dorset and have its roots under the ground in Newcastle. He learnt about hot moss, cold moss, fast moss and slow moss. He learnt how moss grows from the inside out, how it eats itself if it has nowhere else to go and how there is one species that grows only on rolling stones. He learnt that some moss has flowers as big as lilies, and one type of moss eats flies and insects. And he also learnt about the rarest moss in the world.' Mr Glass took a sip of water and cleared his throat again. Then he began to fiddle with the hair of his sideburn with his left hand.

'The rarest moss in the world was very rare. So rare in fact that only one sample had ever been collected, in 1896, and the botanists had been unable to make it grow, so it died. So rare that botanists around the world didn't believe that it *existed*. It was a mystery, a myth, a story that old botanists told young botanists, and the argument over its existence fractured the botanical community. Well, El Professero del Mosso' ('laurensolopez, laurensolopez') 'from São Paulo University fell firmly into the camp that thought it was real. He believed in the rarest moss in the world, so much so that he had dedicated his whole life to finding it. He had searched high and low. He had looked under clouds and he had dived in the deepest, dankest wells. He had travelled the world, from China to Mississippi, but he had not found *Muscus Hirsutus*. He had looked up at the sky and down at his feet. He had talked with astronomers and with geologists. For years and years he had searched, but he had not found it and now his life had passed him by. And when he met Leo Glass he took him aside and said this to him:

' "I have spent my whole life looking for *Muscus Hirsutus* and I cannot travel any more. I am eighty-eight and I still believe that it exists. It is out there, and I think I know where. I need somebody to find it for me before I die, but I can only trust a talented botanist for the job. A botanist who will bring the moss back to me and not claim it as his own. There is one last place that I have not been. I left it until last because I thought it unlikely that *Muscus Hirsutus* would be there. Now I am certain that it is, and I want to ask you whether you will go and look for it for me."

'The young Leo Glass agreed. He was keen to find this moss too, keen to help El Professero. The old professor cleared his throat and looked at Leo. "I have told you that I have been everywhere except for this one place. I have been to India, to New Zealand, to Siberia, to Kenya, to Europe, to Greenland. The one place that I have failed to explore is much closer to my home than all those places. The place where *Muscus Hirsutus* grows is Antarctica. Leo, I need you to go to the South Pole." And with that he shuffled off back into his library.'

Kasia sneezed. Mr Glass nodded. 'You may well start sneezing. It was going to be cold. I had no idea how cold it would be, and if I had maybe I would never have gone there. If anyone had told me before I went that I would not feel my toes for the next eight months then maybe I would have reconsidered. But who knows? I had never thought of going to Antarctica before Lorenzo Lopez put the idea into my head. To be honest, I had probably only spent about ten minutes thinking about the place in my entire life up till then. But as soon as he mentioned it everything changed. To this day I cannot fathom what happened to me, why I reacted as I did. You see, for the first time in my life I fell in love. I was twenty-five, and I fell in love with a place that I had never visited, a place about which I knew nothing. It was more than love at first sight. It was love at first hearing.

'Out of nowhere I became obsessed. I started to read

about it. I read as much as I could, fact and fiction. I committed *The Waste Land* to memory. I read Amundsen's *The South Pole* over and over again. And I thought about it. My mind just could not stop visiting it, entering into the white space, trying to imagine the vast white horizons, attempting to understand the size of the place, the silence of it. And, at that time it seemed like such a secret. Amundsen had got to the South Pole in December 1911, and after that it was almost abandoned, conquered but not really explored.'

Leo turned and looked at Kasia, who sat motionless in her chair. 'I had so many questions about Antarctica. Everything about her fascinated me. All day long I imagined vast snow plains with faint mountains in the distance, or a pale sea. I saw huge white caves with long icicles that glittered in the sunshine. I saw ravines open up in the ice in front of me which were white as far down as I could see, and I saw turquoise icebergs rearing up above me in the sea. The place I saw in my head looked like a huge landscape of whipped cream, sprinkled with icing sugar, all beneath a brilliant blue sky. I found it all so hard to comprehend and I knew so little about it. What path does the sun trace when it is light for twenty-four hours a day? Can you really throw boiling water into the air and watch it land, seconds later, as ice? Which way is north when you stand on the pole? And which way is south? Somehow, you see, categories cease to exist down there, the continent seems to have its own rules. When Shackleton's men were stranded on Elephant Island they ran out of tobacco and smoked penguin feathers instead. Can you imagine? *Penguin feathers*. It seemed to me to be a white and blue paradise, and the pole was a haven, a secret hideaway – a motionless place on a gyrating world. I thought that there, if anywhere on this earth, was the only place that I might be able to stand outside the world and time, and look back at it, a real observer at last.

'Every morning as I woke up I heard the call of the quiet land, and every evening as I lay in bed trying to sleep she would whisper in my ear. And if she had just been beautiful, then at least I could have shut my eyes or looked away, but she was there in my head, in my mind and in the air all around me. I had to listen to her white, secret whispers, and I fell in love with the gentleness of her voice.' Leo looked out of the window. His face was flushed and his thick white hair looked more tousled than usual, with bits sticking up here and there, making him look like a scarecrow. Kasia was silent.

'I had three weeks to wait before I could get a flight out there, and it seemed like three years. I spent the time with Lorenzo preparing vessels and equipment for keeping the moss alive during transportation, packing my film and cameras for recording the moss in its natural habitat, and experimenting with tents and sleeping bags. I could see, every day, how much this trip meant to Lorenzo and how disappointed he was not to be able to come with me. He had, after all, devoted most of his life to looking for his moss. He was so anxious that I find it that he spent the evenings poring over a map of the continent calculating currents and temperature gradients and trying to work out which patch of rock might be the most likely place for it to grow. When I finally left I had the most comprehensively marked map you could imagine – there were twelve points on it where he thought I should look first, and after that I was on my own, although we did discuss places that were, as Lorenzo called them, "unlikely but possible" too. We worked out that I should be there for the entire summer – from mid-October to late February – travelling to the crosses on the map and documenting my journey so that Lorenzo could read it on my return. There were only a few people down there – some British people and some

Chileans – and we liaised with them for accommodation and transport.

'And so I went. I strapped myself into a seat next to the bags of post and slept. I slept through take-off and through the flight over the ocean. I slept through the point-of-no-return (when over half the fuel has been consumed) and only woke for the landing because turbulence made the post bags slide across the floor towards me, coming to rest with their dusty covers inches from my nose. And then I unstrapped myself and got out. I climbed down the steps and looked around me. I could see a glittering white plain. I could hear the wind. But more than that I could hear nothing: there was nothing to hear.

'So I started on my journey and every day I would see something that stopped my breath. I saw grease-ice, immense icefalls, snowsnakes and frostsmoke. I visited the dry valleys where it is so dry that a seal has been preserved for three thousand years, in the position in which it died. I saw a pond where the water was so saline that it wouldn't freeze at −60°C, and it dripped off my ski-stick like molasses. I saw the southern lights, Mount Erebus – an active volcano – and sundogs – bright spots near the sun that are formed by the ice-crystals in the air. It was a tough journey – the food disintegrated when we heated it, and we began to lose all sense of time – but we travelled around in a state of constant astonishment and in our surprise we overlooked the hardships.

'By February I had still not found the moss and I wrote to Lorenzo requesting permission to extend my stay by at least another two months. I could not bear the thought of returning to him empty-handed. Looking for moss was a difficult job because, although I could tell where it would, or would not, grow, we had to tread carefully. It could take up to ten years for a footprint in Antarctic moss to disappear, and we did not want to leave any traces. So I asked for leave to continue the slow work which would mean staying on into winter, being there to see the twenty-four hours of darkness and risk developing what was called "big eye" – a certain kind of insomnia brought about by the endless night.

'One day, about one month into winter, the team in the British base where I was staying were called together for an emergency meeting. I had still not found the moss and was beginning to give up hope. We gathered in the meeting room and one of the other British people present, a middle-aged ornithologist called Alfred, got up to speak. He told us that he was currently conducting an experiment with a pair of spiders that he had brought over from London Zoo. He wanted to see whether they could survive winter temperatures in the Antarctic, so that they could be eaten by skuas in summer and encourage the dwindling population of the birds. He talked for a while about the spiders and their behavioural habits. Their technical name was *Sloof Lirpa*, but they were more commonly known as the "foot spider". And then he told us: when he got up this morning there had only been one spider in the enclosure. One had gone, and he needed us to help him look for it, because otherwise he would not be able to make them reproduce and the experiment would be ruined. The reason they were called the "foot spider" was that they had a soft spot for feet. In fact, this genus of spider was unique in its habit of climbing into socks and nestling between toes – usually between the fourth and the fifth toe – until it was evicted by someone or something. There were a few shudders in the audience for even the toughest men can be afraid of spiders and this was not, after all, somewhere like the rain forest or the desert, where insects were only to be expected. So Alfred asked the entire room to remove their socks and shoes and peek between each pair of toes, and indicate, as quickly as possible, if there was something large and dark, legs folded in, nestling there.

'We did as we were asked. Carefully and slowly, we removed our shoes and socks. My feet were, as usual, like blocks of ice, and it took a little persuading to separate my toes. I started on my right and moved on to my left. And there, between the fourth and fifth toe of my left foot was something dark. I looked at it, my heart in my chest, pulling my toes apart as far as they would go. It was not a spider. It was something else. Something that I recognised immediately.

'It was the moss. I could hardly believe my eyes – all these months, all this cold, and it had been growing between my toes all along. There it was, just a little patch, about the size of a penny, in the dip between my toes. I went to my hideout as soon as I could and carefully transferred the moss into the containers that Lorenzo had prepared for it. Then I sat down to write about the discovery in my diary. I had not made an entry for a good few weeks – I had given up, thinking that I would never find it – and it felt strange to be holding a pen. As I wrote the date at the top I thought of Lorenzo. "1 April 1938," I wrote at the top of my page and then stopped. The first of April. April Fools' Day. And I smiled. I saw the room full of men peeking between their toes and I began to laugh. And I looked at the moss safe in its container and I laughed even more.

I returned to Brazil as quickly as I could, every day staring at the moss for hours on end, just in case it started to die or wither or develop a disease. It took me four weeks to get back and I returned the same way that I had come: on a plane delivering the post to the Chilean base. Each day the moss looked the same as the last, but that did not stop me worrying that it would die the day before I got it to

Lorenzo. I cannot tell you how proud I felt when I reached his street and entered his block. I walked the last few steps up to his door with extreme care, convinced that I would drop the container or sneeze into it or that it would suddenly vanish from beneath my nose. An elderly woman opened the door and looked shocked. I had not thought about my appearance for the last six months – I had a long beard, scraggy hair and I was very thin. She led me in and I explained what I was doing there. She was Lorenzo's sister. She led me through to the living room where I sat down on a leather sofa and she sat opposite in a high-backed chair. She asked me whether I would like to take a bath, but I declined, and repeated my request to see Lorenzo. We sat in silence for a while – I can remember thinking that perhaps he was out and we were waiting for him – when eventually she broke the silence and told me that he had died a few weeks earlier, days before his eighty-ninth birthday.'

Kasia and Leo were silent for a while. They could hear the noises of the city: the roads, the planes, the trains, the sirens and car alarms. Then Kasia spoke.

'So what did you do?'

'I renamed the moss after Lorenzo, *Muscus lopezii*. It's still growing today in the moss house in the botanical gardens of Brasilia. And I tried to think about other things. I was trying to cross two species of clematis and I had, as yet, failed, so I tried to plunge myself into that.'

'But you could not get over the fact that Lorenzo had died before you got there?'

'Oh no, it wasn't that. That was sad, but he was an old man. He was bound to die soon.'

'But he never knew that you'd found it. He must have died thinking that no one had found it.'

'He knew that I'd found it. I don't know how, but he

knew that I had found it. Somehow he knew that before he died. Of that I was convinced.'

'So what bothered you then?'

'In my excitement over the moss, in my preoccupation with the specimen and its well-being, I had forgotten that I was leaving Antarctica. I would never see her again, and I had not said goodbye.'

EIGHT

To burn one's boats – To take an irrevocable step; to commit oneself to an action from which there is no turning back. When invading forces burned their boats they were impelled to conquer or die as there was no returning. Sam read it again, looking at each of the words for longer than was necessary. There were certain parts that grabbed him more than others and he mouthed these over and over: 'no turning back . . . no turning back . . . conquer or die . . . conquer or die'. There was nothing under burning *bridges*, but Sam thought that people used it to mean the same thing. Perhaps it was a more modern version of the phrase, a twentieth century rendering birthed after wars fought on land, over rivers and canyons, with planes and tanks. Sam said the words to himself: burning bridges, burning boats, burning bridges, burning boats. He saw images of large London bridges burning, the flames reaching up into the sky, while underneath them boats glided on the water, platforms of flames, gradually turning to ashes which then lay like a grey film over the water and was carried out to sea.

Lauren was sitting at her desk, talking on the phone. He caught her eye and mouthed 'how are you?' at her. She flattened her palm and tipped her hand from side to side in the air. Picking up a pen she scrawled on a pad of paper and pushed it over to him: *Fuckwit client with an IQ that is only slightly larger than the number of hours sleep I got last night.* Sam smiled and tore off the sheet, crumpling it and tossing it into the bin.

He had run into work this morning. It was a strange thing

to do – running to the office, for while he enjoyed the running part, he did not really want to get to where he was going. He kicked his bag of stuff further under his desk and groped around for the bin with his feet. Angela stalked her way into the office, trying to come in late as inconspicuously as possible. Sam smiled to himself. 'Morning, Angela!' he yelled.

'Fucking hell.' Michael worked on Soma cars. He wanted to be a journalist really; in the meantime he worked in advertising.

'What's wrong, Michael?'

'These fucking clients. Do they think I have nothing better to do with my time than ring up directory enquiries and find out numbers for them?'

'Can't you say something to them?'

'I don't think it would be a very sensible thing to do at the moment.'

'What do you mean?'

'Well, you know. In this climate.'

'What climate? Sam spun around on his chair, pushing himself off on his desk each time he slowed down.

'Don't you know about Chloe?'

Sam shook his head. 'What about her?'

He lowered his voice. 'She's just been fired.'

'Fired?' Sam stopped spinning. He was only talking to her an hour ago. 'What for?'

'Well, made redundant. It's the same thing.'

'You're kidding.'

'No, no. She's gone, for sure. Ask Lauren, she'll tell you. But then Lauren's part of the other side now, so maybe she won't want to slag them off.'

'What do you mean?'

'Well, you know. You can't sleep with the creative

director and slag off management at the same time, can you?'

Sam paused and then decided to pretend that he had already known about Lauren and Zach. He felt sick. Sebastian's sentence kept going round in his head: 'We're going to have to shed some people because of reduced profits, so there may be a gap sooner or later for you to fill. I think Chloe will go first and then Phil.' Sam looked over to Phil's desk. Phil was on the phone, studying a piece of paper in his hand, his feet on the desk. He had no idea what was coming.

When Sam got in that night the flat was a tip and Gray was out. Worse still, there were no plates. Sam couldn't understand it, but he looked in the cupboard where they were usually stacked, in the sink and in the drying rack. He even ventured into Gray's room, but there were still no plates. He ate pasta out of the pan and left a note for Gray: *PLATES?* he wrote, and stuck it on his door.

A message on his answerphone from his grandfather reminded Sam of something he had bought at lunchtime, and he went to retrieve it from his bag in the hall. He pulled out a paper bag, and from inside that a map. He cleared the pan off the kitchen table and folded the map out in front of him, smoothing his hands over the thick paper. Then he sat at the table and looked at the map. He sat there for a long time, his eyes moving methodically around the map, as though he was putting together a jigsaw puzzle piece by piece.

He opened his bedroom window and went and sat on the flat roof outside. He often felt while sitting there that it was a pity that he didn't smoke, because it seemed like the perfect place for a cigarette. He never would smoke, just as he would never eat beans on toast or take any interest in tennis. He stared at the sky, as though he was waiting for something to fall out of it. A new job perhaps, or a different life. A girl come to save him. Or even a star, shooting down to rescue him. He ran his fingers through his hair and scratched his scalp. He was looking for a plan. A plan for his disappearance. A plan for escape. An escape from advertising. But to what?

Sam could barely keep his eyes open. After looking at the sky and the stars he finally gave in and let them shut, resting his head in his hands. He listened to the night hum of the city. There was car noise, train noise, plane noise, electricity noise, faint music, and closer by, the noise of Gray making coffee in the kitchen. Sam hadn't heard him come home. Gray never disturbed Sam when he was sitting on the roof, and Sam was grateful to him for it. He seemed to understand that the time on the roof was the time that Sam treasured most.

The next night Sam got the map out again and a compass, but this time in the privacy of his own room, because Gray was knocking around the flat, trying to decide what to wear to a party in town. Sam liked to watch Gray pick his clothes, because he knew that Gray would never admit to anyone except Sam that he even considered, for a second, what he wore. He liked to give the impression that he flung his clothes on with abandon, the same way that a speeding car sprays you with mud as it passes. But of course Gray selected his clothes with thought and care. He spent hours agonising in front of the mirror about how things made him look. He was the biggest fake Sam knew, but he was also the best fake, the most convincing fake, the funniest fake.

After a few minutes Gray came hurtling through to Sam's room. He had a new pair of shoes – dark red suede loafers and a new shirt – marine blue with red stripes. His trousers were green. He strode across the floor and turned on the spot next to Sam's bed.

'Do you think I can wear these together?'

'I think it helps to wear shoes that match.'

Gray frowned. 'The shoes and the shirt.'

'The trousers are okay.'

'What d'you mean? The trousers are cool. And the shoes are the latest thing. You've just got no fashion sense, that's your trouble.'

Sam eyed Gray's shoes and shook his head gently.

'The thing is, Sam . . . this is hopeless, I need to ask a girl. Where's the nearest girl we know?'

'Well, there's that woman who sells you your fags at the petrol station.' Sam looked at his watch. 'She'll be there now.'

'Yeah, right.'

'What about Aphrodisiac? Isn't she around somewhere?'

Gray shook his head and sat down on Sam's bed, watching his feet as they moved around in their new mobile homes. 'Over, mate.'

'Really? What happened?'

'Well, we had a fight. That's what happened to the plates by the way. She took every one out of the cupboard and flung them at the wall. She wasn't even throwing them at me. I was in my room on the phone the whole time. I just kept hearing crash after crash after crash. There are some dents in the doorframe too.'

'You upset?'

'Not any more. Not after I bought these shoes. There's a lucky lady out there tonight somewhere.'

'Yeah, she'll be the colour-blind one.'

He smiled. 'Hey, why don't you rub some salt on to the knife before you twist it? You're just jealous,' and Gray got up and strutted around Sam's floor, watching his feet.

'I'm off out. Have a good night,' and Gray strolled out into the hall. Sam turned back to his map. He was marking a route, faintly in 2B pencil, across the bottom left quadrant.

'Hey, Sam?' He turned. Gray was standing in the doorway. Sam looked at him. 'Is everything okay?'

'Yeah, fine.' Sam shuffled on his chair. 'Why?'

'Dunno. Nothing. You've got a slightly crazy look in your eyes, that's all,' and he walked away once again. 'Adieu,' he called out as he left.

Sam smiled.

As he sat over the map that night he thought again of his grandfather. When Sam was very young, too young to read, Grandad Moss would tell him and Mark stories. In their bedroom at night they would turn off all the lights and undraw the curtains and Grandad Moss would sit at the window pointing out stars for a while, and then begin his stories. In fact, Grandad Moss was not Grandad Moss before those stories were told. When Mark was still a baby Grandad was plain Grandad. It was one night, when Grandad was away and Mark and Sam could not sleep that he acquired his name. Sam and Mark lay awake for a good ten minutes, and then went downstairs in their pyjamas, to find their parents sitting on the sofa watching the television.

'Where's Grandad?' Mark said, as he slid between his mother and father on the sofa.

'He's in London,' his father replied, patting his head. 'He's giving a talk at a conference.' He held out his hand to Sam who was still standing in the doorway. Sam came over and sat next to him, burrowing deep into the sofa and pressing the side of his face into his dad's belly.

'We can't sleep,' Mark said. 'I want Grandad to tell us a story.'

'Will I do?' asked their father. Sam nodded and put his thumb in his mouth. 'Can you tell us Grandad Moss's story?' he said. His mother and father laughed. He looked at their faces, which were full of smiles, and he felt happy. He didn't really understand why they were laughing. What he had meant to say was 'Grandad's moss story', but Sam had confused the apostrophes. He had confused the 'belonging bee' as his teacher at school called it. So their father came upstairs and began to tell them Grandad Moss's moss story, but it didn't sound like the same story at all. And by the time Mark and Sam fell asleep they were convinced that their dad was thinking about a completely different story altogether.

There was a time when Sam had been embarrassed by his grandad. A time when Leo would, towards the end of the afternoon, be taken by the sudden urge to get out of the house and come up to school, to meet either Sam or Mark or sometimes both. And Sam would dawdle to the gates, perhaps with a group of friends, perhaps even with some girls, and his heart would sink and his skin feel cold when he saw his grandfather, waiting outside the gates, gazing up at the sky, or pacing round in a circle.

Even when he stood still, Sam's grandad still stuck out. It wasn't just his thick white hair that refused to lie flat, and stuck upwards like the crest of a tropical bird. It wasn't just his large hook nose that loomed over his face like a cliff over a bay. And it wasn't just the way he held himself upright, almost like a dancer, only slightly too rigid. It was the way he chose to dress too – his corduroy jackets, with their numerous pockets and large lapels, his matching corduroy trousers with their turn-ups, and his bony ankles sticking out underneath. All this and his jaunty walk made people turn their heads. When Sam saw him he often wanted just to walk right past, to hold his head up high and carry on by, but he knew that he couldn't. And the thought, the feeling, shamed him. So he went over sheepishly, feeling the eyes of his friends follow him, and then examine his grandad, and then seeing them snigger, hands over their mouths as they whispered to each other. And Sam would mumble a greeting to Leo and set off, hunched over, striding along and desperate to get away from school and the critical eyes of his class, willing his grandfather to take larger, faster strides.

It was at these times that Sam wished it was his dad who could come to meet him, and not this strange creature he had for a grandfather. It was at these times that Sam completely overlooked what Leo did for him.

'Sam, how are you?' It was Sebastian, smiling and stale-faced, bounding up the stairs in twos.

'Very well, how about you?'

'Superb. Sam, I've got this great opportunity for you. Now, I know that you're working on a pitch already, and that Shadows and Reynolds are both busy, but there's this great chance to impress Robert, and I'd like to give it to you, because I think you're really going to go far, in a very short space of time. We're going to present our agency credentials to the Heron group. You've probably heard of them, they run things like the Drugstore and Lady Clara. Robert's never been into a Lady Clara, so he's asked if somebody could do a brief report on it – its place in the market, its competitors, some store photos – stuff like that.'

I would rather eat my own fingers, thought Sam. 'I'd love to,' he said. And as he listened to Sebastian's onslaught he thought of his journey into work that morning. He had arrived later than planned because the tubes were delayed. The guard at Angel had apologised for the delays and blamed them on a person under a train at Waterloo. This expression had struck Sam as odd because of its simplicity, because it had factored out all question of motivation, of choice, of volition. It sounded like the start of a children's story: *There is a person under a train. What are they doing there? Did they jump? Did they fall? Were they pushed? Or were they just there because that was where they lived?* As Sebastian haemorrhaged words, Sam felt as if he too was under a train. His own inclination, his choice was irrelevant, but here he was adding 'great', 'fantastic', every time Sebastian paused for breath.

'Listen, I'm late for a meeting but I'm thrilled that you'll do it. Come and see me at the end of today and I'll brief you properly on what we need. Oh and it needs to be done by the end of tomorrow, so make sure that you catch me today. Well done, Sam,' and he dashed through the door. Sam sat down on the stairs. His head was spinning. His pager buzzed: *Reynolds meeting NOW in meeting room 3. Gail.* His phone rang, and he turned it off. Then he turned his pager off. Sitting on the stairs, he listened hard, but there was not much noise here. There were the shadows of arguments and TV noise drifting through the small gaps under the fire doors, but he could block them out. He sat in peace and stillness for a few minutes, his arms crossed and resting on his knees, his forehead resting on the sleeve of his suit. And then he thought: this has got to stop.

'Lauren. On for a drink tonight?' Sam sat down at his desk and put his feet up on his bin.

'I'm shagged out, Sam.'

'That's okay. I only wanted to chat.' Sam raised an eyebrow.

Lauren smiled. 'How come you're so cheery? Is Brian Rod on holiday?'

Brian Rod was a client that Sam and Lauren had invented to represent all clients everywhere. He spoke with a nasal voice and a Birmingham accent, drove a Vauxhall Astra, lived in a Barratt Home, wore maroon V-necks, was balding with a middle-manager paunch, got erections at lap-dancing clubs, thought farting was funny, was five foot four, had feathers for hair and enjoyed bullying people.

'No, he's alive and living in Birmingham. But if you come for that drink I'll tell you what's making me so cheerful.'

'Okay. But I can't stay out late.'

Sam's phone rang. 'Just one drink,' he mouthed at Lauren, holding up his forefinger.

'What are you drinking?'

'A G and T, please.'

Sam and Lauren sat down at the bar and stared at their drinks. After a long day in the office both of them felt drained.

'So,' Lauren started, 'why the happiness?'

'Don't tell anyone, will you? Particularly not Zach.'

She shook her head and blushed. The whole agency now knew that Lauren and Zach were seeing each other, but she didn't talk about it, and Sam didn't bring it up either.

'I'm going to leave,' Sam said, and took a sip of his drink.

'You and the rest of the department. What are you going to do?'

'I don't know yet. But I'll find something. And you should start looking too. I think it would be really cool if we resigned on the same day. We could leave the office and go out to a call-box and reverse the charges to Sebastian's office and tell him. And then never come back.'

Lauren smiled. 'It's a great idea, but you can't just leave. You have to have something else to do, somewhere else to go to.'

Sam was quiet for a while.

'You're right,' he said. 'I know you're right, but I will

find something. When I do, I'll let you know and we'll go together. Is that a deal?' He held out his hand.

'Deal.' Lauren shook his hand and smiled.

The Thermlex pitch had been extended from two weeks to six weeks and Sam had to work at the weekend again. The clients were coming on Thursday to have a look at what McLeod Seagal Gale's finest creative and strategic minds would recommend they do with their brand. Sam would have to be there to make sure that all the nameplates were spelt right, that the teas and coffees were topped up at the right time, that the toilets were clean, that the VHS worked, that the presentation was in the right order, that words still meant the same, that everyone had a pad and pencil, that the lights were at the right brightness level, that it was still Thursday, that the air-conditioning was working, that reception knew the clients' names, that God existed, and that all was right with the world. And that he hadn't forgotten anything (that was the main piece of advice he was given when he started: *always* think you've forgotten something – it was enough to give even the most sure-footed person a breakdown).

When he got up on Saturday and looked at himself in the bathroom mirror he decided that he would run into work. He was a mess. He had had four Burger Kings this week (and something from the petrol station on the other three days). His grandad had rung last week and asked him how his salad days were going. Sam had replied that he didn't have salad days, he had Burger King days, and that was that. He did not have time to exercise. He got drunk every Friday night and he stared at his screen so hard that his eyesight was going. As he looked at himself in the mirror, at his belly and his love-handles, he saw that it was all starting to show. He was developing wrinkles around his eyes and stray hairs were turning grey. Running to work was a start, and besides, he needed to run because he was angry.

There was a strange peacefulness about the office on a Saturday. Sam breathed deeply and looked down at his desk. There was a stack of outdoor magazines on his desk from which he had to tear any competitors' advertising, cut around it neatly and stick it on some board. He sat down and started to look through them. It was a mindless job, and as he flicked over each page he kept getting distracted by articles – articles on trekking in Siberia, survival weekends in Scotland, and one about a man who spent each summer walking from one end of the Pyrenees to the other, starting over by San Sebastián and finishing at Port Bou.

Sam turned the page and there, in front of him, was a full-page advertisement that made him stop. He looked at it for a few minutes, brushing his sideburn with his thumb. Then, in the quiet of the empty offices, he read it out loud, slowly, to himself.

THE BRITISH INSTITUTE FOR ANTARCTIC RESEARCH SEEKS RESEARCH ASSISTANTS

The British Institute for Antarctic Research is looking for five Research Assistants to spend six months helping to observe, quantify and assess the impact of tourism on the continent. Applicants should be able to offer the following:

**• 6 months' expedition experience
• a degree in Biology/Chemistry/Geology/Physics/Botany
• team compatibility**

The Research Assistants will need to raise their own funds to cover travel to and from the Antarctic and will be required to work for at least six months (incl. travel); however, if the placement is a success these posts could be extended for another six months. Applicants need to be physically and mentally fit. Previous polar experience preferred.

**DATES: JULY 20TH–FEB 28TH
(incl. one month's training in New Zealand).**

Please send an SAE to PO Box 518, London, W1R 5GH quoting reference SP78 THD3 for further details.

Sam froze at his desk. The past months flicked through his head. All the days of struggling, all the nights of staring into the sky in desperation. All the days of going for angry walks, of working late, of sleepless nights, of anxiety. All the evenings spent wondering, all the endless, unanswerable questions. All the hours spent chewing his nails, all the hairs that had fallen out, all the wrinkles that had appeared on his face, all the time spent with his face pressed against the cold glass of the office window staring up at the sky. His star had finally delivered. Something had finally fluttered down. His plan had arrived. Each word that he had just read seemed so beautiful to him, as though the entire advertisement was a poem.

He looked round the quiet Saturday office and saw instead the white landscape of his childhood. He saw the place that he had dreamed about since he was small, the place that his grandfather had been to, the place that had always been there, lurking, at the back of his mind. He saw his dad, climbing up on the roof, walking along the middle of it, a determined look on his face. He saw him hold out his hand and say 'come on'. Just those two words, 'come on', and a little nod of his head. Sam saw the crystal desert, the quiet place. The sleeping princess. And he longed to go.

Carefully he cut out the page and propped it up on his desk. He thought of the advertisement that Shackleton had placed in a London newspaper in 1860, that his Grandad had once shown him. Shackleton was trying to staff his boat and he wrote: *Wanted: men for hazardous journey; low wages; intense cold, long months of darkness and constant risks. Return not certain.* Going out there must have changed a lot since then, but there were some things that were still the same – the cold, the darkness, the risky journey. He was about to pick up his desk phone when his mobile rang.

'Hello?'

'Sam, it's Clive.'

'Clive. It's Saturday.'

'Yes, I know. The thing is, Sam, I've just spotted that there's a TV programme on the sanpro market tonight, and someone needs to video it. Do you think you could sort that out for me, Sam?'

'Well, okay. I'm actually in the office at the moment, but I'll probably go home later on.'

'Oh, are you . . . oh right. Do you think you could fax me over a copy of the timing plan for the press promotion, so that I've got it first thing on Monday? And send over some dates for the brainstorming meeting too, because our diaries get full very quickly.'

'Right. Okay.'

'So this series is on BBC2 at half-past seven tonight. Okay? Good.' The line went dead.

'Bye then. Have a lovely weekend. Yes, you too, Sam. Sorry to hear that you're in the office and thanks ever so much for your help. It's really very good of you, and I'll make sure I mention it to Sebastian so that you go very far in a short space of time.' Sam shook his head and raised his eyes to the artificial lights of the ceiling. He looked at the dates on the bottom of the Antarctica ad. *Go very far in a short space of time. Go very very very far in a short space of time.* He smiled. And said out loud, into the empty offices all around him, 'You know Sebastian, I might just do that.'

Sam spent the rest of his Saturday sitting by himself in the office imagining that he was Ranulph Fiennes or Michael Palin or even a combination of the two. Ranulph's gravitas but Palin's success with women. Or better still, that he was Amundsen. Or Shackleton. And best of all that he was Sam Glass, yes, *the* Sam Glass. The amazing, daring, heroic but sensitive, and of course handsome, Sam Glass. When darkness began to fall he called Henry and arranged to meet at their favourite pub around the corner from Sam's offices.

Sam felt excited. He felt something he had not felt in months: he felt enthusiasm, coursing like white water through his veins. He wanted to jump, to shout out loud, to sing, to run. He wanted to smile, and smile he did. Sitting at his desk he just smiled, and anyone watching could have been forgiven for thinking him simple. Even though he had done nothing he finally felt in control. He no longer felt that he was the victim of some terrible practical joke. He no longer felt that he was a passenger in the vehicle of his life. He had taken the wheel and found that he could drive.

'You've had your hair cut,' was the first thing Sam said.

'Yeah, only a trim. Does it look weird?'

'Is it supposed to? What do you fancy?'

'A Stella.'

Sam ordered the drinks and Henry found a table.

'How's tricks?' Sam asked.

'Yeah, all right. I had the police round last night because I thought somebody was being attacked in our alleyway.'

'What happened?'

'It turned out to be the combined shadow of the huge plant we'd thrown out and a black bin liner. I felt really stupid. The thing is, it really looked like a guy and a girl, and the plant pot was stuck against the drain, and squeaked every time the wind blew it. Honestly, from the kitchen window, there was no doubt about it.'

'Why didn't you go and look?'

Henry shrugged. 'It was raining. Oh, and I was scared. The noises were so awful.'

'How's Sara?'

'Dismissed from duty.'

'You're kidding?'

'Well almost. She's not that into me either so it's looking

good. And she's away this weekend, gone away with her friends from college, including her ex, so, bingo, I'm free to inflict myself on the fairer sex.' He looked around. 'Can we move on after this one?'

Sam nodded. 'Course, but I'm not sure which sex is fairer in Soho. The boys are prettier than the girls. And we've got to stay here until eight, I told Gray we'd be here, so he might come and find us. He and Lucy are over too, so we're all free and single again. You enjoying your new freedom?'

'Well, yeah, I guess I will. Sara's not that bad, you know. I just wish she was more understanding when it comes to other girls.'

'And other girls were more understanding when it comes to Sara?' Sam smiled cynically at Henry and Henry nodded.

'Well, it's not too much to ask, is it?'

Sam wiped the condensation off his glass with the side of his thumb, rotating the glass with his other hand.

'Henry, can I ask you something?'

'You just have.'

'I've had an idea.'

Henry nodded. 'Now there's a first.'

Sam thought of his grandad. Sure as the floor, he thought, and, feeling the floorboards of the pub beneath his feet, finally understood what his grandad meant. That was exactly how Sam felt. No matter how hard he pushed he would not move that floor. And Sam would not be moved either. For the first time since he was a child Sam had no doubt.

He slowly took out the advertisement that he had cut from the magazine earlier that day. He unfolded it and laid it in front of Henry, leaning it against his pint. Sam watched as Henry read it.

Henry looked at the ad for a few minutes and took a mouthful of beer. He was speechless. Speechless at Sam's brilliance, at his resilience, at his determination. Sam was smiling. Henry wanted to kiss him. Instead he held out his hand, and Sam shook it. And in that small, quiet Soho pub, early one Saturday evening in May (just when Sam was supposed to be setting the video recorder for Clive the Client), Sam and Henry decided to go to Antarctica.

NINE

It was a few days later that Mr Glass decided the time was right to ask Kasia. He had been thinking about it for a few weeks, and now that they seemed to be getting on, he felt the time was right. And so he asked her if she would mind coming for an extra hour each day to read to him. The extra hour would, of course, make itself felt in her pay packet. She was surprised, but pleased. She was glad to spend more time with him, and flattered that he had asked her.

She still had her job in the shop, and so she came an hour earlier in the morning, at about eleven, to start work, and she would start to read to him for an hour before she was due to leave at about two o'clock. And it was in this way, with Kasia curled up in the blue chair and Mr Glass staring out at the space in front of him, that Kasia first met Dickens, Ronald Blythe, V. S. Naipaul, Charles Darwin, Daphne du Maurier and Lampedusa. It was sitting in this chair that Kasia sometimes forgot she was reading aloud and carried on in her head, desperate to get to the end of the story, and never wanting it to end. Mr Glass would cough a little and she would suddenly be aware of his presence again and remember what she was doing. Then she would flick back a few pages and carry on from where she had become submerged in the story. And it was in this way that Mr Glass won the education battle, without Kasia ever realising it.

She did not want to learn things from him. That was fair enough. But as long as she read these books she could not help but take things in. And Mr Glass chose the books carefully. He asked her to read as wide a range of books as possible, he jumped centuries with abandon and he alternated fact with fiction. At the slightest sign of a yawn or a glazed look he switched books for he did not want her to become bored. Sometimes he even resorted to picking up an old piece of newspaper that was lying around and got her to read from that, although the articles usually made him angry ('I wouldn't even have that wrap my fish and chips,' he would say, and start to look for a new book).

Kasia came to love this part of her visit and this part of her day. It was partly because this was the time she was sitting down, the time that was not cluttered with dozens of tasks and jobs, but also because this was the time that she got to know Mr Glass. She looked at his choice of books, and she suspected that each reflected a small part of him, the way that looking through an album of photos might. She felt that she was being given an exclusive insight into Mr Glass, and she felt privileged to be in that position.

And as she got to know him, she realised that Leo Glass *had things that he said*. Slowly over the years he had built up a bank of phrases and words that he always said whenever he felt they were appropriate, and frequently when they were not. He liked his phrases. They made him feel that things had not changed, although he knew that they had. Some of them he had said since he was a young man, and he liked the feeling of constancy that they gave him, as though through his sayings he could approach, however vaguely, immortality.

Sometimes Leo forgot phrases for years, even decades, only to have them appear in his mind at the most unexpected moments. Kasia had had a doctor's appoint-ment on the Friday, so she came to Mr Glass's on Saturday. She returned from the supermarket with a National Lottery ticket (it was her first, but not her last. She would buy one every Saturday from then on). 'There are three things you have to think about,' Leo had said when she showed him the ticket. 'Three things of a very different nature that you have to weigh up,' he half-whispered. 'They are *chance*, *skill* and *luck*. What are the chances that you will win? Do you have the skill to win? And do you have the luck to win?'

'Yes, I know, but I don't think that I'll win. I just like doing something that everybody else is doing,' Kasia replied, defensive and ready for a fight.

'Oh really?' Leo said, eyebrows raised. 'So you don't think about winning at all?'

'Well, maybe,' Kasia said, and sat down in the chair next to him, the high-backed chair upholstered in blue and suffocated by dust. She turned the TV on and flicked it over to ITV, where she had once seen the numbers flashed on the screen before. 'But even if I do, it's got nothing to do with skill at all. And the chances of winning are so slim that they must be only slightly smaller if I didn't buy a ticket at all. So luck is the one I need, and the whole point about luck is that you can't predict it anyway. If I could I wouldn't be here now, would I?'

Leo smiled. He could barely keep up with her.

'Are you sure about the skill involved? You have to choose the numbers, don't you? Is there no skill there? Careful thought and selection? Methodical examination of all numbers past and present? Desperate searching for patterns, for secret codes? Never an even spread, often two consecutive numbers, that sort of thing,' he said.

She shook her head at him. 'I'm not falling for it,' she said, 'I'm not going to have some pointless chat with you about the lottery.' But now she was smiling too.

Leo leant over the side of his chair and pulled out his bottle of whisky. He raised his eyebrows and held it out to her but she shook her head again. He poured a little into his empty water glass. They sat and looked at the television together.

'What would you do if you won?' Leo asked her, all of a sudden. He was sitting with his large hands hanging over the ends of the arms of the chair, his fingers twitching as though he was playing a modern piano sonata, with time signature changes and modulations all over the place.

'If I won the lottery?' she said, and sat back, stretching out her legs and crossing them at the ankles. They sat in silence for a few minutes, while *Gladiators* happened on the TV in front of them. 'I'd buy a cottage somewhere warm, abroad probably, where there are lemon trees and small flowers. And I'd live by myself with lots of cats, with April's babies.' She stared at the screen and pressed the mute button on the remote control. 'What about you?'

'I think I'd hire a large tent and set up a pancake restaurant. Get a really good chef, ingredients grown locally, and lots of pancakes, tarragon, ham and mushrooms, chocolate sauce, lemon and sugar, maple syrup. And I'd have pancake festivals and competitions and races and so on. And I'd eat myself to death, I imagine,' he said, laughing and then coughing a wheezy cough that made him poke his tongue out of the small circle of his mouth. He stopped coughing. Kasia was staring at the television screen. 'And then I'd give some to the Heart Foundation. My son died of a heart attack many years ago. So I'd do that,' he said.

Kasia nodded, taken aback by the sudden change of tone. She had known that his son was not around. She had not known that he was dead, or that he had died a long time ago. She didn't know what to say. She fidgeted uncomfortably. She didn't dare look at Leo but she could see, out of the corner of her eye, that he was staring at the screen too.

'I'm sorry,' she mumbled. He nodded and turned to her.

She looked back at him but she still didn't know what to say. She didn't want to meet his gaze, but once she had she could see by his expression that her silence didn't matter.

'What about your family? Would you give them any money?' he asked gently, his head inclined, his hand stroking his sideburn. And then, 'I'm sorry. That was prying. Please forgive me.'

Kasia indicated that it didn't matter with a wave of a hand, but she lied all the same.

'I don't have any,' she said, and averted her eyes, so that he would not ask any more questions. She knew this wasn't fair. He had told her about his son. Now was the time for her to explain where she had been, what she had done and why she was here, friendless in a foreign city, looking after old people during the day and working in a shop at night.

She looked back at the television. *Gladiators* was over, and she put the sound back on, so they could watch the advertisements. They sat back and watched a girl run along a beach, beaming because of her sanitary towel.

'Hello, Mr Glass. How are you today?'

'Hello there, oh you know. Old. Well, look at you,' he smiled. 'A real Calamity Jane.'

'What do you mean?'

'Calamity Jane was a cowgirl way out West. Well, she was Doris Day really, but in the film she was a cowgirl. She could ride like a man, shoot like a man, and she always went around in her cowgirl gear. One day she fell in love and put a dress on,' he paused, suddenly conscious of what he was saying, 'and she looked just lovely.' April stretched on his lap and then jumped to the floor. 'You haven't fallen in love, have you?'

Kasia shook her head. 'No, of course not. Who am I

going to fall in love with?' And then added, 'I'm going for an interview.'

'Oh I see,' said Leo, quietly. 'What for?'

'Do you mean why am I going for an interview or what is the interview for?'

'No, no, what's the interview for?'

'To clean somebody's house. Mrs Reaper. She lives in Hampstead. She's got a shop too and she might need somebody to clean that as well, which would be good.'

'Well, it's going to rain shortly, so make sure you've got an umbrella with you,' he said, staring straight ahead at the sky outside.

Kasia paused. 'How do you know?'

'Come over here.' Kasia took a few steps forward. 'Do you see that cloud over there? The big one?' She squatted next to his chair and nodded. 'That's a cumulonimbus. A rain cloud. And if you watch it for more than a few minutes you can see that it's heading this way. Look, you can see that it's darker at the bottom than at the top.'

'What does cumulonimbus mean?'

'Well, nimbus is cloud. And cumulus means heaped up. They're categorised according to their height and the shapes they make. There are three main types: cumulus, stratus and cirrus, or heaped, layered and feathered.' They sat side by side, watching the cloud inch its way through the grey London sky. 'You shouldn't be going for cleaning jobs, Kasia.'

'Why not?'

'Because you could do so much more. You could be a teacher, or a lawyer or a doctor.'

She got up quickly. 'Mr Glass, don't. People would laugh if they could hear you say that. You're so . . . why do you have to say things like that? There's nothing wrong with cleaning people's houses. For me this would be a really good job. So don't start overshadowing it with all your educated jobs. It's not fair.' She walked towards the door, her pace brisk, her footsteps clipped.

Leo dropped his voice. 'I'm sorry. I didn't mean to imply that it was a bad job. All I meant to say was that I think you're very capable and clever and if you wanted to do something else, then you could. I'm sure there's a way.'

She turned in the doorway. 'And I'm sure there isn't. Okay?' and she went through into the kitchen where she began to prepare his lunch, slamming cupboard doors and banging plates down on the Formica surface. She pushed the fridge door shut with too much force and the milk bottles clinked. How had he managed to ruin her day with one quick remark? Didn't he realise how stupid it was to say things like that? Those things could never happen, never ever, and she noticed her hands were shaking as she plucked the vegetable knife from the drying rack.

She was preparing a large beef stew, something that Mr Glass could heat up in the microwave by himself tomorrow. As proper jobs raced through her head she began to slice up the carrots. She thought about teaching. She imagined herself in front of a class of children, trying to arouse their interest, trying to circumnavigate their prejudices and inhibitions, trying most of all to make them feel good about themselves, so they could finally learn something. She began to chop more ferociously, the slices becoming thicker and wedge-shaped, toppling over each other and off the sides of the chopping board. She carried on, throwing more and more haphazardly chopped carrots into the pan. She was so angry that when she took the meat from the fridge she could have torn it into little pieces with her bare hands. As it was she imagined that is was steak from Mr Glass – Glass topside, Glass brisket, or best of all, Glass rump steak.

The stew boiled over as she crashed around attempting to

wash up. She swore, a long stream of expletives, as she noticed flecks of stew on her jacket. She took it off and hung it on the back of a stool and then took a deep breath.

When she finally carried through a bowl of stew to Mr Glass he was watching the tail-end of lunchtime TV, his feet on his little stool, the local paper on his lap. She wondered what would happen if she were to trip and fling the stew all over him. Would the burns kill him? Or would the bowl (a thick, white china bowl) spin through the air in slow-motion and land on, or rather bounce off, the middle of Mr Glass's skull, piercing the skin, drawing blood, causing the bone to swell and, after a few seconds, causing blood to trickle from his ears and nose too?

She had this terrible feeling that she would do it, that she was out of control. It was so precisely what she didn't want to do, that she could see herself doing it. She paused, appalled at the possible consequences. Then felt terrible. She was ashamed at these thoughts, but she was angry too. She felt like being violent. And she knew that throwing the bowl at him was the last thing he would expect. She imagined the shock and incomprehension on his face as he turned towards her in the split second after the bowl had hit home. It was the incomprehension on his face that made her heart race. The same incomprehension that she would see on somebody's face were she, at one end of an empty platform, to push them in front of a Northern Line train. That incomprehension made her fingers tingle, it made her mind lurch and her heart freeze. The last thing she wanted to do was to hurt Mr Glass, and it scared her that she might do just that, might lose control and ruin her life, in one quick movement. It terrified her. And it made her grip the bowl with all her might. As she delivered the bowl to its rightful place she could barely bring herself to open her mouth and speak, she was so tense. She left as soon as she could, eager to escape the damp flat just in case she accidentally on purpose set it alight.

Just as she turned on to the main road, on her way to the interview, the phone rang. Leo slowly put his stew aside and got up. He went through to the kitchen, and by the time he got there he knew that the person ringing must be someone he knew. Otherwise they would have given up by now.

'Hello?'

'Grandad, it's Sam.'

'Hello, Sam,' Leo smiled. 'How are you?'

'Fine, what about you?'

'I'm old, Sam.'

Now it was Sam's turn to smile. 'Old as the hills,' he said.

'Older,' replied Leo.

'Grandad, I just wanted to tell you that if you need anything sorting out for Mark's wedding, just let me know and I'll do it, okay? You know, your suit, present, all that stuff.'

'I was just going to wear my old cord suit.'

Sam paused. 'You are joking, aren't you?' He thought of his grandfather's suit with its wide lapels and the thick turn-ups that showed his ankles.

'Well, I was going to wear the bottom half and give the jacket to Mark as his present.'

'Just let me know, okay, Grandad?'

'Okay, Sam.'

'Hello, Mr Glass.'

'Good morning, Kasia! How are you today?'

'Yeah, fine. How about you?'

'Oh, I'm old.'

Kasia smiled. 'But you're old every day. In fact you're

older today than you were last time I saw you. That's nothing new.' He smiled and played a piano concerto in the air.

'So how was your interview? Did you get the job?'

Kasia looked down at the backs of her hands. 'You know the answer to that question. Why are you asking it? You knew the answer the other day, you just didn't say out of politeness.'

'Why are you so angry?'

'I'm *not.*'

He whispered something to himself as Kasia sat down in the blue chair next to him. She picked up *Rebecca,* a sentence forming itself in her head: 'I don't know what to do,' she thought. Why can't I say that? Just say it, she thought. Say it.

'I don't know what to do,' she said, as she kicked off her shoes and tucked her legs under her like a cat. She tried to make herself look comfortable and confident, when she was in bits inside. She pummelled the arm of the chair with her hands.

'I know you don't. But that's all right. You will know. Something will come along. You should meet my youngest grandson – he doesn't really know what to do either. He's a lovely boy. You two might hit it off.' Leo cocked his head on one side and looked at her.

Kasia shook her head and looked at the palms of her hands, embarrassed.

'I don't . . . he wouldn't . . .' She shook her head again. 'But why do people work anyway? Why do they bother?'

'Well, they need a job. Or in some cases, some jobs.'

'But why? What *for?*'

Mr Glass looked over at her. She had her head on the arm of the chair now, and her hands in fists under her chin. She looked like a child, staring far away into the distance. He wanted to take her back to her childhood and start again there. He wanted to tell her stories and explain things to her, and then watch her while she rubbished his explanations, as children always do. But it was too late for that.

'For money. For their children. For their husbands. For themselves. For pancakes.'

It began to rain. Mr Glass looked at his watch. He angled it so that more light fell on it. It was no good. 'What time is it?' he asked, slightly gruffly.

'Half-past twelve. I should make a start on your lunch.'

'Just as I expected: rain at half-past twelve. Look I wrote it down earlier. On a piece of paper . . . I put it somewhere here.' She sat up in the chair. 'Don't worry about the job. You'll be all right in the end,' he said.

'I don't want to be all right *in the end*. I want to be all right *now*,' she replied, but she couldn't quite muster the bitterness needed to deliver the line properly. Somehow Mr Glass had dissolved it.

Kasia carried the bowl of soup in her right hand and a cup of water and a spoon in her left. She turned the light off in the kitchen by pressing the switch with the tip of her nose, and she backed into the door of the front room which was kept almost closed to keep the heat in (glancing upwards first of all, to check there wasn't a feline presence waiting to leap). It was Friday. She did not work in the shop on Fridays and so stayed at Mr Glass's later than usual, finishing up the chores she had not got round to earlier in the week. Then she would go home and spend the evening by herself. Darkness was falling and she knew that Mr Glass was glad to have company at this time of day. If she thought about it, *she* was glad to have company at this time of day too.

Mr Glass was sitting looking at the television. Those were

his own words. Mr Glass did not *watch* the TV. He *looked* at it. A quiz programme was on. Kasia put the soup, spoon and water down on the floor, cleared his side table of books, cups and tablet bottles and then moved it in front of him, placing it just beside his legs.

'Thank you, Kasia.'

As she looked up she started. A spider was sitting on his shoulder. It was just sitting there, in the middle of his left shoulder, stock still but knees bent as though at any minute it might make a run for it and scamper down his front, or round the back of his neck. It was large – a tennis ball could have fitted into the circle made by its long legs and it looked dark against the backdrop of the linen antimacassar.

Kasia shivered. She had no idea how Mr Glass might react. Had she mentioned it he could have told her how spiders have the ability to remain completely still for long periods of time, a state which was called tonic immobility and which was useful for their survival. Had she mentioned it he could have told her about the time a spider in Brazil made its way on to the roof of his mouth when he was sleeping, and he awoke to a spindly obstruction in his throat, which he washed down with hot coffee. But Kasia did not mention it, instead she thought of what she might do were she to see a large spider on her own shoulder and imagined Mr Glass reacting in the same way. He might petrify and never move again. He might panic and try to leap out of his chair, falling on the floor when his heart failed. For a second she thought of leaving it there, screaming, pointing, shouting, panicking just to see what would happen. But she caught herself, ashamed at her thoughts. She reminded herself that this was Mr Glass and that she had no reason to do any damage to him.

She moved nearer and bent over him, placing her left hand on his shoulder and over the spider. She had to clench her hand into a fist, as tight as she could but also as gently, for she did not want to kill it. The spider panicked against her palm, writhing and poking, threatening to escape through the gap between her thumb and her hand. She wanted to cry out, to shake the thing from her hand, but she stopped herself. A shiver ran up her arm, and for a moment she thought that the thing had escaped and was careering up her arm.

Mr Glass looked at her, confused at seeing her standing beside him, her hand on his shoulder. He turned the TV off.

'Are you okay?' she asked, squatting in front of him and placing her right hand on his right leg. The spider was going to escape. She could already feel some of its legs on the outside of her hand. It was going to escape and scamper all over his face, giving him a heart attack. She clenched her fist as tight as she could, her nails pressing into her palm. It still did not seem tight enough, and she clenched harder.

'I'm fine, Kasia. Thank you for asking.' Mr Glass nodded slowly at her. 'How about you?' The wriggling in her hand had almost stopped. She could feel things – legs, she supposed – tickling her palm and itching between her fingers. Her arm was beginning to ache.

'Yes, I'm fine. I brought you some soup,' she replied, still squatting. There was a silence. She was about to stand when she felt Mr Glass's hand under her chin, as light as a spider's touch.

'Goodness me,' he said quietly, eyebrows raised. 'I had never noticed it before, but you have a star looking over you.' He dropped his hand and gazed at a point above her left shoulder.

'What?' she asked, standing up, her brow furrowed. He paused and continued to stare at the space above her shoulder.

'A star, above your shoulder. Just sitting there, looking over you.'

His eyes were sparkling. She didn't know what to say. She was embarrassed.

'What do you mean?' she asked.

'It means you don't have to worry. It means that everything will turn out all right. It's there, just on your left shoulder. It's keeping an eye on you.'

She paused, and once again felt the spider, wriggling its last wriggle in the fist of her left hand. 'The soup,' she said, 'it's chicken and sweetcorn. I'll just be in the kitchen if you need me.'

She left the room, keeping her left hand clenched in a fist. When she got to the kitchen she turned on the tap and opened her hand. There was a reddy-black mess, some legs still intact, others crushed and smeared and twitching. She could see short hairs on the legs that were still whole. Her nails were black too, the dark exoskeleton embedded between nail and flesh.

She shuddered and put her hand under the tap, watching the larger parts of the body and legs wash off, circle the sink, and disappear down the plug hole. The water rushing on to the aluminium sink and the hiss of the water tank drowned out the noise of it, but were you to have stood in the hallway and looked into the kitchen you would have seen that Kasia's head was bowed and her shoulders a little hunched, and that she was crying. As she peeled pieces of leg off her bloodied palm hot tears were on her cheeks and she was gasping for breath. She was not crying for the spider. She did not care about the spider. Not any more, anyway. She was crying because of what Mr Glass had said about the star. She so wished that it was true.

'Are you rushing off tonight?' Mr Glass croaked, flicking the volume down on the TV.

Kasia shook her head. 'You know, my wife used to call

me "Moderation Leo". You wouldn't think it now to look at me, would you?' he laughed, patting his stomach. 'She thought I did everything in moderation. Sometimes she thought it was good, and at others she thought that it made me mediocre, middle-of-the-road, a jack of all trades. She thought it was spineless to do everything in moderation. Conventional and sensible. And to her those words were evil.'

Kasia raised her eyebrows. At the moment conventional and sensible was all she was trying to be.

'I remember once when I first met her, she went to have her hair cut. Well, we'd only just started courting and I asked her what she was going to have done to it, thinking maybe a permanent or a few waves put in. She said she was going to have it cut shorter. I laughed. I remember saying: "You can't exactly have it cut longer." Maybe it was because I said that, I don't know. But when she came back from the hairdressers she had the haircut of a boy. It wouldn't be that shocking nowadays, but then . . . I didn't know what to do with her. But what could I do? It's the way I am, I suppose.'

'Where did you meet her?' Kasia sat down in her blue chair and pulled the elastic band out of her black hair, combing out the tangles with her stretched-out fingers.

'In Brazil. She was Brazilian. Natália,' as he said her name it sounded rich and deep, as if falling slowly off his tongue, like honey or oil. 'I married her when I was twenty-eight and she was twenty-five. About your age, I suppose.'

'I'm twenty-three,' Kasia said.

'Really? I thought you were older than that.' Mr Glass scratched his sideburn, his slow fingers lingering and pulling at stray thick white hairs. 'She was quite a strange creature. I don't think my parents knew what to make of her. She had the temper of a bear and the will of an ox. But I loved her,' he half-smiled. 'Or rather, *so* I loved her. At the time I loved her a lot.'

Kasia slipped her shoes off and pulled her feet up on to the chair, curling her legs around underneath her.

'We were married in England, in Lincolnshire where I grew up, and then we went to live in Oxford because I had got a teaching job there. She didn't like Oxford one bit. Well, at first she said it was pretty and looked nice in the rain, but after a while she found it stuffy and backward. When it was fine she would put on her red dress and go out barefoot, walking through all the little lanes and over the cobblestones, going nowhere in particular. Of course a lot of people saw her who knew her (Oxford was quite a small place then) and she always ignored them, looking right through the president of the college where I taught, pretending not to see the head of my faculty. I begged her to behave herself, I pleaded with her to show some manners, but it only made it worse of course. I can see now that I shouldn't have said anything. Then she became pregnant with our son and she was happy once again. People still stared at her in the street, but now because she looked so beautiful and so unlikely – this strong dark woman striding down these small English streets.

'When Robert was twelve she went back to Brazil for a holiday. And then when she returned it started all over again. She would rant and rave about how boring England was, how stuffy and unfriendly the people were, how bad the weather was, how tasteless the food. It never stopped, day after day after day, and her behaviour became worse. When it rained she would run through the streets cursing at the sky, and one day she was discovered dancing on the tables in the college library. And she barely spoke to me, she just used to shout at odd things in the house – the cooker, the banister, the armchair. I offered to go and live in São Paulo with her, but she refused. "Then *you* will become *me*," she said and shook her head. When Robert was fifteen she went back again, and this time she didn't return. I wrote to her parents but they did not reply. I wrote to everyone I knew, begging for information, if only of her well-being. No one knew anything. And that was that.' Leo stretched his hand and scratched his face. 'I never heard from her again, and neither did Robert.'

'But where did she go?' Kasia asked, frustrated by the end of the story.

Leo shrugged. 'I don't know,' he said, 'I really don't know.'

It was a clear day. Leo had been sitting for most of the morning waiting to hear Kasia's keys in the lock. He had looked at the sky, marvelling at its colour and talked with April and done nothing much else.

'Have you been doing this a long time then? I mean, do you like looking after grumpy old men?' Leo asked when she brought through his lunch and set it down on his table.

'I needed a job. The local authority told me to do this. Here I am, doing it.' She sat down in her chair and looked at her hands. They were dry and cracked from doing the washing-up without gloves on.

'But if you could do anything you wanted to in the whole wide world, what would it be?' Mr Glass fiddled with the large buttons on the remote control.

'Well, I don't know. It doesn't really matter, does it? I can't do anything in the whole wide world.'

'But you could do anything, if you wanted to. Whatever you wanted. Look at you – you're too clever to be looking after me.' Kasia felt a surge. What was it? Was it anger? She didn't know. She buried it as best she could and turned her head and smiled at him.

'I can't. I can't do whatever I want to do.'

'Why ever not? You're young, aren't you?'

Keep calm, she thought. It's not his fault. Just keep calm.

'Because I have a criminal record,' she shrugged. There, she thought, I've said it. I'll be out of here now and never return. Who, in their right mind, would let a woman with a criminal record look after their old father? Why had she just thrown away a job? Was that what the prison psychologist had meant when he told her she was self-destructive?

There was a silence. Nothing in the room moved. The curtains hung. The prints froze on the walls. The books did not move a muscle.

Kasia was aware, for the first time, of the interminable stillness, of the relentless nothing-happens-ness of Mr Glass's life. Mr Glass tilted his head. 'And what does that mean from a job point of view? Do employers have to know that you have one?'

His question almost took her breath away. She tried not to show her surprise. 'Yes, they know. They need to know what you've been doing with your life, why you haven't had a job before. And you can't really do anything with your life if you're in prison.'

Mr Glass nodded again and they sat in silence for a few minutes, listening to the afternoon traffic on the road outside.

'So what can you do? I mean, for a job?' Mr Glass asked gently.

Kasia fidgeted on her seat. She really shouldn't be saying all this. She had promised herself that she wouldn't. But somehow it made her feel better. She had spent too long sorting it out by herself. 'Well, I'm on a rehabilitation scheme at the moment and I can get jobs through that. These sorts of jobs. Where the company gets money from the government to employ me and they keep a close eye on me and all that. But I can't compete otherwise. I can't really get a job in the normal way. I imagine I'll spend the rest of my life on schemes.' She paused. 'Don't you want to know what I did?'

'Do you want to tell me?'

'But what if I murdered old people or something, slipped poison into their tea?'

Mr Glass closed his eyes. 'It wouldn't matter.'

'What do you mean it wouldn't matter? It would make all the difference to me. For a start, my sentence would have been longer.'

'Yes, I'm sorry, you're right. What I mean is: it wouldn't matter to me. *To me* it doesn't make any difference what you did.'

Something inside her sparked. 'Well, it makes a hell of a lot of difference to me. A huge difference, in fact a whole life worth's of difference. So you can't sit there and say it makes no difference to you. Of course it makes a difference to you, because if it hadn't happened I wouldn't be sitting here now, would I? I wouldn't have to look after old people.' Kasia spat the words out and shot him a glance, an aggressive glance.

His gaze was steadily fixed on her, old blue eyes straining not to miss any footnotes to her expression. She tried to sigh, but she could hear her breath coming out in judders as though she was sobbing. Her hands were shaking and she touched one to her face to check that she *wasn't* sobbing. This was what she always got wrong. This was where things always fell to pieces. This was her Achilles heel, the chink in her armour. She felt ashamed. She *always* felt ashamed. She always took it out on the wrong people. And he had said the nicest thing to her. She had heard it with her own ears. He had said something that no one else would ever say. It didn't matter to him what she had done. *It didn't matter to him what she had done.*

She clenched her jaw in the silence. Mr Glass looked out of the window. Kasia tried to make her breathing even.

'I'm sorry,' she said, looking down at her fingers. At least he knows now, she thought. It might all be ruined but at least he knows. And she suddenly felt more at ease, because nothing seemed to matter. 'You should eat before it gets cold. Would you like some tea?' she asked as she got up.

He looked at her. 'Yes,' he nodded. 'White, one sugar. And no poison.'

He caught her off guard and she smiled. He laughed too, and for a minute she just stood there, wondering where her frown had gone.

TEN

Sam had been surprised that Henry wanted to come with him. He knew that, as a journalist, Henry was always on the lookout for new things to do, new experiences to write about. But still, this was going to be a big commitment. It meant training, learning, getting fit, changing their diets, raising money. That commitment did not scare Sam, in fact he barely thought about it. He was fascinated by the end result, and it was this that occupied his mind. He joined the gym near work and started getting up at six to go in for an hour before leaving for the office. He also started to run more. He ran when he got in at night, sprinting past the drunks lurching along the pavements and sucking in the night air. He pounded the pavements, thrilled with the space, with the sky, with the corner shop, the pedestrian crossing. He ran until it hurt, and then some more. He delighted in what his body could do, in how far he could go if he wanted to. And he forgot what time it was. It didn't seem to matter any more that he would be going to bed at twelve-thirty, after an hour of running. It didn't bother him in the least. What mattered to him was the running, and every time he went out he felt that he could run all night.

Sam picked up a pile of Shadows press ads from his desk and headed for the post room. Each time he went into the post room he thought he was going to die. It was a small room on the ground floor of the agency, with one door which was always shut and a small window where couriers knocked for packages. It was always dark and it smelt bad. As Sam went in now he held his breath, keen not to inhale. Simon was sitting at his desk, surrounded, as he usually was, by various packets of biscuits. These packets were joined by three pairs of scissors, all lying open like over-heating crocodiles, two 'handy' penknives (also open) and a kitchen knife (useful for when vegetables came through the post with instructions to be distributed to more than one person in the building). All along the edge of Simon's desk (everyone called him Stanley behind his back, such was his passion for blades) was a row of drawing pins, points up, like spinning tops lined up for battle.

'Simon, I need a tube. For these posters. Have you got one?' said Sam, all on one breath.

'I've got a penknife,' Stanley replied, stock still in his chair. There was a sound like a fart. Oh please, no, thought Sam.

'Yep, that's good. But what I really need is a tube. I don't want to fold them, you see.'

'Oh, a tube? What about the inside of a toilet roll?'

'Errrr, no.' Sam just stopped himself perching on the edge of Stanley's desk. 'I need a thick one, you know, those ones with plastic ends.' Sam looked around. There were lots of envelopes, but tubes were nowhere to be seen. Stanley picked up a pair of scissors and a penknife. He ran the penknife blade between the scissors.

'Sam, I like you,' he said, increasing the speed of the rubbing, 'so I'm going to let you look for your tube yourself.'

At that point there was a tap on the window, and in one sudden movement Stanley lurched over and opened it.

'Urgent package for Mr Z. Bennett. Sign here.'

Stanley put the small Jiffy bag on a filing cabinet and signed the sheet. The phone rang and he lurched over to the other side of the room. Sam started his prowl for tubes, inching towards the filing cabinet with the package on it. He put his posters down and spotted a box with a plastic lid on top, and sure enough the tubes were inside. He took one, picked up his posters and left the room. Stanley was still on the phone, playing with one of his penknives. The package on the filing cabinet was gone.

Sam stood in the stairwell. Should he go up or down? Did it matter? He had a package to deliver, but would he deliver it? He went into the loo, locked the door, put the seat down and sat on it. He put all the stuff that he was carrying on the floor in front of him. He looked at the package. It was a small, white Jiffy bag. It had no return address and Zach's details were written on it in thick black marker. Why had he picked it up? It was probably just a tape or a catalogue. Zach must get sent all sorts of rubbish. Sam picked it up and felt it. It was surprisingly soft – he could bend it in both directions. He shook it. He smelt it. He held it up to the light (what did he expect to see? It was a Jiffy bag, for crying out loud). He slid his finger into the gap at the end and started pulling the paper. What am I doing? he thought. He looked inside. He couldn't really see anything. He put his hand in and pulled out two small see-through plastic bags. Inside the bags was white powder.

'Oh shit,' whispered Sam. 'Oh shit oh shit oh shit. Cunting shit.' He felt like someone on *Hawaii Five-O*. He sat there and stared at the package, expecting Magnum to burst through the toilet door at any minute. 'Fuckety fuck. What possessed you, Sam Glass?'

He thought over his options as quickly as he could. He could replace the envelope and put it back in the post room (but someone might see him, and then he'd lose his job). He could sell it to people in the agency (but then he would be found out, and he'd lose his job). Better still he could sell it to the agency source, Jake in TV, who was constantly being asked for 'some Charlie for the weekend, yah?' But could he trust Jake to keep his mouth shut? If he didn't Sam would lose his job. He could ring the police (then he'd definitely lose his job). He could hide it, but Stanley would probably remember that he was the last person in the post room, and so he'd lose his job. Look at it this way, he thought: Zach is expecting this. It does not arrive. Stanley remembers me in the post room. I lose my job.

Sam looked at the powder again and then he realised: I've lost my job. And I don't want to lose it, I want to be able to give it back to the people who gave it to me. I want to hand it right back to them: 'Here you are. Have this piece of shit advertising job back – it's no good – I'm going to Antarctica.'

As Sam sat there a while longer other thoughts began to occur to him. He was going to give up his job anyway, so why not have some fun? He could ring Henry – he must have some journalist friends who would be interested. But was it that interesting? *Advertising Hoorays in Snow Snorting Shocker* – wasn't that like running a headline along the lines of *Bankers in Champagne Lunches Scandal, Actors in Resting Shock, Writers in Writers' Block Outcry*? Not for nothing had the industry spawned the line *Coke is it*. And then it occurred to him. If he was going to lose his job over this package of fine powder from Colombia then he might as well do it with panache. If he was going to lose something then the agency ought to lose something too.

Sam was sitting at his desk on both his phones at once when, two days later, on a Wednesday, a large envelope arrived at the Department of Health. It was addressed to Tim Jade, a fat man in his late twenties with thinning hair and a beguiling smile. Among other things, Tim was responsible for liaising with the roster of advertising agencies that worked for the DoH on a number of projects. One of the agencies had done all the YTS stuff years ago. Another had done a small campaign for schools on rubella and tetanus. And currently one agency was working on some anti-drug posters, to run outside schools and in big cities.

On this particular morning Tim was late for work, and when he finally got to his desk (at ten past ten) the envelope was sitting there waiting for him. He turned on his computer, chatted to his secretary and went to make a cup of tea. When he got back to his desk he had a quick conversation on the phone and then started on his post. Tim did not often get large envelopes through the post and he found them exciting. So he put the envelope to one side and looked through everything else first.

At eleven o'clock precisely he knocked on his boss's door with an anxious expression. He showed his boss the large envelope, and then took from within it the smaller envelope, and then took from within that (like Russian dolls, thought his boss) the two see-through bags of white powder. His boss was a calm woman. She told him to lay everything out on her desk, so they could both look over it: the big envelope addressed to Tim (the address label was typed), the small envelope addressed to Mr Z. Bennett and the two clear plastic bags.

'This would be highly embarrassing if it got into the press,' said his boss. 'I can just see it: "Ad agency responsible for anti-drug posters in cocaine haul". We'd both be for it, that's for sure,' she sighed. 'What a shame, I quite liked their work. Are you happy to make the phone call or shall I?'

The application forms arrived the following Tuesday, and Sam ran round to Henry's so they could plan how they would fill them in. He got lost on the way (he usually took the tube) but did not really care – jogging through unknown London streets he felt such a freedom that he thought he might be able to fly. He wanted to yell out, to jump and dive, to rise into the air.

Filling out Henry's form was more difficult than Sam's because, although he had done geography at college, his project had been on Scotland, so he had never been on a real expedition.

'I went to Venice with the school. We were researching *Man and Tides*. Does that count?' he asked.

They filled in the forms with care, and lied or omitted information as best they could. Sam considered adding a footnote about his grandfather ('My grandad went there once! Doesn't that mean that I should go now?') but he thought better of it. Sam looked over at Henry who was chewing his pen and tapping his foot. He was clearly excited. Excited that he was going to Antarctica. A kind of fidgety excitement. A kind of jump-around excitement.

'Henry, there's loads to get through yet, you know. All we've done is fill in forms. That doesn't mean anything,' Sam said, taking off his glasses and cleaning them on his shirt.

'Oh, we'll go Sammy. We'll go. Can you imagine? Can you imagine? Antarctica. All that white. What will my father say? And Sara? Have you told Gray?'

'No, not yet. We have to be careful who we tell, and when.'

'Christ, Sam, you sound like my father,' Henry said, slumping down on the sofa.

'And you sound like a kid. Look, we have to work out how we're going to raise the money. We have to get fit. Really fit, like survival fit. Like no body-fat fit. And we have to read up about the place. What the fuck do you know about it, Henry? For example, how big is it?'

'Big.

'What kind of climate does it have?'

'Snow.'

'Fauna?'

'Penguins.'

'Flora?'

'Snowdrops.'

'Population density?'

'Two Eskimos and a Husky. Shortly to be doubled when you and I arrive'

'Food source?'

'Ice cream.'

'Environmental threats?'

'Currently none. Will I be able to smoke out there?'

'Political state?'

'Calm. Penguin riots in 1979 due to tuxedo shortage and consequent identification problem. Since then only the seals have demonstrated, and these are always peaceful acts where the seals lie on the beach and, taking inspiration from the Greenham Common women, chant "we shall, we shall not be moved".'

'Nearest land mass?'

'Australia. Can you think of two countries less alike?'

Sam shook his head. 'What you know about Antarctica could fit on the back of a stamp.'

'I'm not sure the Queen would like to have my thoughts on her sticky behind. And anyway, I know the important bits. I know that Amundsen just beat Scott to the Pole, and that that Captain on the way back said something about going outside for a while, and walked off to die.'

'Oates. Captain Lawrence Oates. "I'm just going outside and may be some time." And he didn't walk. He crawled out of the tent, without putting his shoes on.' Sam paused. 'It is the coldest, the driest, the highest and the windiest

158

continent on earth. It has a mountain range as high as the Appalachians underneath its polar plateau. It makes up one tenth of the earth's land surface. It is one and a half times as big as the United States. It is at the very bottom of the earth, underneath everything. And, for the most time, it is forgotten. And that is how it likes to be.'

Henry looked at Sam, his eyebrows raised.

'It is a blue and white place. Sometimes the blue is almost see-through, and sometimes it is the brightest blue you have ever seen. The white is bright too, brighter than you ever imagined white could be – as bright as red almost, or as orange. The white makes you shield you eyes. And this white is empty. It stretches as far as you can see and further still, for miles and miles and miles, all empty and all white.

'And I asked you the easy questions – there are a lot more we need to be able to answer: what path does the sun trace when it is light for twenty-four hours a day? Which way do compasses point when you stand at the pole? Can you really throw boiling water into the air and watch it land, seconds later, as ice? Which way is north when you stand on the pole? And which way is south? What is grease-ice? What is a sundog? An icefall? A snowsnake? Where are the Dry Valleys? What is Mount Erebus?'

'Okay, okay, you've proved your point,' Henry said, scratching his scalp and then peering at his fingertips. Sam continued.

'The winter temperature reaches –70°C, and wind speeds are 120mph. The land mass doubles because of the frozen seas, and there is only one mammal that does not flee the continent for the winter – the Weddell Seal, whose milk is 60 per cent fat. Can you imagine? It must be like Häagen-Dazs, like suckling double cream from Mama Seal. There is only one bird in the world whose feathers do not grow in patches on their skin. Only the penguin has feathers growing from every square inch of skin — their feathers grow like fur — and you can guess why.'

'Aren't penguins actually mammals?'

Sam laughed. He handed Henry a large book entitled *Antarctica*. 'Read this,' he said, 'please. Otherwise we haven't got a snowball's chance in hell.'

That night when Sam got in he sat for a while in his room looking over his application form. He noticed when he got to the end of it that he had, rather foolishly, forgotten to sign it. He was frequently guilty of this at work — he had sent innumerable unsigned faxes and many unsigned letters in his time. He cringed every time he noticed it.

He took a biro from the drawer and flicked his eyes over the truth declaration above the dotted line. Then he got up from his desk, biro still in hand, and went to stare at the map of Antarctica, which was now positioned where Asia had been, above his bed. His eyes followed the coastline, which reminded him of the edges of a pancake, but instead of lines on a map he saw cliffs and glaciers and large, white landscapes. So big that he wouldn't be able to look at them all at once.

Maps are pretty, but this map was not good enough, he thought as he looked at it. In fact, no map of Antarctica would be good enough, because Sam wanted to see it in the frostbitten flesh. He wanted to witness this triumph of temperature, and tiptoe through this place where man cannot live, catching a glimpse of the vast secret at the bottom of the world. There was something inside him that buzzed, that trembled, that shook, whenever he thought of the place. He wanted to stand and wonder at its barrenness, its inhospitality, its spirit, its silence. It is the one continent that cannot be tamed, he thought, and with a beating heart he signed his application form.

The next day Lauren turned up at work looking an absolute wreck. She was still beautiful, but she did look wrecked. Her mobile rang the whole morning, and each time it did she left her desk and went to sit in an empty office somewhere, shoulders hunched, door firmly closed. At one point, as she was sitting typing, Sam thought that the briefest brush of her hand across her face was removing a tear, but he glanced at her again and thought that he must have been mistaken. He sent her an e-mail: *Are you OK? Sxx.*

Gail came down from the management floor and reported that the agency had lost the Department of Health Anti-Drugs account, but no one seemed to know why. Sam acted surprised and shocked along with the rest of them, but he was unsure of his acting skills so he went back to his desk. He had an e-mail from Lauren. *Y. Things a little difficult on the Z front. Lunch, darling?*

By the time they sat down to a pizza she was looking decidedly worse. Three separate bollockings and a long argument with a client had darkened the bags under her eyes and paled her skin.

'You look tired.'

'Up half the night again. I got into bed at four, and had to be in at eight for a meeting. And it's only Wednesday. Can you imagine how I'll be on Friday? And then Gordon told me this morning that I was "being childish" over some work that's due to run next month for Hitsui that is exactly the same as some scripts we've just sold to Askhams.'

'Not for nothing does McLeod Seagal Gale get called a

one-horse show. We've rerun one idea across most of our high-profile work for years. What kept you up till four, or shouldn't I ask?'

'Well, it wasn't shagging, that's for sure. You mustn't tell anybody, Sam, so please don't repeat this: I was trying to chuck Zach, I've had enough of it all, but he wasn't having it. He wouldn't let me leave his flat, he wouldn't let me go to bed, he just wanted me to explain myself, over and over again.' The pizzas arrived and they started to eat.

'Are you okay? I mean, he didn't try to hurt you or anything?'

'No, I'm fine. He's not aggressive, he's just – well, to be honest I feel sorry for him, he hates being by himself. And he's in a foul mood in general because of something else too.'

'What?'

'You mustn't tell anybody.'

'I won't,' Sam replied.

'He's the reason we lost the Department of Health account.'

'Oh really? What happened? Did they have some sort of falling-out?'

Lauren shook her head. 'No.' She breathed in. 'Zach frequently gets his charlie biked over to the agency. Someone nicked it, while it was still in an envelope with his name on it, and sent it to the client.'

Sam looked shocked. 'You're kidding.'

She shook her head again. 'He's determined to get to the bottom of it. He really liked the work we were going to run for them, and he thinks they're being naive.'

'Still, I suppose you can understand their viewpoint.'

'Yeah, completely. I'd do the same.'

Sam smiled at her as a shiver went down the back of his

neck. He changed the subject.

'So, Zach won't take no for an answer?'

'He says he's in love with me.'

'Well, that's fair enough.'

'No it isn't. We only went out a couple of times, he's always on planet white powder so he doesn't know what he's doing, and we only shagged three times, for God's sake.'

'Was it good?'

Lauren laughed. 'If you think I'm answering that, you're off your head.'

'Oh go on. You've told me I can't repeat any of this anyway. I mean, how old is he? Forty? Forty-five. Wasn't he a bit . . . droopy?'

Lauren giggled some more.

'That's a yes, then. What about practices? Anything unusual?'

'Depends what you mean by unusual. I don't usually shag people who come too soon, if that's what you mean.' She tried to stop herself smiling. Sam smiled too.

'You're kidding me.'

She shook her head. 'Don't you dare repeat that, Sam, or I'll lose my job. Hey, did you hear about Phil?'

Sam chewed his pizza and shook his head.

'Resigned.'

'Really?' Sam smiled. So the letter he'd sent Phil had worked. 'That is fantastic news. I think we should have some wine to celebrate.'

'Why are you so pleased? I thought you liked him?'

'I do,' Sam nodded, 'and he's better off anywhere else.'

'You've got a point. The funny thing is that he's been going around telling everyone that he got a letter warning him that he was going to be made redundant. Really odd. Like some Sherlock Holmes mystery. I'm expecting an envelope with orange pips in it any day now,' Lauren added, as she pushed away her plate, the crust of her pizza still a perfect circle with the centre eaten out.

'So, Zach then . . .'

'S-a-am, you're obsessed, for –'

'How much does he earn?'

Lauren shook her head. 'Oh no, nothing more. My lips are sealed.'

'Just move your head, then. Two hundred grand? Three hundred? Half a mill?'

'Two fifty.'

'Two hundred and fifty thousand pounds for snorting coke all day and occasionally saying "That, is a good, ad"?' Sam mimicked him.

'Sam, be gentle. Remember, I shagged the guy.'

Sam nodded, his mouth full. 'Yeah . . . why?'

Lauren paused for a second and looked past Sam's face to the street outside. 'I don't know,' she said quietly.

Sam was sitting in a room with Angela. Neither of them spoke. Eventually Kid and Dan ambled in, clearly suffering from being away from their desks and the creative milieu of the fourth floor. They sat at the other end of the large, corporate table.

'Can't stay long,' said Kid. 'Places to go, people to see.'

'Right,' Angela started, 'your Shadows script. You see the thing is, that you really have to think about what women want to get out of a sanpro brand. They need to feel that the brand understands them, that they can trust it and that it trusts them. The boy sticking his finger in the dam isn't about trust, is it? The work needs to use the current brand equities and make the consumer have a warm feeling in their stomach when they think about Shadows.'

'Or a warm feeling in their knickers,' Dan said.

Sam smiled. He couldn't help it. When he looked up he saw Angela looking at him.

'What you don't understand is that we're talking to women on their own terms,' Kid said. 'We're cutting the crap and getting down to business. It's a dialectical materialist script, in fact, it's positively socialist and they'll like that. Its style is like agit prop, it's for the people.' Then he got up. 'I've gotta go,' he said, and left the room.

'So we've all agreed that you're going to rewrite. If you need any creative reference, ask Sam. If you have any questions, ring me.'

Dan grunted and got up. Sam went for the door too.

'Sam . . . a word.' Angela stood up and gathered her papers.

'Sure,' said Sam and doubled back into the room. She looked furious.

'Don't you *ever*, *ever* laugh at me in a meeting again. *Ever*, do you hear? I will not be laughed at in front of people who I have to work with. Is that clear? And don't think for a minute that those guys are your friends. No one is your friend in this industry.'

Her forehead and cheeks had gone red and her eyes glinted like glass. Sam took his cue from the silence.

'I wasn't laughing at you, and if that's how it appeared then I'm sorry. I was smiling at Dan's joke,' Sam replied. 'Fuck off and die, you paranoid old cow,' was what he had planned to say, but somehow it had come out differently.

'Dan's smutty, adolescent, pathetic little joke.'

'As I said, Dan's joke.'

'Which was taking the piss out of what I was saying and undermining my status in the argument. How do you expect . . . ' and that was it. She burst into tears and fled the room. Sam breathed deeply. He didn't care. Someone, somewhere must love her, he supposed. Thank God that it doesn't matter that I don't.

Henry and Sam had arranged to spend Saturday afternoon learning stuff. The 'white cross code' was what Henry called it, and Sam had to admit that it did feel like being back at school. But back at school in a different way. Back at school through choice. When Henry came through the door to the flat Sam had a shock.

'You've had your ear pierced.'

'Yeah.'

'Did you have anything else done?'

'I had a two-inch steel bar through each nipple so that when they find my frozen corpse under four foot of ice in the South Pole they'll be able to winch me out more easily. They might even be able to do it with magnets, or do magnets not work in the South Pole?'

They didn't do any work, of course. Instead they sat around chatting, and then, lying on their stomachs facing each other, started on a game of Risk. Just when Henry was on the verge of conquering China, Gray came in carrying the paper and, in trying to negotiate a route to the sofa, kicked the pieces flying.

'Sorry, guys,' he said, sitting down.

'I was just about to win, Gray, you cunt,' said Henry, picking the counters off the carpet and beginning to reposition them.

'Less of the language, Henry. Girls around and all that.'

'Oh yeah?' asked Sam.

'Yeah,' replied Gray, without looking up. 'Lucy's back.' And he pulled a face that told Sam to shut up.

'That does *not* go there, Henry,' Sam said, looking down at the board. '*I* had Madagascar.'

'No you did not. You had Indonesia. *I* had Madagascar.'

A slender pair of legs now crossed the board and joined Gray on the sofa.

'Hello, Sam.'

'Hello Lucy.'

'I barely recognised you. You been working out?'

'Yeah, a little bit,' Sam nodded and removed Henry's repositioned pieces off Eastern Australia.

'For the benefit of a lady? Or just for yourself?' she asked, sitting on top of Gray and stealing the magazine section of the newspaper.

'Oh, just for me,' Sam replied, moving one of Henry's pieces off Western Europe. 'That was mine too.'

'Hello? Hello? *I* had Western Europe.'

'You should get yourself a woman. It's a shame to let that body go to waste.' Lucy smiled at him and gave a little shrug. Sam blushed. He was beginning to like Lucy, despite the fact that she had smashed all their plates.

'Hey, here's one for you, Sam. "Forty something into second wind, seeks good-looking twenty something full of joys of spring,"' Lucy read, a laugh in her voice.

'She'd get you fit, I guess,' said Gray. 'Fitt*er*, anyway.'

'Let's have a look at that, Gray,' Henry said and he flung the section over. 'Anyway, what about me? I've been working out too, can't you tell?'

'God, what's got into the pair of you?' Lucy asked, looking up from the magazine.

'We're going places,' Henry said.

'Right,' nodded Lucy.

'We're going somewhere that isn't even on this map.'

'Are you going into space?'

Sam shook his head. 'You're not far off though.'

'Antarctica,' Henry whispered.

'You're *not*,' she said.

'We are. We want to anyway. Filled in the application forms, started to read the books, going to the gym, raising the money,' Sam said. Lucy left Gray on the sofa and came to look at the board. Sam could smell her hair as she leant over him.

'What about this one, Sam? "New to London, mid-fifties Libra, likes opera, cooking, walks and art. Looking for like-minded solvent gent GSOH." What do you suppose mid-fifties means? That she is mid-fifties or that she was born in the mid-fifties?'

'I imagine the first one. It wouldn't make much difference anyway, would it? It's still old,' Gray said.

'Yeah, but you know what they say about these women: when they're over the hill they pick up speed,' Henry replied.

'Are you really going there?' Lucy asked, running her index finger along the empty bottom of the board. Sam watched her and wondered how many times he had done the same to the continent. He nodded. 'That is so impressive. I mean that is like shag-me-now impressive.'

Henry looked at her. 'You think so?'

She nodded and knelt down next to them. 'I mean, what a superb chat-up line. It's like James Bond or something.'

'Do you think it's like "two young guys seek girls for good times before departing for trip of their lives"-impressive?' Sam said, turning his head and looking up at her. She smiled and raised her eyebrows.

'Bingo,' said Henry.

'I mean, do you know anybody who's ever done one of these?'

'They're not the sort of people who go out, Sam. They're not the sort of people who know other people, otherwise they wouldn't be advertising in there,' Gray replied. He was not impressed. On his coolness scale placing a lonely hearts ad did not rate highly.

'That's not fair,' replied Lucy. 'One of my friends did it. She got thirty odd responses.'

'And how were they?'

'Okay,' she said slowly.

'In a four limbs, one pulse and they didn't murder her way-okay?' Gray said.

Henry hit Gray's legs half-heartedly with the magazine. 'Look at it this way Sam – what have we got to lose?'

'Your pride, street-cred, self-respect and, possibly, your lives,' Gray interrupted.

'Come off it, Gray. We're not looking for long-term companionship, we're looking for no-strings shags, and as long as we make that clear, then Henry's right, we've nothing to lose,' Sam replied, but Henry didn't hear him. He was already lost in a reverie of waking up one morning to find a queue of beautiful girls waiting to have the honour of giving a few hours of pleasure to the hero who might not return.

Two hours later they were still arguing about the wording. Oddly, for a journalist, Henry claimed that it wasn't that important, that they just had to get across the facts. Sam disagreed, saying that those few words made the difference between someone picking up the phone or not. Then they started to argue about the details, beginning with whether to be specific about their ages or not. 'No one's going to phone because of your age,' Sam said.

'Why not put it down then?' Henry replied. 'So, what are we looking for?'

'Well, young, attractive, fun . . . anything else?'

'Yeah, they either have to be Naomi Campbell, Christy Turlington or Zoë Ball, otherwise I'm not shagging them.'

'Zoë Ball?' Sam looked horrified.

'Yeah, well. She's better looking than that Sandra bird you went out with at college. She had antlers.'

'Antlers?'

'Moose. She was a moose.'

'Yeah, she wasn't that nice on the inside either though it took me a while to work that out.'

Sam was doodling on the paper. He hadn't really been out with anyone since his college relationship with Sandra. She had told him that she wanted to spend her life with him and then walked out of the door two days after her finals finished. Sam had still had an exam to go, and he left it early, his paper blank. Now, as he sat in his living room he was drawing snow-capped mountains one after the other, stopping every now and then to go back and shade in the snow. He felt good. He felt happy with their decision about the trip. He was so keen to go that he kept setting himself silly little challenges: if he had the right change in his pocket for a packet of chewing gum then he would go; if he could make it to the front door of his flat in less than twenty paces then he would go; if the fridge door stayed closed the first time he kicked it then he would go. He knew that these things wouldn't help, but he also believed that they would. He knew that there were some factors he could control, but he also knew that a lot would be down to luck – just like any job interview – sheer, bloody-minded luck.

'This is ridiculous, we're not getting anywhere.' Sam was sketching some trees on his mountains aware that they were out of place: there are no trees in Antarctica. 'Let's just write our own and then amalgamate the two. You go to the kitchen.'

'Okay.'

In the kitchen, eating two Jaffa cakes, one on top of the other, and sitting at the table Henry wrote this:

Two 25 yr old men leaving UK in 2 months for indefinite period seek girls for fun and frolics. We are fit as a butcher's dog and raring to go (one good-looking blond Taurus, one brown). Where are you? Zoë Ball l-a-lks welcome.

Sam, still lying on his stomach in the living room, stared out of the bay windows at the sky for a while and then wrote the following:

We're just going out, we may be some time: Two twenties men on voyage of lifetime to Antarctica. Leaving country in two months and seeking warm and sunny women (20–35) to chase the chill from last months in Britain. No long term commitments.

They finally reached agreement and then went to play football in the park. Eventually Sam went off to see his grandad, and Henry started ringing his friends, telling them to keep an eye out for the lonely hearts section of the paper next week.

The next week at work was glorious for Sam. His desk suddenly looked beautiful, his phone positively radiant, and his pager seemed like a useful tool of communication. Everybody (well, almost everybody) in the office seemed out to help him, out to make his life easier, out to give him a good time. One thing that bothered him was the thought that perhaps he and Henry were tempting fate by placing the ad, that somehow, stating that they were going to Antarctica meant that they would not really go. Although they were both going to the gym and flicking through the odd book, they both seemed to have overlooked the fact that there was a selection process involved. Sam was not supremely confident – it was just that he could not imagine the prospect of *not* going. He could not see it any other way.

On Saturday the following ad appeared in the paper:

WE'RE JUST GOING OUT OF THE COUNTRY, WE MAY BE SOME TIME:

● **TWO 25-YR-OLD MEN** leaving UK in 2 months for Antarctica. Seek warm women and wine to chase chill from last months in Britain. One blond Taurean seeks Zoë Ball look-alike, one dark-haired Scorpio does not. We're fit and fun, where are you?

Henry was quite proud of the ad and he cut it out and pinned it on his kitchen noticeboard. Sam was quite embarrassed by it, but secretly proud of the first line, and he tore out the page that had it on before he got back to the flat, so that Gray wouldn't see it.

As soon as he got in he rang the number they had been allotted and listened to Henry's bouncy voice describing them both. Sam had been too shy to record his own so he asked Henry to do his too. Needless to say, the description of Sam seemed somehow tacked on the end. No one had left them any messages yet, but hell, it was only two in the afternoon. The cutest girls probably hadn't got out of bed yet. And they didn't want anyone too keen, anyway.

Sam hung up and looked at the phone. He rang the number again. His heart quickened and his throat felt dry: it was engaged.

ELEVEN

One day, just after lunch when it was raining outside, Kasia finally told Mr Glass about how she had grown up. He did not ask – in fact, he had never asked – but the silence that followed any reference that she made to her past, his conspicuous lack of questions, made it clear that he felt somehow disadvantaged.

Kasia did not know what made her tell. Maybe it was the weather on that Wednesday in May. Maybe it was the book she was reading to him at the time: Constant's *Adolphe*. It was something she avoided talking about because she did not like to think about it – not that it was necessarily so terrible, just that it was something that she did not associate with herself. She told him about her parents who had arrived from Poland in 1979, able to leave because of a relative in Hull whom they had never bothered to track down. They settled in Birmingham, and her father got a job in a clothing factory. He was responsible for making sure the elastic was in the right place on the waistbands of skirts.

Kasia was five and her mother decided that she would like to educate her at home, making sure that she was taught in Polish. She made no friends in the neighbourhood, and as the years passed the only people she knew were her parents. She asked to be sent to school but her parents refused, insisting on the importance of her native language and certain that she would learn more at home. When she was nineteen her parents told her that they were going to return to Poland: they did not feel they could live in Britain any longer. Kasia decided to stay. Her parents had no money so she would have to support herself.

She came to London and did a variety of jobs, living in hostels but she found it hard to survive and she began shoplifting from time to time. She met a man and lived with him for a while, squatting in Stoke Newington. Eventually they got a council flat together and he got a proper job: working in the photo laboratory at Boots in Islington. She was twenty-one and her life finally seemed to be working out. Everything was fine until the man starting bringing pictures home. He would come in from work and stick photos up all around their mattress. Kasia asked him who they were of and he told her: one was an ex-girlfriend, another an old mate and another was his sister who lived in America. They were all of young girls, about fifteen or sixteen, all taken in different locations: on holiday, at a party, in their rooms, with their cats. Kasia knew that he didn't know the girls in the pictures and once again she left. 'I *definitely* didn't run away this time,' she said. Leo wasn't so sure. She returned to her old life, got arrested for shoplifting and went to a low-security prison for eight months.

'A packet of Shadows, can you believe it? Sanitary towels! It wasn't even chocolate or perfume or a major luxury, but something I needed. But it made no difference to the judge,' she scoffed, hearing in her voice the hard tones of the women she'd been locked up with and whom she'd vowed never to become. Bitter, cynical old cows who shook when they smoked and spat like men.

'And I was released five months ago. On to a scheme. Which is why I'm here now. They pay me less, keep a close watch on me and get a bonus from the government for employing an ex-con.' Again she saw those women in her

head. She added, 'It's a good thing really. A good thing.'
But she did not sound convinced.

'Captain Oates? Captain Lawrence Oates? The one that
went to Antarctica and . . .?' Leo said as he pulled his glasses
down his nose and looked over them at her. She shook her
head. She had come to a passage in the article she was
reading him that compared Princess Diana to a certain
Lawrence Oates.

'Go on, say it, "my goodness, your general knowledge is
terrible".' She paused, but Mr Glass kept quiet. The
afternoon was curious, dark clouds and sunshine, and
somewhere over London, comfortably straddling the huge
city, there must have been a wonderful rainbow. Leo
looked at her and thought for a second that she was like an
opal: the cracks within the stone give it its wonderful
colour, just as Kasia's weaknesses gave her her brilliance.

'Would you do me a favour please?' he said.

Kasia nodded.

'Over there, on the fourth shelf up, can you see all my
maps?'

She went over and ran her hand along the green, orange
and pink maps, stacked up and held from slipping by a
broken clock on top of which sat a girl and boy, kissing.

'The third one in – could you bring it here?'

Antarctica. She took it to him and he unfolded it on his
knee, carefully because the folds were worn and threatened
to give way, splitting the continent into large rectangles that
would flop around by themselves.

'Come here and look. It's a difficult place to map of
course, but this will give you some idea of the place. In fact,
I'm convinced that there's a mistake on this map, and I
wrote to the cartographer, but he's adamant that I'm wrong.

There's no way of settling the dispute I suppose, short of going there and finding out. It's this island which he's drawn south of Berkner Island – there are actually two islands there, and for some reason he's missed one.' Mr Glass seemed to be talking to himself, far away in his own world. 'Anyway the surface area of the continent more than doubles in the winter because of the ice, but look – here is where Scott started, and here is where Amundsen started out and they took different routes through the Transantarctic mountains,' and he traced their paths with a shaky forefinger.

'Scott set out from Britain in 1910. He was going to discover the South Pole. Well, not exactly discover, because they knew it was there, but be the first person there. Just think how it must feel to be the first person anywhere in the world. I suppose in most places, where there were native peoples, the first person there didn't know they were first. They just went to places for food, water and shelter. But the South Pole was different. No one lived there so there weren't any indigenous people. And Scott wanted to be the first human to place a foot, to take a breath, in the middle of the underbelly of the earth. His crew were men who had been to the Antarctic before – there had been numerous failed attempts; it was one of those things that people tried to do, like us now, trying to work out DNA, or to search for life on the Moon.'

Mr Glass shifted in his seat and wiggled his fingers, before taking the map once again – gently – in both hands. 'They started to trek across Antarctica on 24 October 1911. Because Scott felt that dogs had let him down in the past he took ponies to pull the sledges, but ponies are not made to pull sledges in sub-zero temperatures, and Scott and his men shot them once they had crossed the Ross Ice Shelf, just here,' he said, pointing with his right index finger. 'From then on they man-hauled their sledges, growing weaker each day as they did not have enough food with them to make up for such physical exertion. The five of them – Scott, Evans, Oates (who had a limp), Wilson and Bowers eventually reached the South Pole on 18 January 1912, but as they approached they saw something terrible. At the very pole, against the pale blue sky, there fluttered a flag – a Norwegian flag. Amundsen had beaten them to the pole by less than a month.

'Nothing had prepared them for being beaten, and by now they were exhausted, undernourished and dispirited, and they had 1,290 kilometres to go before they would reach the first support hut on the way back. The first man to weaken was Evans who, descending the Beardmore Glacier, died of frostbite and starvation. He had had a fall and was badly concussed as well. A month later, only a few kilometres from their support hut, a blizzard broke out and the four survivors pitched their tent to sit it out. After a short while Lawrence Oates crawled towards the entrance of the tent and told his companions: "I'm just going out and may be some time." ' Mr Glass cleared his throat. 'Lawrence Oates was gone a long time before his companions went out to look for him. When they found him he was two miles from the tent, collapsed in the snow, frozen. He was concerned that his limp would slow down the others on their return journey. And he thought it better for him to die than for the whole team to perish. Can you imagine thinking the same thing in his position? Can you imagine thinking "I slow everyone down, and I eat an equal amount of rations that I don't deserve. They are better without me"? I can see myself thinking that. But to do anything about it? To actually think, right then, I should kill myself and then actually do it? How tempted must he have been to turn round when he was crawling away from the hut? He was giving up his life, after all. His own life. The night he crawled through the blizzard until he froze was his birthday. He had just turned thirty-two. An Englishman if ever there was one. And a hero. A real hero.'

Kasia sat cross-legged in the blue chair and stared out of the window as she listened to Mr Glass.

'So you think that we should all live like that? Dying so that others can live?'

'Well, we don't all get the opportunity, thank goodness. But that sort of thing, yes. I think it's important to think about other people, to be aware of yourself, and the effect you have on other people. You should be aware of the effect you have on me, for example.'

He looked at her and then turned away.

'But how do you know about this bloke?'

'Oates?' She nodded. 'Scott kept a journal. They found it in the tent with the remaining bodies.' He reached into his pocket and took out a small foil packet. Opening it he offered it to Kasia and, when she declined, broke off a chip of chocolate and nibbled on it.

'So Oates only became a hero because Scott wrote about him? It would have been a complete waste of killing himself if no one had noticed, or no one had bothered to mention it.'

'Ah, you mean, like the unknown soldier?' Leo raised his eyebrows at her.

Kasia shrugged. 'You've got to admit. How would you feel if you did something really heroic that nobody knew about?'

'How do you know that I haven't?'

She looked at him, chewing her bottom lip, her face in a stern frown.

'The motivation for heroic action should never be the wish to be a hero. That renders the action, by definition, unheroic. What is heroic is when somebody does something to help somebody else and is completely blind to the consequences, is completely unaware of anything else, of any praise or adulation that might follow. They are not thinking of themselves. Heroism is complete and utter selflessness. It is the act itself which concerns the hero.' April jumped up into his lap.

'But Oates must have known that they would write about him? He must have known that he would become known as a hero. In which case he is not a true hero, is he?' She looked almost pleased with herself, convinced that she had stumbled upon Mr Glass contradicting himself.

'How would he have known?'

'Well, because he must have known that they would come looking for him. And that when they found him they would write it down. There can't have been much going on there. They'd definitely write about a death.'

'But they all died.'

'Then all of them are heroes. He couldn't lose, if you ask me.'

'You're very cynical.'

'I'll tell you what's cynical,' she said, standing up and stretching. 'Thinking about it, I would say that Scott and the others were getting so hungry they decided to kill a member of the team. They chose to eat Oates – because of his limp – and then felt so bad about it that they made up that line so that he would become a hero, and they could sleep at night.'

Mr Glass looked up at her. Then he laughed. He laughed so much that April, rocking to and fro in his lap, gave up the idea of finding any peace and ran off.

Kasia found Leo slumped in his chair, as though he had been deflated. Her heart pounded as she stood looking at him. He was sleeping, breathing heavily. He smelt of sick, and she could see orange pieces of food down the front of his blue cord shirt, starting to darken around their edges where they were drying out. The bathroom smelt of vomit too, and there were splatters around the sink and on the floor.

Kasia cleaned it up, working quietly so as not to wake him. Then she cleaned the kitchen and put on some soup. She wanted to find a clean shirt for him, but his clothes were in his bedroom, somewhere she never went. Could she go in while he slept? Should she go in while he slept? She stood outside the door, listening out for any sounds from the front room that would indicate that he was waking.

She pushed the door and was instantly greeted by the powdery smell of an old man: mints, pyjamas, hair lotion, milk. The room was dark and cluttered. There was a bed, neatly made; a tall wardrobe; and about three tables with all sorts of things on them: cups, pieces of paper, books, old magazines, bottles of pills, leaves. On the wall next to the wardrobe hung a picture which caught Kasia's eye. It was a photo, an old photo, where the blacks are dark brown and the whites gentle creams. It was a woman, not unlike Kasia in her colouring. She had long dark hair and large dark eyes, but her features were stronger than Kasia's: her cheekbones higher, her lips fuller, her eyes wider. She looked like an Amazon: a large, strong woman. Her expression in the picture was one of petulance. Irritation that someone dare take her photograph. Kasia assumed that she was looking at Mrs Glass. Well, she thought, maybe that's why Mr Glass is so patient. Maybe he *had* to be patient if she was anything like she looks. She looks like a dragon. But a dazzling dragon. Kasia was not surprised that the old man next door, snoring with vomit down the front of his shirt, was once able to net such a pretty woman: she had seen photos of him as a young man.

Retrieving a clean shirt and vest, she woke Mr Glass and made him change his clothes. She then made him some tea and hand-washed his dirty shirt and vest. Mr Glass was sheepish, but she did not want him to be ashamed. He was old, after all. He didn't mention the fact that she had been in his room (or perhaps he did not realise?), but either way Kasia was grateful, because she did not want to have to justify her visit, especially when she thought of the time she had spent staring at the angry woman.

'Are you going to be all right? I mean, by yourself?'

'Yes, yes, I'll be fine. I must have eaten something. I'll be fine.'

'I don't know. I'm worried that you might be ill again. Listen, it's Saturday tomorrow. If you like I could stay over on the sofa just to check that you're okay.' He shook his head weakly.

'I don't think you need to. It's nice of you to offer. Thank you.' Out of nowhere he was sick again. It poured from his mouth like cake mixture or cement, coiling down on itself, over his shirt and trousers. Kasia was shocked. Taken aback. She went and fetched a bucket and sat with him until he had finished.

'I'm sorry. I'm very sorry. I've never done this before.'

'That's all right. You poor thing. How do you feel?'

'I've still got some pain in my stomach.'

'I'm going to call a doctor. Is that okay?'

'I don't think there's any need. It's not malaria, I know that.' She smiled. She could probably have worked that out for herself.

'No, and it's not typhoid either. You do say some funny things, Mr Glass. Anyway, just to be on the safe side.'

She cleaned him up again and put him to bed, a towel covering the pillow and a bucket next to the bed. The doctor came and reported a virus that should pass in twenty-four hours. He asked her to stay the night and call him should the vomiting get worse.

She passed the evening in front of the TV, drinking tea and poking around his front room. In all honesty she was happy to be spending a night away from her small room. She got fed up with spending night after night by herself, not once opening her mouth to speak. Even though she was not speaking now, she did not feel the emptiness she usually felt at this time of night. And she felt cosy being here with him, enjoying the knowledge that he was fast asleep next door.

She had never noticed quite how many books Mr Glass had. There were books on almost every surface, and one wall was completely shelved. Most of the books were on plants and flowers: he had a whole shelf full of large dusty books containing nothing but pictures of rare wild and tropical flowers. She took each one out in turn and looked at the exquisitely drawn plants, running her hand over the smooth, shiny paper as though that might help her to imagine the plants in the flesh. One of the books had a piece of pink paper sticking out of the top of it. Opening it at the marked page, she looked at the pictures. On each page was a flower – one light purple, with long thin leaves in a circle, and a centre made up of cream and maroon spindly bits; the other was blue, a kind of royal blue with a hint of turquoise and was clearly the same type of flower as the purple one, although it did not have the inner circle of dots. She cast her eyes down to the bottom of the page and looked at their names: the purple one was called *Clematis William Kennett*, the blue one *Clematis Natália*. Kasia looked at the flower for a while longer and thought how nice it must be to find a flower with the same name as your own. Lucky Natália, she thought, stroking the page once again with her fingertips. What she did not realise was that this was a clematis Leo had bred. A clematis Leo had named. Every now and then she checked on Mr Glass, who seemed to be sleeping. She decided to go to sleep just after midnight, and made up a bed on the sofa. She had none of her things with her, but the flat was warm and she undressed and lay down.

When she opened her eyes she did not know where she was. For a minute she thought that she was back in the bad times. She lay for a second and then remembered Mr Glass, and with him came everything else. She was desperate for a wee. She got out of bed and crossed the room, fumbled down the hall and into the bathroom. She wanted a wee so much that it took her a while to persuade her bladder to let go. She didn't flush the loo, for fear of waking her companion. On her way back to bed she heard a noise in front of her, and suddenly, standing in the hallway, as confused as she, was Mr Glass. He was in his pyjamas. She was naked. For a split second she did not see the old man she had been nursing the previous evening. Instead she saw a man. A man and his desires. And for a split second he did not see the girl who cooked him lunch and with whom he liked to talk. He saw a woman. A beautiful woman. A dark, slight woman whose skin shone in the weak moonlight. And he was cross and frustrated that, as an old person, he had to pretend that sex no longer interested him. He averted his eyes as quickly as he could, ashamed.

'Are you all right?' she whispered, shivering and deciding to ignore her prominent nakedness, drawing closer so that it would be more difficult for him to look down at her. He smiled. Now she reminded him of somebody else. Now, in the middle of the night, when she was intent, determined, to pretend she had her clothes on.

'Yes,' he said. 'I was just on my way to the toilet.' He went back into his room and emerged carrying a bundle. He shook it out and Kasia could see that it was a dressing gown. He held it for her, the way men in old films held coats for women, turning his head away because of her body. Kasia paused. She was surprised, taken aback that he was so uninterested in her nudity. She slipped into the dressing gown – a veritable old man's dressing gown, scratchy and large – and tied the cord round her waist. She shivered again.

'Come and look,' said Mr Glass as he made his way gingerly over to the window in the hallway. The sky was surprisingly light for the middle of the night. It was clear, and the moon reflected pearly white light through space, a brownish haze around its edges. 'That there', he pointed, a weak, old but accurate hand, 'is Ursa Minor. The little bear. Those seven stars there, those two are brighter than the rest, but if you look at it for long enough you can see the shape of the bear. And just underneath it is Ursa Major, the great bear. It's also seven stars, but more spaced out. Can you see how they join?' he asked as he traced the shape in the air with his hand.

'So why are they called that?'

'I don't know. I suppose people used to spend a lot of time looking at the stars. Some people still spend a lot of time looking at the stars,' he said, thinking of his youngest grandson. 'And I imagine it's only natural that people should see animals in them. Then over there,' he leant towards her and she looked to his hand, trembling from being held in the air for such a period of time, 'is the Plough. Those eight stars there. Can you see it? It's a shame we can't see the Milky Way, but that's how it is. Some nights it's just not there. Like an unreliable father, I suppose.'

They stood in silence looking up through the hall window at the spacious sky. The dressing gown was scratchy against Kasia's skin but underneath it she was warm and she felt a kind of cosiness that comes from wearing someone else's clothes.

'It's a shame we can't see the whole sky at once, all flattened out in one long canvas. Then I could tell you all about the stars in the Southern Hemisphere too. There are more there, and there are fewer cities, so the sky is darker, and the stars shine even brighter.' He cleared his throat and dropped his voice to a whisper. 'You know the best thing about stars?' She shook her head. 'The best thing about stars is that, being so far away, the way we see them is not the way they actually *are*. The sun is so far away that the way we see it is the way it looked four minutes ago. The moon is nearer, but still that moon we are looking at is the moon as it looked eighty-five seconds ago. Because the light has to travel so far.' He paused. 'Sometimes I think it would be marvellous if the same thing could happen to us. So that, despite the fact that I'm eighty-six, you would look at me and see me how I was at twenty-five, so light would take sixty-one years to pass from me to you. You would see me as I was then, and never be able to see me as I am now.'

Neither of them said anything. Instead they looked at the airy darkness above them, still and silent. The question of why Leo wanted Kasia to see him as he was then and not as he was now did not cross Kasia's mind. The answer was obvious. The answer was as just as clear as Leo's eyes were cloudy, it was as straightforward as Leo's fingers were bent. It was sitting in every crease and fold of Leo's papery skin.

'How is it you know all this?' Kasia asked at last, transferring her weight on to her other hip.

He shrugged. 'When you're my age you'll know it all too.'

'I sincerely hope not. When I'm your age I want to be in a box under the ground.'

'It's not so bad, you know. There are some things that I still enjoy.'

'Like what? What did you enjoy that you still enjoy now?'

'Well, I still like food. I . . . I still like the botanical prints I have. And I have my family, my grandsons. And I like talking to people. I like talking to you, for example.'

Kasia nodded. She looked at Leo's hands, still now and resting on the windowsill, the left hand holding the thumb of the right.

'Well, I won't have any family. And I don't like food very much, so I can't imagine what I will enjoy,' she said softly.

'Why won't you have any family?'

'I won't meet anyone to have a family with.'

'Why not?'

Because he's too old, she thought. There is only one person. And he's standing here now, a ghost of his former self. His body is a shadow, a reflection, an echo of what it once was, but his spirit is as it always was. And the thought of bearing his children went through her mind. Could he still do it? Was he still fertile? And if the answer was yes, then what? One night of passion? Well, it wouldn't be passion, would it? One night of performance, of instruction and then she could have the children of the man she loved. But they would not have a father, and she would not have a mate. In the intimacy of darkness these were the thoughts that flew through her head.

'I don't know,' she said, staring up at the sky. He looked at her out of the corner of his eye and saw how gently the reflected light lit her face, leaving a delicate silvery glow on her cheeks. He marvelled at her smooth young skin, and the soft light on her hair. He wanted to touch it.

'You will,' he said. Why did he say that? Did he want her

to find somebody? I'm right here, he thought, forgetting that a relationship between them was impossible. Then he remembered that she wouldn't want him. 'There's the star out there for you, looking out for you. You'll find somebody,' he nodded. 'He's out there somewhere,' he said, with difficulty. He had better be out there, he thought. And he had better be good enough. Just as diamonds can only be cut by other diamonds, Leo knew that Kasia needed someone who was equal to her. They stood there in the darkness, next to each other, but not touching.

'So what are stars exactly? I mean, why do they shine?'

'They're miniature suns. They are balls of fire, burning up out there. You see, the moon shines because it reflects the light from the sun. If you were in space and looked at the earth you would see that it does a similar thing. But neither is actually a source of light. Stars, on the other hand, are light-sources,' he paused and looked at her, 'but the light is still light, whether it's reflected or generated. I have never seen one, but it is possible to see rainbows at night. If the air is clear, and it's raining and the moon is out. Can you imagine? A rainbow in the night sky?'

Kasia couldn't. But she found it odd that he should tell her about it, because as soon as he had said it she thought how appropriate it was that *he* told her. For she could see that he was, for her, exactly that: a rainbow in the night sky. He was something wonderful, full of colours and light, something that she had not expected.

'You should get back to sleep. You have to work tomorrow. I've only got to sit in my chair.'

'Are you feeling better?'

'Yes.'

'All right,' she whispered and went to pass him. '*Dobranoc.*'

'*Dobranoc,*' he copied her and carried on. An old man,

fumbling down the hallway, able, because of his age, to ignore the naked woman who had stood before him just now. Able? Able to ignore a naked woman? When he reached the bathroom he had to wait before he could urinate because Kasia had aroused him. Not quite the arousal that he had once experienced, but arousal all the same. He looked in the mirror and saw somebody he did not recognise. The colour of his hair and the liver spots on his skin made him a dirty old man.

The phrase repeated itself in his head. *Dirty old man, dirty old man, dirty old man.* At what point did he change from being a charming, attentive man, an active, virile man, who could make women laugh, smile and look at him with a certain glint in their eyes, to a dirty old man? What age was it exactly? Fifty-five? Sixty? Sixty-five? Surely by seventy he was a *dirty old man.* But it had never bothered him before. It had never bothered him because he had only been aroused by things that were supposed to arouse him. It had been physical arousal, girls-in-short-skirts-arousal. Benny Hill arousal. But this was different. This was a different kind of arousal, an arousal of which he did not want to be ashamed. A true arousal, an arousal that is the consequence not only of attraction but of tenderness too. An intimate arousal.

Mr Glass awoke the next morning to a glorious smell. As he lay in bed and remembered who and where he was his stomach began to rumble and his taste buds tingle to what could only be the smell of fresh pancakes. He got out of bed and couldn't find his dressing gown. Then he remembered the meeting in the night. He sat down on his bed and scolded himself for being a silly old man. He vowed that he would no longer think of Kasia as he had the night before; he would encourage her to meet men of her own age. What did he think he was doing? Who did he think he was, to imagine that a girl of twenty-three might, even for a second, have any interest in the shell of a man that he now was. She would be repelled at the thought of just touching him, he knew that. If only she could have seen him as he once was.

He swore to himself that he would ignore his feelings, but when he left his room and walked to the kitchen he saw Kasia, in his dressing gown, at the oven. He could just hear her humming over the hiss of the butter in the pan. She heard him coming and turned and smiled, leaning backwards and holding the frying pan handle with both hands. She tossed a pancake for his benefit, a low, hesitant throw, and she laughed as she caught it. And as he stood in the doorway he no longer knew how old he was.

TWELVE

'How do I look?' Sam asked Henry, as they waited in the reception area of the British Institute for Antarctic Research. It was a large, beige room, deeper than it was wide. On the table were copies of *National Geographic*, along with the *Financial Times*, but he didn't feel like pretending to read. His hands were shaking, and holding a paper would only make his nervousness more obvious. He had not slept and he had not eaten. He had a dry throat and a headache, and he was terrified.

'Well, your tie is horrible.'

'Yeah, okay. But what about the rest of me? Granted, the tie has seen better days.'

'The tie has seen better ties, I imagine.'

'Thanks, Henry. Remind me to make you feel good too.' Sam left Henry in reception desperately trying to memorise notes copied out, in a scrawl, from his World Atlas late last night.

'Everybody, this is Sam Glass. Sam, this is Professor Greg Hausmann, responsible for coordinating tourism research in Antarctica, this is Emma Smith-Holmes who runs the scheme in Britain, and this is Osh Laird who will be leading the project in the South Pole.'

'Hello,' Sam nodded at everybody. He was scared. And he was conscious of his tie. Imagine if I don't get to Antarctica because of my tie, he thought. Scott probably wore horrible ties too. In fact, Amundsen definitely wore horrible ties. Why the fuck am I wearing a tie anyway? he thought.

'So Sam, tell us, what made you fill in the application form?' asked Jean, the woman who had introduced everybody.

'I filled it in because . . .' he paused, 'because . . .' he shuffled in his chair, his mind a blank, 'because I want to go to Antarctica,' he managed.

Emma smiled at him as though he was five. The professor cleared his throat and made some notes. Jean tried again.

'And *why* do you want to go to Antarctica?'

Sam's mind raced: because I wanted to go when I was a kid. Because my grandad went. Because my dad died. Because it would mean something to me. Because my current job is a waste of time. Because it will be quiet. Because it's Antarctica, for crying out loud. *Antarctica.* Who would *not* want to go there? The answers raced through Sam's mind, but he passed over each of them, looking for one that would make more sense to these strange people. Because my dad hated his job. He spent years doing something he hated and then he died. I owe it to him to do something I want to do. Can you understand that? The silence continued. Emma raised her eyebrows at him.

'I can't really say in one sentence. I mean, I just sort of feel fated to go.' Sam felt his face become hot. He tried to concentrate but all he could think of was his tie and what Henry had said about it. He knew that he was not coming over as a rational, thoughtful person, as the kind of person that could be depended on in a blizzard. He looked at his feet.

'What's the best thing you've done in your life so far? The thing that you're most proud of?' the professor threw at him, obviously bored with the silence.

Sam started to shake his head and looked down at his hands. His breathing became more shallow, and his hands started to flutter in his lap, as though he wanted to make large, magnanimous gestures, but dared not. 'I haven't done anything I'm proud of, don't you see?' his eyes stung. 'That's why I'm here. Because I want to do something good, I want to do something that will make a mark, that will contribute to something I care about.'

He looked at the four people in front of him. They were regarding him like a specimen, like an example of some syndrome or neurosis. They looked confused and slightly intrigued. Sam knew that he had failed. He had failed to make himself understood. The rest of the interview went through routine questions about health and administration. They asked him a few easy questions about the continent – about its size, its seasons, its history, its phenomena – all of which he answered correctly. He knew those answers. He knew that a darkish, brown sky meant that the sea was open and a whitish, orangey one that the sea was frozen – they were the kind of answers he could find in books. They were the answers Leo had given him.

'Thank you, Sam.' Jean stood up eventually and showed him to the door. 'We'll write to you.'

Don't bother, Sam thought. He knew what the answer would be.

As it happened there was one face that Sam did not pay much attention to in that room. That face was Osh Laird's, the team leader, the man who would be out there with the volunteers, distributing duties, coordinating research, nurturing a stunted, frozen morale. Osh was a meteorologist. He had studied physics at Cambridge and gone on to do a PhD in fluid mechanics. He had gone to the South Pole in the course of research for his first job on completing his doctorate and he had been back many times since. The longest he had spent there was eighteen months, but he had been coming and going for a good seven years. Of all the people in the room the day of Sam's interview Osh was not the most important, but he was the most successful when it came to assessing a candidate's mental and emotional health for life in the cold.

When Sam came in the room Osh saw, as clearly as the others saw that he had thick, dark hair, that Sam had everything in place. He had endurance. He had self-reliance. He was used to spending time by himself, indeed, time alone did not scare Sam. He was physically fit, and he had a kind of simplicity, a capacity for logical, clear thought that would go far when it came to organising work and developing methods. Osh could see all these things in Sam. He could also see a drive. A drive that would make Sam wake in the middle of the night. A drive that would make him stare at the sky for long periods of time. A drive that would make him run that little bit faster, last that little bit longer. A drive that distinguished him from his peers. The only thing that Osh wasn't sure about was how Sam would react to others, how he would work with his team. But that could be tested. And Osh was determined that Sam would get another chance to show the skills that Osh knew he had.

When Sam got in from work that night he went on a two-hour run ('Look, people of London. Look at me!') and then came home and looked at his maps. The coastline of the South Pole was now so familiar that he could conjure it up in his mind when he lay in bed at night, carefully imagining every twist and bend, like one of those games at fairgrounds when there is a wire and the player has to move a loop along it, without letting the loop touch the wire. If Sam Glass had to play that game now and the wire was the shape of Antarctica's coastline, he would have no problem.

Back at home he went and sat on the roof outside his window. As he sat there, watching a winged ant crawl across the rough tarpaulin beneath him, he thought about the first time his dad took him up on the roof. They had sat in silence for a while, looking upwards, Sam too terrified to talk, and his father too distracted. And then suddenly out of nowhere, Sam had a question.

'Why do people say that the moon is made of cream cheese? It doesn't look anything like cream cheese.'

Sam's dad raised his eyebrows and dropped them again, to indicate that his son had a good point. 'I suppose,' he began, 'that it is just one of those expressions, those sayings that people repeat to each other so they never go away.' He leant back against the chimney pot and looked upwards into the darkness. 'It's a bit like the one about making a bee-line for something. Have you ever seen a bee fly in a direct line directly towards something? No, neither have I. They hover around, loop a few circles, come in, go out again, and then, eventually, perhaps, land. Quite where that expression came from, I don't know.'

Sam was sitting at the other side of the roof, where his father had deposited him, straddling the tiles of the peak of the roof, and leaning against the other chimney for support. Although the brick was digging into his back he dared not move, and he looked up at the sky so that he wouldn't have to look down at the shrunken garden beneath him. His dad seemed perfectly relaxed, and was humming to himself as he tilted his head at the sky, drumming his fingers on the slates beneath his hands and wiggling his feet, which were resting, like Sam's, on either side of the roof.

'So, Crazy Horse, what's going on up there tonight?'

'Well Captain, there's interference between red star one

and red star two, and an alien occurrence has been sighted by little bear's foot.'

'Good work, Crazy Horse. Do you think he can kick it?'

'Who?'

'Little bear. Do you think he can kick it?'

'I don't know. Can bears kick?'

'Crazy Horse, I don't believe I'm hearing this from you. What do you mean can bears kick? Have you never heard of Vincent the footballing bear?'

Sam shook his head as carefully as he dared. He did not want to fall off this roof.

'What do they teach you in school nowadays? Maths and English and rubbish like that? And you don't even know about Vincent the footballing bear.'

Sam shook his head again. He was starting to feel more comfortable where he was. As he sat and listened to his father tell him about Vincent the footballing bear he looked up at the bears in the sky, and imagined them kicking the sun around, marking goalposts with planets, and scoring hat tricks while the stars cheered them on. And he thought: I like it up here.

The calls started. All over London, girls and women started to phone in, in the hope of meeting two fit young men out for a bit of fun. Sam was flabbergasted when he first rang to check on the messages: fourteen people had left messages in the space of twelve hours. Henry rang Sam constantly on his mobile, telling him to listen to a certain message or asking which ones Sam had arranged to meet. As it happened Sam had not arranged to meet any of them yet. He was still in a state of shock at the enthusiasm of the response, at the explicitness of some of the messages ('Hi, this is Tina. I want to have sex with you both already, and

I haven't even met you'), at what he had done. Henry took to it like a duck to water. He called the good ones back straightaway and set up dates all over the place, sometimes two a day.

The Tuesday after the ad had gone in Sam ventured to make his first phone call. The girl was called Jasmine, and she sounded genuinely nice on her message. He had had to find an empty office to make the call in at work, because he didn't want anyone to hear him, and he dialled the number a few times before picking up the handset and dialling it properly. Halfway through the phone call the owner of the office – a senior planner called Wayne – returned with a visitor. Nervously Sam explained to Jasmine that he had to go; he would call her right back. But he knew how it sounded. It sounded like he had chatted to her for a while and then changed his mind, bottled it, decided she was no good after all. Wayne grimaced at him and he left, only to be accosted by Jeff in the corridor and sent out to a garage in Essex to buy a specific bumper for another Reynolds shoot.

Over the weeks Sam had changed. His frown seemed to have dissolved. His grey hair seemed to turn black once again. His breathing had slowed, and the pain he sometimes got in his heart, as he lay in bed at night, eased. He felt like a coiled spring, like a jack-in-the-box, like a toddler in an elastic harness, desperate to get away from its parents. He imagined himself doing all sorts of physical feats: swimming to France, and then back to England again, climbing Snowdonia and then realising he'd left his glove up there so going back to get it, cycling faster than a car. As he walked around the office he was, depending on his mood, either the world's strongest man or the most famous explorer of the twentieth century, signing autographs, writing his memoirs, advising the MoD. He was, all of a sudden, invincible. He was, all of a sudden, Sam Glass.

Sam arranged to meet Rachel at a bar in Soho after work on Thursday. She had told him that he would recognise her by her shoes ('they're blue, royal blue, you won't miss them,' she had said on the phone). Sam waited in the bar, bobbing his head around like a charmed snake, trying to glimpse the shoes of every girl that came in. He was nervous: it was the first one, and although Henry's had all been fine (in fact more than fine – he had shagged one of them already), Sam was convinced that the girls he arranged to meet would all be a few sandwiches short of a picnic. They would have to be, to agree to meet him, wouldn't they? He was also embarrassed. Embarrassed by the whole affair. Meeting strangers in bars in Soho. Placing ads in newspapers. And he was embarrassed in advance for the women who he did not want to snog, and the way he would avoid it.

'Are you Sam?'

He turned and saw a small girl of about his age.

'Yeah,' he managed. His throat was dry. 'Can I get you a drink?'

'A bacardi and coke, please,' she smiled. A silence descended on them.

'So, how are you?' he said, sitting down, feeling as if everyone in the bar was staring at them. He looked at her, trying to take in as much as possible.

'Really well. Sorry I'm a bit late, but the babysitter missed the bus and I had to wait for her.'

Sam froze. Then he felt bad and tried to act normally.

'Oh right. Terrible when that happens,' he found himself saying.

'Yes, and it's ever so hard to find the right people nowadays.'

Sam glanced under the table to see her shoes. They were black knee-high boots. 'What happened to the blue shoes?'

She laughed. 'I changed my mind. Actually I decided they were horrible, so I threw them away. Then I changed my mind again, and went out to the bins to try and find them, but I think somebody had taken them already.'

'Mmm. Terrible when that happens,' he added. Shit. *Shit.*

'So,' she said, taking a gulp of her drink, 'I'm looking for a man who can satisfy my every need.' She looked straight at him. She had a lot of dark make-up around her eyes and Sam thought he caught a glimpse of metal in her mouth: a pierced tongue perhaps? Or maybe a large filling.

'Right,' he said, nodding. 'Only reasonable, I suppose.'

'Well, you would think so. But a lot of men don't seem to see it that way.'

'I suppose it depends on what those needs are,' he said, thinking that he sounded like a schoolteacher or a newsreader. He wished Henry was here, to make everything easier. Henry always seemed to have a good time.

'Well, would you like to find out?'

For the second time that evening, he paused and replayed the sentence in his head, to check that he had heard it correctly. Then he felt a hand on his leg and her breath on his face.

'I haven't much time, you see. I have to be back before twelve. The babysitter will wonder where I am.'

This time he saw the stud in her tongue quite clearly. She smiled at him, giggling. They got up and left the bar. In the street outside they stood and looked at each other for a while, and then she went for him, and Sam felt physical proof of what he had spied through her teeth. What the fuck am I doing? was all he could think. I have no idea who this person is, and her tongue is in my mouth.

He realised two things, as these thoughts of forced intimacy ran through his head and his mouth was invaded. The first was that he did not fancy this woman, otherwise he would not be thinking these things. The second was that maybe he wasn't your ordinary run-of-the-mill bloke. This was every man's fantasy, wasn't it? To meet unfamiliar, predatory women? Sam could understand how sex with a stranger could be exciting, but not with this particular stranger, and probably not with the majority of the strangers he would meet.

Sam snogged Rachel and then made her go home: he did not want to have sex with her. He met Monica, whom he agreed to see again, though maybe at the cinema or theatre, so that they wouldn't have to talk much. He encountered Tanya and left as soon as he could ('I'm just going outside, I may be some time'). Goldie scared him with talk of tents and crampons and with her idea that they could become an outdoor couple when he returned, with her sensible, flat sandals and her extra-lightweight fleece and so he lost her number. Kezza was cool but Sam didn't fancy her. Shavi was beautiful but she didn't fancy Sam. Scarlet was scarily thin and wore too much eyeliner. Hannah, it turned out at the end of the evening, already had a boyfriend in Antarctica and wanted Sam to take a homemade date and walnut loaf out to him. Daisy, it has to be said, was just plain dull. Carmen didn't speak a word of English, and although that didn't really matter – the ad after all had been fairly clear about the nature of the arrangements – she tried her hardest and it took about twenty minutes to work out which drink she wanted. He had to write Ruth off because he tripped over the doormat in the pub and fell over before he met her so he left as quickly as he could and threw her number away. He never met up with Gaby because he had to stay late at work, and couldn't get through to her to let her know. He was too embarrassed to ring again.

Not that it mattered: every day there were more messages in their message box. A good twenty per cent sounded either depressed or crackpot or both. But that left the vast majority worth a phone call. And because of their jobs, Henry could ring the vast majority of the vast majority first, leaving a few borderline cases for Sam to follow up, days later, when he got a minute to himself.

Whenever Sam was feeling bored, he'd ring up their number just to be entertained. There were a number of mystery messages – people who didn't leave their names, men asking if either of them was interested in a gay encounter before they left and people who had clearly just got the wrong number. 'Hi Steve, it's Jenny, I had a lovely time last week, but I've just got back together with my ex, so I probably shouldn't see you again.' Sam made a mental note of this excuse, just in case he should need it in future. Gray left them messages every few days, ''ello, theez eez Nicole, I would laik to ave you both to ma jacuzzi ce soir, pour helper me with washing the places I cannot reach', and one day a woman from McLeod Seagal Gale's finance department left a message. Sam panicked when he heard it, just in case Henry had already arranged to meet her and might mention Sam's name without realising where she worked. As it turned out Henry was preoccupied with a certain Gemma who had given him a blow-job in the taxi on the way home, and had not listened to the messages for a few days. There was even one message from an academic in Leicester who did not want to meet either of them, but wanted to complain about the fact that they had used

Lawrence Oates' last words as part of what she called 'a desperate appeal for sexual favours'.

After his interview Sam worried that he had somehow blown his chances of going by placing the personal ad. He had lined up a girl for every night of the week, and had had no time to sit on the roof outside his room and stare at the sky, but whenever he did have a moment to himself, on the tube going to the gym in the morning, or on the loo, he became irrationally anxious, terrified that he had done something stupid and unwittingly sabotaged the only thing he ever really wanted to do.

'Henry, you don't think we're tempting fate by placing this ad, do you?'

'Nah, I think we have to think ourselves into the frame of mind that we are going, and then we'll get the jobs, and bingo, we're off.'

'But it is a bit previous, isn't it? I mean, we are making quite a lot of assumptions, aren't we?'

Henry was sitting on his sofa, eating noodles out of a bowl. Both of them had started eating carbohydrates by the bucketload, finishing a whole packet of pasta or rice in one evening.

'Mmn mmn,' he said, shaking his head and swallowing. 'Don't worry about it, Sammy, it's not going to make any difference.'

'Yeah, I suppose you're right.' Sam went over to the window and looked up at the overcast London sky. They were supposed to be learning things again, reading case studies on the effects of tourism in other protected areas like the rainforests, or Alaska. Henry got up and took his bowl through to the kitchen, humming a tune as he went. When Sam had arrived that afternoon Henry had proudly sung his new song to him, encouraging Sam to join in: 'We're off to see a blizzard/ A wonderful blizzard near Oz/ It really is a blizzard near Oz because of the things it does/ A blizzard near Oz it is because because because because because/ Because because because because because/ Because of the wonderful things it does,' Henry sang, doing his best Judy Garland impression, which was poor. Sam smiled, shaking his head.

'And who am I? The tin man?' he asked.

'No no, you've got a heart. You're the one without a brain – you're the scarecrow, the floppy one.'

'But I get a brain in the end, don't I?'

'Well, none of them actually gets anything. They all just get certificates saying they've got whatever they lacked, so they believe they've got it, and bingo, suddenly they can do the things they couldn't before.'

'So I was clever all along, I just didn't believe it? It was just a question of confidence?'

'It was just a question of confidence,' repeated Henry, nodding his head slowly as he spread a newspaper out on the floor before him.

'Henry?' Sam leant against the sofa and stretched out his legs, putting his book to one side. It was nice to be looking at a book again. He hadn't read a book in months. He liked books, and he had loads at home, but he rarely read any of them. He used them as coasters, to prop his bedroom door open, to kill errant insects and, of course, as set-dressing. Sometimes he had a look inside, but not often. He stared ahead of him at his odd socks, both worn thin at the heels.

'Mmm?' Henry was still reading the paper.

Sam paused. He didn't really know what to say. Henry carried on reading.

'Why do you want to come with me?'

Henry stopped reading and looked up at Sam.

'It'll be a laugh,' he said, and went back to his page.

'No, seriously, Henry, I mean. Look, I just want to be sure that –'

'That I'm not just taking you for a ride?' Henry raised his eyebrows at Sam.

'Well, I wouldn't have used those words but –'

'But that's what you mean?'

Sam was silent. He wiggled his feet. Henry sat up and turned the newspaper over. Then he turned it over again.

'I guess I want to go because I think it's a good way of passing six months,' he said eventually, without looking up.

Sam nodded slowly.

'So, I mean, are you going to do all the stuff? Read the books, get fit, all the rest of it?'

'No, I'm going to lie around, read the paper once I've eaten my fish and chips out of it and expect to get a place, Sam.'

'Well, I don't know. You don't seem to be taking it very seriously, that's all.'

'Well, I don't have to *be* serious about it in order to take it seriously, do I? And besides, I've got the whole week to read stuff. I don't go to work every day. You've only got the weekends. I have a lot more time than you, Sam. I don't need to start swotting yet.' Henry looked offended. They stared at each other.

'Right,' said Sam and picked up his book again. They read in silence, Sam aware that he was reading a book he was supposed to read, Henry painfully conscious of the fact that he was reading the paper.

'Henry, I –'

'Forget it.'

'I'm sorry.'

'Forget it.'

Sam looked back at his book and turned the page, following the text with his eyes. Henry stared at his paper and cleared his throat. A bus passed by on the road outside and the flat shook a little.

THIRTEEN

'Hello, Grandad.' Sam bent over Leo and kissed him on the cheek. 'How are you?'

'Very well. How about you? You smell a bit queer, Sam.'

'Yeah, I'm well. Been swimming. And running.' Sam sat down in Kasia's chair and began to unlace his trainers. 'I've put the kettle on.'

'How's your work going? You've got dark rings round your eyes.'

Sam shrugged. 'Oh, you know, okay. How's your current daily? You're looking well.'

'Yes,' Leo said, conscious that he might blush, 'she's fine.'

'Talking to you, is she?'

'Yes, she talks. I don't do much else,' he said, waving his fingers in the air.

'Talking's good, though, isn't it? It's important.'

'Yes, but as you get older your topics become more limited, you know.'

'What do you mean?' Sam said, running both his hands through his stiff hair.

'What do you talk about, Sam, with your friends?'

Sam shrugged. 'Oh, you know, any old thing.'

'But if you had to say what you talked about most, what would you say?'

'Don't know really. What's going on. News, films, perhaps?'

'How do the future and sex sound?'

Sam stopped and looked at his grandad. He took off his glasses and cleaned them on his T-shirt.

'The future, yeah, definitely. We talk about plans a lot. About holidays, about next week, about next year. What we're all going to do, that sort of thing.' He paused. Leo watched him. 'And sex, well, of course. Everyone talks about sex. Yeah, I suppose you're right. Those are the things we talk about the most.'

'You see? I don't mean you to feel sorry for me, but I can't talk about either of those things. I cannot talk about sex – I don't have sex,' he chuckled. 'I haven't for many years. And the future? Well, I can talk about next week, but I can't really make plans. I can't talk about what I will be doing next year. There comes a point where you start looking backwards instead of forwards. Where you start remembering good times, instead of imagining better ones.'

'I see what you mean. I'd never thought of that. So what should I do? Appreciate the fact that I'm young? Live life for today? All those old clichés?'

'Oh, I don't mean you to do anything. It's just an observation,' Leo laughed.

Sam went through to make the tea and returned with a tray on which there was a vase of flowers.

'I brought some cake. And the irises. Lemon and ginger.'

'Thank you,' Leo said, 'that's very kind,' and he bent forward to have a look at the flowers, leaning over them as though peering into a well.

'You know, Sam, I don't want to make you feel bad about yourself, but if you don't enjoy your job you shouldn't do it. If it's money you're worried about then I could give you a bit, to help you while you work out what you'd like to do. Keep you going for a couple of months. I worry about you, that's all.'

Sam poured the tea and handed Leo a plate with a slice of cake on it. He wondered whether now was the right time to bring it up.

'Grandad. I saw this ad the other day. The British Institute for Antarctic Research are looking for assistant researchers,' he stirred in the milk, 'to investigate the effects of tourism on the continent.' Sam had to swallow his excitement. He didn't want to mention that he had had an interview because he felt it had gone so badly. He thought that it would somehow be out of place. There was a silence.

'Sam Glass, I can see right through you,' Leo said, as he reached for his tea and took a sip, but he couldn't stop himself smiling.

'Don't say it, Grandad,' Sam warned him, half-seriously. 'I . . .'

'Don't you dare.'

'I told you . . .'

'Grandad. I'm warning you.'

' . . . so.'

'Yeah, fine. Maybe you did, but it's not something you can say to the teachers at school, is it? "Oh, I'm going to go to the South Pole." "That's nice for you, Sammy, and what are you going to do in the real world?"'

'I know, I know.' Leo smiled, shrugging at the same time.

'Anyway, it's not exactly a career move, and I might not get selected so, you know, it's not a definite.'

'You'll get picked, Sam, don't worry about that. Now, just wait here one minute.' Leo got up and went over to his shelves. He pulled out his map of the South Pole again and returned to his chair, unfolding the map on his knee.

'Was this yours?' Sam asked.

Leo was scanning the map. 'No,' he said slowly, 'it's a more modern one', shaking his head and not raising his eyes from the map. 'Here,' he said, tracing the coast of Berkner Island with the forefinger of his right hand, 'here there is, *I think*, a mistake on this map. You see this island here? Now, look at the one beneath it – that is actually two islands. It looks like one when you approach it, but if you get on to it from the Berkner side and ski to the middle there is a gap of about forty feet right down the middle of it.' Leo looked up at Sam. 'At least, that's what I think. The cartographer tells me that I'm wrong. You see, I definitely remember an island like that, but I'm not sure where it was. My memory lets me down, you know.'

Sam nodded, looking at the map on his grandad's knee. It was a different edition from the one Sam had bought himself, but it was not hard to find all the features that he had stared at for so many hours. There were the mountains, there the Ross Ice Shelf, there was Elephant Island and round the other side the Lambert Glacier.

'Sam,' Leo said ' I need you to do me a favour.'

Sam nodded. 'I know, grandad. That's okay. Of course I'll go.'

Leo nodded back. 'I'd love to know. I'm so sure that I'm right, but there's no way I can prove it.'

'There is now.' Sam smiled at him. 'Shall I phone or send a postcard?'

Leo smiled back. 'A postcard will suffice.'

Leo took a sip of his tea and felt glad that the dream Sam had had as a young boy had not died. The death of dreams was a melancholy affair. It was usually doubt that killed them. Leo had hated watching his grandsons go through their father's death. From boisterous children who doubted nothing they had turned into quiet boys who did their schoolwork and watched their mother anxiously from under their fringes.

'Of course, you know that it's cold,' he said.

Sam laughed and nodded, taking a bite from a piece of cake.

'Cold like you've never known,' Leo continued, 'so cold

that it's almost hot. You'll hate it after a while. You wear thick boiler suits twenty-four hours a day, every day. You'll be cold in bed at night, cold when you wake up in the morning, cold when you eat, cold when you run. You won't be able to remember what being warm is like, what sitting here talking to me is like. You won't remember what it is to be able to feel your feet, to breathe air at room-temperature, air that does not burn your windpipe with its ice. Food is put in fridges to keep it *warm*, Sam. It's too cold to wash. The fish down there have white blood it's so cold.' He took a sip of his tea.

'It's depressing too. Nothing happens. Day after day, you have huge expanses of white outside and huge expanses of time in front of you. The most banal things become interesting: how fast your nails are growing, how quickly wrinkles around your eyes are developing, the differences between the canvas flaps in people's tents. It is a world without stimulation, you know that? Now and again a plane will turn up with some post, months old. The food is terrible, all packaged and out of date. It all tastes stale, and disintegrates when you try to heat it because it has been frozen so many times. People change when they're down there. The weight of time, of nothingness brings out the worst in some people; they feel like they're living in a world without consequence, where they can do anything and not have to pay for it. Some become children again, others stop speaking altogether. You know all this, don't you?'

Sam nodded and took a sip of tea, conscious of its warmth as he swallowed it.

'Yeah, I know that. But you'd go again, wouldn't you?'

Leo paused. His hand reached for his spiky sideburn. 'Yes,' he nodded. 'I would go tomorrow if I could. Prepare to fall in love, Sam,' he said, raising his eyebrows with a warning expression.

Sam looked at his grandad and saw him as he was years ago, in the photos taken of him in the South Pole. He remembered how he looked: full of life, full of success, all bundled up in a thick anorak with a snorkel hood that came right down over his eyes. He had found the moss, and was about to return to São Paulo to Lorenzo Lopez to tell him of his success.

'You won't want to come back either. But you have to remember that man does not belong there. You can look and touch and learn, but you can't live. You must not live there, because we are not supposed to.'

'Well, I might not be going. There are loads of interviews and activity weekends before the final selection.' Sam didn't mention the money side of it. He knew that Leo would have given him his pension book there and then, and he didn't want that.

'Yes, I suppose there would be.' Leo looked out of the window. 'You'll go Sam. It's written all over your face. I just wish I could come with you.' Leo reached over the left side of his chair and sat up with a bottle of whisky. He offered some to Sam who declined, and then sloshed a bit in his own tea.

Sam smiled. 'You can.'

And it was Leo's turn to laugh.

When Kasia finally got back to her flat after an evening at the shop she drew the curtains in her bedroom and took off all her clothes. She left them in a pile on the floor, where they had landed around her feet. She washed her face and hands and made a cup of what she called 'Polish tea' – it was the same as English tea, but with no milk. She turned the television on in her bedroom and lay on her bed, staring at the ceiling.

At work that evening in the shop she had realised something. And as she thought about it now it seemed to make more and more sense: she did not want to be by herself any more. She did not want to spend another evening alone. Ever. But she wanted to be with someone particular. And she wanted to be with him always. She did not know why she had not realised earlier: it explained her excitement as she went up to the house and put the key in the lock, not to mention her pounding heart as she approached the front room. And it also explained the disappointment she felt on leaving, the emptiness, the shadow that fell across the life she led away from the house. She was in love.

As she lay there, naked on her bedcover, arms above her head, knees bent and swaying, idly, from one side to another, she repeated the sentence to herself: 'I am in love with Mr Glass, I am in love with Mr Glass.' A modification occurred to her – I *love* Mr Glass – but she could not bring herself to say it out loud, because it made her feel uncomfortable. She thought about what could happen, what might happen and what would happen, and came to the conclusion that 'nothing' was the answer to all three questions.

There was a thriller on the television and she got up and turned it over. She became scared easily, and if she so much as sat in the room while it was on she wouldn't be able to sleep that night. She found it hard to think of Mr Glass and herself as a couple, as people who acknowledged each other's real feelings. It was quite simple really: their lives had overlapped at the wrong place. The end of his was the beginning of hers, whereas what should have happened was the parallel running of their lives and, at an early point, an intersection. This intersection would, like the shining of a beam of light through a prism, have spread before them a future of such fabulous colours and breathtaking beauty, that they would both have had to stand back and shield their eyes, and feel for each other's hands and hold on tight.

As she lay there, goose-bumps rising on her upper arms, she wondered whether she would ever feel the same way about any other man. Any man of her own generation, of her own time wave. She owed him so much, she felt; he had always been so kind. And she could not banish from her thoughts the scenes she had invented of her and Leo dancing the tango in Brazil, her and Leo talking late into the night under a clear sky, (she could imagine so clearly how he would look, his left arm pointing to the sky, his eyebrows raised, the profile of his nose, the face, almost, of a young boy), her and Leo making love. She had looked at the photos of him as a young man, as someone her age and she had fallen in love. And while she had fallen in love with something that was impossible, that was never going to happen, she had not fallen in love with the impossibility of it. It was not a desire that was born partly of the fact that it could never have happened. It was a true desire, a real desire, a desire born of affection, of care and ultimately of a deep resonance of their spirits.

She wished, quite simply, that she could travel back in time and meet him then, just before he left for Brazil. They could meet and fall in love, in fact they *would* meet and fall in love. She would hear somebody singing ('It's a long way to Tipperary, it's a long way to go') one evening on her way home from work as she passed the end of her street and she would crane her head to see whose voice it was, coming from behind a hedge. And the next evening she would hear it again, but this time the voice would be nearer, and she would clearly see a young man digging in the flower beds as she approached. They would look at each other, and in the moment that their eyes met they would build a world, a world that only they could enter. A world that was better than the one in which they lived.

That was the world he would take her to when she was down. That was the world that she would want to hide in, to disappear in, to live in for ever. It was a world that only they could build, by talking to each other, by laughing with each other, by catching each other's eye. And today, when Kasia looked at the eighty-six-year-old Leo she saw the foundations of this world. She could clearly see that they were the strongest, straightest, most solid foundations that she had ever known. Whatever was to be built on them would stand for years, for decades, for ever. And he saw them too. Between the two of them they gaped at these foundations, amazed by what they had stumbled upon, amazed by the strength of the beams, at the regularity of the bricks. But neither Leo nor Kasia began to build. Though they both had clear visions in their heads for how the building should look, for the name above the door, where the windows should be, what flowers should tumble from pots on the balcony, and, in time, whose small shrieks would be heard throughout the structure, neither of them moved a muscle. Instead they realised what they had come across and tried to look away.

When she looked at photos of Natália she shook her head in dismay. *I* would have stayed with him, *I* would have looked after him, *I* would have cared for him. And she wondered how that beautiful face had aged and whether she too was experiencing a lonely old age. Leo married the wrong woman, that was clear. But how was he to have known that the right woman was almost thirty years away from being even a twinkle in her father's eye?

Kasia peered out from behind a curtain at the night sky. It was hard for her to believe that this time last night she had been with Mr Glass. She looked now, by herself, for the little bear and the great bear, but each time she thought she found part of it – an arm or a nose – she would see another star which ruined the arrangement, a star smack bang in the middle of the forehead for example, or off to one side on a shoulder. As she stood there by herself in the darkness and stillness of the night, looking out over the carpet of roofs, she realised that she couldn't find them. By herself she couldn't see anything.

She was late, as usual, and it was raining. It was less serious to be late for Mr Glass than for her job at the shop – she knew that he wouldn't tell on her, whereas anyone at the shop would – but she took it more seriously, because she knew that he would sit there worrying about *her*, and not just about the sales that were being missed.

As this thought went through her mind she stopped dead in the street, her head tilted against the metal tube of her umbrella. *She knew that he would worry about her.* He would worry about her, she thought to herself. She was a stranger in this large city who spent most of her life in silence in her flat, but here was someone who worried about her. An old woman bumped into her trying to pass her on the narrow pavement, and Kasia was jolted out of her daydream. She carried on walking, faster this time, because although the thought that Mr Glass would worry offered something solid in an otherwise collapsing world, she did not want to worry him – indeed the thought of him sitting there worrying needlessly hurt her.

She turned into the path up to the house and saw that the front door was already open and there were various builders' tools lying around outside. She was fumbling for her set of keys, umbrella in one hand and a plastic bag in the other, when she reached the threshold of the house – and not looking where she was going, she tripped. The next thing she knew she was lying on her front, half on the hallway floor and half on the concrete outside, her right hand stinging and her body numb. Her umbrella lay a few feet in front of her.

She seemed to lie there for a second or so, while her head processed information. Then she got up, feeling unsteady, and as she did she heard footsteps on the stairs in front of her. She closed her eyes – she knew that the footsteps would belong to a builder, or several builders, and that they would more than likely have seen her fall. As she stood and assessed where she hurt she steeled herself for their comments, for their inevitable jeering ('Have a nice trip, love?' 'I know I'm gorgeous but you don't have to fling yourself at my feet, darling'). The top of her left thigh was aching, her palms were scuffed and she had torn her orange coat (her only coat). At least she was still holding her plastic bag. She felt like a child and she wanted to cry, to have someone pick her up. Instead she hardened herself, frowned and looked up to face the group of men.

'Are you all right, love?' The man put his cup of tea down on the stairs and came towards her. He picked up her umbrella and passed it to her. 'You took quite a tumble there.' He was a workman, dressed in light jeans and a patterned jumper with paint below the neck. He didn't touch her, but just stood next to her, an expression of cool concern on his face. She was so surprised that it took her a while to find words.

'I'm fine, thanks.'

He reached behind her and shut the front door.

'Have you got somewhere to clean up? If not, you could –'

'Yes, I have. Thanks.' She nodded towards Mr Glass's door. 'I look after the man who lives in there.'

'Oh, right. Well, I hope your bruises don't come up too bad,' he said, picking up his tea and heading outside.

'Thank you,' she said again, still more stunned by his reaction than by her own fall. She put the key in the lock of the flat and pushed hard against the door where it stuck on the carpet. 'Hello, Mr Glass,' she called out once she had slipped through the door, and she heard his faint reply from the front room. It felt almost as if she might be married. Her voice was still shaking from shock, but her cuts didn't seem to hurt any more. Maybe the world isn't as horrible as it seems, she thought, as she washed and dried the grazes on her hands.

She went through to the front room, taking her plastic bag with her.

'It's here. I didn't forget,' she said, as she rounded the door.

'Hello, Kasia.' Leo smiled. 'You're wet,' he said, looking at the bottom of her trousers. 'Don't you have a . . . what do you call those things again?'

'Umbrella. Yes, but look, I brought you a newspaper. You see, I didn't forget.'

'Umbrella, of course. So you have one?'

Kasia laughed. 'I have an umbrella.'

'Good. You'll catch a cold getting wet like that.'

'I'll make some tea. Would you like a cup?'

'Yes please,' he nodded. 'You know where the towels are if you'd like to dry yourself.'

She blinked at him and left the room.

They had reached a break between books, and Mr Glass had asked her to buy the newspaper instead and read bits out to him ('You can read out the articles and I'll tell you what's wrong with them,' he had said with a chuckle). And so she sat in her blue chair reading out all sorts of stories – political stories that neither she nor Mr Glass understood properly, domestic crime stories that she understood all too well, and other feelgood stories about bronze-age boats and newly born pandas.

After lunch and before she started on the housework they sat together looking through the accommodation section, looking for their dream properties. Kasia chose a cottage in Cornwall which had an outside loo and a stone wall round the garden. Leo chose a house in the Cotswolds, although his decision was motivated by the clematis that was, in the picture, climbing all over the porch. And then they sat there in silence, reading, staring out of the window, digesting.

Mr Glass seemed almost to have forgotten she was there; then he turned to her and asked: 'Did you buy a paper today?'

Kasia paused. She didn't know what to say. She was sitting there with it on her knee at that very moment. She had been idly flicking through the back pages, reading bits here and there. Mr Glass wasn't like this. He wasn't like all the others. She rustled it with her hands, so that he might look at it, and said, 'Yes, it's here.'

'Oh,' he said and nodded gently, turning back to look out of the window. Kasia looked back at the text but didn't read. She stared through the page and wondered whether it was better not to tell old people when they asked questions to which they already knew the answers, or whether it was better to pull them up, and risk shocking and upsetting them.

'Have we read it already?' Mr Glass asked, his head on one side.

'Yes, yes we have,' she said. 'There was the article about Europe, the one about the school with damp, and we picked our dream houses, don't you remember?' She became more animated. 'Yours had a clematis growing over the front porch. Clematis . . . Bate something, I think.'

'Miss Bateman,' he said, his eyes as clear as water, and he nodded like a lucid professor, now seeming to have forgotten that he had forgotten.

They continued to sit in silence for a good hour, Mr Glass staring outside and Kasia reading every word, every last letter in the paper. All these other people having other lives fascinated her. And as she read the columns of flat-hunting ads something caught her eye on the opposite page. Under the title *Men Seeking Women* she saw something she recognised, something that she was proud to spot because it was something that she had learnt. There, in bold type, she saw *We're just going out of the country, we may be some time*. She read the ad and stared at the title for a while. Lawrence Oates, she thought, somebody else knows about Lawrence Oates. Someone else in this lonely big city knows something that I know.

She was so excited that she almost read the advertisement out loud to Mr Glass, but something stopped her. Something made her think that she should keep this to herself. And she thought: maybe this will help me. Maybe Lawrence Oates' last words will help me. Maybe I just love Leo because I have not had a relationship for such a long time. Maybe I would just love anybody that I spent some time with. Her feelings for Leo scared her: she did not want to be in love with an eighty-six-year-old man. And it was because of that fear in her heart that she dog-eared the top of the page and decided to take the newspaper home.

FOURTEEN

Her message had been intriguing, and Sam was sure that Henry would have snapped her up had he heard it first. As it was, Sam had started checking for messages first thing in the morning: he knew he got up earlier than Henry, so he would listen to them all, taking down the details of the best ones and then deleting them. Or occasionally leaving them on for Henry to hear, and recording his own message at the end, breaking the tragic news to Henry that he had already arranged a date with the one with the throaty voice.

When they finally managed to meet on Friday night, Sam again chose a bar near work where nobody from the office went. With its hanging baskets and floral curtains it was looked down on for not being trendy enough. She eyed the place with some distaste, but smiled when she saw him, a small smile with a raised eyebrow and no teeth. How she knew who he was, Sam did not know, but she came over to him and held out her hand. Fuck, thought Sam. Scary.

'Sam?'

He took it and nodded. 'Lorna.' He bought the drinks. He was getting used to this now.

'So, when do you leave?'

'In six weeks. Out to New Zealand in July, get there in late August – spring in Antarctica.'

'Of course,' she said, and took a sip of her drink. 'Six weeks left here. I hope you spend them wisely. Shall we go out for supper?'

He nodded again and they left to find a restaurant. Lorna

was older than any of the other women Sam had met. In fact, she was probably older than the *20–35* they had put in their ad. She smoked too much and wore the expression of a slightly bored and contemptuous cat. One thing Sam liked about her was that she posed. Wherever she went she seemed aware that people might be looking at her, and she pouted and looked alluring whenever appropriate. She expected Sam to hold doors open for her, to take her coat, to light her cigarettes.

They went out to supper at a posh restaurant. The waiter called her 'Madame', and Sam 'the young gentleman' which made them both uncomfortable. She told him that she was married to a banker who never came home, and she spent her days in a large house in Sevenoaks being idle. As a student she had played the cello, but she had all but given it up now, and had little to occupy her time. Sam watched her in awe. She appeared so confident, so sure of herself, that he was amazed she was sitting here talking to him. It gave him a thrill to be with her. She spoke slowly, taking time over each word, and she laughed as though she was gargling – she threw her head back and emitted a deep babbling sound.

Needless to say, her absent husband paid for the meal and she persuaded Sam to come back with her and see the house.

'Come on,' she said, pulling his arm, 'come and see the life of a banker's wife.'

He hesitated.

'What's wrong. Are you scared, Sam?' She dropped his arm.

He smiled at her, unsure. 'No,' he said, meaning yes, and he took her arm in his.

The house itself was not that large compared with the land on which it stood. The taxi from the station drove them all the way up a long drive, lined with rhododendron bushes. There were no lights on the land, so Sam could not see exactly how far it stretched, but the lawn in front of the house disappeared into darkness as though it might become the sea.

'Ssshhhh!' she said as they stumbled through the front door.

'Why?' he whispered.

'Because –'

'Is there anyone else here?'

'My husband's upstairs.'

'I'm going.'

'I'm joking.'

'So, who's here?'

'No one, but we have to be quiet.'

'Can you put on the lights then?'

'No.'

'Why?'

'No lights either. Someone might see.'

'Who?'

'Someone. Anyone.' She pushed the front door shut and the darkness became blacker.

'But there's no one here.'

'Not to my knowledge. Come here.' She took his hand and led him across the hallway.

'In here. This is the best place,' she said, pulling him into what seemed to be a large room. It smelt funny, but he wasn't sure what of. They kissed, slowly for they were drunk, and she started to undo his trousers. She moved him over, nudging him gently, as though sooner or later he would feel something soft on his calves and fall backwards on to a bed. Then she pushed him.

In the pitch dark he had no idea what had happened to him. He fell backwards. He felt cold all of a sudden. An all–

over coldness, a coldness that went round his neck, down his spine, in his ears, around his testicles. He surfaced spitting water. He was in a pool. That was the smell: chlorine. Of course. He could hear her laughing somewhere.

'You . . . you . . . Right,' he said, starting to swim straight ahead.

Then he saw a figure at the edge of the pool. From the way the light fell on her he could tell that she was naked. For a few seconds he imagined that he had come home with a psychopath and not a lonely banker's wife, and she was going to play some hideous mental games with him, or stab him in the pool, or batter him around the head.

He heard the water break and saw her swim towards him. He reached down and removed his shoes, throwing them on to the side. He pulled off his clothes and let them float off, abandoned. Then he went under and swam to meet her, pulling her under by an ankle. And then they made love. She held on to the steps and he entered her from behind, kissing the back of her neck, shiny and wet from the water. She was surprised by his gentleness, by his care and consideration and most of all by his obedience. She was the choreographer, the mistress of ceremonies, of that there was no doubt. She asked him to lie on the side of the pool while she climbed on top of him, and it was she who directed his hands and mouth.

'Can I tell you something that nobody else knows?' she whispered, as she lay with his arm under her neck. They had finally found their way up to bed. He was dozing lightly, but he made a noise which meant yes, and slowly came back to life. As he did he realised that he had been sleeping the way characters in fairy tales sleep – his hands pressed palm to palm and beneath his cheek. He thought suddenly of his father – that was the way his father would pretend to sleep when Sam and Mark burst into the bedroom early on Sunday mornings to make him get breakfast. He used to lie on his back, his head to one side resting on his hands, and he would snore loudly, his mouth open and eyebrows raised.

But Mark and Sam knew exactly what to do to make him stop pretending; it was not to tickle his feet or blow in his ear or pull the covers off him. They would pad over to the bedroom window and look out for a few seconds. Then one of them would shout 'Look! Look! Come here, see there . . . no, there . . . there's a man on the roof!' and the other would make appropriately impressed noises, and add comments here and there, 'Look, he's climbing higher . . . look, he's standing on one leg.' Their father could not bear to hear about somebody else's roof exploits, without being able to watch and criticise, and he would jump from the bed saying, 'Where? Where?' and slide in between them at the window. And although it did not take long for him to realise that they were tricking him, that they were, as their mother would say 'crying roof', the realisation did not stop him falling for it every time. The thought that one day his sons might *not* be lying, that one day he might actually miss a real competitor doing his stuff was too much for him to take.

'You probably don't believe me, but I love my husband,' Lorna murmured as Sam woke up properly. 'I do still love him. What I hate is his job. He works all the time, and I never see him. Maybe if I saw more of him I would have fallen out of love with him by now.'

Sam breathed deeply. He hoped that she wasn't going to tell him something sad. At the moment he felt good. In fact, he felt fantastic.

'I hate the bank, I hate his colleagues, and in a way I hate this house and its gardens, because it is what I have instead of a husband.'

'He must be some guy,' Sam mumbled. 'I think I'd rather have the house.'

She had her teeth around his limp penis before he could move out of the way.

'Okay okay,' he said, trying not to laugh, 'I'm sorry, it was a crap thing to say.'

She lay back down next to him.

'Fuck, you're dangerous, Lorna Bobbitt.'

'So, as I was saying, I do not have any affection for the financial world. And about once a month I have to cook supper for my husband and his colleagues. He always gives me plenty of notice and I put on a small dress, rustle up something suitably impressive and laugh at the right times. A few months ago a journalist who writes a column in the *Financial Times* wrote a piece criticising my husband's department, because of some advice they'd recently given the government. Harry Lapsley penned a particularly poisonous article which made a lot of clients think twice about the advice my husband spends all his hours researching and checking. Anyway, last month my husband told me that Harry was coming to dinner, to help effect a reconciliation between the two of them. It was going to be Jacob Simmons, Peter Murray, my husband and Harry. Plus wives, not that they matter. Wives with one-way mouths, that's what they are. And that's what I am too. Food can go in (but not very much), and penises can go in, but woe betide if anything comes out. Sperm is swallowed not spat out, and words don't have a hope in hell.

'The day before they were due I drew up the menu. Gazpacho for starters, salmon cakes on a bed of rocket with a Hollandaise sauce for the main course, and lemon meringue for pudding. I went to Sainsbury's, bought all the ingredients and six copies of the *Financial Times*. The woman behind the till must have thought I was in it or something. When I got home I boiled the salmon in a large pan until the fish was ruined. Then I took most of the bits of fish out and left the water in the pan. I tore up the newspapers into shreds and dropped the bits into the water that the salmon had boiled in. I shredded all six newspapers, and by the time they had all gone into the pan they had soaked up all the water and I was left with a pinkygrey paste, like very fine papier-mâché. The next day I scooped some of the paste out, rolled it in breadcrumbs and fried it gently. I did this until all the paste was gone, and then I placed the cakes on a bed of rocket and decorated them with a swirl of Hollandaise sauce. And that night, we all ate *Financial Times* cakes on a bed of rocket with a Hollandaise sauce. Harry Lapsley ate his own words,' she laughed. 'Can you believe it? All those men, eating copies of the *FT*. Peter's wife even asked me for the recipe, she said they were so delicious. I had to keep pretending to smell burning so that I could leave the room to laugh.'

She rolled on to her stomach and looked at him, still giggling. He could see the outline of her head in the darkness. He reached over and stroked her hair.

'What do you think?' she asked.

'I don't believe you,' he taunted.

'I'll give you the recipe if you like. But you can only really do it with the *FT* because when you mash it you get this perfect dirty pink colour. With a normal newspaper it goes grey, too grey for white fish, which is a shame, because otherwise I'd do it again.'

'So they all ate them? Didn't they taste horrible?'

'Not too bad. I had a mouthful and then claimed I wasn't hungry.'

Sam smiled in the darkness. 'And the next day, when Harry What's-it went to the loo, his own words were shit.'

And they laughed together, lying side by side in the darkness until she rolled over and lay on top of him, listening to his heart in his chest.

Sam got back to his flat on Saturday afternoon. On the train home there were three words that kept going through his mind. Like a professional. Like a professional. It was silly really, because Sam had no idea what a professional was like – he had never been to a prostitute and he probably never would. He had heard someone at work use the phrase once to describe a woman they had slept with, and now it just kept coming back to circle around in Sam's head. He could not wipe the smile off his face.

Gray was sitting in the kitchen flicking through a London A–Z when Sam came through the door. Gray was on a one-man mission to boost tank-top sales at the moment, and he was sitting there now in a purple one with blue stitching around the arms and neck. He had bought three in the last week, and they, he proudly announced, were only the start of his collection. Tank tops were *in*, apparently, and the reason Sam hadn't seen anybody wearing them was that they had only just come in, and they were so barely in that they were almost out. But they were going in the right direction round the fashion wheel, so Gray had recommended Sam to get some quickly, to boost his cred with his fashion-conscious friends.

'Hiya, mate. How's tricks?'

'Good,' Sam smiled. It was a relaxed smile. An I've-just-had-sex smile. 'How about you?'

'Yeah, good.' Gray paused and looked at him. 'Sam mate, what happened to your clothes? You smell really weird.'

'I bet.' Sam smiled even more as he put the kettle on and sat down to tell Gray all about it.

When Sam got in on Monday night there were four messages on the answering machine. Two were for Gray, both from an increasingly angry Lucy, who appeared to have been stood up. The next was from Sam's mum, telling him to buy some shirts for Grandad Moss and take them round at the weekend. The last message was from Emma Smith-Holmes, inviting him to take part in the next round of interviews for the British Institute of Antarctic Research Volunteer Program ('Good afternoon. This is a message for Sam Glass, this is Emma Smith-Homes calling from the British Institute of Antarctic Research. Sam, you have been selected to attend the next round of interviews for the Volunteer Program. Please return this call on 0207 361 0563 to discuss the details. Thank you'). Sam knew most of the details already because he had read them in the information booklet. This round consisted of a taxing weekend in Wales, where the applicants would have to work in close teams to complete assault courses and solve mental and physical problems. A panel of interviewers observed you the whole time and marked you on a whole range of skills, from food preparation to team motivation.

Sam dropped his bag on the kitchen floor when he heard the message. 'Thank God,' he whispered, a small smile on his lips. He called Henry but his phone was switched off. In the morning he found out that Henry was through too. Sam smiled again.

And so Sam began to think seriously about leaving. He started to imagine his life without him in it. He imagined his flat, empty and quiet when Gray was out. His bed with somebody else sleeping in it. He imagined his friends, quickly finding somebody else to fill the gap he would leave. And he imagined his mother. How would she react? Mark would be left alone to look after her. Maybe now that he had Clarissa the two of them could look after everybody. Clarissa would be good at that sort of thing. And Sam thought about his father.

I can leave, he thought. Moreover, I want to leave. I have to go. Otherwise I will not be able to live with myself. There was one thought in his mind: if I don't go now, I won't go. I will spend the rest of my life, the whole of my life, thinking about it. I will think 'what would have happened if . . .?' and then I will die. I'll meet my Clarissa, marry and have kids. And then it would be impossible for me to go. If I become a father, I will be exactly that: a father. I will father for all the years that I have children. I will father for the rest of my life. And fathering means that you cannot leave. And suddenly Sam could fill in the blanks: he could win the cocker spaniel. *If I hadn't left advertising I would never have gone to Antarctica.* What a sentence. What a beauty.

Sam wasn't sure whether to tell his family yet or not. He would see everybody next week at Mark's wedding but the news, he knew, would upset his mother, and he did not want to spoil her day. The same went for Mark – he would have better things to think about than Sam's possibly imminent departure. That was another thing that bothered him: he didn't want to cry wolf. Just because he had got through the first round didn't mean that he would get through the second. Gray was always talking about his plans – about how he was going to become a DJ, about how he was going to live in New York, about how he was going to set up his own clothing company. He had not yet done any of these things, and Sam couldn't help feeling that by the time he did his friends would be so sick to death of hearing about them that they would barely notice that he had gone. Gray was full of ideas and plans, but he never quite worked them out properly. The first stage of his life-plan was winning the lottery, and the second marrying Kylie Minogue, so his friends did not take what he said that seriously. Sam did not want to speak too hastily. He wanted to tell everybody when he had confirmation himself, when he had worked out how he would go, how he would pay for it, what he would do when he got back. But he knew that that wouldn't give them very much time to get used to the idea.

In the end Sam had shagged Chantale. He hadn't really intended to, but after a few drinks, and a lot of chat on Wednesday night, he went home with her. She was a very good flirt. She looked at him for the whole evening, looking just at his eyes and now and again down at his lips. There might as well have been nobody else in the room, the way she never let her gaze be diverted. And she smiled a lot too, baring her teeth and glancing down coquettishly. Besides, Sam liked her. There were times when he completely despaired with women. Times when he thought that he would never, ever find anyone that he fancied enough to shag, let alone settle down with. And then there were other times when he felt spoilt for choice, and he had three or four hot favourites all at once.

The night with Chantale was one of those times. There were suddenly a lot of girls that he liked, that he would like to kiss, to hold, to make love with. There was Gilly: even though he hadn't seen her for a while he still thought about her a lot. Then, of course, there was Lauren. Sam always found Lauren attractive, and some days he thought that he might have a chance with her. And then there was Lorna, or, as Gray had nicknamed her, Mrs Robinson. Sam had got a lot of cred with his friends for his Mrs Robinson story. And now Chantale, sitting here in front of him with her pretty neck and shoulders bared, ready and waiting for his mouth and teeth.

She was trouble with a capital T, he knew that. He just knew that she was the sort of girl who would break all the rules to break the ice. She smoked a lot, drank in the morning and ran around the flat when they made love, dragging Sam to every room, to every surface, to every window, to every mirror, where they had to do it again. She had tied him up and then gone to the front room to phone her mother (her mother!). She never said yes, and she never said no. She talked about cold steel and then wanted to become his 'blood sister', taking a razor blade from the bathroom cupboard, but Sam refused, claiming haemophilia. 'Really?' she said with a demonic grin and a glint in her eye, 'I'm a necrophiliac,' and she frowned and mimed slitting Sam's throat with the blade. At that point Sam thought it was time to leave.

Sam was on the train on Friday afternoon when it occurred to him. He was carrying an artbag with the creative work for a new press campaign for Shadows. It was due to run in women's weeklies and some teenage titles. Kid and Dan had done some work that tied into their TV script: it was a picture of a dam that was made up of lots of faceless packets of what were supposed to be competitive brands. A packet of Shadows was shown being slotted into the one gap, and the line along the bottom ran: *Shadows. When things need to be kept in.* The commuter train going to the middle of nowhere was almost empty and Sam took the concepts out to think about how he would try to sell it. It was awful work, so he would have to lie.

His phone rang. It displayed Angela's number.

'Hello, Angela.'

'Sam, where are you?'

'I'm on the train,' he said, and knew that that sentence would always remind him of this stage of his life. When else would he say, out loud, into a carriage speckled with passengers, 'I'm on the train'? It was a sentence birthed by the mobile phone. He tuned back into Angela's voice.

'I told you to rearrange that meeting, Sam.'

'I tried. I told you, they couldn't move it.' The words tripped off his tongue almost like a song. He knew that he was provoking her.

'You're doing this on purpose, aren't you?'

'No. They couldn't move the meeting.'

'You shouldn't be going up by yourself. I mean . . . oh God . . . why does this always happen to me?'

'Look, it'll be fine. I told them you couldn't come.'

'Don't tell me whether it'll be fine or not. I've got a lot more experience than you in these matters. Just make sure you sell the work. If that work isn't sold you can forget about coming back to the agency, okay? And don't you ever let this happen again?'

'Okay, bye then.' But she had already hung up. Sam stared at the phone for a while and then noticed a piece of paper on the floor. It was the agency's internal approval slip, which was supposed to be stuck to the back of any piece of creative work, complete with signatures from every department. It was there to prove that the agency was happy with this piece of work, and that everybody, from the creative department to planning to production, was happy that the ad was appropriate. In this case it had just been paper-clipped on to Kid and Dan's badly drawn concepts and must have fallen out when Sam had taken them out. As Sam picked it up and fastened it back on to the pieces of paper an idea came to him. He fished in the artbag and took out a couple of pieces of board. Then he took out a marker pen and began to draw.

It took him a while, because he had to lift the pen every time the train threatened to judder. By the time the station was drawing near he had three boards each with a diagram of a sanitary towel on it. The diagram showed the wings, the stay-dry top weave, the grooves and, in the bottom right-hand corner with the shot of the packs, the individual wrapping. He added a large logo next to the packs, and a money-off coupon. Along the bottom of the concepts he wrote: *Have you ever felt your Shadow?* The end result was horrific. The board looked like a page from an incomprehensible instruction manual. It looked like a maze, like a spatial thinking quiz, like a brass rubbing of a complex and hideous machine. Sam could relax. The client would buy it.

When he arrived at the pub that evening Henry was already there talking to two girls. He was on number twenty-three, and Sam had arranged to meet number twelve. So many of them had asked where the other was (as though they were, not unreasonably, expecting to be given a choice) that Sam and Henry had agreed to go out together. He paused in the doorway and looked at the girls. One was short, with mousy hair in a middle parting and looked young. The other had darker hair and olive skin, with wide cheekbones. She was the prettier of the two. She was also the one that Henry was paying most attention to. Sam had just been to the gym and he felt like a sweaty mess. Gritting his teeth, he approached them.

'Hiya, Sam. Sam, this is Alison.' Henry paused and caught Sam's eye. 'Alison, this is Sam.' Sam smiled at

Alison. She looked very young. 'This is Kasia, Kasia this is Sam, my co-traveller.' Sam looked at Kasia and smiled a little. He felt that he'd seen her somewhere before, but he didn't know where. She blushed, and looked down, and then back at Henry, as if for reassurance. Sam looked away.

He turned to Alison. She was small and elfish and reminded Sam of Henry's kid sister. In fact, she probably reminded Henry of Henry's kid sister, which was why he was turned away, engrossed in conversation with Kasia. Sam started to talk to Alison ('nice day? where've you come from?'), and tried to concentrate, looking at her, making eye contact, nodding when he thought he ought, frowning occasionally. But all the while he was listening out for the female voice over his shoulder, the soft, slightly accented, flattened voice, of which he caught aural whiffs now and again, when she turned her head in his direction. He didn't know why he wanted to hear it. Maybe it was just to confirm (or not) whether they had met before.

He went to buy some drinks, and as he approached their table on the way back from the bar he had, suddenly, a terrific jolt of self-consciousness, as though everyone in the pub was eyeing him critically. He could see himself, in his tatty suit, his large nose, his unsure gaze, his terrible shoes. He felt awkward and gangly, and he wanted to hide.

'I'm a Taurus,' Alison was saying.

'Oh really? So am I,' Henry replied, 'but I don't think they're supposed to go well together. What about you, Kasia?'

'I'm the sea one.'

'What do you mean the sea one?' said Henry.

'The one that lives in the sea, with legs.'

'There are four sea ones, aren't there?' Sam asked gently as he sat down.

'No, there must be three, because each sign is either

water, earth, air or something – what's the other one?' said Alison.

Henry shrugged 'Err . . . bollocks? The other three are bullshit, rubbish and toss.'

'No, it's fire, isn't it?' Alison clearly took this seriously.

Kasia nodded. 'I'm the one with the shell, I walk like this.' She put her hand on the table and moved it sideways towards Henry's pint. Sam noticed that she had fine hands. Hands that looked as if they should do small, intricate things. Sam wanted to take one and examine it – he wanted to see how it would sit on his – to compare the difference in sizes. But these thoughts embarrassed him so he tried to clear his mind.

'Cancer, you're cancer,' Sam said, looking up from her hand.

'Cancer,' she repeated. 'Like the illness?' She frowned.

'Yeah, like the illness. Some Americans call themselves Moon People, because they don't like to be associated with the disease.'

'The moon is a good thing to be associated with. Did you know that it takes –'

'Eighty-five seconds for light to travel from the moon to the earth?' Sam finished her sentence for her. She had, he noticed now as she looked at him, a brightness to her eyes that reminded him of a cat, blinking in the darkness.

'Oh, you knew,' she said, a small smile of surprise on her lips.

He nodded and smiled. 'I'm Scorpio. That's a sea sign too.'

'So we can swim together?'

'Well, we can scuttle together at any rate,' he paused, 'run across the bottom of the sea. I don't think crabs really swim, do they?'

'I don't know,' she said, and looked off into space. 'If

they don't swim,' she said, turning back, 'how do they get to the bottom of the sea? And how do they ever get out? Do they just keep walking, along the ocean floor, until they eventually get to the beach? How do they know which direction to go in? They could set off sideways instead, and find themselves traversing the whole of the Atlantic Ocean.'

Sam frowned, 'But they *do* go sideways.'

'You know what I mean,' she said, with a smile and a small shake of her head.

It was Sam's turn to shake his head. 'No, I don't.'

'Right,' Kasia began, 'this is Britain.' She positioned his pint on the small dark table. 'And this,' she said, taking her orange juice, 'is America. So here,' and she pointed to the space between the two with her forefinger, 'is our crab in the middle of the Atlantic Ocean.'

Henry, chatting with Alison, shot them a puzzled glance and Sam smiled and nodded at Kasia.

'It doesn't have any legs,' Sam said.

'What?'

'It doesn't have any legs. Hang on,' and reaching for his bag he took out a biro. He leant over the table and drew three lines on either side of Kasia's fingertip. 'There we are,' he said, 'now at least it can walk.'

'Right,' Kasia continued with a little laugh, 'so, in order for it to get to shore it has to either go towards Britain or America. But, you see, depending on whether it knows where it is or not, it could go sideways,' and she moved her finger down between the pint and the orange juice. 'Well, then when would it hit land? Probably not until it reached a small island off the South Pole. And then what?'

'Well, then I can stop it, bid it good day and ask it if it can swim. And then we'll know the answer, and when I get back I'll tell you.'

'So, Kasia, what's Poland like?' Henry interrupted,

extending his arm along the back of her chair. Kasia looked up, as though she'd been startled out of a daydream, and then began to answer Henry's question.

Sam went back to talking to Alison, but he couldn't help feeling that he was patronising her. She was from a different generation, Sam could tell, and there was a gulf between them. As he sat looking at her he was suddenly gripped by a fear that he was letting things drift. There were important things to do, and he was just letting himself be carried along by other people's wishes. He was scared that he would pass his life as a dreamer, as somebody with his head in the clouds, someone who would stare at the sky for hours on end and not actually do anything. Alison was starting to look worried.

'How old are you?' Sam said.

'Twenty,' she replied, looking into her half empty glass of Baileys. The ice had melted and the drink had turned the colour of sour milk.

'Are you?' Sam replied straightaway, not meaning to imply that she was lying.

She paused. 'How old do you think I am?' she asked, coquettishly.

It was getting late. Sam looked behind him where Henry and Kasia were still deep in conversation. He felt tense.

'I'd say you were about eighteen,' Sam replied, quietly. He looked at her to watch her reaction.

She paused again. 'I'm fifteen,' she said, clearly embarrassed to be so young. Sam could barely remember the days when all he wanted was to be older. No wonder she reminded him of Henry's kid sister.

'Where do you live?'

'Why?' she said, puzzled.

'What I mean is: how are you getting home?'

'The tube to Angel. Then I walk.'

'Do your parents . . .' Sam caught himself – he of all people should know better than to make assumptions about numbers of parents – 'does someone not worry about you?'

She shook her head and finished her drink. 'No,' was all she said. Sam thought he should ask nothing more.

'I'm going to take you home,' he said. 'Come on, it's late.'

'You don't have to, I –' but she looked relieved. Sam thought that he should talk to her about arranging to meet strangers in central London, but he couldn't think of the right words. He knew that *telling* her she was irresponsible and foolish would only make her want to do it all the more. Now he looked at her more closely he could see that she had patches of short, wispy hair along her hairline. Baby hair, he thought. Another eight years and she would have been a great date.

'Henry, I'm going to take Alison home. See you later.' Henry shot a confused look at the pair of them.

'Tomorrow?' he said to Sam.

Sam shook his head. 'Mark's getting married tomorrow. I'll be back on Sunday. Bye, Kasia,' Sam said, racking his brains for something else to say so that this lovely girl might remember him. Nothing came. He looked at the tip of her finger with the biro lines on it, pressed against her glass. He smiled at her and shrugged a little, conscious of how stupid he looked.

Then he picked up his coat and walked out into the Soho rain, where he offered it to Alison and she took it.

Fuck, he thought. He hailed a cab and they got in.

FIFTEEN

'You look lovely.'

'Oh thank you, Tham,' Claritha responded with a warm smile. And in truth she did look lovely. Her dress was simple with short sleeves and a low round neck which approached her cleavage but, in the modest tradition of middle-class weddings, did not expose it, leaving the exact appearance of her firm breasts and how they joined to the imagination of the many middle-aged men there. It had a very small cotton lace trim along the seams, and it just trailed on the floor, revealing, now and again, white satin shoes. But the best thing about her dress was that it was white. Ivory white. China white. Snow white. Just white and nothing else. And Sam thought it was beautiful.

Mark looked well too – as usual distinctively neat – and as Sam stood in the pew next to his mother and his grandfather, watching the two of them at the front of the church, he suddenly found himself about to cry. His mother had started as soon as Mark had confirmed his name. Sam doubted that his grandad would cry and was glad for that. Seeing Leo cry would make him uncomfortable. And although everything seemed just lovely, he could not understand why his eyes were prickling and his throat tight. Maybe it was Mark's happiness. Maybe it was because he felt bad about having been uncharitable towards Claritha. Maybe it was the weather – a glorious June afternoon. Maybe it was because he was jealous that Mark had found somebody to marry, or because when he had walked up to the church he had looked and seen a roof that his father would have loved to walk on.

Not only did Sam have to give a speech, but Mark had also asked him to look after Andrea, whom Mark wanted to be there for the whole ceremony. Claritha was not that keen on Andrea, and insisted that she be kept in the kitchen at all times. Consequently Andrea had started to fight back, demanding more and more of Mark's attention and insisting that she come to the wedding. She was sitting now at Sam's feet, and every time they stood up to sing she began to get up, tail wagging, creaks of excitement coming from her mouth, thinking that she was about to be released. Sam had to bend down and make her sit again. She was salivating, and a string of spittle was already stretched across Sam's shoe.

As he stood up again, ready to join in the singing, he felt for his pager and then remembered that he wasn't wearing it. Things were so much easier now, and he could hardly remember the evenings of despair that had come before. He had to keep reminding himself that there was still work to be done, there was still a long way to go. The selection weekend was next weekend and he didn't feel fully prepared. Part of him felt that he didn't need to prepare, but then he thought of Leo, and he knew that as his grandfather would have done, he should prepare himself properly. As soon as the wedding was over he intended to put the girl thing on hold while he sorted himself out.

After the ceremony he went, with Andrea, to get a drink. He was nervous about his speech, and he needed something to help him relax.

'Sam!'

'Hello, Janie! How are you?'

'I thought I saw you at the front.'

'Well, I suppose you'd expect me to be here.'

'Yes, I suppose so. How *are* you? You didn't ring me, Sam.'

'No, I'm sorry, Janie, I really did mean to. I'm sorry – it was very rude. I lost your number.'

'Well, you could have called.'

'Errr, yeah . . . So, how are you? You look well,' he said with a flirtatious smile.

'Who's this? He's gorgeous.' She bent down and started to pet Andrea.

'It's a she. Andrea. Mark's dog. I've been charged with dog-sitting.'

'Oh, how wonderful! I love dogs. I always wanted to play with Daddy's hounds, but he wouldn't let me. Andrea is a funny name though.' She pronounced the name differently to Sam, stressing the second syllable instead of the first, making it sound as though she were taking her time over the word.

'Mark doesn't like silly names for animals. He thinks of her as a person I suppose.'

'How odd. People aren't animals, so I don't see why animals should be people.'

They began to walk towards the taxis – the reception was being held at Clarissa's and a carriage had arrived to take the bride and groom to the house. Sam and Janie paused by the carriage for Janie to stroke the horses' noses. One of them shat on the road. Andrea whined.

'So, how's things?' Sam kicked off.

'Really well. So well I can't tell you.'

'That's good. How come?'

'Well, I don't know what happened really. I just sort of decided that I'd better sort things out, so I did, and now everything's brilliant. I've changed accounts at work, I finally managed to move into my flat – the decorators had been in there for months – and then Jamie rang me up and asked me to go for supper. I wasn't expecting anything, I thought he just wanted to chat, but he took me to Utopia for dinner and gave me this.' She held up her left hand. On her fourth finger was a plain ring. 'It's not an engagement ring, it's an eternity ring. Much more romantic, don't you think? And they're terribly fashionable.'

'Brilliant,' Sam said. Should he offer his congratulations? Should he kiss her? What *was* an eternity ring? For some reason all he could think of was his phone in the office, ringing and ringing for ever and ever.

'It's truly wonderful. And I thought it was all over.'

Sam nodded and bent to stroke Andrea. She licked his hand and he stood there and watched her saliva dry on his skin.

There were drinks in the garden and Sam fetched a bowl of water for Andrea and sat under a tree, trying to memorise his speech.

'Don't worry about it, Sam. You'll remember it.' His mum came and sat down next to him on the grass, removing her shoes, and smoothing her skirt underneath her the way women used to.

'Where's Grandad?'

'Oh, he went inside for a lie-down. He's not used to all this.'

'Is he all right?'

'Yes, I think so. He'll be out when it's time to eat. You know, I do believe that he's got a soft spot for his home-help –'

'*Mum*,' Sam said, frowning.

'Yes, I know it sounds silly. But – I don't know – I just get this feeling . . .'

Sam shook his head at her. 'I bet he enjoyed this garden.'

His mum smiled, nodding. 'I hope he comes out to dance later on.'

'What, Grandad?'

'Have you never seen him dance?'

'No,' Sam shook his head and tried to remember whether he had.

'He's a wonderful dancer. Used to put all his friends to shame, and have all the girls queuing up to partner him.'

Sam tried to imagine his grandfather dancing, but he couldn't get past the image of him as an old man, and an old man dancing didn't really work. He found it hard to see his grandfather as someone who had once been his own age. Who had once been cool, who had once sworn and been rude, who had once charmed women and looked to the future.

'What do you think Dad would have made of all this?' Sam concentrated on the lawn beneath him, anxious not to meet his mother's eye.

'Oh, he would have loved it,' she replied, too quickly and with a forced smile. She looked defensive.

'He always liked Mark, didn't he?' said Sam, pulling up bits of grass.

His mother sighed. There was, she realised, little point in pretending that she had not been thinking about him.

'He liked you both,' she said softly. 'He used to ask me who it was that I'd had an affair with to have two such lovely children. He couldn't believe that you two were half of him.'

They sat there for a while, watching the guests mill about on the lawn – champagne glasses, peony blooms and hats everywhere. Both of them felt out of place. This was not the environment they were used to, these were not the people they mixed with, and they could not help feeling that they did not belong. Neither of them spoke. Sam suspected that his mother would feel the same as he did; but his mother did not think for a minute that her younger son would feel anything but completely at home.

Sam's speech went well. The story he had chosen to tell

about the noodles went down better than he had expected. When they were very young Sam and Mark used to have a large collection of dressing-up clothes – velvet cloaks, cowboy hats, alien masks – and in amongst them was a huge pair of women's nylon pants that were frilly and scratchy, and although they were dirty white, they had a kind of iridescent sheen to them, like the flesh of fresh fish. These were *the noodles*.

One day, as an act of revenge against Mark for breaking the bunk-bed ladder and telling his parents that Sam did it, Sam put the noodles into Mark's satchel before they left for school. He couldn't remember what possessed him, and it wasn't with a specific aim in mind that he did it.

Well, as it turned out that was also the day that Craig Hahn had his calculator stolen, and Mrs Tennel (otherwise known as Monkeyhair) decided to keep the whole class behind until somebody owned up to it. The class, as classes are prone to be, was stubborn, and sat there in silence while she sat at the front and watched out for the twitchy ones. Twitching, Monkeyhair believed, was a sure sign of guilt. Mark had always been twitchy ('look at him now,' Sam had said with a smile, 'twitching even on his wedding day', and a tent full of people smiled and turned their heads), and after a few minutes' observation Monkeyhair believed that she had found her culprit. She got up from her desk and picked up her metre rule. She approached Mark's desk and leant on the ruler.

'Mark Glass, stand up and empty your pockets.' Mark did as he was told and emptied his pockets. Mark had very neat pockets and their contents too were neat: there was one clean, folded-up tissue; one shiny fifty-pence piece and a carefully quartered penny-chew wrapper. Monkeyhair snorted and took the boy's unusual neatness as a sign of a criminal mind.

'Empty your desk.'

Mark opened his desk and let her see it. There was really no need to empty it. It too had straight piles of books, carefully stacked stationery, a few pencils, all pointing the same way, lying between the books. Monkeyhair was becoming more and more agitated.

'And now your bag,' she snapped, convinced that he was being difficult on purpose.

Mark calmly took his bag from underneath his chair and put it on the desk. He undid the large plastic clips and lifted the canvas flap, letting it hang down the back of the bag. Monkeyhair looked down with a confused expression on her face. Mark followed her gaze and saw the noodles, lying proudly on top of his lunchbox.

'*The noodles*,' he whispered, his voice full of horror. Monkeyhair leant over him and picked them up, holding them up for all the class to see. Mark's skin flushed hot and cold, the hairs on his arms prickled and he began to sweat. The class roared, Monkeyhair turned crimson and, by the end of the day, the entire school knew that Mark Glass carried old women's pants in his schoolbag.

'You terror,' Leo said, as Sam came over and sat next to him.

'What?' Sam picked up a disposable camera and took his photo. A cousin of Claritha's leant over and offered to take a picture of them both. 'Go on,' she said. 'A portrait of grandfather and grandson', and Sam, blind to the similarities, wondered how she knew. He put his arm around Leo and Leo brushed the crumbs off his hired suit. She pushed the button and the picture was committed to film: two men, one white-haired, the other with almost black hair and both with glasses on their faces and glasses in their hands. Sam looks hopeful in the picture, optimistic and cheery, while Leo is looking straight at the camera, a smile on his face, his hair all over the place. They look almost like the same person, or like twins born years apart or brothers one of whom has prematurely aged, and the effect is quite breathtaking. It is impossible to look at them together and not see their strength, their understanding, their *conspiracy*. They make an impenetrable unit, a bond of genes and common history, an unbreakable circle of similarity. Like a mirror and its reflection, the two could not be separated.

'You haven't mentioned my plans to anyone, have you?'

'No,' Leo said, 'of course not. You haven't forgotten our little project, have you? I've started to write out some notes for you, so that it'll be easy to find the island when you get there.'

Sam nodded.

'Have they confirmed you yet?' Leo continued.

'I'm through to the second round.'

Leo nodded. 'When do you think you'll tell everybody?'

'When I know for definite.'

'And how long will it be?'

'Six months, perhaps a year.'

Leo was thinking exactly what Sam was thinking. They were both thinking that Leo might die while Sam was away. Leo wasn't sure but he felt he could last at least another year. Sam wasn't sure, but he knew that Leo *had* to last another year. At least one thing was sure: he would definitely last until he found out whether he was right or wrong about the split island.

'I'll tell you one thing though, Sam,' and he waved his fingers in the air and looked straight at him, 'if I do die, don't come back for the funeral.'

'Grandad,' Sam reprimanded him, looking away.

'No, I mean it, Sam. Have your own little service out

there, that's what I'd prefer. I'd like to think of someone celebrating my life in Antarctica.'

Sam went over to see to Andrea, who was tied to a peg of the marquee with a bowl of food and water, and found Mark, Claritha and Janie smoking in the darkness. Sam wondered what they would have made of penguin feathers, if they had had to smoke them. Mark was fussing with a sheet of paper, folding it and then refolding it, trying to slide it into his inside pocket. Sam knew that as soon as Mark got home it would be filed, neatly, along with his bank statements, his deeds, his receipts. Mark kept almost every bit of paper he encountered. Sam sometimes thought that if, just for a few seconds, Mark were granted the gift of being able to see into the future, he would not look to see the colour of his children's eyes or the nameplate on his office door or even the day of his death. Mark would look to check that all his papers were still filed alphabetically.

As Sam approached, Janie was showing them her ring.

'Tham! Tham!'

'Hiya, Clarissa,' he said, putting his arm round her, 'how was it? Good day?'

'Fantathtic. We're about to go. Daddy'th jutht getting the car ready. It'th all been too wonderful. Thank you, Tham. Thank you tho much.'

Mark shook his head in an amused way and made a drinking gesture. Sam smiled.

'I'm jutht tho glad I did it. Well, we did it,' she continued, glancing around and looking behind Sam, as though she was expecting someone to approach at any moment. She was staggering too, losing her balance every so often, even though she was in bare feet, dangling her shoes by their straps with her left hand.

'You know, I don't know why people wait. I think you

thould do what you want to do, before it'th too late.'

'That's exactly what I thought,' Janie joined in. 'I mean I thought, what am I waiting for, you know, I should do what I want now. I might die tomorrow, just like that, and then what?'

Mark and Sam avoided each other's eyes. They had both lived through someone dying tomorrow. The fact that it could happen seemed so obvious to both of them that neither would ever say such a thing; it would be like telling somebody who was about to face a firing squad to be careful in case they got shot. Sam *knew* only too well that he might die tomorrow. He would never forget that he might die tomorrow.

First thing Monday morning Sam rang the loveline, as he and Henry called it, for entertainment and to check up on what was new. There were a few new messages, and Sam scribbled down the details in the back of his book. The last message had only just been left, and as soon as he heard it his heart stopped.

'Hello, this is Kasia with a message for Sam. Sam, you left your trainers at the pub the other night and I picked them up. My number is 0208 435 4584, and the best times to get me are before eleven-thirty or between four and six, or after eleven, I go to bed about midnight. Okay, hope to speak soon.' Sam replaced the handset.

What a thing to find – his trainers, of all things. They must stink. Fuck. Sam dialled Henry's number. It rang and rang. 'Fuck,' said Sam, under his breath. 'Fuck fuck fuck.' Henry wasn't in. Where on earth would he be at eight o'clock on a Monday morning? He rarely got up early, and never on a Monday. Sam tried his mobile but it was turned off. As he replaced the receiver for the third time that morning he had a terrible vision of Henry and Kasia, naked and fast asleep, curled around each other in crumpled bedsheets.

Sam knew that she had given him the times she was around to be helpful, but instead they kept going round in his mind. He imagined her getting up in the morning, and come midnight, climbing back into bed. And what did she do in between times? Between half eleven and four? Until eleven at night? What did she do after? And what had she seen in Henry?

'Good morning. How are you?'

Sam looked up to see Lauren arriving, a glass of orange juice in one hand and a bowl of Rice Krispies in the other. Her hair was still wet.

'Hiya. Yeah, good. How about you?'

'Fine. Been swimming this morning, so I'm on for a really self-righteous day,' she said with a smile.

'Sam, you have to get the proofs on a bike before ten this morning,' Angela shouted across the office on her way in. Sam nodded at her.

'Good morning,' he said under his breath. 'Nice weekend? Oh good, how nice. It's quite simple really, it's called people management.'

Lauren smiled again, turned on her computer, opened her work book, clipped on her pager and put her mobile phone on to charge.

'So how was the wedding? Tell me all about it.'

'It was great,' Sam replied, looking at a message on his pager, 'really great. Rural church, big tent, champagne, not that much talent though.'

'Oh it's useless talking to boys about weddings. I want to know everything – the dress, the flowers, the service, the food, the music, the bridesmaids –'

'I'll bring the photos in, shall I?'

'Definitely. How was your speech?'

His phone rang. Sam made a thumbs-up sign at her and got to work.

Sitting at his desk Sam felt excited. He knew he was leaving. And he didn't want to go without a bang. Angela asked him about the work that he had presented to Shadows on Friday and he told her: it was sold, the client loved it. He took the work from the artbag, taking care to reattach the approval stickers to the work that he had not presented.

'Look,' he said, flicking the boards over, 'I even got them to sign it.' There, in the box reserved for the client, were Clive's initials, bold and clear.

'Well, it was obvious that they'd buy it. A monkey could sell that work.'

'Thanks,' he said, thinking of a large white place where a certain person wouldn't be.

'So, sort out an estimate with Helen and get it to Clive by this afternoon. And write the minutes of the meeting. I'll go and see the creatives and tell them the good news.'

Sam returned to his desk. He didn't quite know how the creative work mix-up would resolve itself, but he was going to keep it going for as long as he could. He started to think about leaving his job, the way a cat circles a mouse before pouncing. He thought not so much about the actual day as about the time before, about the weeks leading up to it. And he started to circulate articles on government bills on education, on the EU's monetary policy, on migration in the Dominican Republic, highlighting random sentences, ringing others and inserting exclamation marks in the margins. He sent them to the account teams he worked on, copying them to every team member and putting them in the internal post. He changed Angela's ringing tone on her mobile phone to the one that played a tune. He crafted a letter from the Managing Director (whose scanned-in signature was kept on the communal hard-drive) asking the local shops and restaurants to come in and see them, because McLeod Seagal Gale was interested in doing some advertising for them. He sent the letters to places that McLeod Seagal would never want to have as clients – he sent one to the newsagents on the corner, one to the betting shop next door, one to the travel agents on Regent Street, explaining that although they had limited marketing budgets he was sure that there was something McLeod Seagal could do for them. He printed off the letters in the evening, and put the sealed envelopes in the post room so that, if someone happened to open one, they could not trace it to his floor, let alone to him.

Sam knew that he had to be patient. He knew that he had to bite his tongue, bide his time, keep a low profile until he was well and truly out of the door. He wanted everything to be perfect by the time he left. When Sam finally walked out through reception he wanted to be sure that the storm cloud he could see in the distance, heading in the direction of the agency, had his name on it, hanging in the droplets of moisture, large and clear.

SIXTEEN

Sam had arrived late at the office after getting a minicab because the train was delayed and, after a long research debrief on how consumers might respond to scented towels, he felt nervous when he picked his phone and dialled her number. He didn't know what he was going to say. Well – he had prepared a few lines in his head but they were all shit so he was hoping that, for the first time in his life, inspiration would strike once he began to speak.

'Hello?'

'Kasia? It's Sam, you met me –'

'Oh, hello.'

'Hi.' Sam paused. His heart was pounding. Come on inspiration, he thought, come on. 'So, my trainers –'

'Yes, you left them in the pub.'

'Right. Shall I come and collect them?'

'No, there's no need. I could drop them off at the same pub?' It almost sounded like an order.

'Fine,' Sam replied. His voice had gone high and his heart was beating louder than before. Don't sound keen, he kept telling himself. 'Tonight?' he said.

'Okay, seven o'clock,' she said and then said goodbye.

'Shall we go, Sam?' Jeff stood by his desk. He had bags round his eyes and he looked stressed. His tie was flung over his shoulder and his jacket was creased. He ran his hand through his thinning hair.

'Yeah,' Sam replied, grabbing his stuff. He finished scribbling a note to Gail and headed for the lift. Outside the agency Sam breathed deeply. His stride slowed as they walked towards the car park.

Driving down to see Reynolds Exhausts was a tedious journey. Jeff at least had the pleasure of driving the Soma (Jeff claimed it was a pleasure. Sam had no understanding of the pleasure to be had from pressing buttons and turning a wheel in a big box of steel). Sam had to sit in the passenger seat and watch the rows of dirty London buildings pass him by. In fact, Sam liked a lot of these buildings. In isolation they were striking. They were tall and ornate, with gold lettering carved in stone and large windows and railings at the front. But there were too many of them, and they were all too close together, like penguins huddling to keep out the cold. Only these were old, dirty, flea-bitten penguins.

'So, how are you, Sam?'

'Yeah, I'm fine. What about you?'

'Always start the day with a dump, a snort and a wank, that's what I say. I missed out the wank this morning – didn't think I had time – and look at me now. A fucking wreck.'

Sam nodded and didn't know what to say.

'Apart from that things are fine. Splitting up with my missus, my kids are getting thrown out of school, huge vet bills because our dog has the C word and to top it all there's something wrong with this motor. Listen.' As he changed gear there was a scraping noise, as though the car's belly was, for a short period of time, being dragged along the road. 'I think I'm going to have him put down.'

'It's probably the best thing,' Sam mumbled, 'if his chances are slim.' As he stared out of the window he realised that it was possible to become almost completely hypnotised by the passing buildings.

'Yeah. It's a company one anyway. I've been looking for

an upgrade for quite a few months,' Jeff replied, but Sam was miles away.

'So, still enjoying it?'

'Yeah, it's great.'

'It is the best job, advertising. I mean, you can say what you like about it, but it's got one over on all the other jobs I know. It's fast-paced, cutting-edge, varied, relevant to most people, teaches you a lot about media, it's interesting and demanding – both mentally and intellectually.'

'Yeah, I think you're probably right,' Sam found himself saying.

'I love it, you know. It means so much to me. And I'll tell you this, Sam, when I first joined this industry, I don't mind admitting that I didn't know jack shit about anything. All those terms, all those words, you know, that only the condescenti understand, I couldn't fathom them at all. Brand essence, brand equities, qualitative or quantitative research, heavyweight or lightweight campaign, TVRs, frequency, coverage, penetration, all that stuff.' They stopped at some lights. Jeff turned to Sam. 'I mean, do you think you really understand all that?'

'Err . . . yeah,' Sam nodded and gave a little shrug.

'Well, let me tell you something, Sam, and I know that you went to university and got your degree, and good for you, you must have worked hard to get it. But I've been in the business for eleven years, and I'm *still* not sure about some of those terms I mentioned. It takes a lot of time and a lot of experience before you really understand the difference between qualitative and quantitative research, for example. And I mean *really* understand, Sam, not just think you understand. It takes a lot of work up here', he tapped his left temple with his forefinger, 'before you can get to grips with it. I learnt all those words when I started. I sat down with a pen and paper and learnt them all, so I wouldn't be made to look foolish. And it got me a long way too, Sam. It's something I'd recommend, you know – a tip for the top. A little flower of advice from my garden of experience.'

Sam nodded again. He was doing a lot of nodding. Meaningless nodding. Involuntary nodding. Like a dog on the back shelf, nodding nodding nodding. 'Thanks,' he said, and went back to staring out of the window. Not only were the buildings too close together, but now, driving up the Marylebone Road, he decided that the people were too close together too. The queue for Madame Tussaud's snaked round and doubled back on itself over and over. Hordes of people bunched at pedestrian crossings and underground stations, all crammed together, with no room to walk unless the person in front of them walked first. And at this moment Sam felt he was too close to Jeff as well. He would have liked to be further away, about another car's width away. Or better still, on the train. People needed space, he was sure of it. They needed to be able to spread their arms out and spin round in a circle without worrying about decapitating a passer-by. They needed to be able to move without collision.

Despite Jeff's speeding they were late by the time they reached Reynolds. Ten minutes before they arrived Jeff asked Sam to go over their brief for the meeting, and run him through the new press work they were presenting.

'Hi Vicki, how are you?' Jeff asked coolly. He liked being cool. Sam nodded at her.

'We need to get a move on, we've got another meeting at four-thirty,' she replied, and they bustled through to the meeting room.

'Right,' said Jeff. 'As I'm sure you remember, the proposition we were working to was "upgrade your vehicle with a Reynolds exhaust", the support for which was that the majority of cars fitted with a Reynolds exhaust depreciate at a slightly slower rate than they would otherwise have done. We moved this idea on to upgrading because research showed us that Reynolds has a purely functional brand image – so punters just think of Reynolds exhausts as a product which performs a function and do not consider the *benefits* of having a Reynolds exhaust.' Jeff shuffled in his chair and cleared his throat. He had been out for lunch and spilt curry on his shirt and so he was sitting with his jacket pulled around him.

'At the same time exhausts represent dirty, smelly bits of metal that are not in the least bit glamorous or sexy which is something that we all agreed would be good to change. So, that's the proposition. On top of that we were looking for tonal values that reflected this move to more aspirational advertising, but at the same time did not stray too far away from what is currently recognised as the Reynolds brand – i.e. we had to keep the logo in the same place and you would prefer a copy panel along the bottom.'

Vicki and her colleagues nodded and remained silent. Sam's pager buzzed: *Call Clive asap.*

'So, we're confident that the work we're presenting today fulfils these criterias and will do a fantastic job of elevating the Reynolds brand in the minds of consumers.' Jeff leant behind him and picked up a pile of boards.

'The campaign we're going to present to you revolves around the idea of making your vehicle look better, and at the same time has an ironic dig at the car-parts advertising of the past, making the work something that implies that only a few people understand it, which in turn makes it aspirational work. We are confident that it still has mass-market appeal and will have tremendous cut through. So,' Jeff picked up the first board and turned it around. It was a picture of a woman in a bikini holding a Reynolds exhaust. Jeff read the copyline out to the meeting. 'We don't *need* scantily clad women to show you how good a Reynolds exhaust is. But why say no? Reynolds Exhausts. Exhaustingly Low (Cut) Prices.' He smiled at the assembled group.

'Strong, you see. As we always say, "Information goes in through the heart", and what's closer to a man's heart than this lovely lady? Great advertising. Let's do the ABC test on it. Did it get your *attention*?' He chuckled. 'It certainly got mine. Is it *branded*? Well, your copy panel's still there, your logo's there, and your brand name is in the headline. What more could you want? And last but not least, does it *communicate*? Clear as daylight. Clear as daylight.' And he sat back in his seat to let the group look at it.

Jeff ran through the other boards, each of which featured a woman in a snippet of lycra modelling a Reynolds exhaust. When he had finished he and Sam left the room so that Vicki and her colleagues could discuss the work and then feedback on it.

'They loved it,' Jeff announced, as soon as they left the room. 'They loved it, they'll buy it,' and he sniffed confidently. Sam wasn't so sure, he didn't like the work himself, but Zach thought it was funny, so they had no choice but to present it. He went to get a cup of tea from the machine.

'Right. We've discussed the work and Vicki is going to run through our feedback to you.' Vicki smiled a little and rearranged her notebook in front of her. Sam's pager went again: *Ring your pastard friend when you have a sec.* Sam smiled. Henry was clearly having a quiet day.

'Right, well, on the whole we find this work in bad taste, derogatory to women in general, and we don't think consumers will understand it. We're very disappointed with it. I mean, it offends me, and I'm not an easy person to offend, as you know, so we think that it will alienate our female customer base and possibly some of the male customers too. On top of that most people won't actually understand it, because it's quite a complex line – I mean, the joke bit – it's something that everyone who works in advertising in Soho will understand but Mr Smith in Woking won't.'

She looked at Jeff, pleased with herself.

'On top of that is the fact that you've presented press work. When I had a conversation last week I specifically asked you to present work for bussides. Why haven't we got any work for them?'

Jeff looked at her. 'Yes, I remember that, Vicki, and I passed it on to Sam to deal with. Sam?'

Sam looked up from his notes. Jeff had said nothing to him about bussides.

'I – er – I – er – we thought that this work could work as either press or bussides,' he stammered. As soon as he'd said it he wished he hadn't. The work had a full-length shot of the woman on it. Where would she go on the side of a bus?

'So where would the woman go?' Vicki said.

'We'd shrink her,' Sam replied. He was in a hole and all he could do was try to get out. He would have preferred to tell the truth, but that would have involved telling on Jeff.

'She'd be very small, wouldn't she?'

'About 60cm. Yes, quite small, but still big enough to see.'

'But then you'd hardly see the exhaust. You are aware of our stipulation that a shot of a Reynolds exhaust must make up at least twenty per cent of any advertisement's surface area?'

'Yes, I'm aware of that. We had intended to have a product shot at the other end of the busside too, so that the thickness and calibre of the metal would be clearly visible to consumers.'

'Well, we really need to see a layout then, don't we?' Vicki looked at him sternly.

'Yes. I can fax one over by tomorrow.'

'Wednesday? Okay, by ten a.m.,' Vicki replied.

For the second time Sam wished he could retract what he had just said. It would take at least a week for the creative department to be able to scribble something down that remotely resembled a busside. The meeting slowly disintegrated and Jeff and Sam left as quickly as they could.

Sam left the office at six and went for a swim, and he arrived at the pub with wet hair, smelling of chlorine. The smell reminded him of the glorious evening he had spent with Mrs Robinson, and he tried not to think about it as he waited for Kasia. Angela had rung him at ten past six just as he changed into his trunks to ask where he was. He lied and said he was with a Reynolds client, and hoped that she wouldn't check with Jeff.

Kasia wasn't there when Sam arrived, and he ordered a drink and sat by himself for a while, listening to the messages on his phone and deleting them one by one. He still hadn't been able to get hold of Henry, and he didn't know what he was going to say to her about the whole thing.

'Hello,' she said gently, standing before him.

'Oh, hi, hi,' Sam said awkwardly. He wished that he had seen her coming so that he would have had a few moments to prepare himself. He didn't know what to do. He didn't know her well enough to kiss her, and shaking her hand would be odd, wouldn't it? He just stood up, feeling foolish.

'How are you?' she said, but she didn't smile and her accent made her sound tough. She still couldn't believe that she had suggested this meeting.

'Fine, fine, thank you. Can I get you a drink?'

She nodded. 'An orange juice, please.'

He bought the drinks and sat down again. He recognised the carrier bag on the seat next to him.

They sat in silence, sipping their drinks and glancing around. Then they both started to speak at once. Both stopped, and Kasia started again.

'I just wanted to say that I think it's wonderful that you're going to the South Pole. I know someone who went once and he says that it's an amazing place. Really amazing.'

Sam nodded and wondered whether she was talking about both Henry and him or just him.

'I know. I can't wait. I mean, I still have some interviews to get through, but if I do it will be fantastic. My grandad went too.'

Kasia nodded. 'Do you think, if I gave you my address, you might send me a card from the pole? I mean, if you think that is a cheeky request please say so, I don't want to impose on you in any way.'

Sam smiled. Had she asked Henry for one as well, lying next to him in bed this morning? 'No, of course I will. From one pole to another,' he said and laughed. She laughed too, although more from nervousness than from delight. Henry probably made that joke too, he thought. He looked at his watch and paused.

'Would you like to go to the theatre?' Their eyes met. 'It's just – I'm rarely out of work this early, and I'm starting to think that I should do all those things that I won't be able to out there. But if you've other plans . . .' he said, rotating his glass on the beer mat beneath it.

'No, er – I'd love to,' she smiled. 'I really would.'

They went to the theatre and sat through a terrible play. Kasia slowly and quietly shredded the pages of the programme and Sam shuffled in his seat until the interval. They had ice creams and stood in the smoky bar, both of them still too polite with each other to be honest about the quality of the drama. On the way back to their seats for the second half Sam excused himself and went to the loo. He leant against the wall in the corridor with his phone pressed against his ear, listening to it ring.

'Hello?'

'Henry, where the fuck have you been? I've been trying to get hold of you all day.'

'Uuuuuh, S-am. I was asleep.' Bad sign, thought Sam. No sleep the night before then.

'Sorry. Have you been snogging Kasia?'

'Who, oh – oh no.'

'Did you try?'

'Does the pope shit in the woods?'

'And she refused?'

'She's a lesbian.'

'Is she?' Sam frowned.

'Must be.'

'That's all I wanted to know. Cheers,' and he hung up.

When he came back to his seat Kasia whispered in his ear that she had noticed a man in front of them who looked like he was wearing a wig. Worse still, it looked as though it was on back to front. She pointed him out to Sam. And then started to laugh. She couldn't help it. She found it terribly funny that a man should be wearing a wig.

The lights dimmed and the actors began but Kasia could not stop laughing. It was just a little giggle, like a stream running through her somewhere, but it was there, making her ribs shake. Sam caught her eye and smiled, and she was then beyond saving. Sam listened to her for a minute, trying to concentrate on the unconvincing actors, but after a little while he could not help himself: he started to laugh too. And the two of them sat there, giggling like school-children for no real reason, desperately trying to suppress their laughter. They were giggling so much that they could hardly breathe, their ribs aching and throats sore. And just as they were starting to relax, just as they thought their maniacal giggling might subside, a woman with lipstick and glasses leant over the seats and told them to be quiet.

It was the worst thing that could have happened: both of them erupted in another fit of giggling, delighted and ashamed that they were being disruptive and badly behaved. They could not look at each other, knowing that that would set them off again. Sam slipped down in his seat, pulling his coat up round his neck and trying to cover his mouth with the collar. Kasia covered her face with the shredded programme, which made Sam laugh even more. They stared at the stage, trying to think of serious things: of cold showers, death, concrete. But it only made it worse. They laughed and laughed, snorting for breath, gasping and coughing, tears streaming down their faces, their hands pressed against their mouths and their ribcages shaking like corks on water. In the end they had to leave. They gathered their stuff and ran for the door with such an urgency that someone could be forgiven for thinking that they were going to vomit. In the foyer they leant against the door and laughed and laughed, trying to catch their breath. Outside she turned to him and said, 'In Polish we would call that *mizeria.*'

'Oh yeah? What does that mean?'

'Cucumber salad,' she said.

Sam looked at her, mystified, and they were off again, staggering down Shaftesbury Avenue, drunk with laughter.

She looked at him. He had dark blue eyes which were speckled like birds' eggs and which flashed at her when he laughed. His hair was short and dark and she wanted to touch it, just to see how it felt. Standing on the corner of the street, where they had to part, they talked. She watched him closely, conscious of the silences that fell out of nowhere. As she watched him she was aware of him watching her, and she became uncomfortable. She was not as pretty as he was. That was how she felt. Her face was not formed by such pleasing contours. Moreover she was not as funny as he was. She laughed a lot more than he did, and hers was a shy, defensive laugh. He impersonated people, going on long narrative journeys where he met all sorts of characters and always came up with a punchline at the end. As she stood there was one thought in her mind: I like him more than he likes me. Or rather, he likes me as a friend, but I like him more than that.

They ended up talking about potatoes. About the different types, sizes, flavours. And then her bus arrived and he leant in to kiss her. It was a formal kiss on the cheek. But just as he did he took her in his arms and hugged her. It passed in a flash, and replaying the scene in her head she could not remember how it felt or where she put her arms. Did he think about it? Did he plan it? Did it mean anything?

To her it meant everything.

SEVENTEEN

Sam was woken the next morning by the sound of his mobile phone ringing. He scrabbled around for his glasses and then in his jacket pockets for his phone.

'Sam speaking,' he said, heading back to his bedside table to see what time it was. Seven o'clock. His heart started to pound. It must be something bad.

'Sam, it's Clive.'

'Hello, Clive.'

'Sam, I'm on my way to a conference, and I won't be able to talk to you today.' There was a note of satisfaction in his voice.

'Right. Do you want to talk about something specific?' Sam cleared his throat and wiped the sleep from his eyes.

'Well, you know we're planning to shoot the dam ad at the end of July. We had a meeting yesterday and thought that while we were at it maybe we should shoot a testimonial, you know, to save on production costs and timings.'

'Yeah, right, well that makes sense. And you're still keen on testimonials, are you?' Testimonials were ads where women were interviewed in their homes about the benefits of a certain towel, which was then followed by what was called the 'blue liquid' sequence. The agency disapproved of them, and had advised Shadows not to make any.

'Yeah. The thing is, Sam, I know they're not respected in Soho advertising circles, but they work. And if it's not going to work, we don't want to pay for it, goddamn it '

'Yes, I understand that, Clive.'

'So, I want you to start sourcing women – you know that we always use real ones, don't you, not actresses – so that we have about ten to pick from before we shoot.'

'Oh right, you don't do that yourselves then?'

'No, that's why we pay you twenty-five thousand pounds a month. So that you can do the dirty work for us. Is that clear?'

'As daylight.'

'Bye then.'

'Bye, Clive.'

Sam sat on his bed and looked at the map of Antarctica. He smiled. The map he looked at was so white it almost wasn't a map. Most cartographers started with a blank piece of paper and slowly filled in the squares with all the features that made up the ground. Cartographers of Antarctica started with a blank piece of paper and finished with one that was only slightly less blank.

Sam put his phone on the bed and went to have a shower. As he stood under the pounding water he thought about recruiting the women for the testimonials. Where was he going to find women who wanted to recommend sanitary towels on national television? Who would be willing to appear before all their friends and family chatting about the different features over a cup of coffee. And they would be paid next to nothing too, so it would be no use trying to persuade them to do it for the money. Sam could see it unfolding already. Hours and hours of phone calls just to find one woman who might, if it wasn't raining, be willing to come to a studio and be on TV. And then something occurred to him: I'm not even going to be around for the shoot, he thought. *I'm not even going to be around for the shoot.* And if I'm not going to be around for the shoot, then I can't get sacked when the women don't show. And he smiled.

His phone rang.

'Sam speaking.'

'Hello, my name is Elizabeth Gowden. I'm a teacher at West Bloomsbury Secondary School and I'm trying to organise some work experience for my pupils.'

'Right,' said Sam, 'and you were wondering whether we might have some places here?'

'Well, yes, do you have a scheme or anything?'

'No, we don't. But we frequently take people on over the summer. They don't get paid and it's quite hard work, but it is experience.'

'Do you think it might be possible for some of our students to come in?'

'Yes, yes I do,' said Sam, a plan forming in his head. 'How many girls are there?'

'Well, there's thirty in total, but I don't expect you to take the whole class.'

'No, we couldn't do that. We could take ten, though.'

'Really, that's great news.'

'Yes, no problem. Actually you know, we could take the whole class. Hell, thirty – ten, it's all the same in the end. When would they want to come?'

'Not until the holidays. That is, the end of July.'

'So August then,' Sam said, looking at his diary on the screen in front of him. The survival weekend was this one coming, he would hear the following week, and then hand in his notice, whatever the outcome. He would have to work another month, and that would take him to the second week in July. August would be perfect.

'How about August 7th – that's a Monday,' she suggested

'Perfect,' said Sam. 'I'll write to you confirming the arrangements. I'll also give you another contact name

265

because I'll be on holiday when they come in – the person the girls will have to ask for is called Angela Summers, and I'll let her know that she's to expect them.'

'Angela Summers. Great. Thanks very much for your help.'

'Not at all. I hope they enjoy their time here. Bye.'

'Bye.'

'Hello,' he said, striding up to meet her. He was late. He wanted to run a hand over his hair, breathe into his hand and smell his breath, check that his fly was done up, clear his throat. But Kasia was standing there waiting, watching.

'Hello,' she replied. She didn't know what to do. For a moment she just stood there, waiting to see if he would kiss her. He had rung her – to thank her for a lovely evening at the theatre – and suggested, as professionally as he could, that they meet up again one evening, if she wasn't working. She had been gruff and nervous, but somehow they had managed to fix a date.

'How are you?' he said at last, scanning the street for a bin to put his chewing gum in.

'Mmm. What about you?' They were standing beside a fountain near Piccadilly.

'So . . .' he swallowed his gum, 'what would you like to do?'

'I don't really mind. What about you?'

'What about the cinema?' he said. She nodded enthusiastically and thought: he doesn't want to talk to me. He watched her head bouncing up and down and thought: she doesn't want to be seen with me.

'It's this way,' he said. He set off too soon and almost walked into her.

'Sorry,' she said as he stopped too abruptly before he touched her.

They stood outside the cinema, discussing what they should see, looking at the strangely convex posters as London buses and taxis sped by on the road behind them. Sam didn't want to see the thriller (you've made yourself clear, Kasia thought. You don't want me to hide my face against your chest. And then: So why am I here? What do you want from me?) and Kasia didn't want to see the love story (well, that's a clear signal if ever I saw one, thought Sam).

In the end they went for a foreign film about a child who was abandoned at the start of the Second World War and left to roam the countryside in Germany. They bought tickets and went in to the darkness and warmth. Someone tall came to sit in front of them, and Sam had to lean sideways towards Kasia to see. His screen was still the shape of a jigsaw piece, waiting to have a section slotted into it, but he didn't really notice and spent the whole time worrying that Kasia would think he was trying to make a move on her. Five minutes into the film Kasia dropped her bottle of water, and had to fumble about around his shaking legs to find it. And then they sat there, still and silent in the gentle blackness as they tried to concentrate on the film but could only think of the person they were with.

Towards the middle of the film Sam looked sideways without moving his head and saw the unmistakable glint of a droplet of water on her cheek. I can't believe I brought someone Polish to see a film about the Second World War, he thought, and clenched his teeth. He was frustrated with himself. He sat there for another five minutes, catching sight, every so often, of a drop falling from the edge of her jaw into the darkness. And then he thought: fuck this. Fuck burning boats and bridges, fuck all this embarrassment. Here is a bridge I need to build. Here is something that needs my attention. This shouldn't be how it is. He leant nearer her and whispered: 'Are you okay?'

She nodded, still staring straight ahead. 'I always cry at films,' she said. It was a lie. Celluloid rarely made her cry. She was crying because everything was going so wrong. Because she felt alone and because she thought that perhaps she would never have any friends her own age.

'We can leave if you like,' he said.

'What do you think?'

'Let's go and have something to eat,' he suggested, and they took their coats and left. By the time they got outside Kasia had dried her eyes.

They walked through the wide streets towards Soho, Sam wanting to apologise for having chosen the wrong film, Kasia uneasy because he had, now, after her tears, the wrong impression of her.

'Where would you like to eat?' he asked politely, nervously. He stopped and turned to her.

'I . . . er . . . I don't mind,' she replied, desperately trying to think of somewhere and feeling an apprehension rise inside her, a fear that Sam would choose an expensive and fashionable restaurant.

'What about ice cream?' he said, stepping up and down from pavement to road and back to pavement again.

'What?'

'Ice cream, nuts, chocolate sauce, the whole caboodle.'

'For dinner?'

'Y-es,' said Sam, as though he was speaking to a child.

She was confused and she looked straight at him, as he bobbed up and down on the kerb, staring at his feet. Was he just odd? Was he slightly mad? Or was he mocking her? She didn't know, and the longer she was silent, she knew, the more stupid she seemed.

'Well?' he said, looking up at her, finished with his stepping. She looked straight back and, for a split second, thought she saw him wink.

'Okay,' she said slowly, a gentle smile on her lips, 'ice cream it is. But *you* have to eat the largest one in the whole shop. Chopped nuts, chocolate sauce, the whole . . .'

'Caboodle. It's a fine, glittery-white powder they sprinkle over the top that gives it that extra zing, that extra soft coldness which is so crucial to good ice cream.'

'Yeah, really,' she replied, her voice heavy with sarcasm. 'I look forward to seeing you eat it.'

'Oh, you can't see caboodle,' he said, with a small shake of his head, 'you can't see it and you can't hear it and you can't taste it. No one can.'

'Well then, how do you know that it's there?' Kasia asked.

'You just do,' said Sam, 'you just know.'

Sam had to leave work early on Friday to get to the training centre in Oswestry for the briefing. He and Henry sat on the train reading the SAS survival handbook and learning how to trap, cook and eat hedgehogs, should the need arise. Sam was anxious. *This was it.* This was the make or break weekend, and as he sat there, watching fields zoom by, he tried to make himself remember stuff. Remember not to be stupid. Remember to keep going, and not get out of breath. Remember not to whinge. Remember not to be too competitive or say anything horrible about the other people. Remember that contours close together can mean a dip as well as a hill. Remember Never Eat Shredded Wheat. At the same time he felt such an excitement inside that he thought he might explode. He felt an anticipation, an expectation, a looking-foward-ness which made him buzz inside, like the ticking of a clock, forever inching nearer a chosen time.

He looked over at Henry. Book propped open on the

table, Henry was stuffing a bacon roll into his mouth and humming his song ('we're off to see a blizzard, a wonderful blizzard near Oz'), one hand clutching a paper napkin like a child with a security blanket. Sam considered the option of Henry getting accepted and Sam rejected, but he could not think about it for too long because it made him feel sick. He looked back at his book: *walking/running/sleeping in a storm: what to do* — but he couldn't take anything in.

They arrived at the village of temporary buildings at ten to nine and were directed into the canteen. Everybody else seemed to be there already — about fifteen to twenty youngish people were sitting around drinking coffee and chatting, most of them equipped for the rough outdoors, wearing fleeces, trainers, jogging-suit bottoms, and no jeans. He wondered how long they had all been in training: they looked fit, most of them much healthier than Sam, with his tired eyes and his grey London skin.

He and Henry put their bags down, checked in and surveyed the competition. Sam stopped. He recognised one of the girls, and as he watched her for a while longer he remembered where he had met her. She had been one of his dates — Goldie, the one who had talked about the 'great outdoors' and the joys of lightweight canvas overlay. He approached her.

'Goldie.'

'Oh, hello. . .'

'Sam.'

'Sam.' Fucking hell, he thought, she was the one who rang me for a date and she can't even remember my name.

'So, you're here too?'

She nodded. 'I, er, I just wanted to check out the competition, you know,' she said, 'when I met up with you

. . . it was, well, you know . . .' She was clearly embarrassed.

'Oh right,' Sam replied and looked around. Thank God we didn't snog, he thought. 'Well, I obviously didn't scare you off,' he said, laughing nervously.

She didn't reply, and he went off to get a drink.

That evening was a long one. There were fourteen people on the shortlist, and, so they announced that evening, five places. Osh Laird was there, as was Emma Smith-Holmes, who introduced everybody and ran through the schedule for the weekend. Friday night they would be given a medical and shown their dorms. Up at six on Saturday for a run and breakfast. Then they would pack their gear and be put into teams, blindfolded and driven to a remote part of nowhere. The idea was that they get back to base in time for a quick snack on Sunday, but for the last three years less than half the teams had managed it, so they had to be prepared to spend two nights under canvas.

Sam was expected at the office eight o'clock on Monday morning, so he hoped that his team would do it. Otherwise he might be sacked before he even had the chance to resign. Each team was accompanied by an instructor who would help out in an emergency but was otherwise called upon to observe the candidates and, on Sunday evening, report back to the panel. The instructors would rotate groups on Sunday morning to make it fairer for everybody concerned, and the candidates would be told whether they were through by Thursday of the following week.

Sam looked round the room once again, and suddenly felt completely out of his depth. As Emma explained how the selection process worked, he suddenly felt that he was making a fool of himself. He was yet another advertising wanker who thought he could turn his hand to anything that took his fancy and succeed. He had been lulled into thinking that, just because there was no skill involved in *his* job, just because people in his department got far by bluffing, that was how the rest of the world worked. What an idiot. He could almost feel the contempt that the others would have for him, feel their laughing eyes boring into his back. Thinking he was fit enough just because he went to the gym four times a week! Thinking he had the necessary experience because he had been on an expedition to Nepal! Thinking that he could, for a second, compete with these serious people with their serious beards, sinewy bodies and faces, creased and matt from the sun and wind. He thought about Leo and how he had let him down. He thought about Kasia, and how he would not be able to send her a postcard. He had put so much into all this, only to realise, too late, that he was out of his depth. He was embarrassed and ashamed. Ashamed that he had even dared hope that he would be able to go. But at the same time he wanted it so much. If they were tested on desire and desire alone, he knew that he would have to get through. He was sure (sure as the floor) that he wanted it more than any of these people, and somehow, he had to get it.

There were five people in his team. Dougal, a well-built Scot whom Sam didn't dare ask what he did in his spare time – he was sure it was something like jog in the Cairngorms or lap Loch Ness; Eddie, a tall, quiet man from Norfolk who looked as if he could run for England; Pascale, a gymnast who had pulled a ligament and who wanted to travel the world and Tyra who, like Sam, didn't have much in the way of an athletic background and who had worked for Greenpeace as a fund-raiser. Despite this, she still looked hideously fit.

After the run and breakfast on Saturday they were, as promised, all blindfolded and put into a minibus. They sat in silence for a while as the bus bumped along country roads, as though they were trying to work out where they were going by the bends in the road or the noises of the countryside. Then Tyra suggested that they play 'I Spy', and she kicked off with an easy one ('I spy with my little eye, something beginning with . . . B.' 'Er . . . blindfold,' replied Pascale). But they became more adventurous, moving on to trees, birds, fields, trainers and Janice, the instructor who was accompanying them, started to worry that they could actually see through the darkness.

Like the other two boys Sam was quiet. The worries of the night before had not gone away, and although he had managed the run this morning with little difficulty, he was still waiting to be made to look a fool, as he knew he inevitably would be. Dougal and Eddie scared him. Pascale and Tyra scared him. In fact, Janice scared him and she wasn't even part of the competition. He imagined their lungs to be stronger and cleaner than his, their rest-pulses to be slower, their body fat percentages to be almost nothing. And Sam suddenly felt grateful for the blindfold: it stopped him examining Dougal's hi-tech trainers, it stopped him seeing Eddie's laid-back expression, it blocked out Tyra's toned thighs and Pascale's wind-beaten face, and best of all, it meant that no one could look at him. He could hide, and that was all he wanted to do.

Over the course of the weekend Sam was surprised to find Kasia lurking in his thoughts. He wasn't quite sure what she was doing there, or why he was thinking about her. He not only imagined her writhing beneath him, tousled hair and gleaming lips, or swaying on top of him, moaning softly in the silence of the night, but also he imagined her at home, by herself, watching TV. He wondered about what seemed to be the most boring things: about what socks she wore, how she sat when she watched TV, what her kitchen looked like, how she brushed her hair, how she stood when she was on the phone.

'It's this way, clearly,' Dougal said authoritatively.

'Nah, it's this way. Look at that hill over there, and look, there's a river on the map. I'll bet you anything that in that valley there', Tyra said, pointing, 'there's a river —'

'Look, it's this way. Who's coming with me?' Dougal turned and surveyed them all. 'Well?'

Eddie shuffled over towards him, looking into the distance and nodding his head slowly.

'Hang on. We're not supposed to split up. Why don't we vote on it?' Sam suggested.

'Because I'm right, that's why,' Dougal replied, already striding away.

'Dougal, hang on one sec. Let's just check this through,' said Sam. He didn't have a clue which way it was — he hadn't thought about it yet — 'why is that the right way?'

'Oh really . . .' Dougal exclaimed. 'The *sun*, Sam. It rises in the east and sets in the west. Don't you remember that from your geography lessons at school? The sun is currently about there,' he said, waving his left hand at a patch of cloud, 'and so that must. be north. If you look at the map you can see that we have to go south-east, which is, *therefore*, this direction,' and he waved, once again, in the direction that he was heading.

Everyone was ratty. They had been walking since eleven, trying to get to the forest where they were supposed to camp for the night. They walked from one landmark to the next and had to find sections of the map along the way, so they never knew where they were going until they found the next section. Along each part of the route were various challenges: rivers to be crossed (they were specifically directed away from the places which had bridges), small rockfaces to be scaled, trees to be climbed. In each situation they had to grapple with a number of make-believe problems – an injured team member, only one piece of rope, the added complication of bits of equipment that must not get wet.

It was now four o'clock, and although they had their maps they seemed to lose their way quite a lot, reaching roads or rivers or other landmarks only to look at the map and discover that they were not where they should be. Dougal was the grumpiest, snapping at and losing his patience with the whole team. Tyra was always ready for a fight too, but the other three were generally quiet, until things got bad. At the moment things were bad. Pascale was sitting down rubbing her ankles. Tyra had headed off to her valley to see if there was a river. Dougal was going his own way, Eddie was half-heartedly following him and Janice was watching, listening, observing. Sam felt sick. He hated being observed.

'Dougal . . . Dou-gal,' he called, cupping his hands around his mouth, 'just wait for five minutes, can you? We just need to talk this through with everyone.'

Dougal stopped and turned round.

'Fine,' he yelled back, 'but I'm waiting here. And only for five minutes,' and he folded his arms.

'Thanks, Dougal,' yelled Sam and turned round to see Tyra returning.

'It *is* that direction. The river is down there,' she said, wiping her hands on the front of her trousers.

'Right,' said Sam, 'but how do we make Dougal come with us?'

There was a silence. Sam saw Dougal starting to walk off again. The others saw it too.

'Let's leave him,' Tyra said, 'he's too fucking arrogant for his own good.'

'We shouldn't do that,' Pascale replied, standing up and holding one leg in the air and then the other, circling her ankles. 'Can we persuade him to let us vote?'

Sam shrugged. 'We have to do something,' he said, and they all trooped off to catch up with Dougal, Janice following behind, all eyes and ears.

They eventually set up camp at ten past eleven and made some food. They were in the wrong place, but once it turned eleven they decided to stop looking and Sam and Eddie cooked spaghetti over the gas stove, while Dougal directed the girls on where to pitch the tents. They would find the right place, and the next map, in the morning. They were all tired and sat together round the stove chatting and trying to get along as best they could.

Eddie got out some dope and rolled a joint, claiming it helped him sleep and that anyway, he always smoked on expeditions. Tyra joined him and the two of them started their own little conversation, punctuated by Tyra's loud laugh and silences during which they took it in turns to smoke.

The night was dark and mild, and Sam found it relaxing to be in the middle of nowhere. Dougal, Sam and Pascale washed up and packed stuff away, and then Dougal announced that he was going for a run.

'It helps me sleep, and anyway, I always go for a run on expedition,' he said, mockingly, backing off through the bushes.

Sam and Pascale stared at him blankly, Sam holding a tea towel, Pascale with her rucksack leaning against her knees. Neither of them had the energy to suggest that going for a run in unfamiliar countryside at midnight was not necessarily a good idea. Janice watched with interest and Sam saw her watching. A shiver ran down his spine.

When they woke the next morning it was raining. Sam crawled out of the tent, slowly so as not to wake Dougal, and was greeted by a raindrop on the back of his head. He straightened up and tied the laces of his boots loosely so that they didn't trail in the mud. The air was glorious. It was sweet and fresh and he breathed deeply, trying to banish the ghosts of sleep from his mind. Everything around was lush and shiny, the foliage a brilliant green that no longer looked natural.

No one else was up yet and he headed over into a densely wooded area for a piss. On his way back he stood for a while, sheltering under a large tree, watching the rain fall all around him. He had failed, he knew that. He was truly out of his depth. He did not smoke grass on expeditions, he did not go for a run before bed, he had not joked (as Tyra had) about tying the food in a tree away from the camp, which is what she had had to do when she walked through the Rockies because of the bears. Her comment sparked the three of them (Dougal, Eddie and Tyra) to start on a series of sarcastic comparisons of the Welsh countryside with the larger, scarier places they had been ('I'll watch the camp tonight, like I used to in Nigeria,' said Eddie. 'Yeah, and I'll go look for breakfast in the morning,' scoffed Dougal). Sam remembered the Saturday he had first seen the advertisement in the outdoor magazine at work. It all seemed such a long time ago now, that day when he had sat at his desk for hours and then met Henry in the pub. He thought about Henry and how he was getting along.

Sam looked around him at the rain. His dream seemed to be dissolving, taking his vision of the future with it. He tried to believe that there was something else, some other occupation that would make him happy. He had no idea what it was, or where indeed he could begin to look for it. In fact, if he was honest with himself, he didn't believe it existed. At this moment in his life there was only Antarctica.

When he got back to camp Pascale and Janice were up, drinking tea under a tree.

'Morning,' he said, putting on a cheerful front.

'Hi,' said Pascale. Janice nodded, gulping her tea.

'What time is it?'

'Ten past seven.'

'We should work out our route,' said Sam.

'I looked at it last night,' replied Pascale. 'I think I know where we are. And where we have to get to – it's not that far, it should take about an hour or so.' She looked terrible, the skin dark around her bloodshot eyes.

'Are you okay? You look tired.'

She nodded and drank down the rest of her tea. She was not going to say anything more.

Sam and Pascale started to cook breakfast and soon the camp began to wake up. As it did Sam realised why Pascale had not slept well: out of the girls' tent came both Tyra and Eddie. Of course. Sam hadn't even noticed that Eddie was not in the boys' tent when he got up. Janice, fortunately, had her own tent and so had been spared the stifled groans and moans and giggles of late-night sex in a shared tent.

They got moving as soon as they could and reached point number six at half-past nine. As they looked around for the next part of the map a jeep pulled up and out jumped Osh, there to replace Janice. The team was working less well than it had the previous day, and the rain had not stopped. Dougal was even more insistent that he was right, Eddie and Tyra had lost interest and kept disappearing for blow-jobs in the bushes, and Sam and Pascale battled to keep things together. When Osh joined them they were trying to get hold of the next map, which Dougal had spotted in a barrel, which had a see-through lid, with a hole the size of a ten pence piece in it. The map was in a plastic tube, at the bottom of the barrel. They all looked at it and Dougal started to press on the lid and kick the barrel, seeing if there were any loose bits anywhere.

'I think we're supposed to fill it with water,' Sam said, hoping that Dougal would stop trying to wreck the thing.

'Oh yeah,' he replied, 'good thinking, *Einstein*,' and he opened his rucksack and took out his water bottle. Sam, Pascale, Eddie, Tyra and Osh looked on as Dougal poured the contents of the bottle into the barrel. The water rose by an inch, the map in the tube bobbing on the top. There were another forty inches to go.

'We need to get some more water,' Pascale said.

'Does it have to be water or could it be another kind of fluid?' Eddie asked, with a smirk. Tyra laughed.

'There was the river we crossed this morning. Or we could go on, I guess,' Sam said.

'I think the boys should do their stuff. It doesn't have to be water, and I'm bursting for a piss anyway,' Dougal said.

'I say the river,' said Pascale. 'What can we carry it in?'

'You're insane. It was miles back. I don't believe we can't just break this thing open,' replied Dougal, pacing backwards and forwards. Pascale pulled at a blade of grass and put it in her mouth.

'I don't think we're *supposed* to break it open,' said Tyra, 'even though if this were a real-life situation of course you'd break it open. I think we're supposed to play at solving problems,' she explained to Dougal. 'What about using the tents to carry the water?'

Pascale nodded and the pair of them began to unpack

them again, while Dougal cursed to himself and Sam
scouted about to see if there was any water nearby.

Sunday seemed to drag. There were twenty points to get
through that day, and by lunchtime they were on to
number nine. There was no time to stop, they decided, and
so they carried on through lunch, stuffing things into their
mouths every so often. Towards the end of the afternoon
they had almost stopped speaking altogether, and Sam,
pausing at one point to bend down and retie his boot,
noticed that Pascale was flagging. She was way behind and
she kept pausing to readjust her rucksack. They were
walking along an asphalt road, looking for point number
twelve, which according to the map should have been
somewhere on the right-hand side, just after a small area of
trees. There was nothing around at the moment and the
nearest trees were on the horizon.

Sam stopped to wait for her, brushing his hands through
the roadside grass heads, making the furry ones sprinkle
their seeds before they were ready.

'Hi.'

'Hi,' she replied and carried on walking.

'Are you all right?'

'We're not going to make it.'

'Yes, we are.'

'Sam. We are looking for point number twelve. It is
twenty-past five. There are eight points to do before we get
back,' she panted, almost stamping along the road.

'I know, but we're doing really well. I mean, we might
be a little late but –'

'A little late! Sam, exactly how late do you expect us to
walk?'

'I don't know,' he said, looking into the distance. The
group of trees were drawing nearer, 'but we have to complete

it. If we don't finish it we can't even be considered. And there's no point doing all this if we don't finish.'

They walked on in silence, watching the trees up ahead and stopping occasionally to readjust bag straps or shoelaces. Sam could see the others up ahead. Dougal was leading, Eddie and Tyra still in their own little world some way behind him. Osh was behind them, glancing back now and again to check that Sam and Pascale were still following.

Sam saw him glancing back and knew that he would think that both of them were struggling, that Sam and Pascale were the two that tired the easiest, the least fit. The knowledge that Osh would think that produced a tightness in Sam's chest that interfered with his breathing, and it made him want to run to the front, to lead the party for the rest of the day, to walk the whole of next week non-stop, just to show what he could do. But he stayed with Pascale, swallowing his anger and falling into step beside her.

'I think I should drop out,' she said, pausing for breath.

'There's no need. You can do it, honestly you can.'

'I'm slowing everybody down. Look at you. You were at the front before you decided to walk with me. I don't want to be a charity case.'

'You're not,' replied Sam, feeling guilty about what he had been thinking, 'we're a team. You can do this – there's no rush.'

'But I'm jeopardising everyone else's chances by being so slow.' And Sam thought: *I'm just going outside, I may be some time.* No you're fucking not, you're not going anywhere.

'Forget everybody else,' Sam said, 'it's not about their own chances, it's about us as a team, and you're as much a member of the team as they are.'

They were on to point number sixteen when darkness fell.

It was ten to ten on Sunday night, and Sam was faced with the prospect of the office the next morning. Even though he was walking in the middle of Wales, he was surprised to find that familiar Sunday night feeling creeping over him. His heart sank. He felt almost paralysed by the prospect. The figures of the office came at once into his mind: Lauren, Gail, Michael, Jeff, and his heart sank even lower as he thought of Angela. That world seemed so far away now, and he could hardly believe that he had to enter it again in the morning.

Thinking of it suddenly made his current situation less unpleasant, and he gained energy, taking larger strides as they climbed a hill, and as the burden of the morning bore down on him.

'I have to go to work in the morning,' he mumbled to Pascale. They could barely see where they were going now, and every few minutes one would point something out to the other ('dip here' . . . 'slippy rock there' . . . 'prickly branches'). The others were waiting for them.

'Sam,' said Dougal, 'Eddie and Tyra want to go back to camp.'

'And what do you want to do?'

'I think we should go on.'

'I do too,' Sam replied. 'Pascale,' he turned, knowing the answer to his question already, 'what do you think we should do?'

She paused and looked at Sam. Then she turned to Osh, who was sitting quietly to one side of them all. 'Osh, what happens if we don't complete?'

'Well, it depends on how far the other teams get,' he said softly. 'If you get further than them then you have a better chance of getting through. Although it is dependent on other things too, and not just on how far you get. If you go back now, and the other teams have already finished, or have decided to keep going, then they will get more points than you. You see, there is a certain amount of stamina and fitness required for the real thing. The only rule, as you know, is that you must all stay together.'

Pascale looked at Sam again. She knew that her vote was crucial. Hers was the deciding vote. Sam knew that she had had no sleep, and was probably the least fit of the group. She didn't seem to have eaten very much either. He looked away.

She took a deep breath. 'I think we should go on,' she said, looking at her feet. Sam looked up at the sky. It was a clear night and he could see the new moon and most of the stars. He liked that. He liked the fact that he could stare at the same sky here as he did when he sat on the roof outside his room in London. One of the stars was looking back at him, he knew that. Please let us finish this, he thought. Please let us get through it. He thought of Grandad Moss. We have to go.

'Are you sure?' Sam said.

She nodded.

They got back to the camp at a quarter past three in the morning. Their feet ached and shoulders hung and each of them could barely keep their eyes open. Osh was driving back to London and took some of them in his car, Pascale, Henry and Tyra flopped like ragdolls on the back seat, mouths open, snoring gently. Sam sat in the front and tried to stay awake in order to keep Osh awake, and it was then that Sam noticed that his watch had stopped at half-past ten. There were four and three quarter hours of timelessness, of time that had not been recorded, of time that had passed his watch by, slipping the net of measurement and quantification. And he wondered whether that was what it was like in Antarctica. Did watches stop? Did measurement no longer work? Did she stand outside space and time, like another planet, far away, with her own rules and systems? Sam couldn't help it: he felt his eyelids close and fell fast asleep.

EIGHTEEN

'Clive's coming in at half-past ten. I'll say that you're doing something else, because I don't imagine you'd feel comfortable seeing him like that, would you?'

Sam nodded. Angela was wearing a new skirt of which she was clearly very proud. He could barely bring himself to speak.

'And he wants an update on testimonial women, a timing plan and an estimate for the testimonials. Oh and Sam, go out and buy a couple of cappuccinos for our meeting.' And she swept past in a cloud of *Dune*.

Sam's head was spinning. He had got in at ten to seven, got into the bath and stayed there, unable to move, for a good ten minutes. Then he had got out again, got into his suit and gone to work.

'How do you spell committee?' Lauren asked.

'Sam, do you want to talk to Richard Mimm?' Gail yelled over the floor.

'Can you tell him I'll ring him back please?' Sam yelled back across the floor. 'Double everything,' he said, looking at Lauren.

'Huh?'

'Double everything. Double m double t. Come on,' he smiled at her, 'wake up.'

'No sleep,' she said with a shrug.

'No bed,' Sam replied.

'Oh yeah? Get lucky, did you?'

He shook his head. 'No It's a long story, but today I might actually be more tired than you.'

'I wouldn't be so sure. I took a lot of phone calls last night.'

'Oh yeah? All from you-know-who.'

She nodded, taking a swig of her coffee. Zach had still not got the message.

'I don't know what I'm going to do, Sam. It's getting beyond a joke. Thank God I'm going on holiday tomorrow.'

'Oh, of course, I'd forgotten. So is today your last day?'

'Well, I'm in for the morning tomorrow – my flight's in the afternoon.'

Sam turned back to his monitor and flicked on to his calendar. He counted the weeks, slowly, one by one, until he might be able to leave.

Despite the bath and the suit he still looked a bit shambolic. He had a large bruise over one of his bloodshot eyes, a scratch on his left cheek and a Winnie-the-Pooh plaster on his thumb. Everyone at work thought he had been in a fight, and because he could not tell them the real reason for his cuts and bruises, he didn't correct them or bother to make up a different story. Sam had never been in a fight in his life. Gail had been terribly impressed and spent the morning offering to make him cups of tea. And now he asked her, if she didn't mind, and if she wasn't too busy, whether it might be possible for her to nip out and buy a couple of cappuccinos for Clive and Angela – oh, and sorry for asking her to do such a crap job.

Sam got back to his list of imaginary women: after finding one in Wales who agreed to talk to the camera he now, in his imagination, stumbled upon one in Cleveland who was positively eager to talk about Shadows on television. He made up their names, addresses and ages, which he knew was all that Clive would want for the time being. The thought that Sam had made them up would never, ever enter Clive's mind.

He called Henry at work only to be told that he had called in sick that morning. He rang him at home and got the answerphone. He rang his mobile but it was turned off. Sam left a rude message and hung up, feeling, all of a sudden, that he could drop dead with tiredness. It was late afternoon, and he was starting to feel he could not spend any more time in the building when his phone rang.

'Sam speaking.'

'Sam, it's Kasia.'

'Hello.' Sam's heart leapt to his throat. He didn't know what to say. 'How are you?'

'Very well. And you?'

'Yeah, good. I'm a little tired, but apart from that . . .'

'Oh of course. How did it go?'

Sam looked around. A voice was singing out of Gail's stereo. Someone was watching travel agent ads in Jeff's office with the door open and the volume up. Most people were at their desks. 'It was . . . well, fine. It was fine.' Sam hadn't really thought about it since he had got back. He was still shell-shocked. 'Yeah, fine.'

'Good,' she said. There was a silence on the line. Sam didn't know what to say. He wished he could e-mail her so that at least the whole office wouldn't hear his embarrassed silence. It didn't make sense. Here he was, desperate to get away, to leave, to go where he'd always wanted to go and here was this person, on the other end of the phone, whom he wanted to place, firmly, at the centre of his life. He felt a swelling inside, like a tidal wave gradually gathering water, or a tornado spinning.

'So, what are you up to this week?' He tried to sound as casual as possible. It was the best he could do.

'Oh, you know, working. Nothing much else.' Kasia thought of the emptiness of her free time. She knew, she could tell by the life he led, that he would have no concept of that emptiness. Those long periods of nothingness that in his life, she knew, would be filled with friends, parties, sport, phone calls, family. And she thought of Leo, because she knew he understood them. He suffered from them as painfully as she did, she knew that. Like Leo, she had no friends, no partners to relieve this self-consciousness, this uncomfortable awareness.

'Well, would you like – I mean, shall we – let's go out.'

'That'd be great,' she said, no hesitation.

'Wednesday would be good for me, if you're not working.'

'Great,' she replied.

Sam knew that this week would go slowly. He was due to hear from the Antarctic Institute on Thursday. He spoke to Henry late on Monday night and Henry's team had finished their course and were back at base by midnight on the Sunday. Henry had twisted his ankle towards the end of it, and was now in great pain and forbidden to leave the house for the rest of the week.

It was a mild Tuesday morning. Sam was standing outside Marylebone tube station. It was half-past seven and Jeff was supposed to be picking him up to go to an emergency summit meeting with Vicki at Reynolds. Sam was pacing the pavement, feeling sick. He had gone to bed at nine o'clock the night before, as soon as he had come in from work, but he still felt exhausted. In fact, he felt worse. He was getting older. He could go without a night's sleep at college and barely notice. Jeff pulled up.

'Morning.'

'Morning, Jeff. How are you?'

'Dog's bollocks,' he said and pulled out in front of a lorry.

When Sam got back to the office later that morning Lauren was clearing some of her things from her top drawer. She'd been crying. He was talking into his mobile and tried to catch her eye, but she did not look up and turned and left the room.

Sam hung up as soon as he could and ran after her. He found her in the stairwell, about to enter reception.

'Lauren, what's the matter?'

She could barely bring herself to look at him. Her eyes were red and her hair was messy.

'Why did you tell everyone, Sam? I thought we had a deal.'

'Tell them what?'

'You know what. What do you fucking think? I'll give you one guess.'

'I don't know,' Sam replied. He shrugged pleadingly. 'What's happened?'

She sighed and looked up, wiping a tear from her right eye before it had the chance to escape down her cheek.

'I've been fired, Sam. I've been fired because I don't want to shag Zach any more. And because I've been spreading rumours about him, apparently.'

'Is that what they said?'

She shook her head with contempt. 'Of course it isn't what they said. They said that I was surplus to requirements and they made me redundant. But they hinted. On the day that I'm going on holiday.'

Sam didn't know what to do. He thought he should comfort her, sit her down, talk to her, but he thought that touching her would not be a good idea. She might take it the wrong way, and besides, he wasn't sure that she completely believed him yet.

'Look, Lauren, I didn't say a thing. I haven't told anyone.'

Fresh tears were rolling down her cheeks.

'Do you want to go for a coffee?' he asked, as his pager buzzed.

'I don't know why I'm crying,' she said, 'it was a shit job,' blowing her nose and holding the door open for him. They walked through into reception and headed for the main door. 'I'll tell you one thing, though.'

Sam looked at her.

'They might pretend to care about you and your development and everything, but they couldn't give a fuck. The people who run this place, Sam, they're bastards. Complete bastards.' And she put on her sunglasses in the morning light.

Sam was pushing his way through the crowded pub, a drink in each hand, a packet of peanuts between his teeth and his bag slung over his shoulder when his phone started to ring. He turned to Kasia, who was right behind him. 'In the front pocket of my bag you'll find a dead mouse and my phone,' he said between clenched teeth. 'Could you get the phone for me, please?'

She hesitated, unsure for a second, and then smiled, digging into his bag and taking the phone out and, after a few seconds of scrutiny, answering it. Sam stood there and watched, hoping that Kasia was not about to encounter a client.

'Hello?'

'Hello?' It was a female voice.

'Hello?'

'Is Sam there?'

'Oh, yes, but he's a bit tied up at the moment.'

'Oh,' and then a pause. 'I'll call back,' and the voice disappeared. Kasia suddenly felt insignificant, that she had trodden on toes, that she had intruded.

'It was a girl,' she told Sam, 'she said she'd call back.' She watched Sam's expression turn from curiosity to anxiety, and Kasia became sure that she had taken a call from his girlfriend (as it happened it was Lucy, looking for Gray, but neither Sam nor Kasia knew that). They sat with their drinks for a while, not really knowing what to say.

'Did you hear about the man who drowned in a bowl of muesli?' Sam asked suddenly, as he picked up a peanut and tossed it into his mouth. 'He was pulled under by a particularly strong currant.'

Kasia smiled. She had heard it before. She looked at him and saw how beautiful everything was. How his short dark hair turned into faint stubble on that flat little patch in front of his ears. How the dip in the middle of his collarbone, just visible through the gap in his shirt, promised a flat square chest beneath it. How his clear eyes danced and shone as though they were beams, illuminating everything they saw. And then she thought: stop this, Kasia. This is one-sided, and you're getting yourself into trouble.

'If you think that was my girlfriend then you're wrong,' he said, suddenly, quickly.

She looked down at her hands and shook her head. 'It's nothing to do with me,' she said.

'It is,' said Sam, looking at her, and fiddling with his sideburn. He paused, 'and I haven't got a girlfriend.'

Kasia couldn't get over how lovely his eyes were. The blue was so remarkable, so bright and clear. It was a cold blue, a pure, almost translucent blue and what always surprised her the most was that his eyes seemed so warm, so kind and friendly. She would expect eyes like that to be haughty or contemptuous, or at the very least distant. But every time she looked at his she was astonished by the warmth of his gaze. She could almost bask in it. And of course, Kasia being Kasia, she assumed that this was *his* gaze. That his expression was a constant feature of Sam, that he was like that towards everybody, and she failed to realise that this gaze was something that only came into being when she was in the room.

She liked being with him. It was quite simple. She liked nothing more than to be in the same room as him, to watch him, to listen to him, to talk to him. He fascinated her so much that when she was with him she did not think about herself, and so she was happy. Sam gave her another world to enter: his world. His world of clear blue eyes and dark hair, of smiles and little laughs, of talking and listening, of scratching his sideburn when he was concentrating and of staring off into the distance mid-sentence. Wherever he was seemed like a great place to be.

At the end of their third date Sam walked with her to the tube station. They stood in the street and chatted nervously – a chatter speckled with giggles. The last time they had parted they had kissed each other on the cheek. What now? They were both unsure. Not of their own feelings, but of each other's.

They hesitated, talking about what would be on TV when they got in. Sam leant in to kiss her on the cheek again, placing his hand on her upper arm. His hand slipped down her arm and as he was moving away after the kiss, he caught her hand. She smiled – she could not help herself, but at the same time she was embarrassed. Neither of them questioned what his hand was doing there, what her hand was doing gripping it so comfortably. They just smiled at each other, one minute full of confidence and taken in by the thrill of it all, the next minute doubting the whole thing and thinking they should leave.

They held hands for a while longer, Kasia altering the tension in their arms by pacing backwards and forwards, either nearer to the steps down to the underground, or nearer to Sam and his magical eyes. Eventually they let go of each other, like brambles being disentangled, and went in opposite directions.

Sam stood and watched her head move down the steps, then he turned and headed for his bus stop, frustrated that he was wearing his suit. He wanted to run home. Instead, as he walked up to the stop he imagined that he was Amundsen, taking the last few steps towards the Pole, flag in hand. Kasia smiled in the station, pressing the ticket-machine buttons with a childish glee and bouncing down the escalator. She stalked along the platform, unafraid that people might look at her and wonder why she was smiling.

When she first met him she didn't quite realise the effect that he would have on her. They started to talk, and the more they talked the more she wanted to talk. He was funny. He made her laugh and he challenged her. He took her to task when she said things that didn't make sense. He knew a lot more than her but, thanks to Leo (Lco!), she could just about keep up. She watched his eyes, as they darted about and sparkled at her, and she could practically see his thoughts jumping around like overexcited puppies in his head. Everything he said to her seemed to make sense. He can read my mind, she thought at first, and then realised that that wasn't quite right. It was more than that – it was not a question of mind-reading, but one of mind-writing. Whoever wrote his mind wrote mine too, she thought.

They talked for a long while about lots of things. The

conversation ranged from advertising (Kasia knew nothing about it, but she watched ads and so she knew as much as anyone who worked in the industry) to books to food and living in London. They talked about attitudes, and spent a long time discussing how it was to feel angry and bitter and young, and what should be done about it. They were surprised that they felt similar things. He talked about his disappointment in his job, and although she did not tell him in detail the stories she had told Leo, she felt able at least to imply what had happened, and, if not describe the events themselves, at least sketch in the shadows that these events had cast on her life. He trod carefully when she spoke, and he listened with a concentration that she could almost feel, like salt in the sea air. He reminded her of Leo, a young Leo, and she reminded Sam of someone he had never known. Or someone he had only hoped existed.

Neither of them was in a relationship when they first met. And although they parted with a kiss on the cheek it was on this night that they became intimate. It was on this night, as they sat over plates of pasta in Bloomsbury, that something clicked into action. Had they been in relationships it would be this night that, later on when events were unravelled and blame apportioned, would be pinpointed as the first night of their infidelity. Their lips did not meet, but they talked and smiled, both of them thinking all the time how it would be to touch the other, to stroke the other's cheek, or kiss the back of the other's neck. They talked slowly and their eyes roamed, stopping on fingers, chins, collarbones, earlobes. They wanted to touch. But for the time being they just talked. And talking is always the start.

And when Kasia got home that night she lay in bed and tossed and turned. Something was wrong, something was different, but she did not know what. She was agitated, as though she had eaten something that did not agree with her. Her mind was racing, but when she tried to catch a thought, to work out what it was that was occupying her, it slipped from between her fingers and disappeared into the darkness round the edges.

She turned on the bedside light, got out of bed and stood in her room, to the side of her window because she was naked and conscious that another insomniac might spy her. She leant against the wall, feeling the cold plaster on her bed-warm skin. She closed her eyes and thought hard, listening to her heartbeat. She lay her palms flat against the wall and drummed her fingers. What was going on? Why was she in such a state? She felt like a teenage girl in a comic strip story, excited and unable to sleep before her first dance or her first trip abroad. But that was an adolescence unknown to Kasia. She had never felt like this before.

Her eyes still closed, she tried to slow down To slow her thoughts right down so that she would be able to see recognisable images, rather than the speeded up reel that had been flickering meaninglessly. She stood there for a good ten minutes, breathing deeply. And when things had slowed down she saw a face. A familiar face, but not too familiar. It was Sam's face. And she thought: how did you come to be there?

The next day at work was strange. There was no Lauren to talk to, Michael was on holiday and Gail was sick. Henry kept ringing to see if he had heard anything, but each time the answer was no. Sam's mum rang and he realised that he had not spoken to her since the wedding. He felt bad. As soon as he had put the phone down, Angela descended.

'Sam, where's the document?'

'What document?'

'The *document*. The document that I was just talking about.'

Sam paused and furrowed his brow. 'Which document?' he said.

'*The* document.' She was becoming more and more agitated.

'Which one?'

'The one that was on my desk.'

'I don't know which that is.'

'Oh God. *Why* don't you know? You're supposed to sort all this out. You *should* know.'

Sam shrugged. 'I don't,' he said, pleadingly.

'I think Angela means the research document.' Cath had come up to Sam's desk.

'Oh, right. It should be in here.' He went over to the filing cabinet at the side of his desk. The document was not where it should have been. 'It's not here,' Sam said.

'Well, where is it?'

'I don't know. I last saw it here.'

'And where is it now?'

'I don't know.'

'Sam, you *do* realise that it's one of your main tasks to organise and be responsible for all the filing of information and documents?'

'Yes, I know. But I can't keep track of everything. Maybe someone's borrowed it.'

'Well, you should know that sort of thing. *That's* your job.'

'But how can I –?'

'How can you what?'

Sam had nothing more to say. What could he say? 'Just find it, Sam, *now*, and don't let it happen again.' Sam looked at her. At her dark, flashing eyes. Her curled lip. Her flushed cheeks. Her folded arms. And he saw white. His head was spinning and he saw white.

Sam got in that night and found a couple of letters waiting for him. One was from the Institute for Antarctic Research. He felt it: it was thin. Worse still, it was a letter. When he got through the last round they had phoned him. Disappointing news usually came in print.

He sat down at the kitchen table with a bowl of Corn Flakes and opened the other one first. It was from his bank: they wanted him to take out a loan. He looked at the one from the Institute again. It was a white window envelope with a central London postmark. What if it's a rejection, was all he could think. What then? He couldn't face staying in his job, he knew that. But he had no idea what he would do. What if they rejected him? He couldn't spend his life staring at the sky. After all this, after all the fuck-ups he had begun at work, after all the blind dates, the preparation. He looked at the white milk with cornflake mountains sticking out of it. He just wanted to *see* that vast expanse of white with his own eyes, so that he could stop trying to imagine it.

He thought about asking Gray to open it, but it would be embarrassing to be rejected in front of him. He had no choice: he had to open it himself. He tore the flap at the back and unfolded the letter, racing to try and find the clinching sentence. His heart was pounding. *Dear Sam, Good to meet you properly and spend an enjoyable weekend in the country with you. I hope that you found it productive and that it gave you a clear idea of the sort of tasks that would be required of you for such a position.* Blah blah blah blah blah. Sam's eyes scanned the page. *We were very impressed by your knowledge, physical and mental preparation, team work and initiative on the*

*weekend, and are pleased to be able to offer one of the research
assistant posts to you. Your acceptance of this post is of course
dependent on your being able to raise sufficient funds for the trip in
time for the departure date of July 20th.*

Sam reread it. Then he read it again. Then again. He put
it on the table in front of him and sat back in his chair and
shut his eyes. He smiled. He could feel the white space
around him already. And then he laughed: a distinctive
laugh, like a bird flapping its wings in the night. He could
see himself on top of a mountain. A white mountain, and all
around him was white. He was the highest thing around,
and there was no one else there, no one else at all. He was
free. After all this time he was free. After all these months of
agonising about what to do, about where to go, about how
he should spend his youth. He had finally escaped. It was a
beautiful escape route – an escape route glistening with
snowflakes and blue sky. A quiet escape route. A
meaningful escape route. An escape route that would
change his life. An escape route *to* his life.

The next morning the first thing Sam did was ring Henry.

'Henry.' Sam tried to sound neutral.

'Sammy.' Henry didn't sound happy or sad either.
Fuckety fuck. What should he say?

'Go on, then.'

'You first.'

'I rang you.'

'So. I answered the phone.'

Sam paused. His palms felt sweaty. 'I got one,' he said.

There was a silence on the line. Sam didn't say anything.
He waited. His heart pounded. *Please please please*, he
thought. Then a laugh.

'I got one too.'

'Oh fuck, this is going to be fantastic. Fantastic. Fucking fantastic.'

'Sammy, we need to celebrate. When can you leave work?'

'About half seven, if I'm lucky.'

Henry tutted. 'Sam, that job's shit. You should jack it in and do something proper with your life.'

'You know, Henry, I might just do that.'

Sam did his best to remain sitting down for the rest of the day. He felt like a coiled spring, ready at any moment to jump up and sing, dance on the desks, fly out through the windows and into the huge blue sky, stopping on the way to pay a visit to his guardian star, kissing it, and then flying on, deep into the blue.

'Sam, this is a really important presentation that we saw this morning about digital TV. Copy it around the team and file the master somewhere really safe – we'll need it in about a month when we have our media forum.' Angela flung a huge document on to the middle of his desk and carried on by, striding to her desk to get her phone. Sam carried on typing his fax, his hands now weighed down with 400 sheets of A4, and waited until she had left the floor. Then, with a shiver of satisfaction, he picked up the document and put it in the bin.

It was later that day, while he was sitting at Angela's desk looking for a stapler, that the idea came to him. In fact, it was not really a new idea – people were always doing it around the agency, but for some reason Sam had not thought of it. He reached for her mouse and clicked on to her e-mail. He selected Sebastian's name from the address list and thought about the note. It would have to be subtle enough for Sebastian not to suspect foul play, for him to think that it was serious and sincere. He looked up but there was no one around. *Would you like to go out for dinner?* he typed, and then *A, xxx.* He picked up the stapler, stood and pressed 'send'. He walked away from her desk, giggling like a schoolboy. It occurred to him that he hadn't really had anything to staple; he had planned it all along. This was going to be fun.

As soon as he was out of the office that night, on his way to meet Henry, he rang his grandad. The phone rang a long time at the other end.

'Grandad, it's me.'

'Hello, Sam. How are you?'

'Grandad, I got one of the Antarctic jobs I told you about. I'll be able to go and have a look at that island for you.'

'Congratulations. Congratulations, Sam.'

'I'm so excited.'

'I bet you are. She's an amazing place, Sam. You're in for a treat. Make sure you say hello to her from me.'

'I'll see you before I go. I'm leaving at the end of July. I've got to tell Mum.'

'Be gentle, won't you. Tell her that it's all quite safe.'

'Yeah, I will. Listen, I'll call you tomorrow from home to talk about it properly.'

'Okay, bye.'

'Bye,' said Sam and slipped his travel card through the barrier.

'Hello, Mr Glass.'

'Hello, Kasia,' came the faint reply.

She dropped her things on to the floor and went through to the living room. She was happy. Happier than she had been in a long time, and happier still because she was here.

'How are you?' she asked as she approached and sat in her chair with a bounce.

'Old,' he replied, looking at her face, a little smile on his. He could not help himself.

She laughed. 'You can be other things too.'

'Old and . . . I'm well, today, Kasia. I actually feel well.'

'Good,' she said. 'Today I'm going to cook you a Polish lunch.'

Leo smiled. 'That would be lovely. Really lovely. What are you going to cook?'

'Aha. *That* is a surprise.' She laughed again, shaking her head a little and stretching her arms sideways. 'It's a beautiful day today,' she said, and sang a little song as she went through to the kitchen.

Leo had suspected almost straightaway. Now he knew for definite. She had met somebody, and she was probably in love. He looked outside at the glorious blue sky and wished that he could go out by himself and look at it.

He should have known, he told himself. What did he expect? That she would remain single for as long as they knew each other? That she would dedicate her life to him? He had seen her guilty looks, and they made him feel guilty too. She should not feel guilty. She had made no commitment to him. Theirs was, after all, an unspoken relationship. But Leo could not help how he felt. And he felt a twist inside him. As if a cloth soaked in vinegar was being wrung out all over his insides. As if his stomach was contracting and rising to his throat, about to try and force its way out of his mouth.

'I hope he's good enough,' he mumbled to himself. 'I hope he realises what he has.' And he tried to make himself let her go.

NINETEEN

'So, Kasia, how's Sam in the sack?' Gray asked, an eyebrow raised.

Kasia looked around nervously and didn't know what to say. Not because the question embarrassed her, but because she didn't *know* how Sam was in the sack. Gray assumed a level of intimacy which they had not yet reached.

'Ignore him,' Sam said to her, shaking his head, a small smile on his lips.

'No, come on, Kasia. What's he like when the lights go down?'

Kasia smiled a little, unsure of herself and of the question. 'He's nice,' she said, shuffling in her seat, trying to sound casual.

Sam leant over and touched her on the shoulder. Henry was going to be on television, being interviewed by a travel show about his forthcoming trip, and they had gathered at Sam and Gray's flat to watch it. Henry had promised to cook for them all, but at the moment he was in the kitchen on the phone to everyone he had ever known, telling them to turn on their TVs.

Gray gave a little nod. 'Nice, huh?' he turned to Sam, 'Sam, you're nice.'

'Right. Thanks, Gray. Lucy, would you care to comment on Gray's talents as a lover?'

Lucy grinned. 'You know the weirdest thing about Gray is, what he calls his *hydro-alarm technique*.'

'Oh Lucy,' Gray said. 'That's not fair.'

'What? What the fuck is a *hydro-alarm technique*?' Sam said, laughing already.

'Well,' said Lucy, speaking slowly with a smile in the corners of her mouth, 'every night, just before bed, he goes to have a piss. Then he goes to the kitchen and gets out one of those measuring jugs. Then he works out what time he has to get up in the morning. Then he fills the jug with a certain amount of water – usually quite a lot when he's working – and sits down, takes a few deep breaths and drinks it. He claims it gets him up at the right time, because by the time he's due to get up he wakes up automatically, desperate for a piss.'

She stopped, to let everyone catch up with her and to take a sip of wine.

'What's sad, though, is that he's so precise about it all. It takes a good quarter of an hour, working out quantities and then measuring them. And then sometimes, in the middle of the night, I'll hear him fumbling out of bed, heading for the loo, and he'll come back muttering something about the variation in the capacity of his bladder.'

'*That's* why that measuring jug is always on the kitchen surface,' Sam said, and then, 'You don't *really* do this, do you, Gray?'

Gray shook his head. 'She's exaggerating. Typical girl.'

'You liar,' squealed Lucy. 'Best of all is when he gets really drunk and pisses himself and sleeps right through it. That's the best, because not only does he look stupid for pissing himself, he also looks stupid because he's slept right through being desperate for the loo, which proves that his hydro-alarm technique is all a load of balls anyway.' Gray shook his head and Sam winked at Kasia. She looked bewildered.

'Darling, there's a fine line between being funny and too much information,' Gray said.

'Too much information? I don't think so,' said Lucy, 'I was just getting started.'

'Oh, plates,' said Sam, as Henry put his food in front of him.

'I replaced them,' replied Lucy, sheepishly.

'Lucy smashed all our plates,' Sam explained to Kasia.

'But I had a good reason,' Lucy said.

'Which was?' Sam asked.

'Well, you know how it is, Kasia,' Lucy glanced at her, 'men are supposed to do things for women, you know, fathers, husbands provide for the women in their lives, brothers are supposed to protect and teach, and boyfriends are supposed to give presents – flowers, massages, lingerie, all that stuff.'

Kasia looked at Lucy blankly.

'Anyway,' Lucy continued, 'Gray hadn't bought me anything at all since we'd been going out, so I thought I'd leave him a little reminder to go to Harvey Nichols. And it worked,' she giggled. 'He took the mug of water that he'd put his credit card in out of the freezer and defrosted it. For the whole time that you had no plates he was buying me presents. Now all I have to do is think of a different way of reminding him.'

'Perhaps you could do something more conventional next time, like knot his handkerchief or pyjamas?' Sam suggested.

Lucy giggled some more. 'Oh Sam, *who* wears pyjamas?'

'You okay?' Sam came up from behind her and stood to her side. Even as he did it he could not quite believe that this girl was standing here now in his kitchen. Like new shoes he wanted to wear her all the time, look at her and polish her. And wake up the next morning having forgotten that she was his, thrilled once again by everything about her. She was standing at the sink, starting on the washing up. They had finished eating and Henry's interview was just about to come on.

She nodded, scrubbing at the pan with a brush in her hand.

'Don't wash up.'

'I want to.'

Sam pushed her hair back over her shoulders and tried to look at her face properly. She continued to stare at the pan as though she were hypnotised.

'Why?' Sam said, realising suddenly that the conversation had become serious.

She stared at the wall in front of her and didn't know what to say. What could she say to this boy? She wanted to cry, she wanted to tell him that she hated his friends, that she felt stared at, on display, joked about, excluded. She wanted to tell him that she thought they were obnoxious, arrogant and unfriendly. She wanted to tell him that he would never be placed in the same situation as her – she would never be able to make him feel those things – because she didn't have any friends. But what would he think of her then? He would think her crazy and neurotic and paranoid and then what?

She did not want him to go away. She had only just met him, and she didn't want him to leave her now. She had congratulated him on his success as her stomach fell. She had clenched her jaw and smiled at him, pretending, doing her best to seem as thrilled as he was. And what could she say? She didn't want him to think that she was dependent on him. She didn't want to cling to him.

'I have a bit of headache,' she said, glancing up at him and then back down at the sink, trying to relax the pre-tears tension of her face. 'I'll come through in a minute.'

And he put his hand on the back of her neck and said,

'You can lie down in my room if you want. Or shall I get you an aspirin?'

She shook her head and smiled at him. 'No, I'll be fine, thank you. I think I might leave now.'

'Aren't you going to watch the interview?'

She paused, and then said gently, 'I don't think anyone will notice if I'm not there, Sam.'

Sam nodded. 'I will,' he said. In his mind he took her hand and led her to his bedroom, where he gazed into her eyes and undressed her with his teeth. In reality he stood in the doorway to the kitchen and asked her whether she'd like him to call her a cab. He wanted to take her to bed, but he didn't know what to say or what to do. He did not want to lose her, and he stood there, petrified for a moment, by how serious everything had become.

Sam cleared his throat and paced up and down outside Sebastian's office. The walls to the office were made of glass, and Sam stared through at Sebastian who was sitting at his desk, on the phone. Sebastian looked anxious and stressed.

'He'll be another five minutes or so, Sam.' Claire turned from her desk to look at him. She smiled, 'Can I get you a cup of coffee or anything?' she asked as she stood up to straighten her skirt.

Leaning against the doorframe she watched Sam pace. He was tall and strong, and through his jacket she glimpsed his flat stomach. He paced up and down, rubbing his hand along his chin. He stared at a point on the wall. In truth it wasn't a point because the wall was white and bare. He stared at an area, taking a few steps backwards so that the area became bigger. A large area of whiteness. He felt for his tie, and checked with his fingers that the knot was in place. He buttoned his jacket and arranged the bottom of his trousers so that they fell neatly over the front of his black leather shoes. He was nervous.

'Sam?' He turned and went into Claire's office. He cleared his throat.

'Yes?'

'Please go in,' she said breathily, indicating the door at the other side of the room with a nod.

He held his head up and went in.

'Sam! Hi, how are you?' Sebastian turned round with a smile. 'How's Shadows?' Sam sat down on the large leather sofa. Sebastian sat in his chair.

'Good. We've finally got some TV scripts through the client, and they're good. They'll be great ads. And although Reynolds put their campaign on hold we had a meeting with them and understand why. They should have something up and running by the end of the year. And Thermlex is going well.'

'So, what have you come to see me about?'

Sam looked Sebastian straight in the eyes. He let a moment pass. A pregnant pause. A beat. A moment to worry. A silence to wrong foot. 'I'm resigning,' he said.

Sebastian paused, his brow furrowed, his face flushed. 'Are you certain? I mean, have you thought this through properly? Is there anything we can do that would make you stay?' Sam put his ankle on his knee and bounced his foot in the air, looking at the stitching round the edge of his shoe.

'No.' He shook his head in time with his foot and savoured the word. No, there is absolutely nothing you can do, he thought. And I can't tell you how happy that makes me.

'Are you sure? I know you've wanted to change accounts for a while – we could sort that out. As of tomorrow. Or maybe you'd feel happier in the Planning Department. I

307

know you went to a good university. Or maybe you just need to take a holiday. When did you last go away?'

'It's not a question of holiday.'

'Well, there must be something we can do, something that would improve your life here?' Sebastian was squirming now, desperate to find a solution. 'I mean, you're very popular in the agency, and the client has good things to say about you. Are you sure you want to leave?'

Sam nodded.

'But Sam, have you really thought about it? You're doing so well. You'd be throwing it all away.'

Sam didn't know what to say, so he didn't say anything.

Sebastian sighed. 'Where are you going?'

'Antarctica,' Sam said, with a small nod. A breeze came through the window, making the blinds knock against the frames. Sam felt it around his temples. He looked at the window and, for a split second, was convinced that he could fly right out of it.

'Oh right. Who are they?'

'*They* are a continent. The third largest continent in the world. They are the driest continent, the highest continent, the windiest continent and the coldest continent. They have a mountain range as high as the Appalachians underneath their polar plateau. They make up one tenth of the earth's land surface. They are one and a half times as big as the United States. They are at the very bottom of the earth, underneath everything. For most of the time, they are forgotten. And that is how they like to be.'

'Oh right,' Sebastian said, clearing his throat and looking puzzled. He paused for a while. 'Sam. When we took you on as a graduate we hoped that you'd stay here and make your way up to senior management. We had high hopes for you. We've invested in you, after all. Are you sure that going travelling is what you want to do? It will look a bit slack on your CV. You're supposed to get this out of your system before you start work. And although there's nothing written, you did make a verbal commitment to stay with us and use your skills and experience to help the agency grow. We've paid for your training and now you're off. Not exactly what you'd call a fair exchange, is it? I think you at least owe us another few years.'

'I wouldn't dream of staying here.' Sam lowered his voice. 'I have been let down and disappointed by this agency time and time again. I was taken on as a graduate to be trained, to learn, to develop and one day contribute to making this place one of the best in town. I have learnt absolutely nothing since my first week here. I have photocopied, I have set up meetings, I have been sent out to buy cappuccinos. I have whittled away my days faxing and distributing. I have rarely had to think, let alone form my thoughts into coherent sentences, and I have never had to justify any facts I have produced.'

Sebastian was looking stressed again. Sam was perfectly calm.

'I spent three years at university to order tea and coffee for people whose combined intelligence and talent is less than that of my brother's dog. I have wasted my time, and what annoys me most is that you know full well that I have wasted my time, and yet you refuse to acknowledge it. Everyone pretends that their job is somehow difficult or challenging, or that it requires more skill or thought than it takes to be plankton.'

'Okay. Okay, Sam, I take your point. But is there no job in the agency that you'd consider doing?'

Sam shook his head and looked out at the sky. 'You shouldn't have fired Lauren. She was the best account manager you had.' With that he got up and left.

Claire, who had been looking for a file in the cabinet

next to the door for the duration of the conversation, turned to watch him go. He got into the lift and turned round. Claire was leaning against the doorframe again, watching him. Behind her Sebastian was standing in the middle of his office looking down at his desk. Sam stood there and let the lift doors close in front of him. His mind was racing. He felt as light as air.

The lift stopped and the doors opened. Richard was standing there, holding a copy of *Campaign*, the trade magazine.

'Sam. Hi. You seen this?' Sam got out of the lift while Richard was getting in. With one hand on the 'doors open' button Richard opened the magazine to the centre spread. It was called *New Faces to Watch*, and there, in the bottom left-hand corner was a photo of Richard (24), looking interested and serious, his long fringe flopped over one side of his forehead. 'Bloody brilliant, yah? I've had three job offers already, one for account director on Flamenco. Told you I'd be on six figures by the time I'm thirty. I've got six years to go, and at the moment I'm not settling for anything that doesn't start with a four.'

Sam nodded. 'Like "*For* God's sake, fuck off"?' He looked at Richard.

Richard looked surprised. Then he laughed. 'Yah, right.'

Sam turned and walked out of the agency into the street. 'I wasn't joking, Richard,' he said.

He walked round the square, taking deep breaths. He felt the breeze on his neck. It felt good. Really good. As if he was walking along a catwalk with an orchestra playing at his feet. As if he had just scored the winning goal. He sat on a bench and tried to think things over, trying to calm himself before he went back into the agency.

He had felt sad that morning. It was, he realised now,

nothing to do with the job. Of course it wasn't. Okay, maybe it was slightly sad that he had come to this place full of hope and ambition and he was leaving it dissatisfied, a couple of years later, with wrinkles on his face and cynicism in his heart. Maybe. But what had made him feel sad was the thought that when he left, he would be leaving Kasia. She suddenly meant a lot to him and he seemed hardly to know her. He wanted to spend time with her. In fact, he wanted to be with her now. Here and now.

He wondered where she was. She was probably at work. Sam dialled her number, but there was no reply.

He went to buy a coffee and a croissant. He smiled at the girls in the shop; he smiled at the men in the street – he couldn't help himself. He walked back to the building and went to his desk. The news would not be out yet, he knew. It usually took a day or so to filter down. But Sam had to tell Angela and Jeff, and as he dipped pieces of croissant into his coffee he wondered how he should do it. He looked at his monitor, at the papers all over his desk, at his phone and he felt like sweeping the whole lot into the air, and watching it tumble through space. He wondered for how long he could sit there and do nothing, and realised that it wouldn't be very long. The nature of his job was that everything had to be done there and then, now, instantly, because the deadline was always yesterday.

He piled up all the papers that were strewn across his desk and put them in the bin.

Sam and Henry called each other all day, giving constant updates on their situations. Henry's boss was excited by his news, and offered to pay for part of the trip if Henry would send two hundred words once a month for a column about life on the ice.

Sam called Kasia too, and arranged to meet her that evening, after he had been to the gym. He left a message for Lauren, for her to get once she got back from her holidays, telling her what he had done. All of a sudden there seemed to be so many people to tell. He spoke briefly to Mark and he e-mailed Gilly. Henry rang back to say that he had just arranged a date with the woman with the sexiest voice on earth. Sam said that it was probably a man, and Henry hung up. Sam sat and stared at his monitor for a while.

'Angela, could I have a word?'

'What is it?'

'Err . . . in private?'

'I'm really busy, Sam. It'll have to wait,' she said, and rushed off.

'Sometimes,' said Michael from behind Sam, 'I think that she's like a time-bomb, you know, waiting to go off at some scary point in the future.'

'I'd never thought of it like that,' said Sam, spinning around in his chair, 'but I like the idea.' He went over to the filing cabinet and started to rearrange all the Shadows papers. He devised his own alphabet, and moved everything around according to it. He put F first, because he liked F, and then 'U', followed by C, K, O, and then two more F's because he liked them so much. Then he got bored with alphabets and decided to file the rest of the stuff according to the density of paper that it had been printed on. By the time he had finished he could successfully find nothing. Not one sheet of paper was where it was supposed to be. He stood back and surveyed his handiwork. And then he threw a few folders away for good measure.

At half-past six Sam packed his stuff up and turned off his machine — he was going to the gym. He was twitching already, desperate to get out of the office. He was just getting up from his desk when Angela approached. She had her coat on.

'Oh, are you leaving?'

'Yeah. Off to the gym.'

'But you're coming back in?' she said, with a little frown.

'Err, no I hadn't planned on it.'

'Haven't you spoken to Clive today?'

'Yeah, a couple of times.'

'So he told you about the competitive review?'

'No, didn't mention one. Why?'

She brushed the front of her jacket with her right hand and squeezed the corners of her mouth.

'He wants you to present one in the meeting tomorrow morning.'

'*Tomorrow morning*?'

She nodded.

'Why tomorrow morning?'

'Because he's seeing the Chief Exec the day after and he wants a competitive update from Clive.'

'I can't, I'm busy, I'm sorry,' said Sam, lifting his bag on to his shoulder. 'Did you say we'd do it?'

'We *have* to do it. You can't be busy. It has to be done by tomorrow morning. If I tell you to do it, you have to do it.' She was going red, starting with her cheeks and spreading outwards to her forehead and neck.

'Why can't we fax him a competitive update by the end of tomorrow?'

'We can't, Sam. I told him you'd do this.'

'Well, I'll ring him and tell him I can't.'

'Sam, if you want to get anywhere in this business you're going to have to learn that you have to work late. You're such a shirker, always trying to get out of things. To get to where I am takes hard work, and you're not going about it the right way at the moment.'

Sam sensed that people were listening in, ready for a fight. He could hear pens being downed and telephone conversations dropping a few decibels all around him. Sam had never really had a huge fight with Angela. Not a huge fight. Other people had, but Sam had never got stroppy with her. He looked at her now and saw that her eyes were shining and narrow. He would never forget that face. He tried to focus, but all around him things were swirling. He felt sweet anticipation in his chest.

'I resign,' he said. A murmur ran through the floor. He could see, far away, somewhere else, a white horizon, and just above it an orange sun.

'What?' she said, sneering at him, with a little laugh.

'I'm resigning,' he repeated, gently. He could feel a cold wind on his face, that seemed to wet his cheeks as it whipped past.

'Oh really?'

Sam nodded. He breathed deeply. He could smell water. A clear, cold smell that was barely there.

She took a deep breath. 'Sam, this is a professional environment. I know that you're inexperienced but I would have hoped that in your time here you would have learnt that you cannot joke about such things. You may think it's funny. But let me assure you that it's not.'

'I'm not trying to be funny. I'm trying to tell you something.' And then somewhere, far away, there was a creaking sound.

'Oh yeah – like what?'

'That I'm *resigning*,' Sam said again, eyebrows raised, pleading to be understood. The creaking noise was still there, getting louder, and more insistent. Then suddenly beneath his feet the ice moved, and he was on the edge of a large sheet of white ice that was moving upwards, being pushed higher and higher in the air. He looked around him as he got higher. He looked at all the white, at all the brightness, at all the silence.

'Jesus, Sam. Do you really think that's funny?' she sneered once again, and then, as though it had just occurred to her, 'Perhaps you'd like to inform Sebastian of your decision?' There was a look of triumph on her face. Sam let a beat pass.

'I already did,' he said slowly. 'Earlier today. My last day is 17th July.' And, standing high on his sheet of ice, Sam looked up at the huge cold sky above him. Blue above and white all around. He sucked in the sweet air and felt his hands tingle. A motionless place in a gyrating world. I'm here, he thought. I'm here.

'Hi,' Sam said, and kissed her on the cheek. His lips accidentally brushed hers as he moved back and he blushed, embarrassed that she might think he did it on purpose.

'Hi,' she smiled. They were going out for dinner. It was a date. Clear as daylight, there was, now, no getting away from it. There were no trainers to hand over, there was nothing impromptu about their evening. Before they had gone to the cinema and sat in the darkness, conscious of each other and unable to relax but pretending that everything was completely normal, grabbing some food afterwards, but still pretending that they were out together for a different reason. Their last meeting was a *drink*, where they happened to have dinner since neither had eaten. And then she had come over for supper, to see Henry again and watch his interview. Both felt more comfortable like this, with everything out in the open, with agendas confessed. Sam had booked a posh restaurant during the day because he had become reckless. Perhaps it would be the last time he would go out for dinner in London. And besides, he wanted to take her out for dinner. He wanted to celebrate with her.

They sat and ate together. He watched her lips and she watched his hands. She looked at his eyes too, at those warm blue eyes that took her breath away. As she looked at him she thought of his departure. Was that why he was so appealing? Because he was going? Was it one of those holiday romance-type things, where the finite timeframe warped judgements and dissolved discrimination? She didn't want him to go and she couldn't bring herself to think about being alone again once he was out of the country, just as she didn't want to think about parting from him tonight. So she sat there and put those things out of her mind. And as she sat there, gazing in astonishment at this wonderful creature, she couldn't help but be infected by his mood.

They ordered wine and lobster and things that neither of them had ever tried, giggling over strange words in the menu and speculating on what they might be. When the dishes arrived they giggled even more, poking at this and that and wondering which part of the body might be on their plates. She had felt uncomfortable at being taken out for dinner, but he had insisted so much, threatening her with all sorts of embarrassing public spectacles, that she gave in. After a while they were joined by Henry and girl number twenty-four, an Irish girl with hair the colour of straw, and the four of them laughed and drank their way through the evening.

As they staggered out Sam put his arm around Kasia and she moved towards him, comfortable in his embrace. He announced, with a big grin, that everybody had to come back to his house to continue celebrating Henry's and his imminent departure, but Henry and his girl seemed keen to get home. And so Sam and Kasia wound their way to

Regent Street, crisscrossing small alleys and wide rubbish-strewn streets busy with prostitutes and sex-shops, looking for a taxi.

At a street corner Kasia stopped and looked down. Sam thought that it might be time to lay his cards on the table and kiss her, but as he turned to her she bent down and stretched out her arms in front of her.

'Sam,' she whispered, turning her head slightly towards him, but still looking straight ahead.

'What?' he whispered back, giggling and squatting down beside her.

'Look,' she said, pointing in front of her.

Sam looked. There was a large black bin liner, stuffed with rubbish, a crushed milk carton sticking out of the top of it. There was a cardboard box with pieces of cauliflower in it. There was a beer bottle, still half full of beer. Behind them all were the wheels of a large round metal bin, hidden by all the rubbish. There was a pool of liquid on the pavement beneath it.

'What?'

'There.' She leant close so that he could follow the line of her finger. 'A bird.'

And then he saw it. It looked like a female blackbird, standing there, looking at them. It shat.

'I think it's broken its wing,' Kasia whispered.

'Why?'

'Because it should have flown away by now. It hopped out of my way, and look, its wing is sticking out.'

Sam was silent and watched the bird. It watched them from the side of its head.

'I think we should take it back with us,' she said.

'And do what? I don't know how to look after a bird.'

'Neither do I, but it's better than leaving it to be eaten by Soho cats, isn't it? It might recover.'

Sam shrugged. Kasia took off her jacket and held it with both hands as she knelt down and leant nearer the terrified bird.

'Come on, Birdy, I'm not going to hurt you. Come on,' she whispered as she backed it into the corner and wrapped her jacket around it.

They stood up and Sam took Kasia's bag from her. He looked at this girl whom he barely knew. She had dirt on her knees and she was bending over the bundle of jacket, whispering into it. She was shivering in her thin dress and her skin shone gently in the evening light of the moon. Sam knew that he would have walked straight past the bird. Even if he had noticed that it had a broken wing, he would still have walked past it – too busy and stressed to bother himself with such things. This was central London – who bothered about birds with broken wings? There were deals to be clinched, profits to be made, deadlines to be met. As a young boy he would have picked it up. His grandad, still, to this day, would pick it up. But Sam Glass, this Sam Glass who ran around an advertising agency all day and all night with his mobile phone and his pager, sorting things out, making sure everyone knew what was needed by when, would have walked straight past – he was too important to be bothering with invalid birds, he had too many demands on his time.

Sam looked at Kasia and saw something he wanted in his life. She knows what is important, he thought. She is, in the end, right. He wanted someone who would remind him who he really was, someone who in the grimy, glamorous streets of Soho would stop to pick up and take home an injured bird.

He brushed her hair off her face and put his jacket around her shoulders. She barely noticed as she fussed around the bird, cradling the bundle in her arms like a baby. Then suddenly she stopped, her eyebrows raised.

'You don't have a cat, do you?'

Sam smiled. 'No,' he shook his head. 'She'll be safe at mine. Come on.'

They got a taxi back to Sam's and Kasia let Birdy (which was what she had christened it) wash herself in a Tupperware box in the kitchen.

'She needs some food,' Kasia said, turning to Sam who was standing in the doorway.

'What kind of food?' he asked.

'I don't know. What do you think?'

'I might be able to find an insect somewhere, but other than that I have no idea.'

'Neither do I,' she said, and smiled.

In the end they decided to let the bird decide. They put bits of food in separate piles on a plate – mashed up sardine, crushed up Special K with milk, some small bits of apple and some dry roasted peanuts. Sam lifted the bird out of its Tupperware bath and put it on the kitchen surface where it ran to the back and pressed itself against the wall, not moving. Kasia left the plate in front of it and said that they both should leave the room, so that it might stop being frightened. They went off to find a bed for it, digging out shoeboxes from cupboards, taking bowls from the bathroom and, at one point, picking up a slipper.

'What do you think about this?' Sam asked. Kasia shook her head and shredded some newspaper into the shoebox. She went back into the kitchen and lifted Birdy into the box. She put the box underneath the boiler in the kitchen, next to a bowl of water, and shut the door.

'Do you think she'll be all right?' she whispered, her back against the closed door of the kitchen.

'Yeah, I reckon. She'll be warm, and tomorrow I can ring the RSPB or something and see what they recommend.'

They looked at each other in the hallway. It was half-past two and they were both tired and still a little drunk. They had forgotten what they were doing there. They had forgotten that they had been on a date. Sam leant against the wall and looked at her. She seemed to fit into his life very easily.

'We should go to bed,' he said and added, 'I can sleep on the sofa.' He did not want her to think that she had no choice.

She nodded, thinking that perhaps he wasn't that keen any more. 'No, *I'll* sleep on the sofa,' she said. And then he was sure that that was what she wanted. They stood there in the hall a little longer, both of them trying to work out where they went wrong, where they had made a mistake. They stood there confronted with their misunderstanding, neither of them bold enough to be honest. Then Sam gave her a duvet and a T-shirt and she went to bed.

The weather was strange that night. It started to rain almost as soon as Sam had laid his head on his pillow, large, fat drops that fell with such purpose and resolve that one could only imagine they had been intending to fall in that place for years, waiting for days in the sky before they were set free. Sam drifted off, but he slept fitfully, waking every now and then to the sound of his window-pane rattling in its frame or rain lashing against the glass.

Just as it was getting light Sam woke up properly, a terrible pressure in his bladder and a dryness in his throat. He climbed from his bed and stumbled to the bathroom, passing, on his way, the front room. His eyes still shut, he pissed and, without thinking, flushed the loo. On his way back he stopped in the doorway to the front room and looked at Kasia, asleep on the sofa. She was lying on her stomach, her arms folded underneath her head, the duvet across the small of her back, revealing bare shoulders. The T-shirt Sam had given her was still folded, exactly as he had handed it to her, and lying on the floor.

Sam stood and looked at her. He looked at her hair and her skin, glowing curiously in the half-light as it had the night before in the street. As he looked at her he imagined things: he imagined gently taking the duvet off her and being able to see the small of her back, her bottom, her thighs gently touching, the backs of her knees, her feet. He imagined her kneeling up now, right there in front of him and he thought about the way her breasts would lie, the softness of the skin on her stomach, the shade of her pubic hair. He had an erection, and standing there he could not help himself and he crept over to be nearer her. He sat down at the edge of the sofa and touched her cheek – placing his fingers on her skin and leaving them there, waiting, feeling the urge to touch more of her and fighting to control it. He wanted to touch her all over, not just this cheek, but he did not know what to do, so he stayed there, slightly uncomfortable and motionless. He was breathing deeply.

As he sat there, watching her, feeling his fingers tingle against her skin she opened her eyes. She looked up at him and lifted her head, but she did not seem surprised, and lay down again as she had been. She picked his hand from her cheek, moving it to her mouth, where she nibbled it gently, her fine teeth and nimble lips taking each finger in turn, and then slid his forefinger into her mouth, sucking on it, massaging it with her tongue. Sam knelt down beside her and placed his other hand on her back, feeling the softness and smoothness of her skin. His hand was almost shaking, and he steadied it by pressing on her. He rubbed her shoulders and worked down her spine, vertebra by vertebra, his hand meeting the duvet and sliding beneath, down until he had reached the last vertebrae, where her tail should have been. He stretched out his hand and moved it over her bottom, feeling the soft curves and the gentle join where her legs started. He looked at her, eyes closed, mouth working on his hand and felt such desire that he shook as he moved. And then she knelt up slowly.

Just as he had imagined, she knelt, the duvet falling off behind her, the dawn light falling crossways over her body, showing him her breasts, her olive skin, her dark hair, her smoothness. She crawled off the sofa and on to the floor, opposite him and they started to kiss, taking each other's lips in their own, Sam reaching for her breasts and then lower. She moaned and so did he, rolling backwards so that she lay on top of him, pressing herself to him as he struggled out of his boxer shorts and she pulled his T-shirt off. They could wait no longer – she slid on to him, straddling him and feeling his mouth on her nipple and she came almost as soon as he was inside her, and he followed her.

They lay together on the front room floor for a while, watching the dawn grow brighter, sleeping in bursts, and then, at six o'clock, an hour before Sam had to get up, both of them half asleep, he began to touch her once again, slowly this time and gently as though he almost wasn't there. She lay on her back and sighed at the ceiling, more hesitant this time, and they made love once again. They teased each other, both of them extending their pleasure for as long as they could, and then she lay with her head on his shoulder and stroked his hair until the short hand of the clock on the wall moved gently over the seven and Sam separated himself and went to have a shower. When he came back she was sitting wrapped up in the duvet, looking out of the window.

'I was thinking Sam, is there a word for bird-like?' she asked, knowing that Leo would know what it was.

Sam shrugged. 'Birdal?' he said, towelling his hair. 'Birdistic?' he offered, letting the towel drop around his neck. She threw a cushion at him and he kissed the smile off her lips.

TWENTY

'Sam speaking.'

'It's Clive.'

'Hi Clive, how are you?'

'Very well. Well, I'm at home today because I've got conjunctivitis, but apart from that . . .'

'Oh, I'm sorry to hear that, Clive,' Sam replied. At home because of conjunctivitis? *Conjunctivitis?* If Sam was off for more than a day he was required to get a letter from a doctor explaining what was wrong with him. 'Sorry to hear it,' Sam repeated.

'Sam, I've left my TV file at the office and I need to do some work. Do you think you could get me a pack together with all the scripts, the timing plans, the estimates, probably the brief, oh and the testimonial details. Could you get it all biked to my house before lunch – I might go out for a spot of golf this afternoon.'

'No problem, Clive,' Sam said. He spun round on his chair and ducked his head underneath the phone flex. Gail was standing, barefoot, on a large white piece of paper and drawing around her feet. Michael was taking a Polaroid of Sally next to the window and someone was asleep in Jeff's office. Lauren's desk was empty.

'Does it have to be before lunch? That may be a little tight.'

'I said it had to be before lunch. I wouldn't have said it if I didn't mean it.'

Sam smiled. He could not help it. He thought of Kasia. Lovely Kasia and her glorious body, warm and sunny. And he thought of his departure. Clive doesn't even know I've resigned yet, he thought. The agency wouldn't tell the client until he'd left, he knew that. He wanted to tell him there and then ('I'm leaving, Clive. Fuck you and your conjunctivitis. Fuck you and your game of golf'), but he knew that it would be more fun to wait.

'And Sam.'

'Yes?'

'I haven't seen anything on the press work since you presented it. Isn't it time I saw something?'

'Yes, well I haven't seen anything yet. I'm expecting it at the end of the week, so if it's all right, you can see it at the start of next week.'

'I'll see it at the end of this week, didn't you mean to say?'

'Yes, that's exactly what I meant to say. Thank you for correcting me,' Sam replied, a small smile on his lips.

Now that Sam had resigned he had all sorts of ideas about what he could do to avenge himself on McLeod Seagal. They ranged from the most basic and crude, like burning the offices down or leaving a tap running in a seldom used loo, to ideas which spiralled around themselves and were so complex they made his head spin. He wanted to think of something original, of something that had not been done before, and, whenever he had a spare moment, and frequently when he did not, his mind was ticking over, considering possibilities, thinking of something that would be unforgettable, something that would go down in the history of McLeod Seagal Gale.

As he sat at his desk now he looked at all the things around him, attempting to see their humorous potential. He looked from his computer to his phone to his lamp, to his filing cabinet to his pager and mobile phone. He had three weeks before he was due to leave. He would think of something.

Sam left the gym and walked towards the bench where he had agreed to meet Kasia. As he approached it he saw that she was already sitting there, legs crossed, her face looking up at a tree to her right. Her shape and form seemed so familiar to him already and Sam stopped in the street and watched her. As he saw her look down at the tip of her shoe something stirred inside him that made him uncomfortable. It stirred inside him in a place he didn't recognise (was it his stomach? his lungs? his heart?) and the stirring seemed to constrict his chest, hindering his breathing and prickling his skin. He looked at her form, at her profile on the bench and didn't know what to do. He wanted to go over and talk to her until darkness fell, to describe to her these strange feelings, to tell her everything that he was thinking and what went through his head as he lay in bed at night. He wanted to hear her say that it was the same for her, that she too was discovering places in her body that seemed to have suddenly woken up. But he just stood on the pavement and observed her. He was embarrassed and shy, for although these stirrings were unfamiliar to him, he knew exactly what they meant.

It had been raining, but the sun was starting to appear from behind the clouds, and they sat on the bench by the puddled pavements, the smell of wet air in their nostrils, and kissed. Both wanted more, they wanted to go home and go to bed, but neither would suggest it. Instead they just kissed, embarrassed in front of each other and completely unaware of anyone else around them.

'Let's go to the park,' said Kasia, standing suddenly and looking up at the strip of sky between the buildings, high up above them, swinging her arms about her.

'Which park?'

'Whichever.'

And so they walked up Regent Street, hand in hand past stuffy shoe shops, as though they were a couple on holiday. Past Oxford Circus and past embassies and institutes until they reached the black railings of the park where they slipped through the gate, just as the sun came out to greet them on the light June evening.

'We can't stay out too long. We have to go back and look after Birdy,' she said.

Sam's phone rang and displayed Clive's number. Sam pressed the 'busy' button, knowing that he would have to face the hideous consequences in the morning. But the morning seemed a long time away, and Clive couldn't touch him any more. It rang again. Sam turned it off.

'Do you prefer long or short?' she said, pulling him by the hand towards the edge of the lake so that she could look into the water.

'Short.'

'Sweet or sour?'

'Sweet.'

'Day or night?'

'Night.'

'Major or minor?'

'Minor.'

'Fruit or vegetable?'

'Fruit.'

'Loud or quiet?'

'Quiet.'

'Black or white?'

'White.'

'Right or left?'

'Right.'

'Rough or smooth.'

'Smooth,' he said, with a raised eyebrow and he moved her hair off her face and touched the end of her nose with a fingertip. As they walked through the park they noticed little of what was around them. And then the first raindrop fell, hitting the tip of Kasia's nose just where Sam's finger had been, and then falling to the pavement beneath her feet.

'It's raining,' she said, stroking her nose with her fingers.

'So it is,' said Sam, stopping to look up. 'How extraordinary. I didn't order rain. Did you?'

'I most certainly did not. Not for this evening, anyway. What are you going to do about it?' she said, looking at him, his blue eyes, like brilliant pebbles, seemingly brighter in the rain.

'I'll complain,' said Sam. 'I'll get a refund.'

'But what are you going to do about it now? Now that I'm getting wet?'

'I don't know,' replied Sam as they stood there, looking at each other as they began to get wet.

'Well, you must be able to do something. It's raining and pouring. Haven't you got anything that will keep me dry?' she said, with a challenging glint in her eye. 'Haven't you got an umbrella for me, or a mackintosh or some wellingtons? Can't you magic them from somewhere?'

Sam shrugged. 'I have my wallet,' he said, holding it up with one hand 'and my gym bag', and he nodded his head towards the bag on his left shoulder.

'Let that be a lesson to you, Sam. Always be prepared to help a lady. Now, what have we here,' she said, plucking the wallet from his hand and heading towards a tree. 'I'm going on holiday. I'm going to travel the world with your wallet,' she said, taking out his credit cards as she brushed underneath the leaves of the tree and stood in its canopy. 'I'm going to buy a panda in China with this one, and a tea tree in Australia with this one and a spring roll in Malaysia with this one, and . . .' She was looking at one of the cards, running her fingers over its raised surface. Sam had followed her under the tree and he put his arms around her waist and his chin on her shoulder. She pulled away from him.

'S. L. Glass,' she said and paused. She looked down at the card for a while longer and then back up at Sam. 'You never told me your last name was Glass.'

'You never asked,' he said, with a little shrug.

She looked back down at the card. 'Do you know Leo Glass?'

'I am Leo Glass,' he replied, smiling. 'Samuel Leonard Glass,' he whispered. His own name made him shy and he tried to pull her to him, but she resisted.

She frowned and for a minute she thought that maybe her dream had come true. Maybe Leo had somehow become the same age as her, and this was him. Maybe this was all a dream. Maybe that was all it could be. Nothing before in Kasia's life had been as good as this.

'No, but do you know Leo Glass who's eighty-six? White-haired Leo Glass? He lives in Highbury.'

Now it was Sam's turn to frown. 'How do you know him?' he asked, his mind racing, trying to work out whether he had known Kasia before; whether they had been at school together, whether she was actually his sister. How could she know Leo? No one knew Leo any longer – he was an old man. Most of his friends were dead.

And she looked at him again. At his shining blue eyes, dark hair, the calmness of his expression. They stood there in silence.

'I look after him,' she said after a while, thinking now of Leo, alone this evening with his television, like all the other evenings of the year, and a pulse of guilt went through her. 'I'm his daily.'

'He's my . . .' Sam stared off over her shoulder, 'grandad,'

Sam said, dropping his arms and struggling to place Kasia as the girl that went three times a week to care for Leo.

And as Kasia looked at Sam she realised that Leo had been right of course, that there *was* someone out there for her. And that someone was his grandson. She could not have Leo, he was at the wrong end of life for her, but she could have Sam. And she felt so grateful to Leo, so thankful that he had had a child who had gone on to have a child. It seemed to make so much sense. *Of course* Sam was Leo's grandson. *That's* why he was going to Antarctica. *That's* why she had fallen in love with him so quickly. She was already in love with him before she met him. She was predisposed to the Glass family, she was primed and ready – for a Glass of her own age. And here he was.

And what did Sam think? Sam did not love Kasia any less now that he knew who she was, knew that she fitted into another part of his life as well. But he remembered his mother's voice, on the evening of Mark's wedding as they had sat in Clarissa's garden. He remembered his mother saying that she thought his grandad had fallen in love with the girl who looked after him. He remembered his own reaction to it – how he had thought the speculation ridiculous, and in fact, a slur on Grandad Moss's self-control. And he looked at Kasia, her face glistening from the rain, her wet hair darker than usual, and he thought *I don't blame him. I don't blame him one bit.*

They continued to look at one another. There were suddenly a lot of questions to be asked; there was suddenly something to discuss. Sam thought he should ask how Leo was, but then he thought he should know how Leo was, and the possibility occurred to him that Kasia might resent Leo's family for not looking after him properly. And was there anyone else she had met? How much did she know about the family? Had Leo told her anything about *him*?

330

Had she seen photos of him as a young boy? Did she know who he was when she first met him?

He took her hand as they walked through the drizzle, talking about their new point of contact. They talked slowly and asked questions gently, unsure of how the other felt about what they had discovered. And then the rain moved on and the sun came out, and a huge rainbow rested over London.

'Look,' said Sam, as they stopped to look at it, 'can you see the secondary one, just a little bit higher and a bit fainter?'

Kasia nodded.

'That's caused by a second refraction in the drops of rainwater. When the sun shines through the drops of rain it bends and splits up into colours and comes out the other side. That's how a rainbow is formed. But some of the rays bounce around inside the raindrops a bit more and come out at a different angle, which is why you get a second rainbow further up.'

Kasia nodded again, pulling her hair back into a ponytail.

'And that patch in the middle, between the two, that's called Alexander's dark band,' he waved his hand round in its direction. 'Do you know that it's possible to see rainbows at night-time?'

Kasia smiled. 'Yes,' she said, 'from the light of the moon. But they're a lot paler, aren't they?'

Sam took off his glasses and cleaned them on his shirt. He smiled as he put them back on.

'If you know everything Leo knows then I'm going to be very dull company.'

'I *like* dull company,' she replied and kissed his hand.

Things were rather strange at work once Sam had resigned. Some people began to ignore him completely, not even bothering to say hello or goodbye, barely able to tell him which floor they wanted when they got into the lift and he was already there. Others came to him straightaway and wished him luck and congratulated him on going abroad. He got the feeling that people didn't really believe that he was going to the South Pole, that they suspected that he was moving to another agency but covered it up with some far-fetched story of exotic travel. But surely they can see it in my face? he thought, for he himself had noticed that he suddenly looked healthier now that he was no longer faced with the prospect of years of meaningless toil within these Soho walls. His hair no longer seemed to be turning grey, and it did not fall out in clumps as it once had. The crow seemed to be lifting its feet from his face and he was slimmer and fitter.

Angela ignored him altogether, unable to bring herself even to look at him. Instead she sent him about ten e-mails a day with various orders and requests, most of which Sam deleted without even opening them. Pressing the delete button with his mouse was one of the most satisfying parts of his day. He started to give out her phone number as his fax number, and he would watch from his desk, delighted as she got call after call which just bleeped at her. Jeff still spoke to him, unable to resist the temptation to give him pieces of advice for later life. The others, Michael, Chloe and Gail, looked at him with eyes alight, sick with jealousy that he had managed to escape. They were pleased for him. He was doing something he wanted to do, and not one of them thought that the sacrifice of a career in advertising was too big; each of them would have done exactly the same.

'Henry.'

'Sammy.'

'How's it going?'

'Great. Shag-tastic.'

'What number are you on to?'

'Well, I dallied around number twenty-three for a good few days and then spurted ahead to number twenty-six, which is where I am at the moment.'

'I hope you're careful, otherwise you're going to be leaving an army of fatherless children all over London.'

'Well, that's the plan. I am going to father a whole *generation* before I leave.'

'God, Henry, how are you going to cope when you're out there? There are probably only about two women on the whole continent.'

'That's all right. I only need two. I find it gets a bit crowded with three. Listen, have you spoken to Gray?'

'No, why?'

'He said something about coming home to find a bird in the kitchen. And I don't mean the kind of bird he likes.'

'Oh yeah. Shit, I forgot to tell him. Kasia rescued it the other night, when we went out.'

'Really? And it ended up back at yours? Did you shag her?'

'Three guesses.'

'Was it good?'

'In your own words, Henry, it was shag-tastic.'

Kasia told Leo in the end. She was sure that Leo would be happy for both of them, because she could not believe that he was really in love with her and so it did not occur to her that he might be jealous. She had read to him for an hour as usual (from *Brideshead Revisited,* chosen by Leo for her benefit) and then she put the book down and asked him how he was.

'You look very well,' he said to her at last, and both knew that the other knew. Kasia knew that Leo knew she was in love with somebody. Leo knew that Kasia had realised he knew.

'Would you like to know his name?' she asked, stretching out her legs and pushing her arms into the air above her head. She was embarrassed and she tried to pretend that she wasn't. She lifted up her hair from her shoulders and twisted it up the back of her head, clipping it on top.

Leo shrugged a little. 'Is it a nice name?' he replied, trying hard to pull a neutral expression.

'I like it,' she replied with a gentle nod. And then, 'It's Sam.'

Leo looked down at his hands and then back up at her. He was silent for a little while. 'My Sam?' he said, eventually, and blinked.

'Yes,' she nodded, her expression that of a child seeking praise from a parent.

Leo smiled. His face cracked and he nodded at her, slowly, his fingers twitching on the ends of his arms. It was a painful smile for him. If the name had been 'Richard', 'William' or 'Oliver' – any of those – then it would have meant nothing to him. But it was somebody he knew. It was Sam. It was the same Sam who was going to Antarctica.

'He's good enough for you,' he said, and looked at her.

Leo felt odd. He was, of course, happy for them. His grandson was good enough for her. And she was good enough for him. But there were things that niggled. Sometimes, small thoughts at the back of his mind would elbow their way to the front and he would feel jealous of Sam. Jealous because Sam was young and virile, jealous because Sam was going to the place that Leo loved, jealous because Leo had spent so much time with Kasia and yet he could not have all of her. And that was what he wanted.

But Leo was old, and this jealousy shamed him. I should know better, he thought. I have had my chance, let them go and be happy. He's my grandson, of all people. I can't be jealous of my own flesh and blood, can I? Or is that the worse kind – the kind that really hurts, that grates on your innards, that pales your skin and makes your bile bitter? The kind that is so close to you it is inescapable: there, staring you in the face, day after day. Leo felt it inside. He felt a burning like indigestion and a throbbing as though something was infected. And then he felt shame. A damp shame that spread over him like a wet cloth, making him hang his head and wonder what he had learnt in his life.

And so he smiled at Kasia and discussed her new-found love with her. He chatted with Sam and did his best to share his joy, his excitement, his wonder at this beautiful creature. But now he was an onlooker, a bystander. He was out on his own again. When he was by himself he cried. And whenever he smiled at her his eyes stung.

TWENTY-ONE

Sam let himself in and put the kettle on. As he walked along the hall towards the living room he heard something unusual and paused: there were voices floating down towards him, coming from the front room. Sam listened harder – it was definitely voices, real live voices. Leo rarely had visitors at the weekend, unless it was family, and if it was family Sam would have known about it, wouldn't he? But there they were, drifting towards him. As he stood in the hallway, frozen and brow furrowed, he realised that one of the voices was a woman's, a flat, light voice that he knew. It was Kasia.

For a second he stood there in shock. Then he transferred his weight to his front foot and took a few more paces, about to walk in. Something stopped him. Whether it was the fact that he was standing on the exact spot where his grandfather had stood the night he had looked at the sky with Kasia or whether it was April who rounded the corner suddenly and rested her owlish eyes on him, he didn't know. All Sam remembered was that when he saw April he instinctively put his finger to his lips, the way one might silently plead with a child for no noise. And then he heard Kasia.

'But why do you want me to read it?' she said, using a voice that Sam had not heard before. It was still hers – her vowels were a little out and her consonants solid and flat, and its timbre was unmistakably hers, but there was something else there – a gentleness, a tenderness, a questioning intonation which was unfamiliar to Sam.

'Because I'd like to hear it, that's all. I used to read a lot of his work when I was younger, and now I can't any more.

I'd all but forgotten about him, to be honest, but something reminded me this morning.'

'But I can't read it – I can't pronounce some of these words, and I definitely won't understand what it means.'

'Well, don't worry then, it's all right.'

'Oh,' said Kasia.

There was a silence. Sam transferred his weight on to his other foot and felt ashamed, lurking in the hallway, listening to their conversation. What was he doing? He was about to move when they started again.

'Well, all right,' she said now, 'but it won't be right.'

'That doesn't matter,' his grandfather replied, a lightness in his voice. Kasia began to read, quietly, as though she was reading to herself.

> 'Goe and catche a falling starre,
> Get with child a mandrake roote,
> Tell me, where all the past yeares are,
> Or who cleft the Divels foot,
> Teach me to heare Mermaides singing,
> Or to keep off envies stinging,
>   And finde
>   What winde
> Serves to advance an honest minde.'

Kasia paused and scanned down the page at the rest of the poem. The words meant almost nothing to her, and it frustrated her, it made her throat dry and her lips tight. She started again.

> 'If thou beest borne to strange sights,
> Things invisible to see,
> Ride ten thousand daies and nights,
> Till age snow white haires on thee,

337

> *Thou, when thou retorn'st, wilt tell mee,*
> *All strange wonders that befell thee,*
> > *And sweare*
> > *No where*
> *Lives a woman true, and faire.*
>
> *If thou find'st one, let mee know,*
> *Such a Pilgrimage were sweet;*
> *Yet doe not, I would not goe,*
> *Though at next doore wee might meet,*
> *Though shee were true, when you met her,*
> *And last, till you write your letter,*
> > *Yet shee*
> > *Will bee*
> *False, ere I come, to two, or three.'*

There was another silence. Sam thought again that he should move, should go in, but he couldn't enter now. Not yet. He would wait for them to start speaking again. It was Kasia who spoke.

'It makes no sense to me whatsoever. I might as well have read something in Portuguese,' she said. There was a tension to her voice, as though she was straining to sing.

'Well, I'll tell you what happens.' Leo cleared his throat. 'You see, the first bit is about doing marvellous things. It says that if you can do all these great things like hearing mermaids sing and understand time passing then you could ride for a thousand days and nights to find me a woman who is both beautiful *and* faithful. And then it says that while she might be faithful for the period of time that it takes your letter to get to me, she will have been unfaithful by the time I actually get there because no woman can ever be both beautiful and faithful to one man.'

Kasia paused, trying to follow the logic of the argument.

She frowned and then began. 'But that's preposterous, that's ridiculous, I mean what kind of male chauvinist . . . ?' But the words in her mouth somehow dried up and she felt her throat catch as a picture revealed itself in her mind and shocked her: she saw there, now, very clearly, both Leo and Sam. The two of them, as they had been in the wedding photograph, a patch of ink on one end of a piece of paper, folded in half, and reproduced with exact symmetry on the other side, with time as the dividing line. She saw now how she behaved with Leo, how she savoured his trust, his confidences, how she encouraged his words because (whatever they were) they meant so much to her. And then she saw Sam too, strong dark Sam who was more her equal and friend, her partner, her opposite. Sam whom she could touch.

She shut her mouth, and felt for a moment that both of them, both Leo and Sam, could read her thoughts.

'You're right, of course. It is preposterous,' said Leo and looked out of the window.

Kasia sat there, stunned by the feeling that she had somehow been unfaithful, but she didn't understand how and she didn't know to whom.

Sam swallowed. He felt like a voyeur, watching a woman urinate or carelessly unfasten her bra, believing herself to be completely alone and unobserved. He picked his fingers carefully, one by one, off the windowsill and tried to turn round without making the boards creak. Halfway through the turn, when he was facing out to the hall window, he heard the voices start up again:

'What do they do?' It was Kasia again, asking questions, like a child.

'They're anti-inflammatory pills. For my arthritis,' said Leo, and Sam heard the rattle of a pill bottle.

'How do they make you feel?' asked Kasia, gently, as though she might be daydreaming, as though there was no one else in the whole world, apart from the two of them, in a living room in north London.

'Try one,' replied Leo, and offered her the bottle. As he looked at her she saw a glint of bravado in his eye. A glint that must have been there his whole life, a glint which had not yet been dulled by old age. And she understood how he had gone to Brazil, how he had gone to Antarctica, how he had done all those amazing things.

Sam stood in the hallway, staring into the sky out of the window and strained desperately to hear what was happening. Was she taking the pill bottle from him? Was she reading the label? Or had she just shaken her head, and Leo gone back to staring out of his own window? He could not hear a thing. He could not hear her as she pressed down and unscrewed the top of the pill bottle. He could not hear her drink from the place where Leo had drunk. And he could not hear her swallow. His heart pounded in his ears. He could only hear one thing: this is wrong. This is wrong. And something else: forgive those who trespass against us. Forgive those who trespass against us. Over and over again, as though his heart did not pound with a beat, but with words, which reverberated round his body, resonating in the cavity of his head and bubbling through the blood in his veins.

He turned round slowly and crept towards the door, holding his breath in his lungs. April slunk past him, perturbed and confused by his odd behaviour. What he really wanted to do was to go in and take Kasia away. He wanted to take her home and make love to her. Because she was so lovely, because she was his, because he wanted to be sure of what they had.

And then he heard what he dreaded most. What he heard

weakened his knees and stopped his heart . . . There, just round the corner, he could hear footsteps, coming closer, and yet his body wouldn't move. He turned.

'Hi.'

She jumped.

'Oh, hi,' she said. 'Sam. You scared me.'

'Sorry – I just got here – I – I didn't realise you were here.'

'I didn't hear you come in,' she said again, and looked at him for a second, observing him like a bird, head on one side. Neither was sure of the next move. Neither was sure whose territory was whose.

'Kasia,' a call came from the front room, 'who are you talking to?'

'I couldn't come yesterday so I said I'd come today. I didn't know you were coming,' she said to Sam. 'Sam's here,' she shouted back to Leo.

'Well, no, I didn't tell anyone. I have my own keys,' Sam said.

'Oh,' came the reply from the front room, almost a moan.

She nodded at Sam.

'Hello, Grandad,' Sam yelled. They remained where they were, as though their own relationship might not exist.

'I was just making some tea,' she said, 'would you like a cup?' moving past him, gingerly in the hallway, without touching him. Sam thought for a second of the kettle and how it would already be warm; he had put it on when he arrived.

'Hello, Sam,' came a call from the front room, a cheery note in the voice.

'No – no, I won't stay,' Sam said, unsure for a second as to what to say or do. He dropped his voice and raised his eyebrows. 'Is anything the matter?' he said, taking a step towards her and reaching for her with his right hand. He didn't want her to go through to the kitchen.

She stayed where she was and shook her head. He approached her and kissed her on the cheek – a chaste kiss, a kiss from a brother to a sister. Kasia was frozen. 'I'll just say hello to my grandad and then head off,' he said and slipped behind her into the kitchen, picking the kettle up, pouring the water away, refilling it and flicking its switch. 'Okay?' he said, and made his way through to the front of the flat.

'Janie, it's Sam.' He paused to give her time to remember who he was. She didn't seem to need it. He clicked on to his e-mail to see if he had any new messages.

'Sam! How *are* you?'

'Good. How about you?'

'Tip top. But Janie's not very happy with you, Sam. Sam never calls. Sam bad boy.'

'Janie, I'm going away for a while, for about a year actually.'

'Oh, right. Where?'

'Antarctica. The South Pole.'

'The South Pole? Do you mean the one that Sir Walter Scott discovered?'

'Er, yes.'

'*Are* you?'

'Yes.'

'What for?'

'I got a job as a research assistant, for a group of scientists researching the environmental impact of tourism out there.'

'Wow. Can I come and visit?'

'Er, dunno. Maybe. I'll let you know.'

'It's going to be really cold down there, isn't it? About minus zero.'

'Yeah, it'll be cold.'

'I'm *so* impressed, Sam.'

'I'm having a leaving party. On the 18th of July. Please come if you can.'

'I'd *love* to, Sam.'

Sam crossed her name off his list of phone calls and got on to the next. Henry had insisted that they have a big party, but in true Henry style, he did not want to organise it.

'Sam? Do you want Corn Flakes or Coco Pops with your milk?' she called from the kitchen.

'Cornflakes.'

She climbed back into bed, pressing her kitchen floor-cold feet on to his knees to warm them up.

'Here you go.'

'Thank you,' Sam put on his glasses and sat up, taking the bowl from her.

He looked out of the window and saw bright June sunlight on the clouds. For some reason he thought of his grandfather and how he had spent his life. After Sam's dad had died he had made it his purpose to look after his grandsons and see they had as normal an upbringing as possible. But even before then, his grandfather seemed to have a focus, seemed to know what he wanted to do. Things were perhaps different now, Sam would have to admit (he had no idea that Kasia was now Leo's focus), but before, and for most of his life, he had a clear goal, a direction.

Sam wanted to go to Antarctica too. He wanted to go so badly that his body ached. He couldn't wait to leave, to see it, once and for all. He felt suffocated here, by all the concerns that made up the surface of London life. He knew that he was right for wanting to go.

Kasia put her head on his shoulder and her arm across his stomach. She pressed herself against his side.

'You know, I *am* going to go,' he whispered, the cereal in the bowl in his hand untouched. They had not discussed it. Kasia knew that he was laying plans, that he had a leaving date. But they had not talked about it since they had made love, since they had become different people.

'Where?'

'Go. To Antarctica. I will be going.'

She sighed. In the bed–warm Saturday morning she was calm and relaxed.

'Why?'

'Because I want to.'

She turned on to her back and disentangled her limbs, staring at the ceiling. She didn't know what to say. Everything seemed to have come right, and it was all going to end so soon. Kasia felt as if she had waited long enough. She had spent her whole life waiting for this, waiting for someone with whom she could really communicate, and now she was faced with more of it. At the same time she knew Leo's stories of Antarctica, she knew how he spoke of the place. She didn't want to stop Sam, but she wanted him here, in bed with her every morning when she woke up. She sighed.

'And you think that is a good enough reason? Just because you want to?'

'I have to. Otherwise I won't have a point.'

'There are lots of points you could have. You could retrain as a lawyer or a doctor or a teacher.' Kasia thought of Leo as she said this. She remembered how upset she had felt when he had said the same thing to her. Sam batted it back to her.

'Yeah, and perhaps I will, but at the moment this means more to me than any of those things. I need to go to Antarctica. It's what I want to do.'

344

'Most people spend their lives doing things that aren't what they really want to do. Why do you have to be different?'

Sam shrugged. 'I just can't. I cannot sit back and let myself spend the rest of my life in advertising. It doesn't interest me, there's no point in it for me. What is the point of everything, of being here, if you don't spend your time doing what excites you?'

'And what about me? Am I not point enough for you to stay?'

Sam put his cereal on the floor. This was the question he had been dreading. This was the challenge. As always with Kasia, as always when he talked to this strangely defensive and vulnerable creature, he trod carefully.

'Well, you're the problem. You're the thing I didn't count on. You're the thing they don't mention in all those travel guides that detail preparations for a long trip. None of them say "oh, and by the way, don't fall in love just before you are due to leave". You're the person whose forgiveness I need. And I know that I don't deserve it.'

He was scared. He thought about Leo again. What would he have done, if he had met Natália as he was about to go looking for the rarest moss in the world? Sam knew that Leo would have done the right thing, but didn't know what the right thing was.

Kasia clasped her hands behind her head and breathed out. He looked at her nutty skin, her warm sunny skin and wanted to touch it. But he knew better.

'Do you think I should wait for you?' she said, staring at the ceiling.

'I think you should do whatever you want to,' he said.

'You might never come back.'

'I will,' he said, and leant over to stroke her hair. 'I'll come back. I'll come back, and hope that you're still here.'

'How long do you think you'll be out there?'

'A year.'

Kasia blinked. She knew that the worst thing she could do would be to prevent him from going. He had found something he wanted to do, and that was so rare that it should not be stopped. But at the same time she was cross and jealous. Jealous that he knew what he wanted, jealous that he was going to get what he wanted. Jealous that Leo was his grandfather and had been there for Sam's whole life, caring for him, teaching him things, playing jokes on him.

She felt let down. Of course she had known he was going when she met him, of course she knew that. But somehow she had hoped that he wouldn't really go. She had hoped that he would turn round one day, put his forefinger on the end of her nose and say, 'I'm not going. I'm staying here with you. We're going to have a wonderful time.' She was disappointed, and ashamed of what she had hoped. And at the same time she was convinced that Leo would have stayed. If Leo had met her when he was due to leave he would have cancelled his flight. *He* would have done that for her, wouldn't he?

But no matter how much she wanted it, no matter how much it eased her insecurities, she knew that she was wrong. Could she survive a year without Sam? Could she be an Antarctic widow? I'll still have Leo, she thought. Things will just be as they used to be. She sighed and looked at Sam.

'If you wait for me, I'll never go anywhere, ever again. I promise,' he said, a drop of milk dribbling down his chin. She watched his face. Would he be able to keep that promise? What if he fell in love with the sleeping princess? What then? How could Kasia compete with a whole continent? Would he be able to stop himself returning to her, over and over again, like an unfaithful husband stealing to his mistress in the middle of the night?

They didn't discuss it any more after that Saturday morning in bed. Kasia knew that there was nothing she could do to stop him going, and Sam knew that there was nothing he could do to stop her meeting anyone else.

'Hello, Mr Glass.' She dropped her stuff on to the floor and went through to the front room. He was asleep. She stood and looked at him for a while, at the small veins in the skin on his cheeks, at his large still hands, resting on his lap. She knew exactly how Sam would look when he was old; he would look like this.

April ran into the room and began to miaow, rubbing herself against Kasia's legs. Kasia picked her up and scratched behind her ears, cooing to her gently: '*Koteczku, Prima Aprilisku.*'

'Mr Glass,' she said, looking at him. He did not move. But then Kasia had played this game many times. 'Mr Glass,' she repeated, a little smile on her face. She poured April on to the chair, and reached for Mr Glass's shoulder, bracing herself for his lively response.

She shook his shoulder. It was stiff. Her mind froze. She shook it, holding it with her left hand. He still did not move. She picked up his arm and held his wrist, placing her two fingers over his artery. It was a gesture. When she reached for the arm it too was stiff, and the skin was cold, but she checked for a pulse all the same. Gently she raised her hand and placed it against his veined cheek. That too was cold. She panicked.

'Help!' she whispered, 'help me!', and she ran about the flat from one room to the next looking for something that might help her. She picked up the phone and called an ambulance. 'What's the matter with him?' they asked her down the phone. How should I know, she thought. What

347

am I supposed to say? *I don't know*, was all that she could manage. Then she stopped and stared at the phone for a little while, returning to the front room after a couple of minutes.

She sat on the arm of his chair and looked at him. She looked at his hands waiting for them to flutter around. She looked at his face and willed him to be only pretending. She knew what she had to do. Better than anyone, she had memorised the drill. Slowly she reached for his pocket. She was scared: he frightened her. But she made herself not be. It's Leo, she kept telling herself, he would not want to frighten her. He should not frighten her. She took the list from his pocket. She'd get him back. She'd wake him up. Of all people, *she* would.

She started with point number one, and held a piece of paper to his lips, glaring at it as fiercely as she could. Her hand was shaking, and she could not tell whether the movement of the paper was due solely to her or whether Leo was contributing to its shivering. With some difficulty she picked up his right leg and crossed it over his left. She was surprised by how insubstantial his limbs were – how the flesh seemed to be barely there through the thick cloth of his trousers. Then she selected the book he had specified (*Configurations of the Southern Hemisphere* by P. H. Hamilton), brushing the dust off it, and she started to hit his knee, gently, just beneath the kneecap, taking her eyes off his foot only to check her aim each time.

She shone the torch in his eyes and took his pulse again, and then she put the record on, struggling in the blur to place the needle down in the right position. She sat and listened to his favourite piece of music with him, and she thought of the two of them dancing to it, as she used to imagine. She opened the windows at the same time, and the neighbours were surprised by this sudden sign of life from a flat that had remained the same for years and years. Sitting there, while the fresh air flooded in, she kept watching for a small shiver or a twitch of blanket. She knew that it would come. She set fire to a piece of newspaper and held it to his nose. His cold skin remained pale under the flame.

Wiping the back of her hand across her face she sat down in her blue chair and read the last two points on the list, written in such fine, old-fashioned writing:

8. If all of the above proves fruitless do not give up! Positive results show that I am alive, but negative results do not necessarily mean that I am dead. Fetch a doctor, and then another one.
9. When you are sure, I am sure.

She sat in silence for a while, watching him. She looked around the flat. Nothing had moved. April had gone through to the kitchen in all the commotion. Kasia tried to sigh, but her ribcage shook. Just as he had known all those things, she knew now. There was a stillness to the flat – a lack of presence, an absence of spirit. She could feel that there was nobody else in the room with her. 'I'm sure, Leo,' she said out loud, her voice hoarse and juddery. 'Sure as the floor,' she whispered.

She wanted him to shout out 'wrong again!', to leap up yelling 'fooled you!', to wink at her, to bark at April, to demand pancakes, to grumble and mutter and fiddle with his sideburn. She wanted him to tell her something.

She sat in her chair and looked at him. The flat was silent and still. The sun was slanting through the open windows. The dark velvet curtains still hung like bassett-hound ears at either side of the frames. There was still dust on the piano. Nothing moved. There was a pile of books on the table next to Leo's chair. Nothing had changed. All was as it was every day when she had come. Some of these things had never moved. The plants all still stood there, waiting for water. The botanical prints still hung on the walls. The blue chair she was sitting on was still dusty. There was still a sewing machine which stood at one end of the sofa, a cloth umbrella with frills around the handle leaning against the windowsill, a wooden bowl full of heavy necklaces on top of the piano.

And yet of course one thing had changed. The most important thing had changed. The only thing had changed. She did not understand. How could such a big change happen in such a small space in time? How could such a big change happen and everything else remain the same? The flat shouldn't be like this. It should no longer exist, she thought.

And suddenly she felt uncomfortable in it, it made her feel sick. The quietness of the flat seemed to weigh on her despite the fact that she had spent many hours there sitting in silence with Leo. She felt alone. She was scared. She knew that her life would be different from now on. And it had only just become sweet. She sat in the dusty blue chair and took her head in her hands.

The ambulance arrived and the men poked and prodded around for a while and then brought in a stretcher. They asked her how she came to be there, how she had found him, whether she knew whom to notify. She asked them whether they could leave Leo where he was, just for a day or so. They said they couldn't. She called Sam and asked him to go to the hospital. He questioned her and she remained silent. She told him just to go and then she hung up. And then she watched as they lifted Leo on to the stretcher and carried him outside.

It was as they approached the doorway and had trouble

opening the door wide enough to fit the stretcher through that she collapsed. She slid down against the wall, her hands over her face and cried and cried. She could not bear to see him leaving the flat. In all the time she had known him he had never left the flat. He was always there, always in the front room, that was where he belonged, just as the sky was up above and the earth below. Leo sitting in the front room was part of her life. She could not bear it.

One of the ambulance men picked her up and made her take some tablets. She went in the ambulance to the hospital.

Sam arrived and asked to see the body. 'Have you got the list?' he asked, almost ignoring her grief. She gave it to him and he disappeared through swing-doors and left Kasia alone on a plastic chair.

After a while she got up and followed him, finding him in a long room with no windows, standing over Leo on a stretcher-bed. Sam was looking at him, the list folded up in his left hand, hanging by his side. He took the red-eyed Kasia into his arms and they stood there in silence. Neither of them could understand why he wouldn't move.

Sam Glass did not cry. He held Kasia and stroked her hair. He pressed his face into her hair, breathing deeply and smelling sand and warmth, and he watched his grandfather over her shoulder, hoping for a movement, for a flutter of an eyelid, a twitch of a finger, a flare of a nostril. Sam stared, trying to watch every extremity at once – both feet and hands, face and stomach. And as he watched that body he had no inkling that that was how his own body would look when he was that age. The profile that embraced Kasia fitted almost exactly the profile that was now horizontal. The lips that pressed into her hair were blind to their mirror image on the bed. The nose that smelt her hair did not recognise its twin brother. And the eyes that looked with that same crazy stare that would never again shine from Leo's eyes, continued to look at the stretcher-bed, searching for movement, and saw nothing. Grandad Moss was still.

The Glass family had another funeral. Sam and Mark were now the men, the people to whom others would turn. They looked smart and handsome in their suits and Leo, who always was proud of them, would have glowed to see them. Kasia borrowed some black clothes from Sam's mother and said a prayer in Polish under her breath during the service.

It was a quiet affair, and sadder than it should have been. Sam and Mark could not help but think of their father's funeral, and their mother was the same. Kasia could not believe that he had gone. There was, this time, no coffin to lower into cold ground, because Leo had asked to be cremated (the thought of being buried alive was too much for him). And as they were driven away, the Glass family was aware that its centre had gone. Leo had washed and cleaned and cooked. Leo tied their shoelaces for them, told them stories in bed and watched them while they slept. He kept them all going, kept the record spinning, kept the clock turning. Leo did not cry. Leo *knew* everything. But he didn't know about the island in Antarctica, did he? thought Sam. And now he never will. I can go and look, and I can know whether he was right or wrong, but he will never know. Never ever.

Sam wished that he could have told him. He could not really imagine it happening. Now that he was dead, he could not imagine sending him a card. He could not imagine him receiving the card, looking at the stamps, reading the message, the answer. Sam did not know what he would have said, and although he could guess he did not actually *know*. What would Leo have thought if he had been right? What would he have felt? He was no longer here to know. He was no longer here to see the answer, to pore over the map with it, to use it as he wished. And what can I do? thought Sam. The only thing that is left for me is to believe that he knows.

It was left to Sam and Mark to sort out Leo's flat and deal with the family solicitor. Mark opted for the paperwork, and Sam was left with the flat. He imagined his task many times over before he actually turned up there and started work. He had pictured himself becoming upset by certain objects, finding old forgotten treasures and things that his grandfather had had for years, but when he actually arrived and walked through the silent rooms he knew that that wasn't how it would be. He felt, once he got there and prowled through the rooms, wondering where to start, like a trespasser. He felt as if he shouldn't be there, as if he was burgling a flat while the residents were on holiday.

It was clearly a flat that one person had lived in for a very long time. He knew his grandfather well, but not this well. Not well enough to have known every possession of his, not well enough to be already acquainted with his secret scribblings, to understand the significance of the jet necklace that he had kept, for forty-two years, in a sock in his underwear drawer. Sam did not want to see these things, he did not want to stumble upon them in this flat – private things that had been made by one person for that person alone. It was Leo's den, his hideout, his secret place, and it was not meant to be disturbed.

But disturb it Sam did, and he tried not to look as he boxed objects and filed letters. He took all the boxes back to his room, where they sat gathering dust. Sam did not want to throw anything away. At this point, he would not have been able to forgive himself. He wanted, instead, to pretend that Leo had gone travelling, and had asked Sam to look after his belongings.

At least he had a good innings. The phrase repeated itself over and over in Sam's head, and he couldn't get rid of it. He was embarrassed that such a cliché should occur to him about his grandfather, but there it was anyway, repeating itself in his head. A good innings. What did it mean? Did it mean that the person had achieved a lot, or that they had enjoyed themselves and had a good time? Or did it just mean that they were old when they died – that they had had the opportunity to achieve a lot, even if they hadn't achieved anything?

Sam would not dial his telephone number again. He could cross his address out of his address book (although he didn't – he stared at it for a while and then left it there, untouched). He would enter it the following year too, because Leo had always been the first name in the Glass section and Sam didn't want things to change. Before Sam left the country he ran to Leo's flat for the last time and looked at it from the outside. He had a set of keys with him but he had no desire to go in. Instead he loitered on the pavement, looking suspicious but not caring, and wondering as he stood there where the person who had sat for so many years inside that building had gone.

Sam did not cry in front of Kasia. It was not that he would have minded her seeing him. It was more that he thought he should look after her, make her cheese on toast ('you have to eat'), tell her stories in bed at night. Leo was no longer there, and someone had to take over his role, Sam knew.

They spent time at her flat because they had to look after April, who slept on Kasia's pillow at night and every so often stretched out her paw and placed it on her face. April was all that Kasia had left of Leo, and she spoilt her because of it – feeding her the same food that she ate herself, brushing her every day, letting her sleep on the bed, picking her up to cuddle her whenever she happened to pass by.

Sam had two weeks left and suddenly, after all that waiting, after all those years of killing time, it felt like no time at all. He tried to be as he knew Leo would have wanted him to be. He spoke to his mother, Mark and Kasia about pulling out from the trip, about staying in London and helping, being around, looking after people, but none of them wanted to stop him going, because they knew that Leo would not have approved.

His absence weighed on them all. With Leo gone a whole slice of their lives had disappeared and Sam was left with something that did not even vaguely resemble the time that had gone before. For all of his life Leo had been there. For twenty-five years, he had been part of Sam's landscape. Everything that Sam had known had had Leo in it, had always had Grandad Moss in it. Please bring him back, was all that Sam could think. Please bring him back.

TWENTY-TWO

Sam Glass was out on the roof. He looked up at the stars, imagining himself far away from the busy London that was all around him. He scanned the sky, looking for the constellations that he knew, looking for the star that was watching him back. The moon was a sliver (or, at least, eighty-five seconds ago the moon *had been* a sliver) – a new moon – a moon full of promise. Wherever Leo is, Sam thought, it looks like a nice place.

Sam was talking to himself: muttering under his breath, thinking through what he should do, what was going to happen. There was a week left before he was due to depart. He looked at his nails and at his fingertips and then back up at the sky. It won't even be this sky that I will look at when I am there, he thought. It will be the sky of the southern hemisphere, a different sky, a new sky. It will be the sky that is described in *Configurations of the Southern Hemisphere* by P. H. Hamilton.

The roof creaked beneath him and a police car wailed past. But I am going to see that place, he thought. That amazing place that Grandad Moss loved so much – the sleeping princess. The place that I grew up thinking about. The place I have always wanted to visit. And despite Leo's death, despite meeting Kasia, despite everything, he still wanted to go.

The next few days were strange for Sam. He felt as if he was part of a large experiment on humankind. He went to work and caused as much havoc as he could face for one day. He phoned his mother to check that she was all right. He spent every evening with Kasia, the two of them taking walks through the July London, or sitting in her flat with April and some books. Or they would lie on her bed, where he would read out the titles of her Polish books and she, staring at the ceiling, would have to name the authors. His pronunciation made her smile, a funny, crooked smile with red nostrils above it, and she would teach him how to say the names, making him repeat them over and over.

One evening they were sitting in her tiny kitchen talking over whether Kasia should give up her job in the shop when Sam suddenly stopped and looked up at her. She had tied her hair back with an elastic band and was fiddling with it now, catching stray bits at the back of her head and trying to tuck them under the elastic.

'Do you want to go home?' he asked.

'What?' she said, pulling the band out of her hair and letting it fall around her face. She started all over again, smoothing her hair back with her palms, the band between her teeth.

'I mean to Poland. Do you want to go back?'

She shook her head and frowned. 'No. Why?' she said from between clenched teeth.

'I thought you might want to see your parents.'

She shook her head again and looped the band round her hair, turning it back on itself a couple of times and then putting her hands on the table, happy this time with the result. She had told Sam about growing up with her parents here, and then about them returning to Poland. She had not really told him about the intervening period: she told herself that there had not been enough time, but in reality she had backed out of every available opportunity. Whenever a silence fell between them it would occur to her to bring it

357

up, and so she started to talk about something else instead.

'Are you going to be okay when I'm gone?' he said, clearing away the plates.

She laughed. A single laugh that was, ultimately, a sharp exhalation from her lungs.

'I've managed twenty-three years without you, Sam Glass, I think I can get through one more.'

And he came and stood behind her, wrapping his arms around her and pressing his face against her neck.

Sam's mother had started to phone Kasia too, and he was grateful to her for that. She seemed to sense that Kasia might have been affected more deeply than any of them could have predicted by Leo's death. And Sam went to the gym and worked out with an energy that seemed to come from nowhere. And he ran. He ran for Leo, he ran with Leo, but he no longer ran anywhere near where Leo's flat used to be.

Leo had left him two hundred pounds, and this, combined with his savings, paid off the rest of what he owed for his ticket. Osh Laird rang him a couple of times to check that everything was okay, that he felt prepared, that he had the correct documentation, that he had cancelled the milk. He said that he was looking forward to working with Sam, and, for the first time since Leo had died, Sam felt good.

And he thought about how Leo would want them all to behave. He would not want them to be subdued, to mope around, to mourn and grieve alone in silence. He was, after all, the master of the practical joke. He was the one who taught April to jump off doors, who played possum every second day, who told stories about moss growing between people's toes. He was the one who waved his fingers in the air like a magician, who knew everything about the sky, about plants, about moss, about everything, who always smiled, who always joked. He was the one who did not cry.

'Sam, I've been thinking. Have you bought all your gear yet? Because everyone's saying that next season's colour is grey, but I think they're wrong. I think you should go for purple, you know, purple fleece, purple boots.'

Gray was eating a packet of marshmallows and doing the *Evening Standard* crossword at the kitchen table.

'Gray, I don't really care about the colour of my gear,' Sam replied gently.

'But you should. It's all about forward planning, you see. I can only assume that you want to do something momentous out there, and at some point somebody will be bound to take your photo. And that's where colour comes in. You see, if you're in grey then you'll blend into the background, with all the white and blue. But purple will zing out – just imagine – a deep purple against that light blue sky and all that white. It will look fantastic. And people will know that it's you, because you can never see faces, can you?' he said, biting a marshmallow in half and looking at its middle.

Sam smiled. 'Yeah, yeah I get your point. But I don't like purple, and besides, I just need to get the best stuff.'

'Oh-oh. The first sign of an outdoor-bore. What's nine letters, with a P and a M, meaning the opposite of transitory? What does *transitory* mean when it's at home?'

'Fleeting,' Sam replied. 'Permanent. It's permanent.'

Gray looked up at him, pencil poised over the boxes. 'Can I come and visit?'

Sam smiled. 'Bugger off, Gray, I'm not falling for that one.'

'No, I mean it. I'd love to come and see you out there.'

'Gray, I'm researching into the effects of tourism. What's the suggestion – you come over and I see what effect you have?'

'Now you're talking.'

'But you *hate* the countryside.'

'Yeah, and?' Gray looked at him. His expression was that of a petulant toddler.

'You don't want to come to Antarctica. It's going to be fucking freezing and crammed full of outdoor-bores and there's no sex. None at all.'

Gray shrugged and ate another marshmallow. 'You're probably right. But I'd like to go somewhere, you know. You and Henry are going to have a fantastic time. And anyway, the penguins must shag.'

'Yeah – each other. And anyway, the girl penguins only shag you if you collect enough stones for them, so it's hardly worth it.'

Sam gave Kasia the photo of him and Leo at Mark's wedding, and she put it in the copy of *Brideshead Revisited* on her bedside table. She had not finished reading it to Mr Glass, and now she kept it there, not reading it, but sometimes picking it up and flicking to a paragraph early on, and wondering how could it be that Mr Glass had been alive when she had last read that part of the book.

Sam couldn't understand why she had suddenly started to read loads of old, boring books, but she did not explain herself. She got another old person to look after and she joked about meeting his grandson and falling in love. 'Well, you're going to be away for a whole year,' she teased. 'There are lots of fishes in the sea,' she would say, a small smile on her face as she poured herself some tea, or kicked off her shoes.

'Sam,' she whispered one night as they lay in her bed, in the darkness, 'Sam?' He rolled over and came face to face with April. She purred and put her paw on his nose, pushing him away.

'Yes?' he replied, with as little movement as possible.

'Sam, I'm going to do something,' she said. He listened for a while. There was the noise of occasional traffic, the hum of electricity, the creaks of the flat. He gently removed April's paw, got up and undrew the curtain and then sat at Kasia's feet and the two of them looked at the sky.

'Do what?' he asked.

'I don't know yet,' she replied, stretching out her legs, 'just something.'

He nodded and then, 'What kind of thing?'

'I have no idea,' she said, propping her head up with her left hand. And the two of them looked out into the night, and the night looked back at them.

Sam worked hard for the last few days. He had, after all, a lot to do. He didn't stay late, but he was busy during the day, running around just as much as ever. He filled in all the junk mail coupons he could find with Angela's details, flicking through the back of newspapers in the search for erotic underwear catalogues or leaflets on painting courses in Dorset. He filled in her job title box as *trainee*, which he knew would rile her. When it finally came to his last day at work he could not believe it, and he knew that the realisation would not sink in for months.

'Sammy.'

'Henry.'

'How are you? All set?'

'Just about. You?'

'Yeah, I think so. Are you scared?'

'No,' replied Sam. It was a lie.

'Good. Neither am I.'

Sam smiled. 'I'd be more scared if I was going to the Arctic. Polar bears and all that.'

'Listen, I'm not going to come to your agency bar tonight. I'm going to go straight home and make sure everything's ready there. The music and so on.'

'Fine. I'll probably turn up around nine. When I've finished here.'

'Has Kasia told you yet?'

Sam paused. 'Told me what?'

'That she's a lesbian?'

'Henry, there is one person in this world who would rather go out with me than with you. You're going to have to face up to it sooner or later.'

'You've got to admit though, Sam, it's hard to understand.'

That Friday at work was a write-off. Sam went for lunch and did not come back until half-past five, at which point he went to the bar. He had not drunk much for a while, and he was not used to it. He remembered all his friends arriving at one point, and then going somewhere else. Gail tried to snog him, and Jeff tried to make him take some cocaine, and he told them all that it was he who had sent Phil the letter telling him to resign.

Kasia came to the rescue, kissing him enough to make the others leave him alone. They left and went on to Henry's, where most of Sam's friends were already as drunk as he was, and he was welcomed with hugs from people he had never met before. Sam drank some more and danced with Kasia, and then they went upstairs to make love. When they came back down, Henry was trying to make a speech, standing with one foot on either arm of an armchair, with a toy polar bear on his shoulder.

And as Sam stood there, listening to Henry singing his song to the heckling crowd – because perhaps of his tiredness, or maybe because of the amount of alcohol he had drunk, because he was saying goodbye to his friends, because of Leo, because of his father, because it had all come true, come right – a narrow stream of water that nobody saw squeezed itself out of his left eye, getting only to the top of his cheek before it was wiped away with a swift brush of his hand.

Sam had dedicated Saturday to his grandfather. He had had it planned for a good two weeks now. This was the day that would belong to Leo, the day of which Leo would approve. This was the day when one of those stars in the sky would shine just a little bit brighter.

Sam got into work at about lunchtime and stood before his desk. He started to clear it, keeping cards from friends, a note that Lauren had once written him: *If I had woken up with white-hot needles sticking in my eyeballs this morning I would have been in a better mood. Lxxx*, and various notes he had written himself about burning bridges. Then he took the lift to the top floor – the management floor – and started work. He worked carefully and swiftly, aware at each stage what needed to be done for the next: he had planned his actions, he had, as a good account manager should, planned ahead.

He opened a tin of tuna and locked it in Robert McLeod's bottom drawer. He swapped his African violet that stood next to the photo of his wife for a dope plant he had borrowed from Gray. He changed the time on his clock and tuned the TV into a soft porn channel and threw the remote control out of the window. He went through to Sebastian's office and unpicked the arms of the jacket that was hanging on the door. Then he went down to the edit suite and changed tapes so that the TVs in reception that were supposed to play the agency's ads were playing a Wombles video on continuous loop.

Then he started on the real work. He walked the entire building, taking every internal phone list he could find (two hundred and four in all). He sat at his desk and cut one up, carefully cutting round each extension number so that he was left with a pile of bits of paper, each with four numbers on it. Then he took an old list and stuck each bit of paper against the names, over their old extension. He stuck down the numbers at random – any old number against any old name. When he had finished glueing he copied his new list, and then toured the building again, distributing it.

He took a magic marker and a scourer to the lifts and got inside. He bent down and rubbed each number off the buttons, working as carefully as he could, so as to leave as few tell-tale signs as possible. When the buttons were blank, and steadying his hand by leaning on the silver of the lift wall, he renumbered the buttons in his neatest handwriting. Finally, he put new batteries in his pager and then locked it in a cash box in the finance department. He paged it, and, locked away in its box, it began to vibrate, making the metal box hum.

Then he returned to his desk to start on the paper work. He sent out change-of-address cards to half of the client-list. To the other half he sent a copy of an internal finance document, detailing how much money was never given back to them. The Marketing Director of Soma cars got a VHS of an old ad which the agency had revoiced with an upbeat song about the client being a cunt. He crafted a press release saying that the agency was set to resign its biggest account (Euroair) because of a difference of opinion. He wrote a letter to the BBC, inviting them in for a week 'to film life as it is lived in an advertising agency'. He mailshotted the top ten universities and explained that McLeod Seagal would not be able to take anyone on that year because of internal difficulties. He changed the phone number on the letterhead of three boxes of paper in the post room. Then he went back to his desk.

It was twenty to eight and he was exhausted. His fingers were sore, and his head was spinning. He drank from an empty cup on his desk and then got up. There was nothing more to be done. He had finished his tasks. He had got to the end of everything that he had planned. He went over to the window and looked up at the light July sky. The funny thing about stars, he thought, is that you can't see them during the day.

Sam stood in the street and looked up at the shiny windows of McLeod Seagal Gale. At the decorative balconies and at the swish logo above the automatic doors. He never wanted to see this building again. He didn't even want to to have to think about it. It was no longer a part of his life, and Sam was glad. 'It's going to rain on Monday,' he whispered to himself. 'It's going to pour with rain.'

And as he stood there a small smile crossed his face and he thought that Leo would have been proud. What a shame neither of them would be around to watch the dramas unfold on Monday morning. 'When a man slips on a banana skin, it's not funny unless somebody sees it,' Leo used to say. But Sam thought, it is if you know he's going to slip.

His eyes scanned the shiny glass front, the intimidating face, completely unrepresentative of all the chaos that went on behind its smooth skin. Now that he no longer worked there he did not feel such a venomous resentment towards the place, but he could still remember coming through the doors into the outside world at midnight, night after night. He could still remember, still feel, like a virus in his blood, the stress and panic that went on every day. The pain he used to get in his heart. The stiffness of his neck. The ache in his shoulders. The sweat, the anxiety, the hungry evenings, the waking up at two in the morning consumed with worry that the tape that went to the client had the wrong ad on it.

But as he looked up at all that glass now he felt a certain satisfaction at how he had spent his day. His eyes scanned the outline of the building against the sky. He turned round on the pavement and looked down the street, at couples out for a Saturday night in Soho, at the dark, closed doors of the other office buildings. He took a deep breath. And then Sam Glass walked away.

It was decided that the big farewell would be held on Sunday night since he was leaving on Monday morning. His mother came down, as did Mark and Clarissa, and they ate a meal together in Sam's flat and Sam was given presents – his mother gave him a penknife, Mark and Clarissa gave him a fountain pen and some paper and Kasia gave him a watch with a small box for the date on its face. 'It's a subtle hint,' she said with a grin as she handed it over, and he knew that every time he looked at it he would think of her. 'When that bit says February you have to be with me. And if you're not, you better ask yourself why not,' she told him.

Later that night, when everyone had gone he gave her a map of the stars at night, a map that showed both hemispheres. She spread it out on the floor and cocked her head and looked at it. 'Sam Glass, I can see right through you,' she said as he sat down next to her.

'Go on then,' he replied. 'What was I going to say?'

She got up and looked at the stars for a while, pacing along the edge of the stretch of paper and then announced,

'You were going to say that I should look at this star here,' she bent down and pointed with her finger, 'and you will look at that one there, and then, somehow, even though we're on different ends of the planet we will think of each other and be together.'

Sam smiled. He had met his match.

They made love that night on Sam's small bed, quietly, for fear of waking his mother, who was staying over and was asleep (Sam hoped) in the living room. Kasia smelt glorious: of sand and sun and something more – a sweet smell like a tropical flower out to attract the bees. Leo would have known the smell, had he ever been in a position to smell it. He would have been able to go to his dusty bookcases and select the exact book which had a diagram of the flower in it, and he would have explained to Sam how the scent is made, when and why it is released.

But as Sam lay there, making love to Kasia, he did not think about his grandfather. As she breathed sweetly beneath him, as he watched her eyelashes on her skin, her hair on the pillow, the dip at the bottom of her neck, he thought only of her, and of how lovely she was. Beads of sweat began to appear on her top lip, and he wiped them away with his thumb, moving stray strands of hair off her cheek as he did so.

'Let's go outside,' he whispered and he stood up and opened his window. She came out and made him lie on the tarpaulin. 'It's your idea, I'm not lying on the hard roof,' she said with a smile, and then she climbed on top of him. And they made love on the roof, underneath the night sky. Sam looked up and knew that he wanted nothing more from it.

On Monday morning he got up early and went for a run. His mother fussed about his luggage, making sandwiches which she wrapped in greaseproof paper and gave Kasia to carry. Henry arrived with all his gear and sat in the front room, watching television. Sam changed into his travelling clothes and Gray came through to see them both.

'Bye then,' he said, glancing over his shoulder to check how he looked in the mirror.

'Bye, mate,' Henry replied and gave Gray a hug. Sam followed.

'Take care of yourselves. And write to me, you bastards.'

'Gray,' Sam called out, just as he was leaving the room. Gray turned. Sam shrugged off his jacket to reveal a purple fleece.

'Sammy,' Gray said with a smile, '*very* nice,' and he left for work.

The time had come. After all those evenings of staring out from it, the world had turned enough times for Sam to have to leave. He hugged his mother and was glad that she did not cry (maybe she could, after all, replace Leo?). And then he set off for the tube to Heathrow with Henry and Kasia, both of them carrying rucksacks stuffed with winter and summer gear, to cover their training in New Zealand. Kasia had a small canvas bag, a plastic bag of sandwiches and a book for the return journey.

They sat on the tube in silence, Sam and Henry taking in their last glimpses of grimy, busy London. Sam lifted his hand to his mouth, about to chew his forefinger, and then let it drop. He thought about the last few days and how quickly they had passed. Things seemed to have happened in a blur, and he marvelled at the way that time, seeming to pass so slowly and painfully, each quarter of an hour a lifetime in itself, could suddenly bolt past, like a terrified cat.

The train gradually filled with people and suitcases and

buskers, hoping to catch people at their most vulnerable – either daunted by a trip or saying goodbye – and cajole them into making a donation. Sam held Kasia's hand and he was conscious of its warmth and smoothness, of its delicateness and fine bones, conscious that he would not have a hand to hold for a long time. He would forget the heat of sex, the heat of tears, the heat of wounds. It would become something to dream about, to fantasise about.

A young man got on and glanced at Kasia as he sat down opposite her. He had flaming red hair and a fine, noble face. She looked up at him too, unable to resist such a charming face.

Sam squeezed her hand and she smiled at him, knowing what he was thinking. And as he sat there on the train he thought of Mr Fellows, his old geography teacher. Mr Fellows was the man who had first introduced Sam to maps. One particular day Mr Fellows had taken it upon himself to teach the largely apathetic class not only geography but also English. They had just had exams, and while the content of the essays was good Mr Fellows, skinny in a tank top and tweed trousers at the front of the class, was appalled by the grammar and spelling of the children.

He pulled out a book from underneath his desk and began to tell the class the story of two brothers, one of whom had been a schoolteacher for many years, until he resigned over a difference of opinion. Aged forty-one, he was obliged to make a fresh start in life, and he joined his brother in Guernsey and together they did literary work: translations, guides to language usage and essays. The First World War broke out and both brothers enlisted, but they were old for fighting – one fainted on parade, the other became ill. They returned to Guernsey to continue with their work, but after a year the younger brother died. And so the older continued to work alone, and after his death the book he had been working on, and which was to make him a household name, was published.

At this point Mr Fellows held up *Fowler's Modern English Usage* for the whole class to see, and there were, inevitably, some mumblings about his name not being known 'in my house'. And then Mr Fellows read the preface that Henry Fowler had written for the book that he and his brother were supposed to write, and which Henry dedicated to his brother. Sam could remember that day clearly, but most of all he could remember the first line of that preface, because, at that time, when he heard it, he could not help but think of his dad. As Sam thought about it now, as they pulled into Osterley station, he spoke the line out in his head: *I think of it as it should have been, with its prolixities docked, its dullnesses enlivened, its fads eliminated, its truths multiplied.* To Sam it sounded like the first line of an epic novel, of a fantastic story, of a thrilling narrative, and not the preface to a book about grammar. And it had even more resonance now, now that he was finally leaving for Antarctica and Leo was gone. *I think of it as it should have been,* Sam thought, with Leo here, with my father here, with more time to spend with Kasia. This wasn't how I planned it, he thought. This wasn't how I imagined it. *I think of it as it should have been.*

At the airport they checked in and bought a newspaper. Henry went off to Burger King and Sam and Kasia stood by the ticket desk, checking through his luggage. There was no more time to kill. No more hanging around in the flat. No more ticking off weeks in an office. No more treading water, no more crossing off days, no more clock-watching – although there would be, in the months to come, a lot of watch-watching. No. This was it. Sam cleaned his glasses on his sweater and took a deep breath.

'Forgive me,' he said to Kasia.

Kasia blinked. Sam's eyes looked as though the sun was shining through them. They were the colour of the sky, and Kasia wondered, for a second, whether they were that colour because he spent so much time staring up at it. Or perhaps the sky, the glorious huge blue of the sky, was, in reality, a reflection of Sam's amazing eyes. They embraced. His flight was announced over the tannoy.

'I'll write to you,' he said. And he thought: please smile at me. Please smile.

'I might not reply,' she said, a dimple in her cheek.

'That won't stop me writing,' he said and he brushed her hair off her face. Sam felt in his pocket and pulled out his plane ticket. With it was his travelcard in its tatty plastic wallet, with holes in its corners and a half-torn spine. He looked at it and thought about the number of times he had used it. He thought about the time he had talked about it with Janie. How many times had he slid it through the barrier? How many times would he have used it if he hadn't left now? The Sam that stared back at him from the picture looked young and lost, like someone who didn't know what he was doing.

Sam looked around him and tossed it into a bin. He felt his neck loosen, his shoulders drop, his lungs expand. He looked at Kasia.

'Sam,' she said, holding out the small canvas bag towards him in her right hand, 'your mother asked me to give you this.' Her hand looked small with the canvas strap wound around it. His flight was announced once again.

'What is it?' he asked, looking at the bag.

Kasia shrugged. 'It's Leo's ashes,' she said. Sam was silent. 'I think she wants you to scatter them —'

'I know,' Sam interrupted gently, and took the bag from her. In his head he could see where he would scatter them. He could see the vast white landscape, wider than he could imagine, deeper than he could imagine, stretching for further than he could imagine. That vast white and blue landscape, glittering and glistening in the sunshine. The sleeping princess. *The sleeping princess.* Here, he thought, have your sleeping prince. You deserve each other. And he could see the island, cleft in two as it undoubtedly would be, and he knew that that was where Leo's ashes should fly. The ashes of the sleeping prince should fly high up, in the cold air, over the icy sea, above turquoise glaciers, over penguins and seals and underneath the huge blue sky.

'Do you two already know each other or something?'
Flippancy was what was needed here, I decided. 'I'm afraid so. Marcus once branded me on the forehead with a red-hot poker. Although he wasn't called Marcus then.'
'Abigail sent me her hair in an envelope,' he said, almost smiling. 'She wasn't called Jex then.'

Abigail Jex never expected to see any of the Radley household again. In dramatic contrast to her own conventional family, the Radleys were extraordinary, captivating creatures transplanted from a bohemian corner of North London to outer suburbia, and the young Abigail found herself drawn into their magic circle: the eccentric Frances, her new best friend; Frances' mother, the liberated, headstrong Lexi; and of course the brilliant, beautiful Rad.

Abigail thought she'd banished the ghost of her life with them and the catastrophe that ended it, but thirteen years later a chance encounter forces her to acknowledge that the spell is far from broken . . .

Into the Forest
Jean Hegland

Nell and Eva live alone in the forest. Recently orphaned and completely isolated, they struggle for normality in a post-holocaust world in which the busy hum of society is slowly replaced by the silence of nature. From chaos comes strength however, and through this cataclysmic destruction the sisters discover their hidden power. As they blaze a path into the forest and into an unknown future, they become pioneers and pilgrims – not only creatures of the new world, but the creators of it.

At once a poignant and lyrical portrayal of the power of sisterly loyalty and a horrifying cautionary tale about the future of humanity, *Into the Forest* is a deeply moving account of human nature and our fragile existence on earth.

Praise for *Into The Forest*

'A truly admirable addition to a genre defined by the very high standards of George Orwell's *1984* and Russell Hoban's *Riddley Walker*' *Publishers Weekly*

'Beautifully written . . . impeccably authentic' *Kirkus Reviews*

'[A] beautifully written and often profoundly moving novel' *San Francisco Chronicle*

'a work of extraordinary power, insight and lyricism, *Into the Forest* is both an urgent warning and a passionate celebration of life and love' Riane Eisler, author of *The Chalice and the Blade*

'mesmerizing . . . Hegland's sweet and sadly elegiac tale is . . . engrossing' *Booklist*

Black and Blue
Anna Quindlen

Fran Benedetto's husband beats her. So badly that she takes her son and runs away. Starting afresh in Florida under assumed names, Fran and Robert slowly rebuild their lives – until an accident at a fairground puts Fran into the public eye. Now, she must face up to her worst fear: that her husband will come after her. That he will never let her go.

Praise for *Black and Blue*

'As tensely gripping as a thriller . . . a subtle exploration of love and fear' *Sunday Times*

'It is rare to find a novel at once tender and taut, full of insight, yet with a darkness at its centre – and that's what makes it gripping and real' Margaret Forster

'Quindlen has got so deeply inside her characters that they gave me nightmares' Lisa Jardine, *The Times*

'Quindlen invests her tale with rare pathos and even rarer psychological acumen . . . the honesty of her storytelling is exemplary' *Sunday Telegraph*

'Anna Quindlen pours heart into *Black and Blue* . . . this novel lingers like a bruise' *She*

'Don't miss Anna Quindlen's compassionate portrayal of a violent marriage' *Marie Claire*

'Qualities and shades of love are this writer's strong suit, and she has the unusual talent for writing about them with so much truth and heart that one is carried away on a tidal wave of involvement and concern' Elizabeth Jane Howard

Electricity
Victoria Glendinning

Charlotte Mortimer, a spirited, sensual young woman, is testing the limits of her world. A world bounded by strict conventions, a world on the brink of change. And Charlotte is going too far . . .

Electricity is a tour de force, a fast-moving novel, both funny and moving, about connections, contacts and shocks – electrical, emotional, sexual, intellectual. Set in the 1880s, it is the story of one spirited, sensual young woman's adventure, recounted with wit, candour and an intimacy of closely observed domestic and technical detail.

The novel is also about choices – science versus religion, spiritualism versus rationalism, gas versus electricity – and control, as the young woman, Charlotte, finds her own way of coming to terms with the forces bearing down on her and of resisting the people pressing in on her.

Praise for *Electricity*

'Sparks fly, wires cross and connections crackle throughout . . . a terrific new novel' *Daily Mail*

'A magnificent novel set in Victorian London which illuminates all it touches . . . authentic, engrossing' *Daily Telegraph*

'Glendinning reveals a sense of the past so tangible at times that you can smell it, taste it and feel it' *Independent*

'A literary triumph, a superfine novel about power and illumination' *She*

'Above all, it is in the small things that this novel excels: in the telling social and domestic details that offer a cultural history in miniature' *Times Literary Supplement*

Also Available in Arrow

☐ Learning To Swim	Clare Chambers	£5.99
☐ Into The Forest	Jean Hegland	£5.99
☐ Black and Blue	Anna Quindlen	£6.99
☐ One True Thing	Anna Quindlen	£5.99
☐ Electricity	Victoria Glendinning	£5.99
☐ Ma Polinski's Pockets	Sara Sheridan	£5.99
☐ Truth Or Dare	Sara Sheridan	£5.99
☐ Seesaw	Deborah Moggach	£5.99
☐ Close Relations	Deborah Moggach	£5.99
☐ The Last To Know	Candida Crewe	£5.99

ALL ARROW BOOKS ARE AVAILABLE THROUGH MAIL ORDER OR FROM YOUR LOCAL BOOKSHOP AND NEWSAGENT.

PLEASE SEND CHEQUE, EUROCHEQUE, POSTAL ORDER (STERLING ONLY), ACCESS, VISA, MASTERCARD, DINERS CARD, SWITCH OR AMEX.

☐☐☐☐☐☐☐☐☐☐☐☐☐☐☐☐☐☐

EXPIRY DATE .... SIGNATURE ....

PLEASE ALLOW 75 PENCE PER BOOK FOR POST AND PACKING U.K.

OVERSEAS CUSTOMERS PLEASE ALLOW £1.00 PER COPY FOR POST AND PACKING.

ALL ORDERS TO:

ARROW BOOKS, BOOKS BY POST, TBS LIMITED, THE BOOK SERVICE, COLCHESTER ROAD, FRATING GREEN, COLCHESTER, ESSEX CO7 7 DW.

TELEPHONE; (01206) 256000
FAX: (01206) 255914

NAME ....

ADDRESS..

....

Please allow 28 days for delivery. Please tick box if you do not wish to receive any additional information ☐

Prices and availability subject to change without notice.